Bolton Council

Please return/renew this item
by the last date shown.
Books may also be renewed by
phone or the Internet.

Tel: 0120

www.bolton.g

D1355416

Emily Forbes began her writing life as a partnership between two sisters who are both passionate bibliophiles. As a team, 'Emily' had ten books published.

While Emily's love of writing remains as strong as ever, the demands of life with young families have recently made it difficult to work on stories together. But rather than give up her dream Emily now writes solo. The challenges may be different, but the reward of having a book published is still as sweet as ever.

Whether as a team or as an individual, Emily hopes to keep bringing stories to her readers. Her inspiration comes from everywhere, and stories she hears while travelling, at mothers' lunches, in the media and in her other career as a physiotherapist all get embellished with a large dose of imagination until they develop a life of their own. Emily Forbes won a 2013 Australia Romantic Book of the Year Award for her title *Sydney Harbour Hospital: Bella's Wishlist*.

If you would like to get in touch with Emily you can e-mail her at emilyforbes@internode.on.net

When **Joanna Neil** discovered Mills & Boon®, her life-long addiction to reading crystallised into an exciting new career writing Mills & Boon® Medical Romance™. Her characters are probably the outcome of her varied lifestyle, which includes working as a clerk, typist, nurse and infant teacher. She enjoys dressmaking and cooking at her Leicestershire home. Her family includes a husband, son and daughter, an exuberant yellow Labrador and two slightly crazed cockatiels. She currently works with a team of tutors at her local education centre to provide creative writing workshops for people interested in exploring their own writing ambitions.

THE HONOURABLE
ARMY DOC

BY
EMILY FORBES

MILLS & BOON

Published in Great Britain 2014
by Mills & Boon, an imprint of Harlequin (UK) Limited,
Eton House, 18-24 Paradise Road, Richmond, Surrey, TW9 1SR

© 2014 Emily Forbes

ISBN: 978 0 263 90746 9

Harlequin (UK) Limited's policy is to use papers that are natural,
renewable and recyclable products and made from wood grown in
sustainable forests. The logging and manufacturing processes conform
to the legal environmental regulations of the country of origin.

Printed and bound in Spain
by Blackprint CPI, Barcelona

Dear Reader

Thank you for picking up my latest book. The idea for this story came from an article I read about people who choose to care for ex-spouses who are battling severe and sometimes terminal illnesses. I began to wonder what sort of person would offer to do that. They would have to be selfless and compassionate and, although most of the carers in the story were women, once Quinn came into my head that was it—the story started with him.

He is a gorgeous man—loyal, kind and generous (with amazing blue eyes!). He cares for and respects women, and is just the sort of man Ali needs. She is attracted to his strength of character, his kindness and his sense of moral justice. All he needs to do is convince her that she's the perfect woman for him.

Enjoy!

Emily

Dedication:

For my brother, James, who is a lot like Quinn—
gentle, kind, respectful of women
and a fabulous father.

Growing up with three older sisters
can't always have been easy
but you've turned out pretty well!

Love you xx

Recent titles by the same author:

**These books are also available in eBook format
from www.millsandboon.co.uk**

CHAPTER ONE

Quinn

QUINN DANIELS FINISHED his drink and signalled to the barman for another. His second Scotch would have to be his last for the evening, he was a keynote speaker at the weekend medical conference and his address was on tomorrow's agenda. He needed to keep a clear head.

He waited at the bar, keeping himself a little separate from the rest of the crowd. He let the conversations flow around him, not shutting them out but not totally absorbing them either. They were background noise as he let his attention wander over the room. The bar was in a conference room that was doing double duty as the cocktail reception area and the usual nondescript décor, seen in large hotels the world over, meant he could have been anywhere, but to Quinn's eyes it was the crowd that told him he was home. The room was only half-full but already there were more women in the space than he had seen for a long time. His gaze wandered, watching more out of habit than with any real purpose.

He was still getting used to being in the company of women, women who weren't off limits.

After his second tour of duty in Afghanistan he was still acclimatising to Western life. The Scotch in his hand and the women in the crowd were only two of many differences. But it was enough to change the atmosphere. The sounds were different—the men's voices provided a bass accompaniment to the higher-pitched and slightly louder female voices, and the air smelt different too. It smelt of women—perfume and soap, hairspray and make-up—and the room certainly looked different. In Afghanistan he and everyone else had spent most of their time in uniform. There weren't many occasions to dress up but tonight he was surrounded by men wearing suits and ties and women in cocktail dresses. There was plenty of black and a lot less khaki.

A splash of red caught his eye. In a room of predominantly dark colours the red dress burned like fire, casting a warm glow over everything nearby and drawing his eye. The dress was draped around the most beautiful woman he had seen in a very long time. The dress began over one smooth, tanned shoulder and wrapped across rounded breasts then pulled in firmly at the waist before flaring out and falling to her knees. Her arms were long and slender. So were her legs. She was showing far less skin than a lot of other women in the room but Quinn let his imagination picture what lay beneath the gauzy fabric. She wore her dark hair long and it flowed over her shoulders, gleaming as it reflected the light. Her lips were painted a glossy red to match her dress and the brightness of her mouth stood out in sharp contrast to her olive skin and raven hair. Her colouring was exotic, she was exquisite, and he wondered who she was.

She had paused in the doorway as she surveyed the room. He held his breath as he watched her, waiting to see if she found whoever it was she was looking for. He waited to see where she was heading.

She had perfect posture and a long, slender neck. She looked serene, elegant. Her head turned towards the bar as she scanned the room. Her eyes met his and Quinn felt his stomach and groin tighten as a burning arrow of desire shot through him.

Desire. It was an emotion he'd thought long forgotten and the strength of it took him by surprise. His heart rate increased as blood raced around his body, bringing him to life.

Did she hold his gaze for a second longer than necessary? He knew he wished it were true but as her gaze moved on he knew it was more than likely his imagination.

He waited, hoping she wouldn't find who she was looking for. Wishing she was looking for him.

She stepped into the room and moved gracefully across the floor. Her steps were smooth and effortless and she seemed to glide through the crowd. He couldn't stop watching. It wasn't a case of wanting a second look. He was unable to tear his eyes away and that made it impossible to look twice. He appreciated the beauty of a female form and hers was better than most. Far better. He knew he was staring but he couldn't stop.

She turned towards the bar. The bar was busy. It was early in the evening and people were still arriving and, for most, their first stop was the bar to fortify themselves as they prepared to mingle. He could see her looking for a spot to squeeze in. He moved a little to his left, creating a bigger space, a more obvious space, beside him as he willed her to accept his silent invitation. He hoped she would prefer to wait at the bar rather than in a queue.

He watched her gaze travel along the bar and find the gap. Saw her lift her eyes and felt his heartbeat quicken as her eyes met his again.

Her cherry-red lips parted in a smile, revealing perfect white teeth. His racing heart played leapfrog in his chest as her smile fanned the flames of desire still burning within him.

She took a few more steps, closing the distance between them, and slipped into the space beside him.

'Thank you.' Her voice was soft and sultry. It suited her. Her olive skin was smooth. Her grey eyes fringed by dark lashes. The colour of her eyes was unusual and not what he'd expected at all but it was her mouth that had him excited. Her lips were full, moist and red. Suddenly Quinn was very pleased to be home.

The bartender delivered his Scotch and he held up a hand, getting him to wait. 'May I also have...?' He looked to his left, offering to order.

'A gin and tonic, with a slice of lime, please.'

The top of her head reached just past his chin and he could smell her shampoo or maybe her perfume. It was sweet but not cloying and reminded him of the gardenia hedge that had grown under his bedroom window in his childhood home. The room around him melted into the background. The conversation around him faded and became nothing but subsidiary noise. There was nothing else that could capture his attention.

But he'd learnt the hard way not to let attraction outweigh reason. He was still paying the price for that lesson. Not that he regretted the lesson. He couldn't. That lesson had given him his daughters but there was no denying it had changed his life and now it was no longer his own. An occasional and very brief liaison was all he allowed himself now, just enough to satisfy a need but not long enough to allow any attachment. But it had been a long time since he'd felt desire.

Desire was dangerous. The way he felt right now he knew desire could outweigh reason. He knew he could lose himself in this woman.

Perhaps that would help to wipe away memories of Afghanistan. Perhaps it would help to bring him back to the present. He would still have the dreams but sex was always a good distraction. This woman might be the perfect solution. But sex to satisfy a need was one thing. Sex and desire was another combination altogether.

Ali had noticed him almost the moment she had entered the room. He had an interesting face but extraordinary eyes and it was his eyes that had made her look twice. He had maintained eye contact, almost daring her to look away first. And then he'd moved, just slightly, just enough to make space for her at the bar. Was it another challenge or was he being chivalrous? It didn't matter. She didn't want to linger alone, she didn't want to look out of place or conspicuous, so she was grateful for his silent offer. She hesitated, only ever so slightly, before his eyes convinced her to accept his offer. He had the bluest eyes she had ever seen, so bright their colour was clear from metres away. Hypnotic. Mesmerising. She felt as though he'd cast some sort of spell over her until her feet moved, almost of their own accord, and carried her across the room and she found herself beside him, accepting his offer of a drink.

He was watching her intently, almost as though he was committing her features to memory, but his attention didn't make her feel uncomfortable. It wasn't intrusive; somehow he made it feel like flattery.

His confidence was attractive. Her own confidence had been shaken of late and her pulse quickened as she met his eyes. A sense of excitement raced through her as she looked into his eyes, so blue they appeared to be made from azure Cellophane, illuminated from behind. They were intense, compelling, captivating and she was riveted. The external borders of his irises were a darker blue and the change in colour reminded her of a tropical sea as it deepened and darkened as it left the white sands of the shore.

He handed her a tall, cold glass, its contents garnished with lime. 'Will you let me keep you company while you wait for your friends?' he asked as she thanked him for the drink.

'How do you know I'm waiting?'

'I saw you arrive,' he replied. 'You looked like you were meeting people but you also looked like you were the first one here.'

Somehow in a room rapidly filling with people they'd seen each other at the same instant. She wouldn't call it fate, she had once been a big believer in fate, though she wasn't so certain any more, but even she had to admit there was a nice symmetry to this chance meeting. She smiled. 'One of my many bad habits, I confess. I'm always early.'

'I can't see how that's a bad thing.'

'It makes others feel guilty because they think they were late.'

'Well, I hope they take their time.' He smiled at her, bringing little laugh lines to the corners of his incredible blue eyes.

Was he flirting with her? She hoped so but she didn't completely trust her judgement.

He extended his hand. 'I'm Quinn Daniels.'

She knew who he was. Captain Quinn Daniels. She recognised his face, only from a photograph but that was enough. He was one of the conference keynote speakers. She planned to attend his session on infectious diseases and immunisation tomorrow. She knew from his short biography in the conference program that he was an army medic. An army captain. But the black and white head shot in the conference notes didn't do him justice.

He was six feet, maybe six feet one, of solid muscle. He looked fit. His shoulders were broad and his arms filled out the sleeves of his suit jacket. She could see the muscle definition of his deltoids and biceps under his jacket and his pectoral muscles were firm against his shirt.

He wasn't typically handsome; his face was broad, his blond hair cropped short, his jaw firm and clean-shaven, his chin strong. He was rugged rather than handsome but there was something about him that made it difficult for her to look away. It was more than just his eyes. It was something deeper, something powerful, something confident. He looked as though he could take care of himself and by association anyone else he chose to protect.

The bridge of his nose was slightly flattened, as if it had once been broken, but Ali sensed that if it had happened in a fight it had been the other guy who would have come off second best. But despite his size and the sense of strength she didn't get a feeling of menace. She got a feeling of raw masculinity but not danger. He might not back down from a fight but she got the sense he wouldn't start it. Although she was certain he would finish it. He wouldn't stand by and watch. He would go to help.

He seemed strong. Interesting. He made her feel brave. She put her hand into his. 'I'm Ali.'

His fingers closed around hers, his grip firm but gentle and sending an unexpected rush of excitement racing through her. She didn't want to let go, it had been a long time since she'd been excited about anything.

'It's a pleasure to meet you, Ali,' he said, and something in his tone made her believe he meant every word. 'You're a doctor?' he asked. She nodded in reply. She didn't think she could speak, not while he still had hold of her hand, her senses were overloaded. 'Are you Brisbane based?' he added as he released her hand.

Ali shook her head and found her voice. 'No, I'm from Adelaide.'

'Ah, I should have known.'

'Why?'

'South Australia has more than her fair share of beautiful women.'

He was definitely flirting.

'Have you been to Adelaide?' she asked, hoping that he had a legitimate reason for his flirtatious comment and that he wasn't just spouting platitudes.

'Many times,' he replied. 'Do you like living there?'

'I do.' Ali nodded. She loved her home town and although many of her friends had moved interstate she had never thought she'd prefer to live elsewhere. 'But I must admit the opportunity to escape our winter and head north for some sunshine and the conference was too much for me to resist. I'm looking forward to hearing your address tomorrow.'

Quinn smiled. 'You're attending my session? You're not going to ditch me in favour of lying by the pool and working on your tan?'

'I try not to play hookey until the second day,' she quipped before she sipped her drink, conscious of the fact she was flirting in return but surprisingly without apprehension.

His phone rang, interrupting the flow of their conversation. He pulled it from his pocket and glanced at the screen. 'Would you excuse me? I need to take this.'

She watched as he took two steps away from the bar. She wondered who it was. Wondered who had the power to make him search for privacy.

He paused and turned to face her again. 'I'll be back,' he said, before leaving her to watch him walk away. As he left he took with him the air of excitement she'd experienced and the evening dimmed a little. She wondered if he would be back. She had no way of knowing.

Ali was enchanting. There was no denying she was beautiful but it was more than that. It was more than attraction, more than desire. There was a sense of grace about her that fascinated him, a calmness about her that drew him to her. He knew he needed calmness after his months in Afghanistan and he longed to stay at the bar and let her soft, sultry voice soothe his weary soul. While he listened to her he was able to breathe, to relax. He didn't want to walk away but he couldn't ignore this call. His family were more important to him than anything else. They would always take precedence.

'I'll be back,' he told her. He wanted to ask her to wait but that would have been presumptuous. He told himself he would find her when he returned.

He moved away from the bar to answer the call, not because he didn't want to be overheard but so he could ensure he could give his full attention to the call. He knew if he stayed beside Ali he would be distracted. He wanted to turn around, to retrace his footsteps, to return to her side, but duty came first. He had never shirked his responsibilities before and he couldn't start now.

He answered the call but the voice on the other end of the line was unexpected. He had been expecting his daughters but instead he got his mother-in-law.

'Helen? What is it? What's the matter? Is it one of the girls?' It was unusual for Helen to ring him. Their relationship was perfectly amicable but there was never a real reason for them to speak. His daughters kept him in the loop and anything important he would discuss with their mother. Helen could only be ringing with bad news.

Quinn kept walking out of the room and into the hotel lobby. He needed to get away from the bar, suspecting he would need some peace and quiet. His heart was lodged in his throat as he waited for the reply. His breathing laboured.

'It's Julieanne.'

His wife.

Ex-wife, he corrected automatically.

He was certain now the phone call was not good news but hearing that the call wasn't about his daughters relaxed the muscles in his diaphragm and allowed him just enough air to speak. 'What is it? Has there been an accident?'

'No. It's her headaches.'

Julieanne had always suffered from headaches and Quinn knew that of late her headaches had become more frequent and more severe. He'd asked her to speak to her doctor but Julieanne had been convinced that she could manage them by experimenting with her diet and exercise routine.

Helen continued and Quinn could hear her voice catch with emotion. 'She had a seizure today.'

The last vestiges of calm that he'd felt when he'd been speaking with Ali vanished as Helen's words forced their way into his head. He could almost feel his mind resisting her words. He didn't want to hear this.

This is serious, he thought. He closed his eyes as he

rubbed his brow with his free hand. *This isn't about diet and exercise. I should have insisted she see someone.*

There was an ottoman in front of him, tucked into a corner of the lobby, and Quinn collapsed onto it, his elbows on his knees, his head in his hands, and forced himself to take a deep breath.

'Where is she? Tell me what happened.'

He listened as between Helen's sobs she told him what had transpired. 'We're at the hospital now. The doctor has just come to speak to me. She has a brain tumour.'

A tumour.

The rest of the conversation was a blur as Quinn spoke first to Helen and then to the doctor. He forced himself to concentrate as they discussed Julieanne's condition but he knew he'd only registered the basic facts and they were far from good.

When the conversation ended he stood up from the ottoman on shaky legs. His hands were shaking too as he pocketed his phone. He was struggling to breathe. He could feel his larynx spasm as he tried to relax his diaphragm and take a breath. He needed air. To his right was the hotel entrance. To his left was the conference room. He looked back towards the bar, back to the room where he had left Ali. But he couldn't go back into the bar. Not yet. He needed fresh air.

He pushed open the hotel's front door, not waiting for the doorman's assistance. The hotel was built on the banks of the Brisbane River and Quinn crossed to the embankment in three long strides. He gripped the railings at the river's edge, anchoring himself as he gulped the fresh, evening air and tried to make sense of the conversation he'd just had. But even as he was trying to get things straight in his head he knew there was no making sense of it. It was a horrible, unimaginable situation to be in.

He stared blankly into the depths of the dark water swirling below him. Growing up on the Sunshine Coast of Queensland, he'd always had an affinity for water and it was something else he'd missed while stationed in Afghanistan. Normally he found water soothing but tonight it wasn't allaying his fears. It wasn't soothing. It wasn't calming. He'd been craving calm since his return from Afghanistan but now he couldn't imagine things ever being calm again.

He had no idea how long he stood there, staring into the water, but gradually he became aware of people around him, couples and groups strolling along the pathway, giving him sideways glances as they passed by. He made himself relax his grip on the railing. Relax his shoulders. He knew he couldn't stay outside hoping the water and fresh air would revive him. He didn't have the luxury of time. He had things to do. He had plans to make. He had responsibilities.

He retraced his steps to the hotel. The doorman saw him coming and opened the door. Quinn nodded without really registering the service as he passed through. He headed for the bank of lifts adjacent to the conference room where he had been minutes before. He hesitated at the door, searching for a flash of red. His eyes ran along the length of the bar. Nothing. He scanned the room and found her.

He wished he could go in. He could do with some of the serenity that seemed to envelop her but she wasn't alone. Her friends had arrived and she was gathered within their circle.

He wished he could go in but he had no right to interrupt her. No right to demand her attention. She didn't need his problems. He had thought his life was complicated enough twenty minutes ago. If only he could have that life back. But in the space of twenty minutes his life had changed irrevocably. There was no going back.

He took one last look at Ali's red lips and wished he could taste them. Just once. But he couldn't go back. He could only go forward. He had to do what he had to do. His daughters would need him and, as always, he would put them first. He turned his back on the bar and headed for the lifts with heavy steps.

The lift doors closed, cutting him off from Ali, taking him out of her life.

Quinn took another deep breath as he prepared himself for what lay ahead. There was no time to think about anything else. There was no time for ifs, buts and maybes. There was only reality. His present no longer consisted of raven hair and cherry lips. His present consisted of responsibility and duty.

CHAPTER TWO

Ali

ALI PUSHED OPEN the clinic door and unwound her scarf
as she felt the warmth of the waiting room begin to
defrost her face. She was so over winter. It had been
unseasonably cold and long, even by Adelaide Hills
standards, and the few days she'd spent in the Brisbane warmth for the medical conference seemed a
lifetime ago. Her skin had forgotten the feeling of the
Queensland sun over the past six weeks and she couldn't
wait for summer.

She undid the buttons on her new winter coat, a scarlet, woollen swing coat that she'd bought to lift her
spirits and help her get through the last weeks of cold
weather. Her spirits needed lifting, she needed something to look forward to. She loved her job but lately
it had lacked excitement. It had become routine. The
last time she'd felt excited about anything had been in
Brisbane. The night she'd met Quinn.

She sighed. Her life was a pretty sad state of affairs if
a ten-minute conversation was the highlight of the past

few months. But there was no denying she'd enjoyed it and no denying she had spent far too much time thinking about him. Wondering why he hadn't come back. Wondering what had happened to him.

Despite telling herself she no longer believed in fate, she hadn't been able to shake off the idea that they had been destined to meet. But even she wasn't delusional enough not to realise she was romanticising things. Quinn had probably had no intention of coming back, he'd probably thought she was dull and ordinary and had been desperate for an escape, whereas she'd thought he was interesting and charismatic.

She'd spent so much time thinking about him that on occasions since getting home her subconscious had tricked her into thinking she'd caught fleeting glimpses of him. But of course it was just her imagination working overtime because when she'd look a second time she would see it was just another solidly built man with cropped blond hair or that the person had disappeared from view completely.

Imagined sightings, unfinished conversations and scant memories were all she had.

She knew she wanted to find love but she was sensible enough to realise it wasn't going to be Quinn Daniels who would sweep her off her feet. No matter how much she wished it. Daydreams weren't going to change anything, she thought as she shrugged out of her coat. It was time to move on.

She glanced around the waiting room. There were a couple of patients sitting quietly but no one she recognised. She wasn't actually due at the clinic for another hour as she'd finished her nursing-home visits earlier than expected so she assumed they weren't waiting for her.

'Ali, there you are.' The receptionist's chirpy voice greeted her as she emerged from the back of the clinic. It sounded as though Tracey had been waiting for her but Ali couldn't imagine why as she was well ahead of schedule. 'Your mum wants to see you as soon as you get in,' Tracey added.

The medical practice had been started by Ali's mum when Ali and her brother had still been in nappies. The building that was now the surgery had been their family home but as the practice had expanded their family had moved into a bigger house nearby and the clinic had taken over the building. Ali had spent many hours in the practice, playing in her younger years and helping out with various odd jobs as she'd got older, and she'd always known she wanted to work there one day. Her mum had shown her it was possible to balance a career and a family successfully and that had been Ali's dream too. Until recently.

Until recently Ali had been quite content working as a GP. She enjoyed knowing her patients and being a part of their lives and the community. But until recently she hadn't ever expected that she might never have more than this. She was twenty-six years old and at a crossroads in her life. She was restless. Her future lacked direction and excitement and she was at a loss as to how to remedy this.

'Do you know why?' Ali asked.

'She wants to introduce you to the locum. He's in with her now.'

'He?' The locum position was a part-time one, to cover for Ali's mother who was accompanying her husband to an overseas conference followed by a short holiday. Ali knew her mother was hoping that if things worked out she could then persuade the locum to stay on, allowing her to reduce her working hours further. Ali had assumed, incorrectly apparently, that the job would go to a female doctor as part-time hours were highly sort after by working mums, but perhaps the new doctor was also nearing retirement age, like her own mother. 'Is he old?'

Tracey grinned and Deb, the practice nurse, laughed. 'Not by our standards,' she said, 'but every minute you stand out here he'll be another minute older. If I were you I'd be hustling in there.'

Ali gave a quick glance over her shoulder at Tracey and Deb as she headed for her mother's consulting room. They were giggling like a pair of schoolgirls. She frowned, wondering what on earth had got into the two of them.

She knocked and opened her mother's door. The physique of the man in front of her was instantly recognisable and he was far from old. Her heart leapt in her chest.

Tall, solid and muscular, he stood lightly balanced on the balls of his feet. His hair was longer, not so closely cropped, and the blond was touched with flecks of grey that she was certain hadn't been there six weeks ago. He looked a little leaner and a little older but when he turned to face her she saw that his eyes were unchanged.

They were the exact same extraordinary, intense, back-lit, azure blue.

His name slipped from her tongue. 'Quinn?'

He stared at her. Did he remember her?

Her heart was in her throat, making it impossible to breathe. She had dreamt of meeting him again but in her dreams there had been no hesitation. In her dreams he hadn't forgotten her.

'Ali?'

She exhaled. 'You're the new doctor?'

He nodded.

'You two know each other?' her mother asked.

Ali had barely noticed that her mother was in the room. She only had eyes for Quinn. She forced herself to turn her head and look at her mother. 'We met at the conference in Brisbane,' she explained.

'Good.' If her mother noticed Ali's preoccupation, she gave no sign of it. She was already moving ahead, pressing on with the next issue. She very rarely stopped and today seemed to be no exception. 'Alisha, I have patients waiting, can I leave you to show Quinn around the surgery and let him get settled into his consulting room? He starts with us tomorrow.'

Her mother didn't wait for her to agree or to argue. She shook Quinn's hand and hustled out the door to call her first patient, leaving Ali temporarily frozen to the spot and at a loss for words. Her brain was full of questions. There was no room in it for motor functions. Her body appeared to have shut down as she stood and feasted on the sight of Quinn and struggled with the questions that were racing through her head.

What was he doing here? What about the army? His proper job? What on earth would he want a part-time locum job in a small clinic for? Why had he left her at the bar? Why hadn't he come back?

Quinn couldn't believe his eyes. Ali was standing in front of him. Ali of the raven tresses, grey eyes and cherry-red lips. After the chaos of his last few weeks, to see her standing a few feet away was nothing short of amazing. To say he was surprised would be an understatement. Astounded, perhaps. No, flabbergasted, that was a better word. He'd never had an occasion to use that word before but it was the perfect word for this situation.

He'd just been employed by Ali's mother? The petite, colourful Indian woman was Ali's mother?

That would at least partly explain Ali's unusual colouring, Quinn thought as he absorbed the fact that she was here, in the flesh, in front of him. He'd suspected Spanish or maybe Mediterranean heritage but an Indian lineage made sense too.

He hadn't taken his eyes off her. He couldn't. She was even more beautiful than he remembered. She was wearing a red silk shirt that exactly matched the colour of her lips. He hadn't forgotten those lips. The colour had imprinted itself on his subconscious and had not faded in his memory over the past weeks. He didn't think he'd ever be able to see the colour red without thinking of her.

She looked healthy and vibrant. Her olive skin glowed. It looked warm and soft, alive.

She hadn't moved. He had no doubt she was equally as surprised as he was. He knew not all surprises were good ones but from where he was standing this surprise was all positive. He hoped she agreed.

Seeing her made him feel that applying for this position had been a good decision. For the first time in a month and a half he felt as though his life wasn't completely out of control. He recalled the sense of calmness he'd felt on the night they'd first met. Now, more than ever, he could use some peace and serenity.

He watched as her frown deepened. He could see the questions in her grey eyes.

'I don't understand. What are you doing here?' Her soft, sultry voice caressed his senses. He wanted to close his eyes and relax and let her voice wash some of his troubles away. 'Aren't you with the army?'

'It's a long story.' And a complicated one. Quinn knew that, as surprised as Ali was to see him, his reasons for being here would surprise her even further. It wasn't something he could explain in a couple of sentences. He needed time and no interruptions. 'Can we go somewhere else? Your mother will want her room; I'll explain but not in here.'

She nodded and led him into the corridor and across the hall. He followed and his eyes were drawn to the sway of her hips, which made the hem of her black skirt kick up, exposing the tops of a pair of long black boots. Even though he couldn't see her legs he could remember the shape of her calves, the narrowness of her ankles, and he felt the unfamiliar kick in his stomach that he knew was desire.

Ali opened the third door on the opposite side of the building and turned to face him. He made himself focus, dragging his attention from her backside as she spoke to him.

'This is the spare consulting room. It will be yours while you're here.'

She sounded far from convinced and he couldn't blame her. It was an odd situation to find themselves in and it was obvious neither of them quite knew how to handle it. But he'd have to do his best to explain his circumstances.

By silent consent he took the chair in front of the desk. The desk was positioned in front of the window and he was vaguely aware of a view onto a side garden but he was having difficulty dragging his gaze from Ali. Her hair was tied back in a ponytail that spilled over one shoulder and she sat in the chair beside the desk and crossed her ankles, tucking her feet under the chair. She was sitting very upright, her posture as perfect as the night he'd met her, but he sensed that now it was more of a conscious effort. Her shoulders seemed tense, as though she was holding herself together, keeping up appearances, and he wondered what it was about the situation that was making her nervous.

'What are you doing here?' Ali repeated her earlier question. 'Have you left the army?'

He shook his head. 'Not exactly. I've taken leave, carer's leave.'

'Carer's leave?' she parroted. 'Who for?'

'My wife,' he replied.

'You're married?' He saw her glance at his ring finger. It was bare. Just as it had always been.

'Ex-wife,' he corrected quickly. 'We're divorced.' Their marriage had hardly been a textbook one but even now he struggled with the 'ex' part. Not because he still wanted to be married but because it was a reminder of his failings as a husband. For someone who was, by nature, a perfectionist, it bothered him that he hadn't been able to keep a marriage together.

Ali was frowning again. 'You're caring for your ex-wife? Why?'

'It's complicated.'

'I'm sure it is.' She smiled, inviting him to tell her more. But telling her more would wipe the smile from her face. He had no doubt about that. And he wasn't sure if he wanted to be the one to make her smile disappear. If Ali was smiling he could pretend that things were fine with the world.

'You're not doing a very good job of explaining why you're here.' Ali spoke into the silence that stretched between them.

Quinn pinched the bridge of his nose and ran his thumb and forefinger out along each eyebrow, trying to ease the tension he could feel through his forehead as he summoned the strength to tell her what she was waiting to hear. He was yet to find an easy way to deliver this sentence. 'My wife, ex-wife,' he corrected himself again, 'has a brain tumour.'

He was relieved when she didn't gasp or hesitate or stammer something inane, like most people did. Being a doctor, she grasped the situation better than most.

'What grade?' she asked. Her question was matter-of-fact. There was no room for emotion, just the facts.

'A GBM IV.' He could see by Ali's expression that she understood the poor prognosis. Her olive skin paled slightly. Ali didn't know Julieanne, she didn't owe her any sympathy, but Quinn could see that she felt for her. Astrocytomas were the most common primary brain tumour in adults but their characteristics and prognoses varied widely. Glioblastoma multiforme IV was a fast-spreading, highly malignant tumour. It was not the one you wanted to be diagnosed as having.

But Julieanne's condition still didn't completely explain his reasons for being there. 'My mother-in-law has moved in with them,' he continued, before Ali could ask more questions, 'but she can't manage to care for Julieanne and the children. I'm doing it for my kids. After all, they are my responsibility.'

'Children?'

He'd forgotten Ali didn't know about his daughters. Forgotten she knew virtually nothing at all about him. There was a part of him that felt as though he'd known her all his life. An idea in his head that they'd shared more than just a brief conversation many weeks ago. He nodded. 'Two girls.'

Her shoulders relaxed as she leaned forward in her chair, closing the distance between them, letting her guard down. She stretched a hand towards him, as though to touch him, before she thought better of it. Her hand dropped into her lap and Quinn's heart dropped with it. The movement served to highlight to him how much he wanted to feel her touch. How badly he needed to be connected to another person. To Ali.

'Oh, Quinn, how terrible for them. I'm so sorry.'

Her response surprised him. He realised he'd expected her to ask him about the girls but instead her first response was one of empathy. He appreciated that curiosity wasn't first and foremost in her mind. He took her empathy as a show of support. She didn't find it strange that he would drop everything to care for his ex-wife and he had a feeling she would have been disappointed in him if he hadn't.

Ali wanted to comfort him and she was almost tempted to reach for him before she realised that might be inappropriate. No matter how she imagined him, no matter that seeing him again made her pulse race and a bubble of excitement build inside her, the fact of the matter was they were strangers. He probably didn't need or want her comfort.

Her own problems shrank in comparison to Quinn's. Her own disappointment about the recent events in her own life she could, and would, overcome with time, but Quinn wasn't going to get a happy ending to his tale and neither were his children. He had two daughters, girls who would be left without a mother, maybe not immediately but in the not-too-distant future. Ali knew how unfair life could seem at times and her heart went out to Quinn's daughters. How would they cope with losing a parent at a young age? No matter what might have transpired between Quinn and his wife, no one deserved this.

'Oh, Quinn, how terrible for them. I'm so sorry.'

She felt for him too. The situation must be a night-mare for him but she didn't know him well enough to put her feelings into words. She needed time to process what he'd just told her, time to work out how to react appropriately. Shock and surprise were making it difficult to know what to say.

It was a shock to see him again. A shock too to find he was divorced and a father. Her imagination hadn't pictured that scenario. In her dreams he was a dynamic, GI Joe type, athletic but intelligent. Daring but sensitive, and a bachelor. Most definitely a bachelor.

But some things hadn't changed. She was still aware of a raw sexuality about him, a ruggedness, a hard, firm maleness, but there were also lines in the corners of his eyes that she didn't remember seeing before. She wanted to reach out and smooth the lines away but she resisted the urge, sensing she would be overstepping the mark.

She searched frantically for something to say, some-thing that would steer the conversation towards less emotional waters. 'I still don't understand why you want this job, though,' she said. 'Won't you have enough to keep you busy?'

'The girls are back at school now after the holidays. My mother-in-law and I will care for Julieanne in shifts and as long as I can be home when the girls are there I don't need to be there all the time. I want to be busy. I need to be busy. I'm in Adelaide because people need me but Julieanne and I don't need quality time together. Our marriage ended a long time ago and nothing is going to change that or change the situation.'

'Yet you're going to be her carer.' The situation was unusual, to say the least.

'Our marriage ended because of circumstances, bad timing and bad judgement, but we've stayed friends. We're committed to our children. I can do this for Julieanne. I want to do it.'

It was obvious he still cared for his ex-wife. Did he still love her? Ali wondered. Not that it was any of her business but his reply confirmed her opinion of him as a strong and compassionate person and she suspected he was going to need every bit of that strength. She couldn't think of too many other people she knew who would offer to care for an ex-partner. In contrast, she knew of many who would struggle to care for a current partner in the same situation.

'Is Julieanne having treatment?'

Quinn nodded. 'Radiotherapy.'

'Is it working?'

He shrugged and his gesture reminded her of Atlas trying to balance the world on his shoulders. 'The oncologists are not optimistic at this stage.'

'What have they told you?'

'That this could be her last Christmas.'

It was early August and Christmas was less than five months away. Quinn's voice was heavy and Ali had a second overwhelming urge to try to ease his pain. But she resisted again. Six weeks ago they had shared a drink, half a drink really, and that was the extent of their acquaintance. Even if the excitement and interest she had felt had been mutual, she knew the goalposts had shifted since then. Quinn was now out of bounds. He had enough going on in his life. But that didn't mean she couldn't offer to help in some way. It didn't matter how much inner strength he had, he was going to need help and Ali resolved then that she would do whatever she could. Even if she didn't yet know what that could be.

'What do you think?' Ali's mother asked. 'Did I make a good choice?'

It was several hours later and Ali was sharing lunch with her mother. She was still trying to come to terms with the idea that Quinn was suddenly in her life. After weeks of replaying their first conversation in her head, all ten minutes of it, to have him here, in her town, in her office, felt surreal and she had no idea how she was going to deal with it.

'I have to admit his appointment took me by surprise,' she replied. 'I was expecting the job would go to a female doctor, someone with kids who wanted to work part time.'

Malika shrugged, a gesture that made the numerous gold bangles adorning her wrist chime. 'Quinn is all of those things, just not female.'

Definitely not female, Ali thought.

'Besides,' her mother continued, 'it might be good to have a male doctor on staff. You have to admit we're rather lacking in that department.'

Ali couldn't disagree. Both receptionists were female, as was the practice nurse and the other part-time doctor. There wasn't a male amongst them. It could be a very good appointment *if* Ali was convinced her mother had found the right male. 'Don't you think he has enough on his plate, without working too?'

'That's his decision. Not mine,' Malika said as she poured them both a cup of jasmine tea. 'What reservations do you have?'

None she was prepared to voice, Ali thought. She just knew it would be difficult to keep her feelings in check but that was her problem and one she would deal with. She couldn't admit she was nervous about working with him, worried about her ability to remain professional, but she had to think of something to say and she had to think of it quickly. 'He told me he's taken leave from the army so it doesn't sound as if he plans to be here permanently.'

Malika nodded. 'No, and that's a shame. I was hoping the locum position might develop into something more permanent. But I can see why this job is attractive to him at the moment and I'm happy to have him. His experience is excellent, and I want to do this for him. He's going through a tough time. If we can help each other then that's a good thing. As long as he can cover for me while I go to that conference in Barcelona with your father, that's the minimum commitment I need.'

'Are you sure he's the right fit for the practice? You don't think he'll be bored working here? You don't think he's a bit over-qualified?' In her opinion an army medic was likely to find general practice work rather mundane.

But Malika wasn't easily dissuaded, about Quinn or most other matters, and Ali should have known she was clutching at straws. 'It's only a short-term locum position at this stage and I think he could use a break from the stress of the army and his overseas postings,' her mother responded. 'I think it will do him good to have some routine medicine. He'll have enough stress at home and he might enjoy coming to work for a break.'

Ali couldn't argue. The surgery was, after all, still her mother's, the decision was Malika's, and Ali knew, professionally, it was a good one. It looked like she would just have to get used to the idea of working with Quinn.

Ali dictated the last referral letter, pushed her chair back and stretched her arms over her head to get the knots out of her shoulders. It was time to go home. She was the last one at the surgery, it was dark and she was tired. She stood and collected her handbag and red coat from where they were hanging behind her door but a sudden noise made her pause. Someone was coming in the back door.

She wasn't expecting anyone and the light from her room spilled out into the corridor like a beacon against the darkness of the rest of the clinic, highlighting her presence to whoever had just entered the building. Ali heard two footsteps, light, not heavy, and her heart missed a beat before lodging itself in her throat.

'Hello?' The footsteps were accompanied by a voice. Quinn's voice. For a solidly built man he moved lightly.

Ali's heart skipped another beat. Her fight-or-flight response was in top gear thanks to the adrenalin that was kicking around in her system, but now the adrenalin transformed into a flurry of excitement instead of fear.

She stepped out from behind her door.

'Quinn, what are you doing here?'

He was casually dressed in old, soft jeans and a blue woollen jumper that made his eyes gleam as the light from her room shone on him. His jeans stretched firmly across the muscles in his thighs. His legs were muscular, powerful and very male. Ali blushed as her gaze swept across his groin. Very male. Quickly she averted her eyes and lifted them to his face, hoping he hadn't noticed her transgression.

'I wanted to drop off a few things and get myself a bit organised before I start consulting tomorrow.' In his arms he held a cardboard archive box. 'Am I disturbing you? I didn't think anyone else would be here.'

Ali shook her head. 'No, I was just finishing up.' She followed him into his room and watched as he dropped the box onto his desk. It sounded heavy. He'd made it look light. 'Would you like some help?' she asked as he began to empty the box. She'd trailed after him without thinking about what she was doing and only now did she realise he might not want company.

'Sure. Do you want to find a spot to hang this?' he asked as he handed her his framed medical degree.

There was an empty hook to the left of the window, above the desk, and Ali hung the frame there, right where patients would be able to see it. If he was bothering to unpack, did that mean he was thinking of this as more than a locum position?

When she turned back to Quinn he was still pulling certificates from the box. She looked at the certificates as he stacked them in an ever-increasing pile on the desk. Trauma, underwater and hyperbaric medicine and chemical and biological defence followed his traditional medical qualifications. She had suspected he was over-qualified for the job but she hadn't realised by how much.

'You carry these around with you?' she asked.

'No.' Quinn shook his head and grinned at her. 'They've been gathering dust in Julieanne's attic. The army moves people around so often it's been easier to store stuff with her,' he replied, as he picked up the pile of frames and put them on the floor, leaning them against the wall.

Ali wondered where he'd been but before she could ask she was distracted by a photograph of two girls that he was lifting from the box.

'Are these your daughters?' she asked as he set the picture on the desk. 'They're twins?'

Quinn nodded. The girls were identical from what she could see. With white-blonde hair and Quinn's extraordinary blue eyes, there was no doubting who their father was, but they were older than she had expected. She knew they were at school but she'd imagined them as only just old enough. Judging from the photo, they'd been at school for a while. 'You got an early start.' She'd learned from her mother that Quinn was only thirty-two. Six years older than she was.

Quinn ran his fingers along the top of the photo frame. 'They caught us by surprise. They turned nine a few months ago.'

'What are their names?'

'Beth and Eliza.'

His voice was soft and Ali could hear the love as he spoke his daughters' names and her heart ached with loneliness and loss. But she couldn't stop to dwell on her own feelings right now. She couldn't afford to be swamped by disappointment. She suppressed those feelings; she'd deal with them another time. She was getting quite adept at that. She knew she needed to address the issue, she couldn't just continue to ignore it, she knew that wasn't healthy, but she didn't have the strength to do anything else. Not yet. So she continued to talk, keeping the focus on Quinn.

'Pretty names,' she said. 'Which one is which?'

Quinn smiled. 'It's hard to tell in a photograph unless you know them, but Beth is the extrovert, she's usually the first one to talk and she's just cut her hair. Or, more correctly, Eliza has just cut Beth's hair. Beth said she was tired of people not being able to tell them apart so she convinced Liza to chop it off. Of course, then they had to go to the hairdresser to fix it and Beth now has a bob, I think they call it.'

She looked again at the photograph. Even though they were older than she'd expected, they were still far too young to be going through this nightmare. 'How are they coping with everything that's going on?'

'Better than I am, I think.' He sounded sad.

'You probably know more about Julieanne's condition than is good for you,' she told him. 'Sometimes ignorance is bliss.'

'It's not Julieanne I'm struggling with. It's parenting.'

Ali frowned. 'What do you mean?'

'I haven't spent much time with the girls. I was still

studying when they were born and then the army has kept me busy, then the divorce. Julieanne has been the constant in the girls' lives so far and I'm on a pretty steep learning curve.'

'You didn't share custody?'

'I couldn't. The girls were here, I've been in Queensland or overseas.'

'Peacekeeping missions?' Ali knew that army medics would have to accompany soldiers on any mission.

'Some.'

His answer was vague enough to arouse suspicion. 'War zones?'

Her heart was racing at the thought of Quinn being in danger but he was grinning at her, his blue eyes sparkling as he replied. 'That's classified.'

'What, you could tell me but then you'd have to silence me?' She found herself smiling in return.

'Something like that,' he teased. 'Let's just say I'd much rather be here.'

Did he mean in Australia or right here, with her? Ali's mind was turning in circles, trying to decipher what his smile, his dancing azure eyes and his words all meant.

He laughed. 'I can't believe I've been thinking about you and you've been under my nose all this time.'

He'd been thinking about her. 'What do you mean, "all this time"?'

'The night we met, at the bar,' he explained, 'the phone call I got was from my mother-in-law, telling me about Julieanne. I had intended to come back to you, I wanted to come back, but everything else took a back seat. I flew out the next morning, straight down here.'

'So that's why you didn't give your keynote address.' Quinn nodded.

'You've been here since June?' Ali asked.

'I've been up and back to Brisbane a few times but I've been here for a few weeks now.'

She thought back to all those fleeting glimpses, all those moments when she'd thought she'd caught sight of him. Perhaps it hadn't been her fanciful imagination. She couldn't believe he'd been here all that time. Not that it would have made any difference had she known. Despite his intentions, she was sure his priorities would have been elsewhere.

'If I'd known you were here I would have searched for you,' he said.

'Why?'

'Because I find your presence cathartic.' He smiled at her and Ali's insides all but melted.

'Is that a good thing?'

'You make me feel calm and I need that right now. I needed it when we met but for other reasons. You make me forget about all the unpleasantness, the stress. I feel as though I can breathe properly when I'm with you.'

That was ironic, Ali thought, considering that when he was near her she almost forgot *how* to breathe. When he looked at her with his brilliant blue eyes it made her breath catch in her throat, made her feel light-headed and excited, as though the world was full of possibilities. She could get lost in his eyes. They shimmered like pools of clear blue water that tempted her to dive in and never resurface.

'I'm glad I'm here,' he repeated, and this time his meaning was clear.

He was perched on the edge of the desk, watching her mouth. Was he waiting for her to speak? Her gaze travelled from his eyes to his mouth. He was almost close enough to kiss. If she dipped her head their lips would meet.

Her breath caught in her throat and her lips parted as she struggled for air. She could imagine losing herself in his eyes, losing herself in his lips. She was glad he was here too and she quite liked the idea of escaping from reality for a while. Of losing herself in Quinn. But now wasn't the time.

Ali stepped back, away from temptation, and changed the subject.

'Why didn't you quit the army and follow your family? You could get work anywhere.'

'It's more complicated than that. The army paid for med school, I can't just quit. There's a thing called return of service,' he explained. 'I have to repay them in time for every year of study they supported me for plus one year. It was that or buy out my service and I couldn't afford that. I've got four months left.'

'What are you going to do then?'

'I don't know.'

Ali had hoped he'd say he was planning on staying here but she knew it would depend on other factors. Julieanne's condition would be the decider and no one was in control of that.

She took one last look at his mouth. She couldn't do it. She couldn't take the chance. She wasn't brave or courageous, certainly not enough to get involved in something that was complicated, potentially messy and tragic. She wasn't strong enough for both of them.

Fate had brought them together again, even if she didn't want to believe it, but circumstances would keep them apart no matter how much she wished things were different.

CHAPTER THREE

Julieanne

JULIEANNE WAS EXHAUSTED. It hadn't been a particularly strenuous day but she found any day that she had to go to appointments stressful. The drive through the hills from Stirling into the city, waiting for the appointment, waiting for results, they all took their toll. She'd had scans today. Scans that showed that, despite the radiotherapy, the tumour continued to grow. She hadn't been surprised. She could feel things weren't improving yet a tiny part of her had been hoping she'd been wrong. That was exhausting too, trying to keep positive when she knew things weren't getting better.

And just because the bad news wasn't unexpected didn't make it any easier to hear. She tried not to dwell on the statistics but she knew the odds were not in her favour. Survival rates were pretty well non-existent with this type of tumour, fewer than three per cent of people survived past five years and the average life expectancy, even with treatment, was between seven and nine months. She was approaching five months. But she wasn't ready to give up yet.

She lay on her bed, listening to the sounds of the twins in the bath. They'd had netball practice and a late dinner, neither of which Julieanne had had the energy for. There was so much she was missing out on and this was just the beginning. She hated the thought that she was going to miss out on the rest of their lives.

She was grateful to her mother and to Quinn for stepping in to help. She didn't know how she would manage without them both but then Quinn had always tried to do the right thing. He was the type of man who took his responsibilities seriously.

Sometimes she wondered why she couldn't have been happy with Quinn. Why she'd had to go looking for some excitement. What was wrong with her that she couldn't be satisfied with a man who wasn't only attractive but also intelligent and kind and decent?

But he hadn't often been around.

Julieanne knew she'd embarked on the extramarital affairs as a cry for attention. She'd felt weighed down by the responsibility of motherhood, she'd felt as though she'd lost her identity. Quinn had been busy, he had been studying and fulfilling his defence force training commitments, but she hadn't been able to see that he'd been suffering with the same feelings of pressure. She'd only seen that he'd got to escape from the constant, unending world of crying, sleepless babies who had forever needed changing and feeding. She knew now that her expectations of him had been unrealistic. He had been trying to finish his degree and at the same time keep a roof over his family's heads. She knew a lot of other men would have never taken on the responsibility in the first place yet at the time she'd been so caught up with her own needs that she hadn't stopped to consider Quinn.

When he hadn't even noticed the first affair she'd embarked on another and another. It had given her a chance to feel like a woman again instead of just a mother. She hadn't pretended she'd felt like a wife. A wife wouldn't have behaved the way she had. She'd known she was playing with fire but she hadn't been able to stop. She'd got bolder as she'd waited for him to notice. Waited for him to beg her to stop. Waited for him to tell her he loved her and that her affairs were breaking his heart.

But those words had never come.

She waited and waited but it was a long time before he found out. They were living in army accommodation where there wasn't a lot of privacy, people saw things, people talked, and eventually someone told Quinn. But even then he didn't profess his love. He just asked her what she planned to do. He didn't throw it in her face that he was working and studying hard to provide for them and this was her way of thanking him. He didn't accuse her of childish or selfish behaviour or of any of the things that he could have accused her of. *Should* have accused her of. She knew she'd behaved badly but she wondered now if he'd seen it as a way to get out of his commitment. Not to the children but to her. Would their relationship even have lasted if she hadn't fallen pregnant? Was an unplanned pregnancy the only reason their relationship had lasted as long as it had?

The whine of the hairdryer interrupted her thoughts, the high-pitched noise competing for room in her brain. She had noticed she was having increasing trouble concentrating and any extraneous noise only compounded the problem.

She blocked out the noise as she asked herself a question she'd asked countless times before but had never been able to answer. Had she destroyed their relationship or would it have eventually run its course anyway?

She knew the answer was most probably yes. They'd been young. Too young. And naïve. She suspected it would have run its course but she would never know for certain.

Whatever the answer, she still couldn't believe she'd behaved so appallingly. She'd treated Quinn so badly and yet here he was, back beside her, offering his help and support. Even if he wasn't offering his love, he was doing more than she deserved. But she knew he was doing it for his children.

He may not have always been there for them but he was here now and she needed to prepare him for what would come next. She needed to prepare all of them. This was going to be her last gift, her attempt to right all the wrongs she'd done to Quinn. To make amends. Her last chance to try to leave them all in a good place.

Someone switched the hairdryer off and the irritating whine was replaced by the sound of her daughters' giggles. They skipped into her room, decked out in pink pyjamas, their cheeks still flushed from the heat of the bath, her blonde hair, Quinn's brilliant blue eyes. Julieanne felt her spirits lift. She and Quinn may have been a mistake but she had no regrets. That mistake had given them these two gorgeous girls and despite her early struggles she loved her daughters. She knew they were the best things that had ever happened to her and she needed to do her best by them now.

'What's so funny?' she asked.

'Granny was teaching Dad how to wash our hair.'

'How did he go?'

'He didn't use enough shampoo.'

'He said it's 'cos he hardly has to use any 'cos his hair is so short.'

'Your hair looks pretty to me.' Their hair fell in glossy, healthy sheaths to their shoulders, Eliza's still longer than Beth's. 'Did he get all the knots out?'

'Granny did.'

'Can you brush it for us?'

'Sure. I'll do yours first, Liza, then you can swap with Beth.'

Quinn stuck his head around the door and as Julieanne looked into his blue eyes she wished again that she hadn't messed things up. 'Are you okay?' he asked.

Julieanne nodded. This was a relaxing activity. A good one to do as they wound down for bed.

'I'll just go and clear up the dinner dishes and then I'll read to the girls,' Quinn said.

'What's Mum doing?' Julieanne asked him.

'Ironing the girls' school shirts.'

Between them they were doing all the things she used to do. Routine things that she had done, day in, day out.

She'd once wished, on some days, that she'd had someone to share that load, someone to do those never-ending tasks, but now she wished she had the energy and the attention span to do the ironing or to stand at the kitchen sink.

She brushed her daughters' hair as she listened to their chatter. They didn't need much input from her, they were content with each other's company and Beth, in particular, didn't look for her input. Julieanne was happy to sit and listen. Happy just to be part of their lives.

'Who's ready for a story?' Quinn was back.

'Would you mind reading it in here?' Julieanne asked. 'The girls can lie with me and listen.' She wasn't ready for the girls to leave her yet. She was feeling melancholy.

Quinn nodded. There was an antique wing chair in the corner of the room and he folded himself into it and draped one leg over the arm. Julieanne tried to ignore how out of place he looked in her room. She had redecorated earlier in the year and while it wasn't frilly or fussy it was very feminine with a lot of accents of her favourite colour, pink. Quinn looked far too rugged and large for the dainty chair and the fabrics of his surroundings.

Julieanne closed her eyes as he started to read. She had one twin on each side of her, their warm bodies pressed up against her. She could breathe in their clean, apple scent from the soap and shampoo.

'Can we sleep here with Mummy?' Beth asked as Quinn finished the second chapter.

'Please, Daddy, you can sleep on the couch,' Eliza added.

Julieanne was still amazed at how the girls had never really noticed that their parents were divorced. She could only suppose that because Quinn had spent so little time in the country over the past two years they were more used to him being absent than present, so divorced or away was really no different. And because he went to bed after them and got up before them, they didn't notice that he slept in the study.

Quinn nodded as he stood and picked up the cashmere blanket that was draped over the back of the wing chair. He spread the rug over the girls and Julieanne. 'I'll carry you to your beds later, though, okay,' he told them, 'so that you don't disturb Mum with your wriggling.'

Julieanne stirred when Quinn returned and lifted the blanket off the sleeping trio. She opened her eyes and watched as he scooped Eliza off the bed. She looked as light as a feather in his arms. Eliza turned her face into Quinn's chest, tucking herself against him. He kissed her forehead as she snuggled against him. She was the more affectionate of the girls, the one who needed more physical attention. The one who was most like Julieanne.

There was more of Quinn in Beth. She had the same determination, the same courage of her convictions. Once she made a decision she very rarely changed her mind. She was loyal but she didn't need constant reassurance. She was more likely to give it to others.

Julieanne hoped that when the time came, when the

girls were without her, Beth would get comfort. She would need it as, despite her independent nature, she was only nine. Eliza would be fine, she would seek solace and love and reassurance, but it wasn't in Beth's nature. Julieanne would have to remember to tell Quinn to watch out for her.

He came back for Beth. He gathered her into his arms and kissed her lightly on the forehead too. Julieanne relaxed when she saw Quinn take this opportunity to kiss her while she slept, it wasn't often offered when she was awake.

Quinn loved his daughters. Julieanne knew that. The three of them would be okay. She knew he doubted his parenting ability but he was a good father.

He was a good man.

She wished she could ask him to sit with her while she went back to sleep. She wished she didn't need to ask. She wished he would offer. But their time was long past.

She wished things were different.

Julieanne was vaguely aware of soft footsteps on her bedroom floor as she waited for sleep to reclaim her.

'Jules? Are you still awake?' Quinn's voice was quiet and for a moment Julieanne thought she was dreaming.

She opened her eyes.

'I'm sorry,' he apologised, 'but I wanted to talk to you about your appointment today. I read the copy of the report,' he told her, as he sat on the edge of her bed. 'How are you feeling?'

'Disappointed. Angry,' she admitted. 'But not really

surprised. I thought I was ready to accept my fate but every time I have a scan there's a part of me that still hopes for some good news. It's not going to happen, is it?'

Julieanne could feel the tears in her eyes and this annoyed her. She wasn't looking for sympathy from Quinn, he was already doing enough. But that didn't stop her from wishing that something would fall in her favour. She wanted to go back to when it had been okay to throw herself into his arms. Back to the days when he'd known the right things to say to her. Back when he'd wanted to be the one to comfort her. But those days were gone.

He shook his head and reached for her hand. 'I'm sorry, Jules.' His touch was comforting but she needed more. 'Did the specialist have any other treatment suggestions?'

'No. He's doing everything he can. But he started talking about hospice care. I'm not ready to think about that. Not yet. I want something to look forward to and that's not it.'

'What are you planning?'

'The girls want to throw a birthday party for you. I want to help them organise it.'

'I don't need a party.'

'I know. But the girls want to do it. I know I don't have any right to ask this of you but it'll be fun for the girls. We need to make sure they have some happy memories of this time. Their lives can't stop because of me, and neither can yours. I appreciate everything you're doing, but, please, let us do this for you.'

'What did you have in mind?'

'Nothing yet. It's your birthday, we'll let you have some say,' she teased, thinking that if she sounded relaxed he'd be more likely to agree to her requests.

'Where are you planning on having it?'

'Here.'

'No.' He shook his head. 'You're not well enough.'

'I'm not well enough to go out,' she argued, 'but I'd like to be able to see you blow out your candles, and if we have it here I can manage that.'

'Can I think about it?'

'Are you going to ring the specialist to see if I'm up to it?'

Quinn started to shake his head before he stopped, a guilty expression in his blue eyes.

'We'll keep it small,' Julieanne negotiated. 'Manageable. The girls would love it. I'll plan it and Mum will help. I don't mind asking her if it's just a small party. You just tell us who you'd like to invite.'

'I don't have anyone to invite.'

'What about some people from work?'

'Why would they want to come to a party for me?'

'Why wouldn't they? Besides, I'm sure if the girls invited them they would come. The girls can be very persuasive.'

'I know.' Quinn smiled. 'How about if I agree to at least let the girls make a cake. We'll celebrate as a family, even if we don't have any extra guests.'

'Okay.' That was a start. Julieanne knew the girls would talk him round. A party was just what they all needed, it would be something to look forward to. 'Thank you.'

'Now, you need to sleep.' He stood up and the mattress sprang back into shape. He leant over and kissed her gently on the forehead. Julieanne closed her eyes as his lips brushed her skin. She knew his kiss was more of a reflex than anything else but she missed the comfort that physical contact could bring. She wondered whether Quinn had anyone in his life to comfort him. She'd have to remember to ask him tomorrow, she thought as she drifted off to sleep.

Quinn successfully managed to avoid the topic of his birthday for several days. There were far more important things to worry about and he really wasn't in the mood for celebrating. Although he did understand Julieanne's point of view, he just didn't know how they could possibly imagine hosting a party, no matter how small. He was still struggling on the home front; it was a perpetual juggling act and he just hoped and prayed that parenting would eventually become second nature to him.

Work was his one salvation. The one place where he still felt in control. Where he still felt capable. It was relaxing in its own way. At work he was busy worrying about other people's problems, which left him no time to dwell on his own. If it wasn't for Helen's help at home he didn't know how he would manage. Everything seemed to take twice as long as it should and he knew he would never get the girls fed, organised and where they needed to go on time without help. Today was a case in point. The minute something took Helen out of the equation things immediately seemed to go pear-shaped.

He hung up the phone and rubbed his brow as he tried to work out how to tackle the latest issue. He closed his eyes and sighed.

'Is everything all right?' Ali's smooth, sultry voice interrupted his musings.

He opened his eyes. She was standing in the doorway and he took a moment as he ran his fingers through his hair just to look at her. 'It's fine.'

He recognised the expression on her face. Lately everyone expected to hear bad news and bad news only. Julieanne's condition had everyone he knew balancing on a knife edge, waiting for the day that the worst would happen. But today wasn't that day. He knew his brief reply wouldn't have given enough reassurance so he added, 'Nothing major. I just need to reshuffle some things.'

'Is there anything I can do to help?' Ali had offered assistance before but he hadn't yet taken her up on her offer. He was trying to pretend he had everything under control.

'No. Thank you. Julieanne and Helen have been delayed in the city. Julieanne's radiotherapy treatment is behind schedule so I need to make some arrangements for the girls after school. I've got a late list today as Helen would normally collect the girls midweek.'

'I started at seven this morning so I'm due to finish at four,' Ali told him. 'I can take over your list if you like and you can take the girls home.'

'Thanks, but I don't want to muck my patients around. I've got a few coming in for follow-up appointments and I wanted to offer them consistency of practitioner. They've already had to see me instead of your mother.' He had applied for this job with the idea that he could manage to be father, carer and employee—after all, how hard could it be compared to what he was used to?—and he didn't want to give anyone reason to think he had taken on more than he could handle.

'So what will you do? You're stretching yourself thin as it is.'

Did Ali already suspect that he wasn't coping? 'Julieanne has given me the numbers of a couple of mums from school who are happy to take the girls home with them.'

'So you're sorted.' Her tone suggested she knew he was struggling.

'Mmm.'

'What is it?'

'I don't like feeling indebted.' That was true, but he couldn't think of another solution.

'Quinn, you don't have to do it all by yourself. People offer assistance as a gesture of goodwill. There's not much anyone can do for Julieanne except help to look after her family. Her friends will feel better if you let them do this.'

'I get that but I feel I should be able to manage.' He didn't want anyone to think he wasn't up to the task. 'And I hate it that the girls get foisted off onto other people. I feel I'm letting them down. Constantly.'

'Why don't you get them dropped off here, then? They

can play in the garden—you can keep an eye on them. There's an old swing in the oak tree in the garden outside that I used to use when I was little. You can see it from here.' Ali crossed the room and leant over the desk to point out the window. Her arm brushed his shoulder and he was enveloped in her perfume. The fragrance that transported him back to his childhood, a simpler, if not necessarily happier time in his life. He wanted to close his eyes again and let Ali's voice and scent soothe him and allow him to forget about the world for a moment. 'They'll be safe and occupied out there,' she said, reminding him of his responsibilities with one sentence.

Quinn thought Ali's plan had merit until the girls arrived, tired, hungry and grizzly. There was no appeasing them and their whining had him at his wit's end. He needed to get back to his list. At this rate he'd be working until midnight and the girls would be ten times grumpier.

Ali appeared in the doorway of the clinic kitchen, a remorseful expression on her beautiful face. 'I'm sorry, was my plan a bad one?'

Quinn shook his head. 'The girls are just letting me know of a flaw in my parenting skills. Of another one,' he amended his comment. 'I forgot to organise an after-school snack.'

'I can fix that.' She pulled out a chair and sat at the table in the kitchen that doubled as a staffroom and lunch room. 'Hello, Beth. Hello, Eliza.' She looked at each girl in turn. 'I'm Ali, I'm one of the other doctors here. I'm finished for the day so why don't I take you both to the bakery and you can choose something for afternoon tea?'

Quinn was impressed that she not only remembered his daughters' names but that she was able to match the right name to the right girl.

'How did you know which one of us is which?' Beth asked. Quinn smiled. Julieanne always said Beth was a smaller version of him and it seemed she even thought the same way.

'Your dad talks about you all the time when he's not busy with his patients and he told me about when you got Eliza to cut your hair,' Ali explained. 'He's been working really hard so why don't we let him finish his work while we get something to eat.'

Ali let the girls set up their afternoon tea on the table outside near the oak tree. Winter was finally considering giving way to spring and it was mild enough to be in the open air. The first of the daffodils were flowering in the garden beds and the girls had picked some and put them in an old vase to decorate the table. Everything else on the table was in various shades of pink—pink doughnuts, melting-moment biscuits with pink icing and glasses of strawberry milk. Pink, they informed Ali, was their favourite colour.

By the time Quinn finished consulting the girls were fed and were happily putting the swing to the test. He joined them in the garden and Ali made them each a cup of tea and convinced him to sit and enjoy it and let the girls play for a little bit longer.

'That swing looks in good nick. Has it really been there since you were young?'

'What are you suggesting? That it's ancient or just that I am?' Ali teased, pleased to see that Quinn had relaxed now that the crisis had passed. 'I asked George, our gardener, to replace the ropes earlier in the week and he sanded and varnished the seat. I thought it might get used sooner rather than later.'

'You did that for the girls?' he asked.

I did it for you. 'I told you, people want to help. If there are some things to keep the girls occupied here after school, it may make it easier for you all. George suggested they could replant the old veggie patch if they're interested.'

Quinn looked around the garden. 'Did you spend a lot of time here growing up?'

Ali nodded. 'This used to be our family home. Mum started a part-time clinic here when I was two and as a teenager I used to work here in term breaks, covering for the receptionists' holidays, filing, doing that sort of thing.'

'Did it influence your decision to become a doctor?'

'I suppose so,' she answered, 'but I didn't really know anything different. Mum and Dad are both doctors, so is my older brother.'

'Where do your father and brother work?'

'Dad's a neurologist in the city. Tomas is in Melbourne, doing his orthopaedics speciality.'

'Did you ever think about *not* becoming a doctor?' He was smiling at her and the lines around his blue eyes deepened, but his eyes looked happy now, not exhausted, and Ali's heart lifted in her chest as though it was smiling back at him.

'No.'

'Was it expected?'

'Expected? No,' she answered with a shake of her head. 'Encouraged? Definitely. And I love it.'

Despite the fact that she'd felt it had lacked a bit of excitement of late, she did still love it, which was fortunate as she had nothing else in her life. She had always been quite content working as a GP, enjoyed knowing her patients and being a part of their lives and the community, but she hadn't ever anticipated that she might never have more than this. She was twenty-six years old and at a crossroads in her life but if she didn't have her career at the moment she knew she'd be totally miserable. She had to love it, it was all she had.

'I'm very glad you became a doctor.'

'You are? Why?'

'I wouldn't have met you otherwise.'

The twins jumped off the swing in mid-air and ran to the table, interrupting Ali before she could respond.

'Dad, we think we should have an afternoon tea party for your birthday,' Beth said.

Eliza turned to Ali. 'It's on Sunday. Would you like to come?'

'We're having cake,' Beth added, conversing in the tag-team manner Ali had grown accustomed to throughout the afternoon.

'It's your birthday?' Ali asked Quinn.

He nodded and looked at his daughters. 'But I thought it was just going to be family.'

'Dad...' Beth gave a long-suffering sigh. 'That's only five people, that's not a party.'

'It's enough for Mum.'

If Quinn expected that to be the end of the discussion he hadn't counted on the double-teaming that Ali suspected the girls were very good at.

'But we think we should have afternoon tea, just like we had with Ali today. That way you don't have to cook,' Eliza said.

'Dad's a terrible cook,' Beth added in an aside to Ali.

'We can buy some pretty pink things to eat at the bakery.'

'And a cake.'

'You can't cook?' Ali asked.

'I can,' he protested.

'As long as it's a barbecue,' said Beth.

'I think you've given away enough of my secrets for one day,' Quinn said. 'Five more minutes on the swing and then we are going home.' The girls both took another biscuit and ran back to the swing.

'Who does the cooking if it's not you?' Ali wanted to know.

'Helen, my mother-in-law,' Quinn replied. 'But I'm not completely useless. Beth was right, I can barbecue and I do the washing up and some of Julieanne's friends, mothers from school, have organised a food roster so a couple of times a week someone will drop off a meal. It's very generous of them and makes me feel a bit guilty. I know the girls want to celebrate my birthday but I can hardly ask Julieanne's friends to make me a cake. And I'm not sure that Julieanne is up to a party anyway.'

'What has she said?'

'She agrees with the girls. She thinks it would be nice to celebrate a happy event.'

'So you're the only one with objections.' Ali smiled.

Quinn rolled his eyes. 'And to think I used to lament the lack of women in the army. I've forgotten how good you all are at getting what you want.'

'This isn't what I want. It's what your daughters want. But does that mean you'll do it?'

'I don't have anyone to invite.'

'Invite us.'

'Us?'

Ali waved one arm towards the clinic. 'The people from here,' she explained. 'That way Julieanne can meet everyone and she won't worry when the girls come here after school. And what about those mothers who are helping with meals? Are they the same ones who pick up the girls?'

Quinn nodded. 'Yes.'

'Well, why don't you invite them as well? Julieanne might like to see them and I bet they'll offer to bring some food too. We'll all bring something and that way you won't have a chance to poison us.'

Ali had offered the idea in an attempt to be helpful but as the words came out of her mouth she wondered if she really wanted to surround herself with Quinn and his daughters. Was she making things more complicated? Not for him, but for her. Should she be getting involved in his life?

CHAPTER FOUR

Ali

BUT WHEN QUINN agreed to go ahead with a party Ali couldn't resist the invitation. It would be rude not to go, wouldn't it? Of course, she told herself, it had nothing to do with her curiosity and absolutely nothing to do with wanting to meet Julieanne. She was going as a show of support.

Her habit of being early meant she was the first one to arrive. She stalled outside until her watch told her it was three o'clock exactly but when Quinn opened the door with a semi-inflated balloon in his hand it was obvious that they weren't quite ready for guests.

'Sorry, am I still too early?' she asked. 'I told you it was a bad habit.'

'No, your timing is perfect, my jaw muscles are beginning to ache. You can take over the balloon-blowing for me while I tie some to the front fence.' He grinned and a warm glow suffused Ali. He looked pleased to see her.

Ali retraced her steps. She placed her basket on the

ground and took a balloon from Quinn's hand. Their fingers touched, flooding Ali with heat that pooled low in her stomach. His eyes were locked on her face, his fingers entwined with hers, the contact wrapping them in a capsule of time when only the two of them existed.

Ali didn't know how long they stood there, silently connected, but it was long enough for her to start to feel dizzy from a lack of oxygen. She was the first to break eye contact. She had to look away so she could remember to breathe.

She looked vaguely at the balloon pinched between her thumb and her finger, as if wondering how it had got there. Quinn still had a handful of fresh balloons, all of them pink.

'Was there a special on pink balloons?' Ali asked. 'It's not very manly.'

Quinn shrugged his shoulders and grinned. 'I'm living in a house full of women, and if you can't beat them…' He hadn't taken his eyes off her and they sparkled like he had a secret he wanted to share, but before he could say anything further the twins appeared from inside.

'Are you finished yet, Dad?' Beth asked.

'All done,' he replied.

'Hi, Ali,' Eliza said. 'What's in the basket?'

'Hello, girls.' Ali lifted a covered bowl from her basket and handed it to Eliza. Nestled inside the bowl were dozens of pink spheres. 'I made coconut burfi.'

'They're pink!' Beth exclaimed.

'What are they?' Eliza wanted to know.

'They are an Indian sweet,' Ali told them, 'and they

are delicious. You can make all different sorts. Sometimes I make chocolate ones but I thought pink would be best. I don't know what your dad's favourite colour is so I went with yours.'

The girls ran back inside with the bowl, leaving Ali and Quinn alone again. Ali delved into her basket a second time and lifted Quinn's present out.

'This is for you.' She handed him the gift and as his eyes met hers and held her in their spotlight she decided his favourite colour should be azure blue, to match his eyes.

Her present was a potted herb garden containing a red and a green chilli plant, coriander and mint. An envelope was tucked amongst the plants. 'Open the envelope,' she told him.

Quinn slit the envelope with his finger and pulled out a sheet of paper. 'Cooking lessons?'

'We were talking about people wanting to feel useful. I'm offering to teach you to cook. Nothing fancy, just some easy dishes that you can do with the girls.'

'On a barbecue?' he asked hopefully.

'Maybe.' Ali laughed.

'It's a great idea. I love it, thank you.' He smiled at her and Ali held her breath again as she let Quinn's charm work its magic.

This time the spell was broken not by Ali but by the arrival of the girls from work. Ali's first thought when Tracey and Deb arrived was disappointment that she no longer had Quinn to herself, but when they went inside her disappointment turned to relief. She was about to meet Julieanne, and surely it was better to meet her with company. What if Julieanne could somehow read her thoughts about Quinn? That would be a little inappropriate.

A pot-belly stove warmed the room which had been festooned with more pink balloons. The dining table had been pushed up against one wall and standing proudly in the centre was a chocolate cake decorated with toffee shards. Ali smiled. It was possibly the only item on the menu that wasn't pink. Oversize suede couches were clustered around the fire.

Julieanne was seated on one couch and as Quinn made the introductions all Ali could think of was that Julieanne was not what she'd expected. She was blonde, that wasn't unexpected given the twins' colouring, but she was petite. A cheerleader type but without the boobs. Ali had expected someone a little more robust, someone who could match Quinn, not in size but in energy. But then Julieanne smiled and Ali could see her strength of spirit and her heart sank. If Julieanne was Quinn's type, there wasn't much hope for her. Tall, curvaceous, brunette and mixed-race Ali was about as far from the all-American type as you could get. The only thing she and Julieanne had in common was nice teeth.

The twins were perched on the couch either side of their mother and Ali's heart sank further and a surge of envy ran through her veins. It was odd to be envious of a terminally ill woman but Ali couldn't help her feelings. She longed to have what Julieanne had. She longed for children. Even though Julieanne's marriage hadn't lasted, she was still a mother and no one could take that away from her. Ali's dreams of motherhood had all but been destroyed. She knew it could still happen but not in the traditional way. If she was lucky enough to have a family of her own it would be a long process, an arduous one, and she still had to find someone who would take that path with her. She couldn't do it alone.

Her gaze sought Quinn. He was greeting more guests, the school mothers, Ali supposed. Every adult female in the room had experienced motherhood, excluding her, and with that realisation her sense of loss intensified. She'd thought she was dealing with it but obviously she was only managing to ignore it.

Somehow she smiled and chatted and pretended she was enjoying herself but it was a struggle. The only thing that kept her from fleeing was Quinn. She escaped to the kitchen by offering to make cups of tea but her seclusion was short-lived. 'Let me take over for you,' Tracey said as she came into the kitchen. 'Julieanne has asked to speak to you.'

Ali had no idea what Julieanne would need to talk to her about but she could hardly refuse. She returned to the lounge area and sat on a couch opposite Quinn's ex-wife.

'I wanted to thank you for giving Quinn a job,' Julieanne said.

'That was my mother's doing but it's working out well for all of us, I think. Quinn is an extremely competent doctor.' *Well done,* Ali congratulated herself, *you've managed to keep things professional.*

'You like him, don't you.' Julieanne made a statement, not a question.

'I...' Ali had no idea what to say. What was the right etiquette for this situation?

'It's okay,' Julieanne reassured her. 'I've seen the way you look at him. He's a very likeable man and he's going to need people soon. More than he realises. I was hoping I was right about you, I was hoping your feelings might work in my favour.'

'I'm not sure I'm following you.'

'Quinn will need a full-time job eventually. Would it be a possibility to stay on at your clinic?'

'I guess so.' Ali frowned. As much as she liked the sound of it and she knew that her mother was hoping for that outcome, it wasn't her decision. 'But what about the army?'

'His return of service is up at the end of this year, which means he can quit the army. He's been trying to decide what to do. I don't want him to stay in the army, it's not good for the girls and he's going to be raising them alone. I want him to stay here. He's going to need my mum's help or vice versa. Neither of them can do it alone once I'm...'

Julieanne didn't need to say anything further. Her meaning was self-explanatory.

'I'll see what I can do.' *What else could she say?*

Eliza and Beth rounded the guests up to sing 'Happy Birthday' to Quinn and Ali was pleased to have a reason to end the conversation. The girls dragged Julieanne to the end of the table to stand beside Quinn. Eager to put as much distance between them and herself, Ali stood at the opposite end of the table. Unfortunately this put her in the perfect position to become chief photographer and at the girls' insistence she had to take several shots of Quinn, his daughters and his ex-wife. Ali's heart sat heavy and sad in her chest as she looked at the image of the Daniels family through the viewfinder. At the perfect family portraits. She snapped one last photo of Quinn as he blew out the candles. As she watched him cut the cake, she could only imagine what he wished for.

The twins passed plates of cake around to the guests. It looked delicious but could have been cardboard for all Ali noticed. She was ready to go home. She wasn't sure she could handle any more happy family moments, even though she knew Quinn would tell her it was all for the girls' benefit.

Fortunately it became obvious to all that Julieanne was tiring quickly and when she excused herself to lie down the guests began to leave. Ali offered to help Quinn clean up but Helen shooed them both out of the kitchen.

'It's Quinn's birthday, I'll do the dishes and, Quinn, you can see Ali to her car.'

'I didn't drive. I walked, it's only a few blocks,' Ali said as she collected her basket and her red swing coat.

'I'll walk you home, then,' Quinn told her. 'I need some exercise after all that sugar, not to mention some fresh air after all those women.'

'You were rather outnumbered, weren't you?' Ali laughed, her spirits buoyed by the thought of having Quinn to herself for the short walk.

Quinn helped her into her coat. As he lifted her hair from her collar his fingers brushed the back of her neck and Ali thought she might melt at his feet as heat flooded her belly and her limbs. He opened the front door and Ali felt a burst of cool air on her face. The sun was low in the sky now and the temperature was dropping rapidly, but at least the cold, fresh air did wonders for her racing pulse and flaming cheeks.

They turned the corner into the main street of Stirling. The streetlights were on and the shop windows were lit but the pavements were virtually empty. Most other people were inside in the warmth. The pub was busy, though, packed with diners and people enjoying an evening drink in the bars.

'Do you know what I'd really like to do?' Quinn said as they stepped into the pool of light being cast from the hotel onto the dark pavement. 'I'd like to finish that drink we never managed to have.'

'Now?' Ali asked.

'Why not? It's my birthday, I should get to celebrate in the way I choose, don't you think?' He smiled at her and she felt the heat return to her cheeks under the intensity of his blue eyes. 'Would you care to join me?'

He crooked his elbow and gave her a look as though almost daring her to accept.

Ali tucked her hand through his elbow. 'It would be my pleasure.' He didn't need to ask her twice.

He ordered their drinks, a Scotch for him, red wine for her, and then found them a seat. The room was warm, an open fire glowing in the fireplace, and was almost full, the press of bodies adding to the heat. Ali shrugged out of her coat. She was wearing a red wrap dress, which matched her lipstick and hugged her curves, and her favourite long black boots.

'That dress looks amazing on you.'

Ali noted the appreciation in his azure eyes. She

was glad she'd removed her coat as the warm glow was back and heat flooded through her. Perhaps he did like women with curves.

'It's the same one I had on earlier.' She smiled as she teased him.

'I know. Don't think I didn't notice but I didn't have a chance to say anything earlier.' Quinn relaxed back into the armchair. Somehow he'd managed to find them a secluded corner. 'This is exactly what I wished for when I cut the cake, to have some time with you.'

'Really?' Of all the things he could have, *should have* wished for, this was what he'd wanted?

'I know you think I should have wished for a miracle but Julianne isn't going to get better. If I only get one wish a year I wanted there to be a slight chance it might come true.'

She was surprised by his wish but also secretly pleased. 'Maybe you should have been a bit more ambitious with your wish, you've got another three hundred and sixty-four days before you get another one,' she replied.

'I'm a simple man.'

'Is that why you joined the army?' she asked.

Quinn laughed and Ali felt it vibrate through her, adding to her already inflated bubble of happiness.

'No. The defence force offered the best solution to the predicament Julieanne and I found ourselves in. When we found out she was pregnant I applied for a scholarship. It was the only way I could think of that I'd be able to afford to finish my degree and support a family. But it turned out to be both a blessing and a curse.'

'How so?'

'I was putting in eighty-hour weeks for the last few years of my study, you know how it is, and after I graduated from uni I had to complete my military training. I was committed to the army and had to go where I was sent. I was sent on disaster relief missions throughout Australia and posted overseas while Julieanne stayed behind in Brisbane.'

'So what happened? How did Julieanne end up here?'

'She's from Adelaide. We met when I was in fifth-year medicine at Brisbane Uni. Julieanne was a nurse. When she graduated she moved to Queensland to have a change of scenery, to have some fun. I was a very serious, conscientious med student and Julieanne made it her mission to introduce me to a social life. She was like a shooting star, vivacious and fun, and I'd never really met anyone like her before. I think I'd always avoided them, knowing I'd get burnt. And then I got her pregnant.

'Julieanne had never intended on staying in Brisbane permanently, and getting pregnant definitely wasn't on her agenda. Once she'd had the babies she wanted to be back in South Australia with her family but I wasn't so flexible. I was still studying, still committed to the army, so she stayed for a few years and tried to keep our family together, but we were both exhausted and swamped by the reality of parenting when we weren't mentally prepared for it. We didn't know ourselves well enough, let alone each other. I couldn't give her the attention or company or help she needed and she was lonely. Her family and most of her friends were in Adelaide, not Brisbane.

'She went looking for company and she found it. We both know that we never would have lasted as a couple if Julieanne hadn't fallen pregnant. Apart from the girls, we didn't really have much in common when it came down to it. We got divorced, she moved back down here and we're trying to do the best we can. Which brings me to you.'

'I have nothing that can compare to that.'

'I find that hard to believe. No broken engagements, no ex-husbands, no jealous boyfriends?'

Ali shook her head. 'A couple of ex-boyfriends but they're ancient history and certainly not the jealous type. My life sounds incredibly dull. In fact, it actually is depressingly dull.' She wondered what he would say if she told him that meeting him had been the most exciting thing that had happened to her in a long time.

'Maybe I can spice things up for you.'

'I've no doubt you could,' she replied with a smile as she finished her wine.

'I'd like to offer you another drink but I'd better get home,' he said as he checked his watch. 'Can I take you out again, though? Properly? For dinner?'

He was asking her on a date! A proper date, she thought as she stood and let him help her into her coat. Her heart was beating so furiously she was convinced everyone in the room must be able to hear it. She tried not to let her excitement show as she said, 'It sounds lovely but are you sure you have the time and energy for that?'

'You give me the energy,' he said as he took her hand. Her heart raced as his fingers wrapped around hers. His hand was warm, his grip firm but gentle, and Ali was quite happy to let him hold her hand as he walked her home.

'Everything else is taking a piece of me, bit by bit, and at times I feel as though I'm in danger of disappearing, but when I'm with you I feel that everything will turn out okay,' he said as they stopped at her front door. 'Can we make a date for next weekend?'

'I'd like that.'

Quinn reached towards her with his free hand and tucked a strand of hair behind her ear before he bent his head. Ali held her breath. Was he going to kiss her? She wanted to close her eyes, ready to savour his touch, but she forced herself to keep her eyes open, waiting and watching to see what he would do. She waited until his lips met hers before she shut her eyes and allowed herself to get lost in his touch. She parted her lips in response to his urging and allowed herself to get lost in his taste.

He tasted like whisky, of malt and warmth. His lips were soft but the pressure was firm. He wasn't asking her permission, he was taking what he wanted, but she had no objections. She was more than willing to give herself to him.

The scratch of his stubble was rough in contrast to his lips but not unpleasant. Definitely not unpleasant. She pressed up against him, wanting to feel his body against hers. He let go of her hand and pulled her closer to him, his hand on her bottom, holding her hips against his. She could feel his arousal, his hard maleness pressed against her stomach. She wound her hands behind his neck as he increased the pressure of his tongue against hers. His short spiky hair was soft under her fingers, much softer than she'd expected.

She didn't know if the kiss lasted one minute or ten and she didn't care. All she knew was that it was the best thing that had happened to her in a long time and when he stopped all she could think was, *No, don't.*

He was breathing deeply, his eyes dark under the night sky as he looked at her. Ali was panting, her breaths coming in rapid, short little bursts.

'I really have to go,' he said. 'I'll see you at work tomorrow but don't forget...' he was grinning now and he looked just like she felt, excited, full of anticipation and expectation '...we have a date next weekend.'

That wasn't something she was likely to have trouble remembering.

He kissed her again. Briefly this time. 'Sleep tight.'

Ali wrapped her arms around her chest, hugging herself, wanting to prolong the feeling of euphoria that spread through her as she watched him walk out the gate. She knew she had a ridiculous cheesy grin plastered on her face as she closed the front door but she didn't care. She was going to savour this moment and enjoy the memory for the rest of the night. 'I won't forget,' she whispered to herself. 'I won't forget any of it.'

CHAPTER FIVE

Ali

'HI, COME ON IN.' Ali opened the door and Beth and Eliza bounded into the house while Quinn followed at a more sedate pace. He let the girls skip ahead and put one hand on Ali's hip as he bent his head and kissed her on her mouth. Her lips parted in response to his pressure and her heart rate skyrocketed as Quinn deepened the kiss. He tasted warm and sweet; all traces of the maltiness of the Scotch had long since disappeared but he still tasted wonderful.

'I've been looking forward to that all week,' he said as his mouth left hers.

'Me too,' she replied. Her cheeks were flaming and her heart was still beating wildly in her chest. She could feel it beating against her ribs, making her breathless.

'These are for you.' Quinn handed her a bunch of magenta-coloured lilies.

Ali raised her eyebrows. 'They're not pink.' Her hands shook as she took the flowers from him. She was full of nervous anticipation at the idea of having him in her home, even if they weren't going to have privacy.

'That's because I chose them without the girls. The colour reminded me of your lips. They're to say thanks for having all of us.'

The week since Quinn's birthday had flown by but he'd had no free time. She had seen him at work but they had both been busy, which had left no time for anything more than a shared smile and a longing, heated glance. Today was supposed to be their first date and Ali hadn't planned on sharing it with the twins, but when Quinn had phoned to tell her he would have the girls with him Ali had quickly adapted her plans and decided she would give Quinn his first cooking lesson. There was no reason why the girls couldn't join in too.

'And to apologise for ruining our first date,' he added.

'Don't be silly, it's fine.' Ali was disappointed, she had planned on having Quinn to herself, but she consoled herself with the fact that this was better than nothing and shelved her lustful thoughts for what she hoped would be another time. 'How's Julieanne feeling?'

'Tired,' Quinn replied. 'I'm worried about her.'

Ali knew that Julieanne had fallen over a couple of times in the past few days . Her balance was being affected by the tumour as her condition continued to deteriorate. 'Do you want to leave the girls with me and go home?' Ali asked. She still felt weird discussing Quinn's ex-wife with him but she couldn't ignore her existence or her illness. Julieanne was the elephant in the room, albeit a very tiny one.

Quinn shook his head. 'Quite the opposite,' he said. His extraordinary blue eyes held her gaze, leaving her in no doubt as to how he felt. Ali's heart skipped a beat as the intensity of his gaze melted any resistance she might have had. 'I'd like to have you to myself but Julieanne wants peace and quiet, which means she needs the girls out of the house for a while. Helen is with her, she doesn't need me.'

'That's good news for me, then,' Ali said as she stepped back to let Quinn into her home.

The girls had found their way to the family room at the back of the house, adjacent the large, modern kitchen. Displayed on just about every horizontal surface around the family room were ornamental elephants. Beth was gently holding an elephant that had been embellished with an ornate pink head covering.

'Do you like elephants?' she asked Ali.

'Those belong to my mum.'

'Why are they in your house?'

'This is my mum and dad's house,' Ali told her as she filled a vase with water for Quinn's flowers.

'Where are they?' Eliza asked.

'They're away on holiday,' Ali replied.

Eliza picked up a photo frame from a bookcase. 'Is this them?'

Beth pointed to the man standing beside Ali in the photo. 'Is that your husband, Ali?'

'That's my brother. I don't have a husband.'

'Why not?'

'Girls,' Quinn reprimanded, 'stop asking so many questions. Ali doesn't have to have a husband.'

'Of course she does,' Beth argued. 'Don't you want to have kids?' she asked Ali.

'You don't have to have a husband to have kids,' Eliza said, directing her comment at her sister.

'I know that but Mum says it's easier if you have a husband.'

Ali knew that comment would have hurt Quinn. She knew it weighed on his conscience that he hadn't made a success of his marriage. She wondered if he'd ever be prepared to go down that path again. She wondered, not for the first time, if she was making a mistake by getting close to him. And his girls. But she couldn't seem to help herself. She was irresistibly drawn to him.

She glanced at him. She could see the shadow behind his blue eyes. When he was deep in thought his azure blue eyes darkened, as though someone had turned down the light that usually shone from behind them.

'Mum might be right but only if you have the right sort of husband,' he told his daughters.

'What's the right sort?' Eliza asked.

'Someone who isn't scared of spiders,' said Beth.

'Someone who can open the jar of strawberry jam,' Eliza added, then both girls dissolved in fits of giggles.

The girls' comments made Ali and Quinn smile. 'What about someone who can cook?' Ali asked.

The girls' giggles intensified and the subject was changed. 'Dad can't cook.'

'I thought that's why we were here,' Quinn teased. 'If Ali teaches you two how to cook, I won't have to learn.'

'Dad!'

'You're *all* going to help me,' Ali told them.

'Really?' Beth and Eliza asked in unison.

'Yes. I've picked easy, yummy dishes that I used to help my mum make when I was much younger than you. They're so easy even your dad will be able to handle them,' she said, making the girls giggle again.

Ali had spent the morning working out what to cook and gathering the ingredients. It couldn't be anything too difficult, she didn't want to frighten Quinn, and it had to be something the girls would eat.

'What are we making?'

'Chicken kebabs with a dipping sauce and naan bread,' Ali answered the twins. 'I thought the two of you could make the bread and your dad can barbecue everything.'

'Can you teach us how to make those sweets you brought to Dad's party?'

'Burfi?' she asked, and then nodded. 'After we've prepared everything else, okay?'

Ali handed aprons to everyone and instructed them all to wash their hands. She set up two work stations, one for the girls and one for Quinn. She pulled things from the fridge, passing a parcel of chicken thighs and two bowls of marinade to Quinn before putting a handful of bamboo skewers in water to soak.

'You can dice the chicken for me,' she told Quinn. 'You're aiming for consistent one-inch cubes. Then you're going to thread the chicken onto the skewers and spoon the marinade over.'

'Why wouldn't I just buy ready-made skewers?'

Ali sighed and shook her head in mock despair. 'Because this tastes so much better and you get the satisfaction of making something yourself.' She had pre-made the marinades for the chicken, one tandoori and one tikka, but she had planned on letting Quinn take one short-cut, and one only. 'I'll tell you which pre-prepared marinades you're allowed to buy but you're much better off using fresh chicken that you prepare. You know how dicey raw chicken can be. I've got extra marinade so if you like it I'll send that home with you.'

Ali had planned to share a beer with Quinn while she taught him his way around the kitchen but instead she had to leave him to get on with his tasks while she helped the girls with the naan bread. They measured and mixed the ingredients and then Ali let them take turns to knead the dough. As a child she had always loved getting her hands messy and the twins were no different.

'Okay, the dough has to rest now, which means you leave it to sit and rise. It'll get bigger as long as we leave it somewhere warm and while we wait I'll teach you how to make the dipping sauce.' Ali covered the dough with a tea towel and set it on the kitchen bench.

'I'm done,' Quinn said as he put the final skewer into the dish and spooned the marinade over.

'Good. Now you can make a green salad,' Ali said as she covered the dish.

'What? I don't get to escape to the barbecue now?'

'Not yet. The meat needs to go into the fridge for a bit to give the flavours time to get into the chicken.'

Ali put the dishes into the fridge and passed Quinn the salad vegetables. She sat at the kitchen bench and supervised Quinn as she simultaneously instructed the girls how to make cucumber and mint raita.

Ali had spent many hours at this bench, watching and helping her mother cook. In her family, preparing, cooking and sharing meals was one way they expressed love and affection so, for Ali, today was more than just about teaching Quinn how to cook a healthy meal, it was a way to express her feelings without words. She enjoyed cooking and as much as she had been looking forward to spending the afternoon with Quinn she found she was enjoying the girls' company too. She let herself imagine, just briefly, what it would be like to have a family of her own. What it would be like to have a husband and children. It was still something she longed for and knowing it wasn't possible wasn't enough to stop the dreams.

'Does this pass muster?' Quinn's question interrupted her daydreaming.

Ali inspected his salad. 'Not bad. *Now* you can barbecue.'

Once she had given Quinn the items he needed for the barbecue and shown him outside to the patio and barbecue area, she gave the twins their final task. 'Beth and Liza, you can roll out the bread now.' She floured the bench and plopped the dough into the flour. 'Use your hands to roll it into a log so that it looks like a cardboard tube and then slice it into twelve equal pieces.' Ali started rolling as she spoke, her hands working automatically to shape the dough. 'Then roll each piece flat so it looks like a pancake.' She pulled a small piece from the end to show the girls what she meant before merging it with the rest of the dough again. 'Put them onto this tray and when you've done them all bring them out and your dad can cook them on the barbecue.'

It was a simple task, one she thought they could manage unsupervised, leaving her free to have a few minutes alone with Quinn.

'I think you deserve this,' she said, as she went out to the terrace and handed him an icy-cold beer. He had the first of the skewers cooking on the hot plate and the spicy tandoori aromas were beginning to permeate the air.

'Are you okay?' Ali asked, as Quinn took a long draught of the beer. 'The girls' comments didn't upset you?'

'Their comments about what it takes to be a good husband?'

Ali nodded her head as she sipped her drink.

'I don't think they meant it personally,' he replied, 'but I have to admit I wasn't a very good husband.' He shrugged and added, 'But Julieanne wasn't a great wife. We were not a match made in heaven, as they say, and I don't think we were meant to get married. We wouldn't have married if it wasn't for the pregnancy. We thought, *I* thought, we were doing the right thing but it was a mistake. The marriage, not the pregnancy,' he clarified. 'The pregnancy was unplanned but we have never told the girls that. I didn't want them growing up thinking they weren't wanted. That's not something a child should ever hear.'

'Are you sure you're okay?'

'Sorry.' He smiled, his brilliant blue eyes flashing, 'I'm fine, just remembering why I insisted we get married. My father instilled a sense of duty in me from a very young age. He married my mother because he got her pregnant and he made no secret of the fact that he felt it was his duty and that he hadn't planned on having kids. I spent my life trying to be the perfect son to make up for ruining his life but then I met Julieanne and something about her triggered a rebellious streak in me. And then, when Julieanne fell pregnant, I found myself trapped by duty in exactly the same way my father had been. Until then I had spent my life trying to make myself into the perfect son, someone a father could love and be proud of, and then I ended up repeating his mistakes.'

'But he must be proud of you all the same?'

'I'll never know. He never said as much. My parents were killed in a light plane crash before the twins were born. The girls are named after my mother. She would have loved being a grandmother and maybe becoming a grandfather would have mellowed my father. I just don't know. I'm not sure if he was ever proud of me but I think he wasn't disappointed.' Quinn shrugged his shoulders as if to shake off the memories. 'Anyway, I had a vision of the type of father I'd be but it's harder than I thought. I just hope I'm a better father than I was a husband.'

Ali wondered if his past history had put him off marriage permanently but she wasn't about to ask. There was no subtle way of posing that question so she chose to reassure him about his other concern. 'If it makes you feel better, Julieanne thinks you're a good father.'

'I hope she's right.'

'Do you want to ring and check how she is?'

'No. Helen will ring me if there's a problem. Let's just enjoy the few moments we have to ourselves. I've been looking forward to this all week.'

Ali smiled. She had to agree. The afternoon was turning out to be almost perfect.

Dinner was pronounced a success. The girls had made short work of the barbecued chicken skewers and mopped up their raita with the naan bread and Ali was thinking about clearing the table when Quinn's phone rang.

Ali could hear from his side of the conversation that it was Helen and she could tell by Quinn's expression and the darkening of his eyes that something was wrong.

'Girls, why don't you go and wash your hands to get ready to make the burfi?' she suggested, wanting to get them out of earshot. She stood too and gathered a couple of plates to clear, wanting to give Quinn some privacy.

She returned to the table just as he was finishing the call. Quinn was pacing, his azure eyes dark with worry.

'What's happened?'

'Julieanne has had another seizure. The ambulance is there, they're taking her to hospital.'

'Do you need to go?'

Quinn nodded.

'Do you want me to drive you?'

'No. But can I ask another favour? Would you look after the girls for me?'

'Of course.' Ali didn't hesitate. She would do anything for him. 'Leave me your house key, I'll take them home a bit later and put them to bed.' Quinn unhooked his car key and handed her the remaining keys. Ali raised herself up on tiptoe and kissed him on the lips. A kiss that was meant to bolster his spirits and let him know she was there for him. She couldn't put her feelings into words, not yet, she could only show him through her actions. 'Go. I'll tell the girls something.'

By the time Quinn got home Ali had put the girls to bed and was curled up on the couch by the pot-belly stove. She had lit the fire and the room was cosy and warm. She stood up as Quinn came through the back door. His eyes were dark and tired and he looked as though he needed cosiness and warmth. She wrapped her arms around him, hugging him tight, relishing the feel of his muscles under her fingers, relishing his size as she tried to bolster his strength.

'How is she?' Ali asked.

'The specialist ordered another scan, there's a second tumour.'

'Another one?' She stepped back, releasing Quinn from her arms as she sought out his face. 'The radiotherapy isn't working?'

Quinn kept his arms around her as he shook his head. 'It appears so.'

'Do you want to go back to the hospital?' she offered. 'I can stay with the girls.'

'No. Helen wanted to wait there and I just need to stop for a moment. I need time to make sense of all this.'

His voice was heavy and flat, he sounded more than

tired, and Ali wondered what she could do to help. What would he need?

'Do you want me to go?' she asked. 'Do you need to be alone?'

Quinn shook his head. 'Can you stay? I can focus better when you're near. I can breathe and my mind feels clearer.'

Ali nodded. Her heart was singing—he needed her.

'Thank you,' he said. He dropped his arms from her waist only once she agreed to stay. He crossed the room, heading towards the kitchen. There was a bottle of cabernet sauvignon on the kitchen bench and he took a wine glass from the cupboard and filled it. 'Do you mind if I just have a quick shower? I want to get the hospital smell off me,' he asked as he handed her the glass of red wine and put the bottle onto the coffee table in front of her.

Ali reached for the glass. 'Do you need me to wash your back for you?' She smiled, only half-joking. Her confidence was soaring, bolstered by the idea that he needed her, that he wanted her to stay.

His blue eyes flashed and they were back to their brilliant azure best, all traces of shadow gone as he grinned at her. 'That's a hard offer to refuse but what if the girls wake up and come looking for me? I'm not ready to explain this to them.'

'Of course. I understand.' And she did. But it also made her wonder what they were doing. It was hardly the right time to get involved with him. She knew that for Quinn she was probably a good distraction, something pleasant in an otherwise fairly torrid time in his life, but what if it was nothing more than that? Did it matter? What did she want?

Quinn headed for the shower as Ali considered what she wanted. She didn't need a knight in shining armour but she was a romantic and she did believe in happy endings. She didn't need rescuing but she did want to find love. She wanted to be loved. Cherished. Adored. But she didn't know if Quinn wanted that too. He'd been down the road of marriage and babies before. She wondered, not for the first time, if she was making a mistake. Did he really have room in his life, in his heart, for her?

She didn't know the answer but she realised she was prepared to wait to find out. She didn't need to know right now. Time would tell.

She flicked through the pages of a magazine as she waited for Quinn to shower but she wasn't reading the articles, she wasn't even aware of the pictures as her mind wandered. She sipped her wine, which was smooth and fruity, but she barely tasted it.

She wished she could be the person to make it better for Quinn. She wanted to tell him everything would be all right but, of course, they both knew it wouldn't be.

Quinn had showered and changed into a pair of soft, brushed cotton pants that sat low on his hips and an old blue T-shirt. On anyone else the look would have been untidy but the T-shirt hugged his chest and arms like a second skin and the contours of his muscled upper body were clearly defined. He looked divine and Ali felt a flutter of desire as she ran her gaze over him.

He poured himself a glass of Scotch and refilled

her wine glass before joining her on the couch. He sat close enough so their thighs were touching and pulled her in against his side, his arm around her shoulders. He played with her hair, weaving the strands around his fingers and then letting the weight of it fall to her shoulders.

Ali's heart was racing as his fingers grazed her skin, his touch sending her nerves into overdrive. She wondered what he wanted. Did he want conversation? Silent company? Physical comfort?

He sighed. She knew Quinn's feelings for Julieanne were just ones of affection, not love. He'd told her that was the case and she believed him but, of course, he would still worry. And not just for Julieanne but for the girls too. She wanted to eliminate his worry.

'Did the specialist give you any idea about what he might be able to do for Julieanne?' she asked, deciding against silent company, knowing he'd tell her soon enough if he didn't want to talk.

'He'll do more tests tomorrow. We'll know more then. She's tried everything along with the radiotherapy. Vitamin D3, fresh fruit and vegetables, increasing her seafood intake, green tea. Everything. There's not much left.'

'What about Avastin?' she asked. Cancer treatments were not her forte, her experience was limited to the few individual experiences of some of her patients, but she'd done some research. She'd wanted to understand what Julieanne, and by association Quinn, was dealing with.

Quinn nodded and Ali felt relieved. He had obviously heard of this drug; perhaps her research had been correct. 'I'll speak to him about that tomorrow but I have a feeling it's going to be too late,' he said. 'But right now I don't want to talk about Julieanne. I just want to be here with you and pretend that my life is under control. I will worry about everything else tomorrow,' he added as he drained his Scotch and put the glass down on the coffee table.

Ali waited to see if he got up to refill his glass but instead of standing he repositioned himself so he was lying on his back with his head in her lap. His posture evoked a strange sense of intimacy and familiarity. His T-shirt had ridden up to reveal a narrow band of skin above his waist. A thin line of blond hair ran vertically from his navel to disappear beneath the waistband of his cotton trousers and Ali was amazed at how distracting that tiny glimpse was.

She dropped her hand to his hip, which allowed her fingers to rest on his naked flesh. His skin was still warm from the shower and Ali traced lazy circles with her thumb over the ridge of his abdominals.

His eyelids closed, shielding her from view, and with the sense of anonymity she grew braver. She slid her hand under his T-shirt and ran it higher, resisting the temptation to slide it lower. She wanted to feel his skin under her touch. She longed to feel the firmness of his muscles.

Julieanne, Beth and Eliza were all forgotten as Ali focussed on Quinn. Her fingers ran across his stomach, up and over the ridge of his abdominal muscles to where they merged into his firm pectoral muscles. His chest was lightly covered with hair, just in the dip lying over his sternum. Ali's fingers moved out, away from his centre, and she felt his nipples harden as her fingertips brushed over them.

His eyes snapped open as he reached down to adjust his trousers. His movement caught her attention and her eyes were drawn to the unmistakable bulge in his pants. Ali's hand itched to move lower, itched to trace the outline of Quinn's erection, itched to feel the length and thickness for herself.

'I think I either need to get back into the shower, a cold one this time, or we need to move this into my bedroom.' His voice was low and deep and every word was thick with desire.

Ali knew the consequences if she allowed herself to follow him to his room but her body ached for his touch and she wasn't prepared to pass up this opportunity. It had been months since she had been intimate with anyone, months in which she hadn't even thought about sex, but now she was fit to burst. She was aware of an ache between her thighs and she could feel herself becoming moist, and one way or another she needed to release the tension. Her body was waking up, crying out for satisfaction, and she longed to let Quinn have that pleasure.

He rolled up from her lap and stood before her, the bulge of his erection level with her eyes. She could imagine how he would feel as he slid inside her, filling her, satisfying her. She wasn't about to resist. She needed release and she needed to experience this.

She forced herself to lift her eyes and saw him reach out and offer her his hand.

She placed her hand in his and let him pull her to

her feet. He reached behind her with his other hand and pulled her close. Her stomach was pressed against his groin and she could feel his erection through her clothing. Her head felt light and her legs were shaky as blood rushed to her own groin in a flood of desire.

Before she could collapse into a quivering mess at his feet Quinn dipped his head and claimed her mouth with his. His lips anchored her to him and kept her afloat but this kiss wasn't gentle or polite. It was hungry and desperate and demanded a response.

Ali's eyes closed and her lips parted and a little moan escaped from her throat as she offered herself to him. Quinn accepted her invitation and deepened the kiss, claiming her, exploring. She clung to him, relying on him not to let her fall as she lost herself in the warmth of his mouth and the taste of Scotch on his tongue.

His hands were under her jumper, hot on her back, and her heart was racing in her chest. Between the hammering of her heart and the heat of Quinn's kiss she was completely breathless. She needed to come up for air.

'Does this mean you're staying?' he whispered into her ear as he kissed her earlobe.

'For a little longer,' she whimpered. 'But I don't think I can walk,' she said, certain that her jelly legs wouldn't support her.

Quinn didn't reply. He just scooped her up, lifting her to his waist, and Ali wrapped her legs around him as he carried her from the room.

The study where he had been sleeping was adjacent the family room and it was only a matter of a few steps before he was lowering her onto the sofa bed. The distance had taken no time to cover and certainly hadn't given her enough time to change her mind. Not that she intended to. She'd come too far to back out now, there was no way she was leaving until she'd had her fill of Quinn. No way at all.

Quinn was lying over the top of her, his hips between her thighs, pinning her to the bed, but as her legs were still wrapped around him it was obvious she had no intention of going anywhere. Their position was intimate but they had far too many clothes on. Ali tugged at Quinn's T-shirt. She pulled it over his head and tossed it to one side.

Quinn shifted his weight, freeing her legs as his fingers deftly and swiftly flicked open the button of her jeans and slid the zip down. He eased her jeans down her thighs as she lifted her hips to speed up the process, as eager to shed her clothing as he was to remove it. Her shoes were lying out by the couch so she was able to kick her jeans off her feet as soon as they were at her ankles.

He ran his hand back up the inside of her thigh, setting her skin on fire, and Ali gasped as his fingers and palm cupped the mound of her sex. The thin lace of her red underwear did nothing to protect against the scorching heat of his hand.

He lifted himself over her leg until he was lying between her thighs again. His hands slid under her cashmere top, tracing a path from her waist, over her ribs to her shoulders as he gathered her jumper under his fingers. His mouth followed his hands. He ran his lips over her skin as he revealed it. Ali arched her back, lifting her arms above her head so Quinn could slide her top off.

She lay before him in her underwear and let his lips explore her flesh. He pushed aside the lace of her bra, exposing one breast. His head dipped as he took her breast in his mouth, flicking his tongue over her nipple. Ali moaned with pleasure as his hand found her other breast.

Quinn reached behind her and with an expert twitch of his fingers popped the clasp on her bra. His tongue flicked over her nipple again and Ali's knees dropped apart as she opened herself up to him, heat from his lips and his fingers consuming her. She could feel his erection pressed between her thighs, against the lace of her underwear, pulsing with a mini-heartbeat. She lifted and lowered her hips, sliding his erection between her thighs, and her movements were rewarded with a groan.

She could feel Quinn's hand moving across her stomach, felt his fingers slide inside her underwear, seeking her warmth. She was slick with moisture as his fingers slid inside her. She tensed, ever so slightly, waiting for any discomfort, but there was none, only intense pleasure as his thumb found the switch to trigger all her nerve endings and made her gasp. It had been almost a year since her surgery, almost a year since she'd had sex, and it was a relief to find that her body still worked. A relief to find she hadn't lost the desire or the capacity for sex.

She was almost naked but Quinn needed to shed some clothes. She reached down and slid one hand under the waistband of his trousers. He wasn't wearing underwear. There was nothing to hide his desire. Her fingers ran through the golden hair that travelled from his navel to his groin and curled around his shaft. He gasped and Ali felt his erection enlarge even further under her touch. Within seconds he had shed himself of his last piece of clothing, leaving only Ali's knickers between them. But not for long.

Quinn slid her underwear down and buried his face between her thighs. Ali moaned and arched her hips as his tongue found her centre and flicked her over the edge into a frenzy of desire.

As her excitement continued to build Ali knew Quinn would be able to bring her to her peak just like this, but she wanted the whole experience. She wanted the whole of him.

Physically she knew she was healed, both internally and externally. Her scars had faded. Quinn would never notice. She needed to test the waters.

Physically she was ready, more than ready, and emotionally she needed this.

She was ready for Quinn. It was now or never.

She wrapped her hands around the back of his arms. His triceps were solid and tense from supporting his weight and they felt like stone under her touch. Warm stone. She pulled against him, urging him to lift his head, bringing him up to her.

'I want to feel you inside me,' she told him.

CHAPTER SIX

Quinn

HIS BRIGHT AZURE eyes watched her closely and the deep blue rings around the outside of his irises were almost black as he asked the silent question. *Are you sure?*

Ali nodded. She'd never been more certain of anything. She knew she couldn't stop now. Neither could she let him stop. She was ready to explode and she wanted to explode while her body was wrapped around his. While her legs were wrapped around his waist and while he was deep inside her.

He reached into the drawer beside the sofa bed and retrieved a foil packet. Ali watched as he ripped the little packet open with his teeth. She took the condom and rolled it along his shaft, her fingers firm with pressure as she protected them both before she guided him inside her.

She exhaled as his length filled her, arching her hips again to take as much of him inside her as she could.

She relaxed as he entered her. Her body may have

let her down in the past but as he plunged into her she knew she was made for this. Made for him.

Quinn moaned and buried his head into her neck as his hips thrust against her. She timed her movements to match his, making sure their rhythms were in tune.

She pressed her lips against his shoulder. He smelt of soap but tasted salty. The heat that was building between them had brought out small beads of sweat on his skin. She licked the salt from his body as she ran her hands down his back to cup his buttocks, keeping him buried within her.

She felt his lips around her nipple as his mouth found her breast again. She heard herself cry out as all the nerve endings between her breasts and her groin exploded to life.

'Now,' she gasped, 'I can't wait any longer.'

Quinn increased his intensity just a fraction and that was all she needed to push her over the edge, to move her on from desire and into satisfaction. His cries joined hers as they climaxed together. United in pleasure until they were breathless and spent.

They lay entwined as they caught their breath until eventually Quinn eased himself from her and rolled onto his back. He pulled Ali over so she was lying on her side with one leg draped across his stomach. It was just as well he was strong enough to move her, her limbs were heavy and she doubted she could have moved herself.

She closed her eyes, happy just to lie beside him as she listened to the beat of his heart and the deep, steady sound of his breathing.

She felt good. In equal parts relieved, sated and contented.

She heard Quinn's breathing slow and felt him relax under her. She propped herself on one elbow to look at him. The lines of tension had disappeared from his forehead and with his eyes closed, hiding the intensity of his blue gaze, he looked completely relaxed. His breaths were even and deep—he'd fallen asleep.

Their lovemaking appeared to have helped him to forget his troubles, even if only temporarily. At least now, she thought, he might be able to sleep soundly and wake up refreshed and ready to face tomorrow and whatever it might bring.

Ali knew she should leave. She couldn't stay and risk being caught in flagrante delicto with Quinn but she couldn't resist just sitting and admiring him while he slept. His body was firm, he had no visible body fat but his sculpted muscles were rounded, which stopped him from looking hard. He looked like a warm Adonis. He reminded her of a Renaissance figure but made of a richer, darker marble. The only thing he needed to complete the picture was a typical Roman nose.

She lifted one hand but resisted the temptation to run her fingers along his nose. She wondered if it had once been aquiline, back before it had been broken in the sparring incident he'd told her about. She didn't care that the bridge was now slightly flattened and a little crooked, she loved his nose. Everything else about him was faultless but his damaged nose stopped him from being too perfect, without detracting from his looks. In her opinion it added to his air of ruggedness and was one of his nicest features, after his incredible eyes, of course.

Her eyes travelled south. Back over his chest and his abdomen, retracing the path her fingers had traversed just minutes ago. Down to the line of blond hair below his navel, which now disappeared under the sheet that was draped across his hips.

Ali sighed as she fought the urge to wake him up and have her way with him all over again. She wasn't inexperienced but she had never had sex that good before and she was eager to try it again.

But she would have to wait.

She climbed out of his bed. She was careful not to disturb him as she knew he was exhausted and needed his sleep, although to look at him she suspected that a bomb could go off without waking him.

Quietly she gathered her clothes and got dressed. She found a piece of paper and scribbled a note. Even though she assumed he'd figure out why she couldn't stay, she didn't want him to wake up and find her gone with no explanation.

She kept it simple. *Thank you, sleep tight.* That was all she wrote before she folded it and left it propped on the bedside table.

She opened the door and ducked into the family room, hoping that Helen had stuck with her plan to stay at the hospital as she certainly didn't want to bump into her as she sneaked out of Quinn's room at this late hour. The coast was clear, the house was sleeping, so she took a moment to tidy away any evidence. She put the bottle of wine back on the kitchen bench and rinsed and dried their glasses before putting them into the cup-board and letting herself out.

Her muscles ached as she walked to her car but it felt good to have used them.

Maybe their paths had crossed for a reason. Maybe her life was about to turn around. Maybe they could be good for each other.

In an ideal world she would find a man who loved her despite her faults. Despite all the things she couldn't give him.

Maybe Quinn could help heal her.

Maybe Quinn could be the right man.

She felt as though she had been waiting for him all her life. She knew she could fall in love with him. She thought perhaps she already had.

Maybe he could be the right man. He already had children, maybe he wouldn't need more. But she wouldn't know until they had that conversation. She wouldn't know how he felt until she told him the truth. And she couldn't bring herself to tell him that she couldn't have children. Not yet.

The external scars had only just faded and, after to-night, she knew that physically she had recovered, but emotionally it was a different story. She wasn't ready for that discussion. Not yet.

Maybe he was the right man for her but Ali knew this wasn't the right time.

Quinn had existed on the bare minimum of sleep over the past week. It had been like his intern days. He put his hours in at the clinic, then picked the girls up from school and took them to see their mother, then home for dinner, a bath and a bedtime story as he tried to maintain some sense of routine for them all. Helen was spending most of her day at the hospital with Julieanne. That was her choice and Quinn didn't begrudge her that, but he was aware enough of his own limitations to realise he wouldn't manage without the help of Ali and the girls at the clinic who had become willing babysitters, not to mention the help he was also getting from the school mothers.

Ali's parents had returned from their trip and Malika was due to be back in the clinic at the beginning of next week. She had offered to come back early to leave him free to spend his days at the hospital but Julieanne was sleeping twenty-one hours a day and the girls were at school. If he didn't go into the clinic he would have nothing to do for the majority of the day. He thanked her but declined her offer. He preferred to be busy.

But being busy didn't leave much, or any, time for Ali. He was too tired to do anything other than collapse into his bed at the end of the day. He would have loved to have her there with him, he knew he would sleep better if she was beside him, but it wasn't possible. Not with the girls there too. He knew they still thought of their parents as married. Quinn and Ali had been very careful not to let the girls see any show of affection between them and they certainly didn't need another thing to deal with.

His schedule meant he was lucky to catch a glimpse of Ali in the clinic between patients and they hadn't had a moment alone since they had shared his bed. The memory of that night was helping to sustain him but he knew it wouldn't last for ever. He was desperately trying to work out how they could be together again but he feared there wasn't going to be an easy solution.

He was just finishing the paperwork for his final patient before his lunch break when his mobile phone beeped with an incoming text message. Fearing the worst before realising the hospital would hardly text with bad news, he picked up his phone. The message winked at him.

Leftover rogan josh for lunch if you'd like to join me. A xx

A flash of red caught his eye as he read the message. Through the window in front of his desk he could see out to the garden. Ali, wrapped up like a Christmas present in her red coat, was sitting at the outdoor table with two steaming bowls of leftovers in front of her. She saw him looking through the window and she smiled and waved and gestured at the food.

He nodded. He didn't need to be asked twice and grabbed his jacket from behind his door. The early spring sun was starting to get a little bit of warmth but it was still cool enough to need an extra layer even in the middle of the day.

He was outside in a matter of seconds, eager to make the most of this opportunity. It was the first chance they'd had to be alone in five and a half days. The first moment they'd had alone since he'd woken up after making love to her and found her note beside his bed.

He was grinning like the village idiot as he sat down opposite her. He wanted to gather her into his arms and kiss her senseless, but while his consulting room and Ali's both overlooked the side garden so did the nurse's. Who knew who might be looking their way.

'You have perfect timing,' he told her.

Ali blushed and Quinn knew she was thinking back to Saturday night. He felt a stirring in his groin as his mind replayed the evening too.

'I meant with lunch,' he teased.

'Oh.' She grinned as her blush deepened further. 'That just took a bit of forward thinking. I had to shuffle my diary three days ago to match up our lunch breaks. I'm amazed it worked.'

Quinn was touched that Ali had changed her schedule just to be able to share some time with him. Until Ali had come into his life it had been a long time since anyone had done anything just for him. He'd grown accustomed to his solitary lifestyle and more recently to trying to take care of Julieanne and the girls, and he'd forgotten how nice it was to have someone do something for him just because they wanted to. His life was rapidly becoming divided into two parts—Before Ali and After Ali.

'Thank you,' he said, thinking what an inadequate attempt at expressing his gratitude that was. Maybe he could express his thanks in other ways later? Next time he had a spare hour maybe, whenever that might be.

He resisted the temptation to lean across the table and kiss her and instead bent his head over his bowl and picked up the fork that lay beside it. 'This smells fantastic. I can't remember the last time I sat down to eat.'

'Have things been that bad?'

Quinn nodded, his mouth full of lamb curry. He chewed and swallowed the tender meat before replying. 'I haven't been ignoring you, it's been completely crazy. I have a whole new respect for working mothers and single parents.'

'How is Julieanne?' Ali asked. 'What did the specialist say about the Avastin?'

'Have we not even had that conversation?' He was so tired and frantic that he couldn't remember what he had and hadn't been doing half the time.

Ali shook her head.

'According to the specialist, Julieanne is living on borrowed time and there's nothing else he can do,' he told her, 'but I'm not sure I would call lying in a hospital bed and sleeping for ninety per cent of the day living.'

'So this is it?' Ali's voice was soft and gentle. She knew the answer already.

'She won't be coming home,' he said. 'Every time the phone rings I expect bad news.'

'And what about you? How are you coping?'

'I'm not sure, to be honest. I'm just doing what I have to for the girls' sake but I do feel guilty.'

'Guilty? What about?'

'About everything,' he admitted. 'I feel I should be doing more of something but I don't know what. I feel I should be doing more with the girls, or spending more time at the hospital or comforting Helen, but I'm not sure that any of that would make a difference. We're all just biding our time, Julieanne, Helen and me.'

'Do you want to hand over your hours at the clinic? I'm sure Mum would come back to work early. She's due back next week anyway.'

Quinn shook his head. 'That's not the problem. She's already offered to come back early but with the girls at school and Julieanne sleeping most of the day I don't actually know what I'd do with myself. It's not that I'm short of time, it's just that I'm not used to having to work to other people's schedules. At the moment I have to factor in so many other people's needs and it's becoming quite a juggling act. One I don't feel I'm getting right, and that's why I'm feeling guilty. I feel like I'm letting people down.'

Ali reached across the table and squeezed his hand, knowing once again just when he needed to feel that connection to her. 'I think you're being too hard on yourself. You have to prioritise and, right now, work is something that can come way down your list. You don't have to try to do it all.'

He smiled. 'I know, but I like having something in my day that I feel I'm doing well. I know what I'm doing when I'm at work. I spend so much of the day feeling out of my depth that it feels good to come to work, it gives me a sense of achievement.'

'But you need to give yourself some time too. You'll get sick if you overload yourself and being sick is the last thing you can afford right now. I suppose you're going straight to the hospital from here tonight?'

Quinn nodded. 'I'm going to collect the girls from

school and take them down to town. I don't know what else to do. I'd love to have some time to myself, well, not myself exactly. In all honesty I'd love to just be able to go home with you, but I just don't see how that's going to be possible.'

His body was aching for more of Ali but for now he would have to console himself with mental images. The contrast of her red lace underwear, bright against the milk-chocolate colouring of her skin, was still vivid in his mind's eye. The tension in her thighs as she'd wrapped her legs around him, the curve of her bottom under his hand and the sweet taste of her under his tongue, the length of her neck as she'd arched her back when she'd orgasmed and the touch of her hand were all indelibly printed on his brain, but there was no time for indulging in pleasures of the flesh. Not at the moment.

'That's not what I was hinting at. Not that I wouldn't enjoy it…' she grinned '…but I understand. I don't expect you to have to find time for me too. I can wait.'

They both knew it wouldn't be long before there would be one less person needing Quinn's time, but what he didn't realise was just how much would change and not all of it would be what he expected.

The first surprise, while unexpected, was at least a pleasant one. It was Saturday afternoon and Quinn was leaving the hospital with the twins when his phone rang. The number displayed was one he didn't recognise and even though he'd left Julieanne's bedside less than ten minutes before, his first reaction was still one of trepidation. The lack of sleep combined with the unrelenting stress had him constantly on edge.

Rebecca, one of the school mums, was offering to have the girls for a sleepover. She apologised for the late notice but Quinn didn't care. All he could think of was that this could be his chance to spend some time with Ali.

Did that make him a bad father? No, he decided, he needed some time for himself. Time to get his head straight and Ali helped him to do that. Ali was his constant. He convinced himself it would do the girls good to spend some time with friends, being normal kids. This was an opportunity as much for them as it was for him.

He rang Ali and offered to take her out to dinner but once she discovered that his ex-mother-in-law was using the child-free night to stay at her own recently neglected house, Ali had insisted on staying in. She told him it was a more relaxing option and a chance to have some privacy so they compromised with the idea of takeaway in front of the fire at Julieanne's.

Quinn stretched and wrapped his arms around Ali, revelling in the sensation of her warm body tucked against him. Her curves moulded to his side, she was a perfect fit. He smiled as he remembered how nervous he'd been just a short time ago as he'd paced around the room, waiting for her to arrive. The house had been much too quiet. He didn't think he'd ever been alone there before and it had made him feel a little jumpy.

But the minute Ali had walked through the door all his edginess had vanished as a storm of lust had surrounded him. She was gorgeous. Her raven hair had spilled over her shoulders and her expertly applied make-up had made her grey eyes seem enormous beneath her thick, dark lashes, but as usual it had been her red lips that had promised all sorts of pleasures and set his pulse racing.

He'd offered to take her scarlet coat but she'd insisted on keeping it on until they'd been near the fire, and when she'd removed it, revealing that she'd been wearing very little underneath, he'd promptly forgotten about dinner, forgotten about everything except Ali.

He could scarcely believe their plans had come to fruition. Well, almost—they'd never actually got around to ordering dinner.

'I suppose it's too late to order takeaway now?' Ali said as they listened to the hungry rumblings of Quinn's stomach.

'There'll be containers in the fridge—Julieanne's friends are keeping us well fed. I'll heat up something in a minute, when I can drag myself away from you.' He was in no hurry to get out of bed. No hurry to move away from Ali's warmth. The house was quiet but now it was a peaceful quiet. Ali's presence was all he needed to settle him into a peaceful state. And the amazing sex didn't hurt either.

He could get used to this. Being with Ali felt right. It had since the moment he'd met her. He was a free man, sort of, and just for one night he planned to forget about responsibility and duty. Just for one night he would enjoy pretending that this was his future.

He settled himself back into the pillows and Ali

rolled slightly away from him as he moved. The light reflected off a small, pale scar just below and to the left of her belly button. It gleamed like a spot of strawberry ice cream against the milk chocolate of her skin. He'd never noticed it before.

It looked recent. Not fresh, but recent enough not to have faded completely. He recognised it as a laparoscopy scar.

He reached out and traced it with one fingertip. He felt Ali tense under his touch.

'What's this from?' he asked.

Ali had felt herself tense as Quinn's finger had trailed across her scar. It wasn't sore but her first instinct had been to pull away. To pretend he hadn't just discovered it. 'Just some gynae surgery,' she replied, attempting to keep her tone light.

'Nothing major, I hope?'

She knew he wouldn't even be able to begin to imagine the story those scars told. She wondered if he could handle the truth. Should she tell him? Now would be the perfect time. But she hesitated. She wasn't prepared for this conversation. She needed to plan it out. She needed to work out how to tell him.

There was no such thing as the perfect time. She knew that. There was no perfect time to tell him she was a damaged woman.

Quinn's phone vibrated at that moment, jumping about on the bedside table and startling her. He had turned it to vibrate but he hadn't turned it off. Ali hadn't expected him to as there were too many people relying on him.

The vibrating continued. It wasn't a message coming through. The phone was ringing.

It was half past ten at night. It wouldn't be good news but it would distract him from their conversation and buy her some time. She reached out and picked up the phone and passed it to Quinn.

Quinn sat up in bed and Ali lay watching the rise and fall of his broad, bare chest as he spoke. She could hear half the conversation. It seemed to be something to do with the twins, which at least meant nothing had happened to Julieanne.

'That was Rebecca,' Quinn said as he disconnected the call. 'Eliza can't sleep and she wants to come home. I'll have to go and fetch her.'

Ali knew what that meant. It meant she would have to go home too. She'd been toying with the idea of staying the night. She'd wondered whether Quinn would ask her to but now she'd never know.

She sat up and began to reach for her clothes before she remembered she'd hardly worn any. She retrieved her underwear as Quinn said, 'I'm sorry, this isn't how I wanted our evening to end.'

'It's fine,' she replied. 'The girls are your first responsibility. I understand. I'm not going to ask you to shirk your duty.' She shrugged into her red coat, using the action to avoid looking at Quinn. She wasn't fine, she was disappointed, but it was what it was and there was nothing she could do about it.

Quinn watched and waited as Ali climbed into her car and drove down the street.

Responsibility and duty, she had said. Would he never escape those two words?

He'd been a fool to think he could have a moment to himself, a moment with Ali that wasn't interrupted. Would it ever happen? Could it ever happen?

Responsibility and duty.

The two words were constantly rearing up at him. He wasn't about to reject either of them but it would be nice to be able to squeeze some other things into his life on a regular basis, and some quality time with Ali would be a good start.

But one thing he knew for certain. He couldn't walk away from her.

He just hoped she would wait for him.

Quinn steeled his nerves as he approached the hospital. Every time he arrived his apprehension increased as he wondered how much Julieanne would have deteriorated since he'd seen her last, and the past few days had seen a rapid decline in her condition. There was no denying she wasn't getting better. The problems with her balance were worsening and she couldn't get out of bed safely or walk unaided any more. Along with the huge number of hours she was sleeping, he knew it was the beginning of the end. The only thing he didn't know was when the end would come.

Helen was waiting for him as he arrived with the twins.

'Julieanne is asking for you,' she told him.

'She's awake?'

'Yes.' Helen turned to her granddaughters and held

out a hand to each of them. 'Come, girls, we'll go and get you an after-school snack and then I'll bring you back to see Mum.'

Quinn pushed open the door to Julieanne's room. The window blinds were half-closed, the lights were dim and the room was only half-lit. She was propped up on pillows and despite the amount she was sleeping she still looked tired. Her eyes were pinched and strained and her face was grey. Julieanne had been voluptuous when they'd met, now she was skin and bones. He thought she looked even thinner than she'd looked yesterday.

Quinn kissed her cheek. 'Do you have a headache?' he asked.

'Constantly.'

'Do you want me to call for pain relief?'

Julieanne shook her head, the movement making her wince slightly. 'No. The pain relief makes me drowsy and I don't want to sleep, not yet. I wanted to talk to you.' Her voice was soft, her words punctuated with pauses. 'I wanted to apologise.'

'What on earth for?'

'For leaving you to deal with all of this.'

Quinn sat in the chair by her bed. He hadn't been sure what she'd wanted to speak to him about but he was pretty sure this wasn't it. He picked up her hand, which felt cold and fragile in his palm, and he squeezed it very gently as he tried to reassure her. 'I'm fairly sure you didn't plan to do this.'

'No.' Julieanne gave him a half-smile and he knew it was all she could manage.

'We don't need to talk about this now if you're tired. We can talk about it tomorrow.'

Julieanne gave the smallest shake of her head. 'I haven't finished. I'm sorry I wasn't a better wife too.'

Quinn lifted her hand to his lips and kissed her fingers gently. 'You were as good a wife as I was husband. We both had our failings. We weren't ready to be married with a family but I am grateful to you every day that you chose to go through with the pregnancy. Our girls are the best thing that's ever happened to me.'

'Better than saving lives?'

'Lots of people can do that. But only you and I could create Beth and Eliza.'

'I was always glad that if I had to have an unplanned pregnancy you were the father. You will look after our girls, won't you?'

'I promise you I will take care of them. I love them with every ounce of me.'

Julieanne smiled, a proper smile this time, but there were tears in her eyes.

'What is it?' he asked.

'I used to wish you'd say those words about me. That's why I asked for a divorce. I was hoping it would make you say you loved me. That you didn't want to be without me. That you'd forgive me for my affairs.'

'Oh, Jules, I did forgive you. I know you were lonely. I'm sure there are plenty of things we both wish we had done differently but beating ourselves up about it won't change the past. We were always better friends than husband and wife, but we did make beautiful daughters and you've done a fabulous job of raising them. You are a great mum and I love that about you.'

'Thank you.' Julieanne's hand was still resting in his palm and now it was her turn to give his hand a gentle squeeze. 'You're a good man, Quinn. I want you to be happy. The girls need some happiness.' She lay quietly for a moment and Quinn knew she was catching her breath.

'Can I ask you something?' she said when she'd recovered.

'Of course.'

'Is there anyone special in your life?'

'Why?'

'I thought maybe you fancied Ali.'

He'd thought they'd been so discreet but had someone seen something? Said something? 'What gave you that idea?'

'I've seen the way you look at her. I don't think you ever looked at me like that, not even in the early days.'

'Like what?'

'As if she's the reason you exist.'

'And what about her? How does she look at me?' He couldn't resist asking.

'The same way. Making sure you're okay was the last thing on my list but it was one of the hardest. I just thought it might be nice for you to have someone special. Ali could be a good choice and the girls seem to like her,' Julieanne said with a slight shrug. 'Will you think about it?'

Quinn nodded. He'd already done more than think

about it. Much more. But Julieanne didn't need to know that.

'Can you bring the girls in now?' she asked. 'I want to say goodbye.'

'Don't you mean goodnight?'

She shook her head. 'No, Quinn, it's time. I'm tired. I want my family around me.'

Quinn's heart sat like a lump of lead in his chest, weighed down not by regret but by sorrow. Not for himself but for his daughters.

He called the twins and when Helen brought them in he watched, amazed, as they didn't hesitate to clamber up onto the bed beside Julieanne. He wanted to protest, she didn't look strong enough to take any buffeting, but she caught his eye and he stopped. He knew she wanted this.

'Can you take a picture? One of the three of us and one with each of the girls on their own with me?' she asked him.

Quinn took his mobile phone from his pocket and took three pictures before handing the phone to Beth for the twins' approval.

'When you look at these photos I want you to remember that I love you,' Julieanne said to the girls. 'More than anything in the whole wide world.'

Her speech was becoming laboured and her eyelids were drooping. She needed to sleep and Quinn wanted to call the specialist. He knew she didn't have much longer.

'Give Mum a kiss goodnight,' he said to the twins. He couldn't bring himself to say goodbye.

'Let them stay with me, please,' Julieanne asked. 'I want you all to stay.'

Helen kissed her daughter and gently brushed her cheek. She sat beside Julieanne but kept her face averted from the twins and Quinn knew she was crying.

Julieanne hugged Eliza and Beth into her, cradling them against her body. She kissed them both and whispered, 'Goodnight, my darlings. I love you.'

She closed her eyes but didn't let go of her daughters. She moved her hands to their heads and stroked their hair, her movements slow and rhythmical. Quinn knew the repetition would be calming for Julieanne as well as for the twins.

Quinn sat opposite Helen, with Julieanne and the girls between them. He wanted to call the specialist but he was afraid to leave the room. He knew there wasn't much time.

He chose to stay.

He pushed the call button for a nurse and sat watching Julieanne breathe.

Sat watching the slight rise and fall of her chest.

Until it stopped.

Until she was gone.

CHAPTER SEVEN

Quinn

QUINN WALKED THE streets. The girls were in bed and asleep. He had brought them home, driven them up the hill in a state of numb exhaustion and put them to bed. He probably shouldn't have driven, he probably should have made other arrangements, but he'd just wanted to get the girls out of the hospital. He couldn't face any questions. He didn't have any answers. He didn't have the words to tell them their mother had died.

He'd have some explaining to do tomorrow but he couldn't face it tonight. He was exhausted. They all were. But while the girls slept he knew sleep would elude him for a while yet. He was too tired to think but he couldn't settle so he walked the streets.

The roads were dark and virtually deserted. It had rained earlier in the evening and people had stayed indoors. The footpaths were damp and slippery and the air was cold but Quinn was oblivious to his surroundings. If anyone had asked him where he was going he wouldn't have been able to tell them. He wandered aimlessly, his mind blank.

The air was fresh and clean and newly washed but he was unaware of it. His intention had been to get some fresh air, thinking it would revive him, but once he was outside all other conscious thoughts evaporated as he strode the footpaths. He thought he was roaming with no specific destination. He assumed he'd walk for a while and then return to Julieanne's house, but as the temperature dropped and the chill began to permeate his clothing and seep into his skin, it concentrated his focus. He stopped to get his bearings and was surprised to find himself only a few streets from home, right outside Ali's front door.

He had no idea how long he'd been walking. He had no idea what the time was. Was it was too late to call? He was about to pull his phone from his pocket to check the time when he realised the porch lights were on. He decided to take that as a signal that it wasn't too late for visitors. It hadn't been a conscious decision when he'd left Julieanne's to walk to Ali's house but he recognised that it might have been an unconscious one. Ali would help him to make sense of the events of the day.

He knocked, quietly, as he wondered how he was going to explain what he was doing on her doorstep. He didn't think he could talk.

But he didn't need to.

Ali opened the door, took one look at his face and opened her arms. He stepped into her embrace. Her arms wrapped around him as he ducked his head and buried his face in her hair. A sense of peace draped over him. He could feel the haze that had settled over him dissipate with her touch as his head began to clear and the events of the past few hours reassembled themselves into something that he could make sense of.

'Julieanne?' she asked.

He nodded. Ali's arms tightened around him and he knew she'd felt his answer. He should have known he wouldn't need to explain. He should have known Ali would understand what had happened.

He lifted his head and saw Malika standing in the passage, watching silently. He'd forgotten Ali's parents had returned home. He had been focussing on other things and he wondered if turning up unannounced wasn't appropriate after all. Was he assuming things about his relationship with Ali? She was generous with her time and comfort but what had he given her in return?

Ali took her arms from around him and he was aware of the cold air seeping back in. He was chilled to the bone. Were his new-found fears about to be realised? Was he welcome or not?

'Are the girls with Helen?' she asked.

When he nodded Ali stepped back into the house and said, 'You'd better come in.'

He breathed a sigh of relief and followed her inside. He was unable to do anything else. He felt like a man floundering in heavy seas, caught in a rip, and Ali was the only thing that could save him. He needed to keep her close.

He stepped inside and Ali closed the door. She took his hand and he followed her into the lounge room.

Malika watched them go. She still hadn't spoken and

he wondered why, but then again what was there to say? It seemed no one had many words to speak tonight.

A log fire burned in the grate. Several table lamps were lit, their soft light banishing any darkness from the corners of the room. Two large couches with plump, generous cushions squared off on opposite sides of the fire but Ali led him to an armchair that sat by the hearth. He folded himself into the chair, his knees almost buckling beneath him, collapsing with exhaustion and shaky with adrenalin. His bones felt cold, his body numb. He watched Ali and tried to concentrate on breathing as he let the heat of the fire warm him.

A highly polished antique sideboard was tucked beside the fireplace with several crystal decanters lined up on its gleaming surface. Ali crossed to the sideboard, her movements graceful, giving the appearance again that she was floating. She took a glass from the cupboard and poured a drink from one of the decanters. She passed him the glass.

He could smell the golden liquid. A Scotch, aged and expensive.

'Drink this,' she said. 'I'll be right back.'

Ali was gone long enough for Quinn to drink the contents of the glass. The whisky warmed him, defrosting him from the inside. When Ali returned she was carrying a tray. She pushed the door closed with her foot and set the tray down on a small table beside him. A bowl of soup, a plate of cheese and some fat slices of bread were arranged on the tray. The soup was thick with meatballs and dumplings. His stomach grumbled as the flavours of thyme and onion wafted through the air.

The warmth of the whisky had taken the chill from his bones and enabled him to speak. 'You don't need to feed me.'

'It sounds as if I do,' she answered as his stomach continued to rumble. 'Besides, it's what my family does whenever something major happens. We eat when we celebrate and we eat when we commiserate.' She handed him the bowl of soup and smiled, her cherry-red lips parting. 'My father is Danish. This is one of his mother's recipes. It makes a change from Indian food and I guarantee you won't be able to resist it.'

'I—'

Ali put one of her hands over his and interrupted him. Her hand was warm, matching the heat of the bowl. 'Eat first and then we'll talk.' She passed him the soupspoon and took his glass. She refilled it before dragging a smaller armchair to his side. She sat and waited patiently as he tasted the soup. Her presence was calming and Quinn relaxed and did as he was told. He didn't want to argue, it would waste the little energy he had, and, besides, he was starving.

She was right. The soup was delicious and he didn't stop until it was finished. The soup and the whisky and the fire combined to begin to chase away the chill that had enveloped him but he knew it was Ali's presence that was really warming him and making him feel as though he would manage.

'Does that feel better?' she asked as she stood to take the empty bowl and return it to the tray.

'Much,' he replied, as he relaxed back into the chair. It wasn't his intention to let her wait on him but he wasn't sure his legs would support his weight yet. He needed a little longer to absorb Ali's energy, a little longer to let her calmness work its magic and restore him.

'Are you okay?' she asked.

He frowned. He knew people would expect him to be upset but that wasn't his overriding emotion. He took a moment to work out exactly how he was feeling.

'She just gave up,' he said, as he realised that was what was bothering him. He'd known Julieanne was dying but he hadn't expected her to go so soon or so quickly.

He didn't feel devastated. He wasn't upset. He was upset for their daughters but he wasn't mourning. He was shocked.

It wasn't the fact that Julieanne was gone that surprised him but rather the timing. 'I expected her to fight harder but tonight she just gave up.'

Ali had stacked the tray and was now standing in front of him. He took her hand and pulled her onto his lap. He needed her close. He wrapped one arm around her waist and let her curl against his chest. Her bottom was round and firm in his lap, the thin fabric of her pants barely separating her from him. He could feel himself coming alive as desire began to obliterate shock. She was warm and soft and smelt of gardenias. She was just what he needed after the clinical harshness and chemical smell of the hospital.

'What did you want her to fight for?' she asked. 'For you?'

Quinn let his hand slide under Ali's shirt, seeking her warmth. Her skin was silky smooth under his fingers. 'No. Not for me. But I thought she'd fight for the girls.'

'She wasn't going to get better.' Ali voice was soft and gentle, her words realistic and reassuring. 'She was tired. Does it matter when she chose to go? Does it matter that she gave up now? This day was inevitable.'

'I know but I wasn't ready.'

'Not ready for what?'

'To deal with telling the girls.'

'The girls don't know?'

Ali tilted her head up and Quinn could see the surprise in her grey eyes.

He shook his head. 'No. We were all there. Helen, me and the twins. Julieanne had a chance to say goodbye to all of us but Beth and Eliza just think she went to sleep. I'll tell them tomorrow but I couldn't do it tonight. I didn't know what to say.'

'The girls knew it was coming.'

'Yes,' he agreed, 'but not when. None of us knew when and I know I'm not ready to deal with it. I don't know how to tell them.'

'Just tell them she died in her sleep. Don't tell them they were there. Take them outside when it's dark and let them look at the stars, do it again the next night and ask them to find a new star, one that wasn't there the night before. Tell them that star is their mother going to heaven.'

'They'll probably argue over which star,' Quinn smiled.

'Trust me, it will help, but most of all it will remind them of how much Julieanne loves them. That's what they need to hear.'

Quinn sighed and rubbed his head. 'God, how am I going to manage all of this? How am I going to manage being both father and mother? At times I feel I can barely manage the fathering part.'

Ali's head was resting on his chest. She could hear his heartbeat under her ear and the steady, rhythmical pulse was relaxing, but she could also feel Quinn's anxiety. He was wound tight and even though he had wrapped his arms around her again, his body was hard and tense under hers.

She lifted her head and met his eyes. 'You can manage and you will,' she said. 'And not only because you have to.'

She reached up one hand and rested it lightly against his cheek. The day's growth of his beard was rough under her palm but he let her hold him and she felt the muscles in his jaw relax just slightly under her touch.

She watched transfixed as the colour of his eyes changed. When he'd arrived tonight there had been dark shadows behind his azure eyes but they were back to their bright best now and she knew that, despite his stress, he would hear her. 'I think Julieanne waited as long as she could,' she told him. 'She knows you can manage. She trusts that you can and will take care of the girls. She would never have doubted that. You'll work it out. And we'll all help you.'

Ali didn't hesitate to offer help yet again. She fully intended to be there for Quinn for as long as he needed her. If he needed what she *could* give him, maybe he wouldn't worry about the things she couldn't give him.

She put her head back on his chest. She was pleased he was there, pleased he had come to her for comfort, even while a small part of her wished things were less complicated. How different things could be if he didn't have his other responsibilities, his other obligations. How simple it would be if it was just the two of them.

But it wasn't and she knew the girls had to be his first responsibility, and that started with sending him home. Quinn's daughters weren't Helen's responsibility. Especially not tonight.

Ali wondered how Helen was coping with the reality of Julieanne's death. Knowing it was coming was quite different from living through it. As much as she hated to see Quinn go, Ali knew he couldn't stay. Not tonight.

'I don't want to kick you out but you should go. The girls might need you and Helen might like some company.'

'I don't want to leave you.'

'And I don't want you to go,' she told him. 'I wish I could come with you. But I can't. Not yet.' She reached up and put her hand behind his head, pulling him down to her. She kissed him, hard and firm, hoping to give him enough strength to face what was coming. 'I am here for you but your girls need to know you are there for them. They need you.'

She wished he could stay the night with her, take comfort with her. But they didn't have the luxury of that privacy in either house. He had to go back to his daughters.

Ali felt Quinn's absence as though a part of her was missing, as though he took a piece of her with him each time he left. She knew the secret to not noticing he was gone was to keep busy. She tidied the lounge room and carried the tray into the kitchen, where Malika was finishing the dinner dishes. Ali thought her mother would have been in bed long ago and she knew the only reason she wasn't was because she was waiting for Ali.

'I didn't realise the two of you had grown so close,' Malika said.

'What do you mean?' Ali asked as she began to stack Quinn's empty plates into the dishwasher.

'I didn't realise you had the sort of relationship that meant he would come to you first when his wife died.'

'She was his ex-wife,' Ali corrected. She didn't want Malika affording Julieanne status she had no longer held, and Ali felt it was an important distinction.

'I'm not accusing you of anything improper, although you must admit the lines seemed blurred at times.' Ali knew her mother was right but she wasn't about to admit as much. 'I'm just surprised,' Malika continued. 'Is it serious between you?'

'I think it could be. It feels as though it's meant to be. It feels easy.' Ali continued stacking the dishwasher in order to avoid eye contact with her mother. She was fairly certain she knew what she was thinking.

'I would think it will be far from easy, especially at the moment.'

'He feels right for me. I'm excited by the possibilities of being with Quinn.' Ali tried to explain her feelings, tried to make her mother understand. But she couldn't put her feelings into words. How could she describe the way her heart expanded in her chest when he looked at her, or how her body came to life when he touched her or how she felt as though his azure eyes could see into her soul?

'Excited enough to cope with the fact that he'll never be completely free? That he'll never be completely yours?' Malika asked.

'I'm not waiting for him to be free,' Ali replied. 'I know his daughters come first but this might be my only chance of having any sort of family of my own.' Ali was aware that the familiar ache, deep in her abdomen, had returned, but she wasn't going to think about that now.

'Oh, Alisha, I know, despite everything, you have a romantic view of the world. You've always looked at people through rose-coloured glasses but, even if it does work out, an instant family is not necessarily easier. Is that what attracts you to him?'

Ali knew this conversation was far from over. She closed the dishwasher and sat at the kitchen bench, deciding she may as well finish this discussion now. She shook her head. 'The girls are gorgeous but they are a bonus. There was something between us from the moment we met, before I knew about his children, before I knew anything at all about him.'

'But are you sure you're ready for this? It seems very complicated and I expect Quinn will need a fair amount of support.'

'He came to me tonight, didn't he? He feels better when he's with me.'

'That's partly what worries me. It'll get worse before it gets better. Julieanne's not even buried yet.'

'They are divorced. Their relationship ended a long time ago. He's ready for more.'

'Are you certain? He's going to have a lot to deal with. I'd be surprised if he has any idea about what he's going to do, about how he's going to manage. His circumstances are going to be quite different from what they were a few months ago. Do you have the energy, the reserves to give him that support?'

Ali knew what her mother was referring to but she chose to ignore that topic of conversation. 'I don't know, Mum, but I guess we'll find out. I'm not going to walk away now. Not if he needs me.'

'And what happens when he doesn't need your support?' Malika asked. 'What happens when he gets through this? What then? You need someone who can be there for you too. A relationship is about give and take. You've had a tumultuous year and you're still recovering from everything that's happened to you. I'm worried that you haven't recovered enough to support Quinn unless there's some give on his part too. Does he have the capacity to support you?'

'I'm fine.'

'Darling, you had major surgery nine months ago. I know physically you are healing but your emotional reserves were exhausted. You need someone who can take care of you, who will give you the time and space to replenish your reserves. I know the surgery has left a hole in your life. I'm worried that you're trying to fill that with Quinn and he might not be the right fit.'

'I think he is.' Ali was almost certain that meeting Quinn had been her destiny. 'I think I've been waiting for him all my life.'

What if Quinn *was* the perfect man for her? She wasn't about to pass up the opportunity despite her mother's misgivings. She knew her mother only had her happiness in mind but what if Quinn was the one person who could bring her happiness?

'Does he know about your hysterectomy?' her mother asked.

Ali shook her head.

Hysterectomy. How she hated that word. It was a reminder of all that had been taken from her. Yes, it had been her decision but it was the fallout from that decision she hadn't been prepared for. The reality of life after surgery. The dissolution of her dreams.

She'd revised her dreams and she'd thought she had the perfect back-up plan but that hadn't turned out quite the way she'd anticipated.

'No, there hasn't been the right time to tell him.' She'd had a very small window of opportunity but it was hardly the sort of topic you'd bring up on the first date. Or even the second. She fiddled with some papers lying on the kitchen bench, aligning them so they lay in a neat stack as she avoided her mother's eye. She knew what she would say.

'What are you afraid of?' Malika asked, right on cue. 'If he is the right man for you, don't you think you should tell him?'

'Quinn has enough on his plate right now. I don't want to burden him with my troubles.'

'Focussing on Quinn's problems won't make yours go away.'

Ali knew that. The realisation that she would never bear children was still a physical ache in her belly. She could feel the empty space where her womb had been and she could feel the empty space in her heart that was waiting to be filled by a mother's love. She knew her mother was worried about her, that was a mother's prerogative, but it didn't make her right.

But being with Quinn made Ali forget about the empty spot in her heart. He filled it and her mother was wrong, he was the right fit.

'Don't sacrifice everything for Quinn. You did that for Scott and when you needed his support he left you, left you to deal with your loss.'

Ali couldn't argue this point with her mother. This time she *was* right. Ali's dreams of bearing children had been shattered and then Scott had delivered the final blow. He had left her and taken the rest of her dreams with him, her dreams of having a husband and family to call her own. Her revised dreams had included surrogacy and adoption but she had never contemplated the option of not having a family until Scott had left her and made her wonder if she'd find anyone who could give her what she wanted. Having a family was not something she could do on her own. Not without a womb.

But she knew things could be different with Quinn.

Scott hadn't wanted Ali badly enough. He couldn't, or wouldn't, put her before his other dreams and desires but Quinn had dropped everything to be there for his ex-wife. To Ali, that spoke volumes about the sort of man Quinn was. He was as different a man from Scott as Ali could imagine, and she wouldn't be told otherwise.

'Quinn isn't Scott.'

Julieanne was buried on a beautiful Wednesday in spring. The sky was blue and clear and the air was scented with the perfume of flowering bulbs and fruit trees. It was a beautiful day, one Julieanne would have loved.

Quinn stood at the front of the church, his shoulders squared and his spine stiff and straight. Helen and his daughters sat to his left but he was too restless to join them. He had known this day was inevitable but he still hadn't expected it to happen so soon. Organising Julieanne's funeral had become his responsibility. There had been no one else. He couldn't expect Helen to handle it, that wasn't a task for a mother, but he'd been worried about how he would manage to do all the things that were expected of him so he'd been extremely grateful to find Julieanne had left very detailed instructions with her lawyer, outlining how she wanted her funeral to be conducted. Quinn supposed that was one of only very few upsides to knowing your time was coming to an end. It had given Julieanne time to prepare.

He could have used more time to prepare. Despite the fact that Julieanne had virtually organised her own funeral, there were a lot of things that were falling to him and he didn't feel as though he was doing a very good job. Usually he thought of himself as an organised person. Army life was routine in a lot of ways and when it wasn't—for example, when he was on deployment—the way to cope was by being highly organised.

But at the moment there was no routine and he was finding it difficult to organise his family's life. He realised he was really only used to organising himself. Even after the divorce and while she had been sick, Julieanne had still organised the girls and Quinn had just fallen in with her plans. Following orders with regard to the girls had suited him but now it was up to him. Today was the last day he would be able to count on Julieanne's help. It was time to say their final goodbyes.

The coffin was in his peripheral vision. He tried to block it out but one glimpse was enough to remind him of all his failings. As a husband and as a doctor. He should have paid more attention to her headaches. He should have insisted she see someone when they'd escalated. Although he knew that earlier intervention would not have saved her life it might have given them more time. He'd done the best he could as a husband, now he just hoped he didn't fail as a father too. Ali had told him that Julieanne had trusted him, Julieanne had told him the same thing, but he wasn't sure he believed them. Not yet.

He glanced to his left, down the aisle, towards the door. The church was almost full, packed mostly with people he didn't recognise. Julieanne had asked that people wear something bright—pink, preferably, as it was her favourite colour—as she hadn't wanted her funeral to be a sombre, sad affair, and the colourful crowd made the church resemble a hothouse of flowers.

A flash of red caught his eye. A darker, more dramatic colour, it clashed with the varying shades of rose, strawberry and fuchsia.

Ali.

Seeing her in red lifted his spirits. It reminded him of the night they'd first met, when the splash of red against the greys and blacks of the conference cocktail party had caught his eye. Even though the competing colours were brighter today, she was still the one his eye was drawn to. She was his constant.

She made her way to a seat in a pew near the back. It was fortunate she wasn't closer to the front, he wanted to go to her, he wanted to speak to her, to touch her, and if she'd been nearer he didn't think he would have been able to resist. But he couldn't push through the crowd. Even he knew that was wrong. She looked up at him just before she sat down. She smiled at him, her beautiful red mouth smiling just for him, and he immediately felt better. He would get through this.

He took his seat beside his daughters but throughout the service he could easily pick Ali out and he held onto the thought that he could catch a glimpse of her whenever he needed to. Whenever he needed to find a bit more strength he could turn his head and see her. He knew Ali thought he was strong and capable but lately he'd been gaining a lot of his strength from her. He was strong enough to cope with Julieanne's death but he still wasn't sure if he was strong enough to get the girls through it too. Ali had told him they would look to him for guidance, that they would draw their strength from him, but what if he wasn't strong enough for them all. What then?

His attention was captured by a photograph of his daughters. Displayed on a screen that had dropped down at the front of the church was a slideshow of images. Pictures of Julieanne's life. The photos were accompanied by music. Songs that Quinn assumed were some of Julieanne's favourites. He knew her favourite colour was pink but he had no idea of her favourite songs and most of the photos were not depicting memories he had shared with her. These were things and moments Julieanne had shared with the girls. Things he had missed out on.

How on earth was he going to fill the hole that Julieanne's death was going to leave in his daughters' lives?

The church had been almost full when she arrived. She recognised a lot of the people. The Hills community was a relatively small one and a lot of the faces were familiar, but they hadn't held her attention for long. She was there for Quinn.

Ali was surprised to see him wearing his army dress uniform. She had almost forgotten about that part of his life, almost forgotten he still belonged to the army. His khaki trousers and shirt were immaculately pressed, his black shoes highly polished, and several medals adorned the left side of his chest.

She wondered what he was going to do about his job. She remembered the conversation she'd had with Julieanne, remembered that she hadn't wanted Quinn to stay in the defence forces. Ali wondered whether Julieanne had told Quinn how she felt.

On the opposite side of the church from her, one row from the front, she noticed half a dozen other men in uniform. Strangers in uniforms. Army uniforms. She figured they must be Quinn's friends and the thought pleased her. She wasn't the only one here for him today.

They all stood with perfect posture in their perfectly pressed uniforms but none of them looked as good as Quinn. Ali longed to wrap herself around him, to hug him to her and support him through the day, but it wasn't possible. It wasn't her place. From this distance all she could do was smile at him. He was scanning the room, nodding at people as they caught his eye. His gaze landed on her and even from the back of the church she could see his azure blue eyes brighten as their eyes met, and that was enough to lift her spirits. She could only hope it did the same for him.

As the service began he took his place at the front of the church with his family. Her gaze drifted over Beth and Eliza. They sat between Quinn and their grandmother, wearing identical pale pink dresses. They could have been flower girls at a wedding, except there was no bride or groom. She couldn't watch the girls, those poor motherless girls, that was too sad. She returned her attention to Quinn.

He looked strong and composed but she could see the tension in his shoulders, could see the effort he was making to hold himself together. What was going through his mind? Was he lamenting wasted time? Worrying about the future? Wondering how to be both a father and a mother? She had no idea.

As the minister finished speaking Quinn turned and kissed his girls before standing. He crossed to the lectern and for the first time since the service had begun he looked out to the mass of people gathered in the pews and made eye contact.

His voice was rich and deep and he didn't miss a beat as he spoke about Julieanne.

'Julieanne would be smiling if she was standing where I am now. You make a colourful group and I thank you all for making the effort to wear bright colours, as she requested. As you know, she was a people person and the two people she loved most in this world are our daughters, Beth and Eliza. She also loved a crowd and a party, especially her own, and she'd be sorry that she's only here in spirit, but in true Julieanne style she organised everything, leaving detailed instructions for me and her mother, Helen, which we have done our best to carry out. Along with leaving that list, she also left a note that she asked me to read.'

Quinn reached into a pocket on the front of his uniform and pulled out a piece of paper. He unfolded it and began to read.

'I know this is the last time I will have your undivided attention. I want to thank you all for your love and support and for helping my family to get through this. I couldn't have asked for better friends. Please talk about me and remember me to my girls. Love and laugh and make the most of every day. I will see you again.'

Quinn paused.

Ali didn't know how he was still able to read. All around her she could hear people sniffing and sense them searching for tissues as tears ran down their faces. She couldn't look at Quinn. She couldn't look at anyone as the tears rolled down her cheeks. Julieanne may have wanted her funeral to be a bright occasion but she sure knew how to tug at the heartstrings and she wasn't finished yet.

Quinn continued to read. '"Thank you, Mum, and

thank you, Quinn. I know you'll take care of my babies. Beth and Eliza, always remember Mummy loves you."'

Quinn folded the note and put it back into his pocket. He nodded at the line of uniformed men and, as one, they rose to their feet and stood, waiting for Quinn.

'Julieanne's final request,' he said, 'was to be laid to rest beside her father behind the church, but rather than following her pallbearers she would like everyone to gather on the steps out the front instead.'

Quinn's friends stepped forward and that was when Ali realised they were going to be the pallbearers. Quinn returned to his daughters and took their hands as his friends picked up the coffin and, with military precision, carried it outside.

Helen followed her daughter's coffin. She leant on the arm of another elderly woman, who looked remarkably similar and who Ali guessed was her sister, as they walked out of the church. Quinn and the twins went next and everyone else filed out behind them.

As the crowd gathered on the steps Ali realised that Julieanne had orchestrated this so that Beth and Eliza wouldn't witness her being put into the ground. They'd be able to visit her grave later when it was covered with grass and looked less fresh but would be spared the reality and finality of death for today.

Two women stood waiting outside the church, one on either side of the front doors. Ali recognised them from Quinn's birthday party. They were two of the school mums, Julieanne's friends, and they each held a large bunch of pink helium balloons. Quinn took two balloons and handed one to each of his girls. Together Beth and

Eliza released them and watched them float away. The colour of the spring sky was almost identical to Quinn's eyes and the girls' balloons were bright against the brilliant blue.

As the balloons drifted away on the breeze Ali knew everyone was remembering Julieanne. Maybe her mother was right, she thought as she looked at their faces. How was she going to compete with a dead wife? Even a dead ex-wife. Julieanne had wanted to be remembered and that was only right, but did that leave room for *her* in Quinn's life? Did it leave room for her in Quinn's family?

She wasn't sure and that was what she really wanted. She wanted to be loved not only by him but by his daughters. For the first time since meeting Quinn she thought perhaps she was hoping for too much.

She felt the air stir beside her and knew he was there.

'I'm glad you didn't wear pink. Red is your colour.' His words were soft, spoken just for her, and the deep richness of his voice sent a shiver of longing through her core. Was it wrong to feel desire at a time like this? Was it inappropriate? She didn't know but she couldn't help how she felt.

'Hi.' She smiled at him, hoping that her presence would have the same effect on him as his had on her. 'How are you holding up?'

'Better, knowing you're here.' His eyes were bright blue, their colour intense, and he looked at her as though she was the only person he could see, as though all the others had vanished into the atmosphere. The sense that they were alone almost had her leaning towards him intimately, until she remembered where they were.

'Will you come back to the house?' he asked. 'Have something to eat? Please?'

Ali had noticed he never called it his house. He'd told her he'd bought it for Julieanne and the girls and he'd paid for it, but it was in Julieanne's name and in his mind it obviously had nothing to do with him. Ali wondered who the house belonged to now.

She went to Julieanne's wake in the vain hope she'd get to spend some time with Quinn but, of course, the house was full of people and Quinn was busy and they didn't have one moment alone. But despite the occasion Ali couldn't help feeling a sense of hope. She accepted that Quinn hadn't been in love with Julieanne, not of late and maybe not ever, but recent circumstances had meant he had been emotionally bound to his ex.

But as of today there was no denying this was the end of a chapter. Now Quinn would be truly free to move on with his life and she hoped he would chose to move on with her. She might need to be patient but she was prepared to wait. Some things were worth waiting for and Quinn was one of them. Life was for the living and an occasion such as this only served to reinforce that point. Ali intended to have a life worth living.

CHAPTER EIGHT

Ali

ALI HAD SLEPT fitfully, her dreams full of strange images and of Quinn. She hadn't seen him since Julieanne's funeral three days ago. She assumed he was busy with the girls or his army mates or other things that kept him away from her, but he made regular appearances in her dreams, albeit in rather odd situations mostly involving her and him being naked in strange places, and this latest dream had been no exception.

She had never had erotic dreams until Quinn had taken her to his bed. Quinn had woken something primal in her and she was beginning to think she was completely corrupted. She stretched and rolled over. The subconscious version of Quinn was nice but if she was going to be sleep-deprived she'd rather she was losing sleep with the real thing in her bed. She tossed and turned for a while before deciding she was too restless to go back to sleep. She got out of bed and went downstairs, and did what she always did when she was edgy—she cooked.

She was just piling the last of the pancakes onto the stack when she heard a soft knock on the front door. She knew her parents had gone for their early morning walk and she wondered if they'd forgotten their key. But when she opened the door it wasn't to find her parents. Quinn was standing on the other side, with the twins.

He looked a little the worse for wear. A day's growth of stubble covered his jaw and his eyes were hidden behind sunglasses, yet her heart still gave an odd little kick at the sight of him. He was paler than usual and she suspected there might possibly be a few new lines on his face, but to see him standing in front of her, the breadth of his shoulders filling the doorway, and knowing that she could reach out a hand and touch him, feel his warm flesh under her fingers for the first time in three days, gave her a thrill that sent a shiver of longing through her centre.

His head dipped as his gaze travelled from her head to her toes as he took note of her outfit. Her feet were bare and she was wearing yoga pants, a red T-shirt and no bra.

Was he mentally undressing her?

Images from her most recent dream took shape in her head and she felt a tingle of excitement surge through her and take control of her body. Heat pooled low in her belly at the junction of her thighs and she felt her nipples harden. Fortunately the girls were too young to notice her reaction to their father's scrutiny but she crossed her arms over her chest just in case.

'Did we wake you?' he asked.

'No.' Her voice sounded breathless. Just one glance

from him made her heart race so fast that she was panting and desperate for him to rip her clothes off and have his way with her. She cleared her throat and tried to pull herself together. 'You're up earlier than you should be, judging by the look of you. Late night?' She knew the last of his army buddies were due to leave today and she assumed he'd had another night out with them.

Quinn nodded. 'And an early morning, thanks to two girls who need to get out of the house.'

'Did you want to come in?'

He gave a careful shake of his head and Ali wondered if she should offer him some paracetamol.

'We're on our way to the beach,' he explained. 'I need some fresh air and we thought it might be a good way to spend the day. We were hoping you might like to come with us. Are you busy?'

'Not with anything that can't wait,' she said. 'A day at the beach sounds lovely. Why don't you come in while I get changed? I've been making pancakes if anyone is hungry.'

'Pancakes!' Beth exclaimed.

'We love pancakes,' Eliza added, as if further clarification was necessary, before they bolted to the kitchen.

Quinn wasn't so quick off the mark. He removed his sunglasses and Ali saw that his eyes were tinged with red. She raised her eyebrows at him and said, 'Do you want me to have the girls for the morning and you can go home to bed?'

'I like the sound of those words but not necessarily in that order.' He grinned before he stepped inside the door and kissed her.

Heat flooded through Ali as her nipples pushed against the fabric of her T-shirt and the heat in her groin intensified. She moaned and was tempted to take him up on his suggestion but now was not the time or place. Unfortunately the chance to have Quinn to herself didn't happen all that often, and now that he was a sole parent as opposed to a single one, Ali could only assume that they'd have even fewer opportunities to be alone. 'If you've got energy spare to fool around then I think you can manage a day with the girls by yourself,' she teased.

'I'd rather you came with me,' he said as he ran his hand down the front of her T-shirt and rubbed his thumb over one erect nipple before sliding his hand to her bottom and pulling her in close. Ali could feel he was as aroused as she was and there was no doubting the double entendre of his words.

She'd woken up aroused and ready for sex and now his touch threatened to send her over the edge. She would love to sneak him upstairs to her room and strip him naked and make love to him but she would have to wait.

She stepped away from temptation. 'Stop it,' she panted, still fighting to catch her breath. 'That's not fair.'

'Sorry.' He grinned, looking anything but.

'If I come to the beach, will you promise to behave?' she asked.

'Where's the fun in that?'

'You're right,' she agreed, 'but do your best.'

'Anything for you,' he said, as he dropped another

kiss on her lips then walked casually past her on his way to the kitchen.

Ali watched him for a moment, enjoying the view as she caught her breath, before she followed him down the hall.

She set the three of them up in the kitchen with the pancakes and all the accompaniments—maple syrup, lemon, sugar and strawberries—before she went to change.

She dressed carefully. It would be too cold to swim but sunbathing might be an option, so she started with a red bikini—it didn't hurt to stack the odds in her favour—and then pulled a T-shirt and jeans over the top. She tied a pair of red canvas lace-ups and threw a pair of shorts, a jacket, a hat and a towel into a bag.

By the time she joined them downstairs Quinn had tidied the kitchen and stacked the dishwasher. They were ready to go. Ali sent the girls to use the bathroom, giving her a moment alone with Quinn. While the girls are out of earshot she asked, 'Whose idea was the beach?'

'Mine. The girls need to be kept occupied and I'm feeling a bit restless. I grew up by the ocean on the Sunshine Coast. I figure I either needed some time by the water or some time with you. If I can have both, even better.'

'So which beach did you have in mind?'

'You're the local, I thought I'd let you choose. All I need is some sea air and maybe a wave or two.'

Ali made a decision to take them to Victor Harbor via Port Elliot. As a destination it ticked all the boxes.

The weather forecast was perfect, still cool, which was to be expected at this time of year, but no wind, which would make a day at the beach far more enjoyable, and if the weather turned sour there were plenty of activities that didn't involve the beach.

She offered to drive, which allowed Quinn to catch up on some sleep. He looked like he could use the extra hour and she doubted that even after her own interrupted, rather sleepless night she'd manage to relax enough to sleep if Quinn was sitting just inches away from her.

The weather forecasters had got it right. It was a glorious day on the South Coast. The water was glassy and smooth and Ali's favourite stretch of beach was almost deserted, except for a few late-morning walkers and their dogs.

Quinn and the girls wasted no time in diving into the water. They tried to entice Ali to join them and she bravely rolled up her jeans and got her toes wet before declaring the water far too cold. The sun might be shining but the sea still held a winter chill.

She shook out her towel and sat on the beach and watched the girls playing with their father. Quinn lifted them onto his shoulders, one at a time, and they dived into the water from his man-made platform with squeals of delight. Ali could have sat there for hours, admiring Quinn's physique. The water gathered in shiny droplets on his skin and his muscles flexed and bulged as he lifted his daughters.

The girls didn't swim for long but they kept themselves busy building sandcastles while Quinn swam laps up and down the beach. The view wasn't quite so spectacular now that all she could see of him was his head bobbing in the water and his arms striking up and over as he pulled himself through the sea and Ali was able to turn her attention to other things. The day had warmed up enough to make it uncomfortable to stay in long trousers and she stripped off her jeans and changed into short white shorts and wandered along the water's edge, looking for marine treasures for the girls to decorate their sandcastle with. She delivered several pretty shells and a couple of rocks worn smooth by the sand and sea to the girls just as Quinn emerged from the water.

She lay on her towel and watched him walk up the beach towards her. It was her turn now to hide behind her sunglasses and admire him. His hard body was slick with water and it glistened under the sun. He picked up his towel and lifted his arms above his head to rub his hair, affording her a very pleasant view of rippling abdominals. Her eye was drawn to the line of blond hair running into his board shorts and her fingers itched to reach out and follow its lead.

Before she could move he spread his towel out on the sand beside her and flopped down onto his stomach. He propped himself on his elbows and the muscles in his arms bulged as they supported his weight.

'Better?' she asked.

Quinn turned his head to look at Ali. She was lying on her back, her breasts jutting up, round and firm against her tight T-shirt, and her tiny shorts barely covered her hips. Even though she was fully clothed, in his mind's eye he could picture her in that exact pose but naked. Her posture was so seductive he felt himself becoming aroused. He longed to reach across to slide his hand under her shirt, to feel her warm skin under his fingers and to pop the button on her shorts. 'Much,' he replied.

Ali rolled onto her side and dropped her top leg towards him, drawing his eye to the long, lean length of her thigh. Even at the end of a lingering, cold winter her leg appeared lightly tanned, courtesy of her Indian heritage. He itched to run his hand up her leg and under the frayed hem of her shorts to seek her warmth.

The combination of the sea, the swim, the sun on his skin were soporific, but far from feeling relaxed the vision of Ali lying stretched out in front of him stirred his senses and made his pulse race. He longed to lean closer to taste her lips. He longed to have her all to himself. He longed to strip off her tiny white shorts and make love to her.

If he had been ten years younger and hadn't had two daughters in tow, he'd have tried to convince her to sneak off into the sand dunes with him. But he was older and wiser now, he could exert some self-control. They had plenty of time. There was no need to hurry. He would do things properly.

'Stop looking at me like that,' she said, interrupting his carnal daydreaming.

'Like what?'

'Like you haven't eaten for a week.'

'Swimming always makes me hungry,' he said as he let his gaze travel down the length of her, pausing on her lips and her breasts, 'but I'd settle for a taste of your mouth.'

He was pleased to see a blush stain her cheeks and her pupils expand, darkening her grey eyes, as she watched him devour her with his gaze.

'That, I'm afraid, you'll have to wait for, but I can take you to the bakery if you're starving.'

'Is that your best offer?'

'Afraid so.'

'All right, but you owe me a kiss.'

Ali just smiled as she began to gather their things. Quinn called the girls and then watched as Ali bent over to cram the towels into her beach bag, affording him a fabulous view of red bikini bottom and rounded buttocks underneath her white shorts. Quinn made some adjustments to his board shorts before picking up the bag and carrying it to his car.

Ali took them to the Port Elliot bakery for lunch then they drove into Victor Harbor and she resumed her role of tour guide. She parked on the foreshore and took them to ride the horse-drawn tram to Granite Island. The girls had done this before but it was a new experience for Quinn. The tram was an old, renovated, wooden double-decker carriage with an open top that was pulled by a very placid Clydesdale. The girls got to feed the horse an apple and then raced up the curved staircase to the top level to sit in the open air. As the horse began its slow, steady journey across the causeway to the island, the girls delighted in hanging over the side railing and waving to the people who were walking beside the tram.

Ali thought the girls looked adorable and as if they didn't have a care in the world. Their blonde hair was being ruffled by the breeze and with the town, shielded by massive Norfolk Island pines, sprawled along the coast behind them they looked like a tourist advertisement.

Quinn treated them all to an ice cream on the condition that they walked up to the lookout and then back to the mainland to burn off some energy. The girls bounded ahead and Quinn and Ali followed at a more sedate pace. Quinn tucked Ali's hand into his elbow.

His actions surprised her. 'What are you doing?'

'Making sure you can't get away.'

'What about the girls?' she asked, conscious that they weren't aware of her relationship with their father.

'They're too busy having fun to notice and I'm not going to feel guilty about enjoying your company.'

But Ali wasn't so comfortable. She was very aware that they might run into someone who knew Julieanne and who might think their behaviour inappropriate. She looked around to see if anyone was watching them.

'You can relax,' Quinn told her. 'No one knows us here. It feels good to be away from town, to be somewhere I can just be myself, instead of feeling like I have to behave according to everyone else's expectations.'

'What do you mean?'

'Everyone in Stirling is treating me like a bereaved widower. I couldn't hope to get away with walking down the main street in town holding your hand—not yet, everyone would think it's scandalous—but I should be able to. They forget Julieanne and I were divorced.'

'You must understand how they feel, though, in particular Helen, her sister and the girls. It might not be the right time to go public.' As much as she loved the idea of walking hand in hand with Quinn, she realised that others might need a bit longer to come to terms with the development.

'I do understand and I will respect their feelings,' Quinn replied, 'but I don't have to like it. I know they're all in mourning. I'm upset too, but I'm upset for my girls. I will respect the girls' feelings and I will respect Julieanne's memory but I won't deny myself you. I can't keep you out of my mind. I've had enough feelings of guilt over not being a good enough father and husband and I refuse to feel guilty about wanting to spend time with you. Julieanne was my ex-wife, I'm not going to put my life on hold out of some misguided loyalty to her. I've always done the right thing by everybody—don't I deserve some reward?'

'Am I your reward?' Ali asked.

He smiled at her and his eyes sparkled like the sea that surrounded them. 'I'd like to think so,' he replied.

Ali spent the rest of the afternoon trying not to let her imagination get carried away. Trying not to leap ahead to her happy-ever-after. But knowing that Quinn wanted her meant she spent the rest of the afternoon in a bubble of euphoria that lasted through a game of mini-golf and a fish-and-chip dinner and into the drive home.

They weren't far into the return trip before the girls were fast asleep in the back of the car, exhausted by the day's activities. The sun had set and the black sedan seemed to melt into the bitumen as the German engine propelled them quietly through the night. There were no other cars on the roads, no streetlights and only a sliver of moon. The darkness was complete and out on the open road it seemed as though they were the only people in the world.

Ali rested her head on the seat as Quinn steered the car through the twists and turns of the country road. She turned towards him. In the glow of the dashboard lights she could see his profile. He felt her gaze and glanced her way. He reached across and rested his hand on her thigh. She had changed back into her jeans but she could still feel the heat of his hand through the denim.

'I had a lovely day, thank you,' he said as his thumb stroked the inside of her thigh, and Ali felt her muscles liquefy under his touch.

She closed her eyes as the heat travelled from his fingertips to reignite the fire that seemed to smoulder constantly in her belly whenever he was near. She felt his fingers move higher up her leg. She covered his hand with hers—she didn't want to stop him but this wasn't the time or place to give in to her desire. She opened her eyes as the car headlights illuminated a roadside sign for a bed-and-breakfast.

'That would be the perfect end to today,' he said as they buzzed past the stone cottage, 'if we could just check in there and spend the night.'

Ali laughed and relaxed her hold on his hand. 'Aren't you forgetting about the two little people in the back seat?'

'No, but a man can dream, can't he? Don't discount it for another time, though.'

'You'll still have the problem of finding someone to look after the girls. Or is Helen planning on helping you?'

'I'm not sure what she plans on doing,' he said. 'I don't think she knows. She's okay but she doesn't have the energy to deal with the girls on top of her grief. It's going to take time. But Julieanne has plenty of girl-friends who have offered to have the girls overnight if I need help.' He raised his eyebrows and Ali could see his blue eyes sparkling in the dim light.

'I'm not sure their generosity would extend to mind-ing your daughters while you took me away for a dirty weekend,' she quipped.

Quinn sighed. 'No, probably not. So, considering I'm not going to be able to take you out on a date ever, or at least in the foreseeable future, we'll have to come to some other arrangement.' He gave her a quick grin and while he had disarmed her with a smile he slid his hand higher up her thigh and nestled it in her lap.

'Are you trying to impress me with your powers of persuasion?' she asked as she felt her body begin to dis-solve under his hand.

'I will try to impress you with whatever I can,' he admitted.

'In that case, maybe I can find a babysitter who doesn't have any history with your family and who won't pass judgement.'

'Sounds good to me. Do you think you could find someone before I self-combust?'

'*You're* going to self-combust? What do you think you're doing to me?'

'Shall I pull over and put you out of your misery?' he teased.

'As tempting as that sounds, I think we'll both have

to find some self-control somewhere, and may I suggest you go for quality, not quantity, in your date nights?'

But Ali's nerves were buzzing with the prospect of having time alone with Quinn; she was as eager as he was. Perhaps Tracey, the clinic receptionist, would agree to babysit. She'd ask her tomorrow.

'Don't forget to tell any potential babysitters what angels the girls mostly are. If you can distract them with the girls' charms then maybe they won't give a thought to what we're doing.'

Ali smiled. 'I will do my best.'

Quinn glanced at his sleeping angels in the back seat. 'Can you believe I thought I'd like to do this all over again?' he said.

'Do what?'

'Have more kids. But from what you're saying, I'll be lucky to have the time to go on a date, let alone have more kids.'

'You'd like more children?' Ali asked as her heart plummeted in her chest.

'I would love it. The girls are the best thing that's ever happened to me but I was so panicked and stressed out by the reality of finishing my studies and paying for a wife and two kids that I didn't have time to enjoy the whole experience. I missed most of Julieanne's pregnancy. I've missed most of the girls' lives until now. I always swore I'd never be like my father and while I've never regretted having the twins I have still been a pretty absent dad. And I regret the fact that Julieanne and I couldn't make our marriage work. If I ever get a chance to do it again, I'm going to do it properly.'

Quinn's declaration exploded the little bubble of euphoria that had surrounded Ali all day, leaving her sitting in stunned silence. She really hadn't expected him to be prepared to do the whole babies thing again. She hadn't thought he'd need to. She couldn't believe he wanted to. Why couldn't he be content with what he already had? Surely he could concentrate on being father of the year to the two daughters he already had. Why did he need to do it all again?

Ali knew his reasons weren't important. All that mattered was that he wouldn't be able to have those experiences with her. If he wanted to experience a pregnant wife, he wouldn't choose her. There would be no point.

She sat in silence. Quinn had said he wanted to spend time with her, that he wanted to take her away for a dirty weekend, but that was hardly the same as saying he wanted her to have his babies. She didn't think he was looking for the next mother of his children right now so there was no need to tell him she wasn't in contention. There was no need to tell him she couldn't bear children.

Her day had begun so well and the middle had held such promise before it had all come crashing down, before reality had reared its ugly head. Perhaps she should just bow out gracefully now. Would that be best? To go now before they got any more involved? Was it better to give up any dreams of a future with Quinn? Because why would he want her?

CHAPTER NINE

Ali

IN AN EFFORT to keep occupied, hoping it wouldn't leave her time to think about Quinn and his dreams for the future, dreams she couldn't be part of, Ali buried herself in her work.

Quinn hadn't returned to the clinic, although the girls had gone back to school. Helen's sister had flown back to Hong Kong and Quinn and Helen were using the time to start to sort through Julieanne's things. Ali knew he was busy too and she used the excuse that because he wasn't working she was swamped with the extra patient load. That wasn't quite true, she had volunteered to take on extra work, giving her mother a bit of spare time and ensuring she kept herself busy.

When he asked her about date-night plans she told him she hadn't found a babysitter yet. She was glad she hadn't voiced her idea that Tracey might be willing to babysit. She was glad of an excuse as to why they couldn't be alone.

Keeping ultra-busy worked for a few days. For three

days she was able to resist the compulsion to call in and see him but on the fourth day she needed more than work to keep her mind occupied and off Quinn. She went home and started cooking. She cooked up a storm and as she layered samosas into foil containers, bagged up chicken and coriander pies and put the lids on the tubs of lamb rogan josh, she resisted the urge to take the food straight round to him. Maybe if she could resist for one more day the urge would pass.

But the following day at work visions of all the containers sitting in her mother's fridge kept popping into her mind. They would never eat all that food. She'd *have* to freeze it or take it to Quinn. It would be wasted otherwise. And she'd hate to see it wasted. She decided to give in and take it to him after work.

Deb, the clinic nurse, stuck her head around the door, catching Ali just as she was about to shut her computer down for the day.

'Ali, are you rushing out the door or do you have a second?' she asked.

She was going to call in to see Quinn but she had no other plans. What had she done before Quinn had come into her life? She couldn't think.

This had been her life. Her work. And it would be again. It would have to be.

'No, it's fine. What's the matter?' Maybe whatever Deb wanted would be enough of a distraction that she'd forget about her plans to call in at Quinn's. Maybe whatever Deb wanted would keep her so busy that she wouldn't have time. But never in a million years did she expect to hear Deb's next words.

'I've got Quinn's mother-in-law here with the twins. One of them, Beth I think it is, is complaining of stomach pains. Can you take a look?'

Of course she could. After all, she was first and foremost a doctor. She didn't want to dwell on the thought that this was all she might ever be. It was best just to get on with doing what she did and ignoring the things she couldn't change.

Ali nodded and Deb opened the door wider to admit Helen and the twins.

Quinn's daughters but not Quinn. She could do this.

'Hello, Helen, hi, girls, how was school today?'

'We didn't go today,' Eliza told her.

'Beth started complaining of stomach pain after breakfast so I kept them both home,' Helen replied. 'I thought it might have been a psychological pain but she vomited up her lunch and the pain seems to be getting worse. Usually once three o'clock comes and school has finished for the day these pains miraculously improve, but that hasn't been the case.'

'Where's Quinn?' Ali asked, wondering why he wasn't taking care of this situation.

'He had meetings in the city,' Helen explained. 'He doesn't know the girls are home. He had to see Julieanne's lawyer and accountant, along with the bank and the financial planner. It was going to take most of the day and initially I didn't think this was a major problem, but it appears otherwise now. I rang the girls' usual doctor but they said they didn't have any free appointments. I'm sorry to turn up unannounced but I didn't know what else to do.'

'It's fine,' Ali told her, trying to ease Helen's concerns. 'Of course I'll take a look.'

Seeing Eliza and Beth side by side, it was obvious to Ali that Beth wasn't making up her symptoms. Something was troubling her. She was pale and her eyes were dark. It appeared that the twins had inherited the same natural barometer in their eyes as Quinn had. They too had eyes that gave an indication of their feelings, happy, sad, worried or unwell.

'Can you show me where it hurts, Beth?'

Beth rubbed one hand vaguely across her belly button. 'Here, sort of,' she said, 'but it moves around a bit.'

'Can you climb up onto the bed and I'll see what I can find.' Ali turned to Helen as Beth clambered onto the bed. 'Has she had a bowel movement today that you know of?'

Helen shook her head. 'Yesterday apparently.'

'Temperature?'

'It was normal when I took it this morning but it was up a little just an hour ago,' Helen replied.

'Lie down on your back, sweetie, I'm just going to take your temperature again.' Ali held a tympanic thermometer in Beth's ear but the reading was normal.

'Can you bend your knees?' Ali asked as she put a small pillow behind Beth's knees to help to relax her abdominal muscles. 'And show me your tummy.'

Beth lifted the hem of her T-shirt and pulled the waistband of her leggings down. Ali carefully inspected Beth's skin but there were no external signs, no bruising, swelling or marks of any description.

She picked up her stethoscope. 'I'm just going to

listen to your tummy. Can you breathe in and out for me, nice deep breaths. That's right, good girl.'

Bowel sounds were present and normal and Ali moved her examination on to palpation. She pushed gently on Beth's abdomen, starting on the left side just beneath her ribs. 'Tell me if this hurts at all,' she said to Beth. Beth shook her head as Ali worked her way down the left side. Ali tested for Rovsing's sign in the left lower quadrant but there was no referred rebound, but it was a different story on the right side. As Ali quickly removed her hand from Beth's right lower quadrant the young girl flinched and grimaced.

'Was that the pain?' Ali asked.

Beth nodded, tears welling in her eyes.

'I think you have appendicitis.'

'Is that bad?' Eliza wanted to know.

'It feels bad,' Beth told her.

Ali smiled. 'It does, doesn't it?' She pointed to an anatomical chart hanging on the wall. 'See this tiny little thing here that looks a bit like a mini-sausage? That's your appendix. It's part of your intestines, where you digest your food. No one really knows what it's doing there as you don't need it, but sometimes it gets infected.'

'And then what happens?'

'A doctor can take it out and that will fix it. But you will have to go to the hospital to see the doctor.'

'No.'

Ali initially thought the refusal came from Beth but it was Eliza's voice, quiet but determined. She turned to look at her.

'Eliza?'

'I don't want Beth to go to the hospital. I don't want her to see a doctor there.'

'Why not?'

'Because Mum went to the hospital and she didn't come home.' Eliza's voice caught on a sob. 'I don't want Beth to die.'

'Oh, Liza,' Ali said, as Helen knelt down and wrapped her arms around her granddaughter. 'Beth is going to be fine. The doctors can fix this.'

'No. They didn't fix Mum. Doctors are stupid.'

Eliza had the same stubborn set to her jaw that Ali recognised in Quinn. She knelt on the floor to bring herself down to Eliza's eye level. 'Your mum had something that couldn't be operated on. They can fix Beth. I know the doctors at the children's hospital, they do this surgery all the time. You must know other children who have had their appendix out?'

Eliza shook her head.

'We do, Liza,' Beth told her. 'Sophie Abbott had hers out and she's fine.'

'What do we do now?' Helen asked.

'We need to ring Quinn, tell him what's happened and get Beth down to the children's hospital. I've finished consulting for the day and I know some of the surgeons there so I'm happy to meet Quinn there and speak to the doctors if you want to take Eliza home. I'm pretty sure they'll want to remove Beth's appendix. Eliza can come down and see Beth after surgery.'

Ali and Helen bundled Beth into Ali's car. Ali waited for her phone to connect to the hands-free device and then called up Scott's contact details. She hadn't told Helen that one of the surgeons she knew was her ex-boyfriend. She was sure Helen couldn't have cared less who her contacts were. For a brief moment Ali wondered about the psychology of still having her ex-boyfriend's number in her phone but she didn't have time to dwell on that now. Did it matter? Not when he was the person Beth needed. Ali couldn't think of too many other reasons why she'd even contemplate calling him, not after everything that had happened. But desperate times called for desperate measures and she decided it was fortunate she'd never got around to deleting his details.

She looked at the list of contact numbers. She had everything from his mobile number to his home landline, direct office, secretary and hospital. She knew she was unlikely to get Scott himself, not because he might see her number and choose not to answer but because he was always difficult to get hold of. She dialled the number for his secretary instead.

'Sonia, hi, it's Ali Jansson,' she said as the call connected. 'Is Scott about? I need a favour, it's an emergency.'

Sonia, bless her, didn't waste time quizzing her. 'He's not consulting at the moment,' she replied. 'He's over at the hospital but hold on and I'll see if I can get him for you.' Her tone was as friendly as it had always been. If she knew the finer details of Ali and Scott's break-up she wasn't letting it show.

Ali drove down the freeway, heading for the city, as she waited to hear if Sonia could track down Scott. She kept one eye on Beth but she seemed to be coping.

'Ali?'

'Scott, I need a favour.' She had no time for pleasantries and she was certain he wouldn't expect them but surely, after all that transpired between them, he owed her one favour. 'I'm on my way down to the hospital. I have a friend's nine-year-old daughter with me, suspected appendicitis and the symptoms are escalating. Can you see her?' There had to be some benefit to having an ex who was a paediatric general surgeon, even if she had sworn never to have anything to do with him again.

'How far away are you?'

'Twelve minutes.'

'I'll need parental permission.'

'Her father's meeting us there. Quinn Daniels, he's an army medic, based in Queensland. I'll tell him to ask for you.' Scott didn't need any more information than that.

'Okay.'

Ali breathed a sigh of relief. She didn't know why she'd been worried. Scott was a doctor, just like her, and patients would always come first. It was just fortunate that he wasn't already in surgery. 'Thank you.'

By the time Ali phoned Quinn he'd already spoken to Helen and was on his way to the hospital. As Ali pulled into the ambulance bay she saw him pacing to and fro in front of the automatic doors. His strides were long, as if by hurrying his paces he could speed up Beth's arrival. His spine was stiff and straight, he was holding himself rigid, but the moment he spied her car she saw some of the tension ease from his shoulders and the worried crease between his eyes softened a little. She forgot all the reasons why she was trying to keep her distance, forgot about the things he wanted that she couldn't give him. All she could think of was jumping out of the car and wrapping her arms around him, hoping to ease some of his burden. Seeing him so worried and still keeping her distance was going to be more difficult than she imagined.

He had the passenger door open the moment she stopped the car. 'Hello, princess,' he greeted Beth as he unclipped her seat belt, before looking across at Ali. 'Thanks,' he said simply. 'Are you coming in?'

Ali nodded. 'I'll park the car and meet you inside. Remember, ask for Scott Devereaux.' Ali didn't tell him anything more. She wasn't deliberately avoiding a discussion but her history with Scott was irrelevant. He was an excellent surgeon and that was all that would matter to Quinn. She was pretty certain he wouldn't think to ask how they knew each other and she wasn't going to volunteer the information.

By the time she'd parked the car and made her way back to Emergency, Beth was already being prepped for surgery. It seemed as though her diagnosis had been correct and Scott wasn't wasting any time. Ali was pleased. It meant Beth would be taken care of and she wouldn't need to see Scott.

'Can you wait with me?' Quinn asked.

He was permitted to accompany Beth to Theatre but would then have to wait alone while Scott operated. Ali nodded. She would stay until Beth came out of Theatre.

She wouldn't leave Quinn alone. She would stay until she knew everything was okay.

'I can't believe this has happened,' Quinn said when he returned. 'The first day I've left them alone since their mother died.'

'You didn't leave them alone. You left them with Helen. This isn't your fault,' Ali tried to reassure him. 'Beth will be okay, Scott knows what he's doing.'

'God, I hope you're right.'

'I know I'm right.' Ali didn't doubt Scott's surgical skills but for the first time she could truly imagine what it must be like to be so dependent on another person's ability, and it wasn't a good feeling. She reached across and held Quinn's hand. 'Beth will be fine but I do need to speak to you about Eliza.'

'Eliza?'

Ali held onto his hand as she told him about Eliza's fears. 'She was really concerned. You'll have to ask Helen to bring her down to see Beth as soon as she's allowed visitors. I don't think either of them will settle until they've seen each other,' she concluded.

Quinn sighed and tipped his head back to rest it against the wall. 'I can't believe I was starting to think about going back to work. How do people manage this sole parenting thing? How will I work and manage if things like this come up? How will I ever manage army life?'

'You're staying in the army?' Ali knew his return of service was almost up but after speaking to Julieanne at Quinn's birthday party she had assumed Quinn would leave the army.

'I don't know. I don't really have any idea what I'm doing. About anything. Julieanne and I used to make decisions based on what was best for the girls but knowing that Julieanne would be there for them. I know it allowed me to be quite selfish in terms of my career. I told myself I was being the provider and that no one was suffering, but now I have to do it all and I'm going to need some time to figure it out.'

'Whatever you decide to do, don't imagine that you'll be able to do it alone. You're going to need help,' Ali said. He would definitely need a nanny or another wife or his mother-in-law's help. 'Have you had a chance to talk to Helen?'

Quinn nodded. 'I've spoken to her but she's still not coping very well. She's going to spend some time with her sister in Hong Kong. She thinks she just needs some time away from the house. She will be back but we haven't talked about what she wants to do then. Raising my daughters isn't her responsibility. I'm going to have to figure out how to manage without her. Or at least plan for that eventuality.'

Ali was about to agree with him when she was distracted by the sight of a familiar figure appearing over Quinn's right shoulder. Scott was coming their way.

He looked just the same. He was slightly taller and thinner than Quinn. He had a long-distance runner's build, green eyes and a rectangular face topped with immaculate thick, dark hair. She knew she was comparing him to Quinn and she found him wanting. He was cool and focussed and self-absorbed while Quinn was warm, open and generous. And Quinn made her heart race and her body burn in a way that Scott never had.

She waited, curious to see how she felt, and was surprised to find her anger had faded. But the hurt was still there. Scott was entitled to his feelings but it hurt to know she hadn't been enough for him.

She saw him glance at their hands as he walked towards them. Quinn rose to his feet as Scott approached, letting go of Ali's hand as he stood. Scott nodded in acknowledgement at Ali but his conversation was directed at Quinn. Ali wasn't sure what she'd expected but to be virtually ignored, treated as if they barely knew each other, wasn't it.

She sat and waited as Scott spoke to Quinn and behaved as though she was unimportant.

She shouldn't be surprised. She hadn't been important enough for him to build his dreams with rather than without nine months ago, so why should things be any different now? But it annoyed her that his attitude still hurt. It annoyed her that he could still affect her like this.

He was just a man. A man who hadn't supported her, who hadn't listened to her, who hadn't tried to understand her heartache. Instead he'd used her failings as a woman as a reason to end their relationship. When she had needed him to put her first he hadn't, and that was when it had really hurt. She refused to let him upset her any more. She wasn't going to spend any more of her energy concerning herself with him. She straightened her back and stood up.

'Everything has gone smoothly,' he was telling

Quinn. 'I removed her appendix. It was inflamed but hadn't burst. She's in Recovery. You can go through and see her. '

'There you are. Are you finished?' A thin, blonde woman in three-inch heels and skinny black pants, a jacket draped over her arm, perfectly groomed but heavily made up, was walking towards them. It took Ali a moment to figure out she was talking to Scott.

'Just about,' Scott replied.

Ali looked her over again. She was wearing a hospital ID badge, one that indicated she was a nurse, but she wasn't dressed like a nurse and she wasn't talking like a nurse. Was she Scott's new girlfriend?

'We have to be at dinner in twenty minutes,' the woman said as she looked at her watch. As she rotated her wrist the sparkle of an enormous diamond ring caught Ali's eye. An engagement ring, brand-new and ultra-shiny, adorned her finger. Not a girlfriend, a fiancée. Was she Scott's fiancée?

Ali felt sick. She couldn't speak but fortunately no one seemed to expect anything from her.

'I just need to get changed,' Scott replied to the woman, before turning back to Quinn. He only half turned, effectively avoiding any chance of eye contact with Ali as he spoke to Quinn. 'I'll see Beth in the morning. The hospital can contact me if need be but I don't anticipate any problems.'

'Thank you. I appreciate it.'

Ali stood, still and mute, as Scott ignored her. As Scott took the woman's hand and walked off with her.

She could feel her heart hammering in her chest. She was afraid she was going to start hyperventilating.

Scott was engaged. He had found someone else. Someone who would raise the family Ali knew he wanted.

Gradually Ali became aware of Quinn still standing beside her. She'd forgotten he was there, she'd assumed he'd gone to see Beth in Recovery.

He was watching her closely. 'That was awkward,' he said. 'I thought you knew him?'

'I do...did.'

'And?'

'And what?'

'Why were you both so uptight?'

'I'm not uptight,' she protested, but even she could hear the tension in her voice. Her throat felt tight and she had to physically force the words out. 'I didn't know he was engaged, that was all. I was just surprised.'

Quinn raised his eyebrows. 'But that wouldn't have been a surprise to him and he was just as uncomfortable.'

Ali could hear the question in his voice. Was her history with Scott such a secret? She knew it wasn't. Quinn could ask any number of hospital staff and it would take him five minutes to find out how she knew Scott. 'We used to date,' she admitted.

'When?'

'We broke up nine months ago.'

'Did it end badly?'

'No, it's not that...' Well, it was partly that and Ali

knew it was obvious that they had issues, but she wasn't about to get into those details here and now.

Quinn was frowning, clearly trying to sort out her odd reaction. 'People move on. You've moved on, haven't you?'

Ali hesitated. She had moved on, of course she had.

So what if she still had Scott's number in her phone. She hadn't spoken to him in nine months.

So what if she was jealous of his fiancée. It wasn't because she had Scott, it was because her life had all the possibilities that hers didn't.

Seeing Scott again had reminded her of the things she couldn't have and reminded her of why no one would want her. But she didn't want him.

She had most definitely moved on from Scott.

Quinn was still watching her intently. 'I have to go. I need to see Beth.' He turned on his heel and began walking away.

He hadn't waited for her answer.

Ali wanted to call him back.

She started to call his name but as she lifted one hand to reach out for him, to bring him back, she realised he *had* waited but that she had taken too long to respond.

What was he thinking?

She wanted to call him back but what could she say?

That she'd moved on.

That Scott had left her because she couldn't have children.

That she didn't want Scott. She wanted him.

It was all true.

She wanted Quinn more than anything she'd ever

wanted before. But it didn't matter. She had nothing to say that he'd want to hear. He wanted children. He wouldn't want her.

She was frozen to the spot. Speechless, overwhelmed. She had nothing to say.

The ache in her heart and the ache in her belly were back. But this time her heart wasn't aching for the children she would never have, it ached for Quinn.

She couldn't stand the thought of telling him about her flaws. She couldn't stand the thought of being rejected.

Not again and not by Quinn. So she let him go.

She stood and watched as he disappeared through the doorway. Watched until he was gone and she was alone.

CHAPTER TEN

Ali

ALI COULD FEEL herself unravelling. She had to get away from the hospital. She couldn't fall to pieces in public. She had thought she was resigned to the fact she couldn't bear children but the hollow, nagging ache in her belly told a different story.

She managed to keep the tears at bay until she got home. The house was dark and she was grateful for the solitude. She stripped off her clothes and stepped into the shower. In the privacy of her bathroom she could let her tears run freely as she cried for the life she wasn't going to have. She didn't want Scott but that didn't stop her from being jealous of the fact that he and his fiancée were going to be living the life she wanted. They would get married and have babies and she would be old, single and childless.

The old, familiar ache in her heart was accompanied by a newer, sharper pain and she knew that was the place in her heart that belonged to Quinn.

She stood under the running water as her dreams dissolved in her tears and washed away.

Ali was coming out of her en suite bathroom when her mother knocked on the door.

'I just wanted to find out what happened with Beth,' Malika said when Ali called her in.

Ali really didn't feel like talking but she knew that Beth's emergency would have been the main topic at the clinic at the end of the day and her mother deserved to know the outcome. 'All good,' she replied, attempting to keep her tone light and cheerful as she tightened the sash on her dressing gown. 'It was her appendix, it's been removed.'

'Who did the surgery?'

'Scott.'

'Did you see him?' Malika asked.

Ali nodded.

'Are you okay?'

Ali wondered if her mother could tell she'd been crying. She thought the shower had helped to prevent the tell-tale blotchiness but her eyes felt puffy and mothers always seemed to sense these things. 'Not really,' she admitted, 'but it's not Scott's fault.'

'It's not?'

Ali shook her head. 'No. It's Quinn. It's over.'

'Why? What happened?'

Malika sat on the edge of Ali's bed and Ali picked up her hairbrush and started to pull it through her hair with long strokes as she avoided her mother's eyes. 'Seeing Scott again reminded me of what went wrong and

brought back all the feelings of pain and loss and rejection. I remembered how he thought I was flawed.
How I wasn't enough for him. What if Quinn feels the
same way?'

'If?' Malika asked. 'You don't *know* how he feels?'

Ali shook her head. 'No. I haven't told him. I'm not
going to tell him.'

'Why ever not?'

'I can't stand the thought that he won't want me. I
don't know how I'd cope if he rejected me. I'd rather
not tell him.'

'So instead you're going to walk away?'

Ali stopped brushing her hair and turned to her
mother. 'There's no point in telling him. He won't want
me.'

'How do you know?

'Because he wants more children.'

'You know you have other options besides natural
conception.'

'I know, but neither adoption nor surrogacy are easy
and what if he's not interested in that? What if he left
when the going got tough? He left his marriage.' Ali
knew she wasn't being fair. Julieanne had forced his
hand with the divorce but could Quinn have fixed things
if he'd wanted to? Had he taken the easier option?

'But he came back to help Julieanne when she needed
it. I imagine the past few months have been extremely
difficult for him but he's done what he needed to. He
must be dealing with a lot of stress already so perhaps
this isn't the right time to have this discussion but I
think he deserves to know.'

Ali shook her head. She couldn't see what difference it would make. Maybe this wasn't the right time for them but maybe it never would be. Quinn wanted to have more children and he wanted the whole experience, starting with a pregnancy. He wasn't going to want her.

'Do you love him?' her mother asked.

'Yes.' Her feelings hadn't changed. Even though she couldn't see a future with Quinn, she still believed he was the one for her.

'Then I think you owe it to him to tell him. Let him decide.'

But if he decided he didn't want her, if he rejected her, there wasn't enough left of her heart to cope with that. Her heart was missing too many pieces. A piece for the babies she would never have and now a piece for Quinn. Her heart was already breaking and she didn't have the strength to mend it. If it suffered too many more blows, it would shatter. She wasn't strong enough to persevere with such a damaged heart. She took herself to bed and stayed there.

'Liza, have a look at this,' Beth said as she held out a small specimen container to her sister. 'It's my appendix.'

'Ew, that's gross.'

'Is not.'

'Is too. What do you want to keep that for?'

'I'm going to take it to school.'

'Yuk, you're disgusting.'

'Am not.'

'Are too.'

'Girls, that's enough.' They'd done nothing but argue since Helen had brought Eliza to visit, and it was driving Quinn crazy. Of course, they paid him no attention, choosing to continue their bickering instead.

'Quinn, can I have a word?' Helen asked, indicating with an inclination of her head that she wanted to speak to him in private.

Quinn followed her into the corridor, grateful to have an excuse to leave the girls to it. He loved them dearly but sometimes they were hard work.

'Can I make a suggestion?' his mother-in-law asked, waiting until he nodded before she continued. 'Eliza is missing Beth. It's pretty quiet at home with just her and me and I think she feels that Beth is getting all the attention. That's why she's being so argumentative, it's a way of getting noticed.'

'I don't see what I can do about that. Beth is terrified of staying here by herself,' he replied. Quinn had promised Beth he wouldn't leave her and he'd slept at the hospital for the past two nights. 'I'm not going to leave her here alone.'

'No, I understand that, but why don't you take Eliza across to the park or at least to the café downstairs for a milkshake? I'll stay here with Beth and you can spend a couple of hours with Liza.'

Quinn was exhausted. Camping on a fold-out bed in a children's hospital was hardly conducive to a good night's sleep. What he'd really like was to spend a couple of hours sleeping or better still a couple of hours in bed with Ali. That would improve his mood, but he knew it wasn't possible and he knew Helen was right. His girls were his first priority.

He hadn't seen Ali since the day of Beth's surgery. He knew she'd phoned the hospital for an update but she hadn't been back to visit Beth. When he'd phoned her she'd told him she had a bad cold and didn't want to expose Beth to any germs. She had sounded stuffy but that didn't stop him from wanting to see her. He wanted to talk to her about Scott. He'd made some assumptions about her feelings for her ex and he was beginning to feel he should have given her a chance to answer his question. But he'd been so jealous that he had stormed off without listening and he owed her an apology. He wanted Ali to himself. He didn't want to share her. He was tired and grumpy and angry with everyone.

He was angry with Julieanne for dying and leaving him to cope with girls. He was angry with Helen for planning a trip to Hong Kong and effectively abandoning them. Angry that Ali might still have feelings for her ex, angry with the girls for fighting and angry with Eliza for needing his attention.

But he wasn't so angry that he didn't realise he was being unfair. No one was deliberately trying to irritate him and he recognised that anger was one of the stages of grief, and that Helen and the girls were all grieving too. He would get through this. He just needed to take a deep breath and calm down. But Ali was the best person for keeping him calm and circumstances were conspiring to keep him from seeing her, and that was another thing that made him angry.

Enough, he told himself. This wasn't helpful. He

needed to deal with the most urgent matters first. He needed to deal with the things he could control. He wanted to see Ali, he needed to feel her arms around him, he needed to taste her red lips, but all that would have to wait. Responsibility and duty, as always, came first. He'd promised Beth he would stay with her and the only way he could leave with Eliza was if Helen remained behind, as she'd offered to. She was leaving for Hong Kong in a few days so he'd better accept her help while he still had that luxury.

He took a deep breath. Ali wasn't here to calm him down, he'd need to manage on his own. His daughters needed him and he'd promised Julieanne that he'd take care of them. He wasn't going to let her down. He would do his best.

He thanked Helen and went to fetch Eliza as he forced himself to put Ali out of his mind for another day.

Ali was nervous. Her hands were clammy and her heart was racing. She washed her hands and dried them, trying to wash away the dampness. She held her cool hands against her cheeks and took a deep breath. One more patient for the day, which was no big deal except for the fact that the patient was Beth. She was booked in for her post-op review with Ali, her referring doctor, and more than likely she'd be accompanied by her father, which meant that Ali was about to come face to face with Quinn for the first time in a week.

She opened her door, intending to call them through. She could hear Quinn's voice and his deep tone sent a shiver of longing through her. She stuck her head into the waiting room. Quinn was leaning on the reception counter, chatting to Tracey. He was casually dressed in soft jeans that hugged his bottom and her favourite blue jumper that highlighted his eyes.

'So when are you coming back to work?' Tracey was asking.

Ali paused in the doorway. As far as she knew, he hadn't yet committed to a return date and she was interested to hear his answer. Very interested.

'I don't have any firm plans yet,' he said. 'It's something I need to discuss with Malika. If she has space in her diary she wanted to see me after we finish with Ali.'

Tracey was nodding. 'That'll be fine. I'll let her know you're here.'

Now was as good a time as any to interrupt, Ali thought as she called them through.

She tried to focus on Beth as she started her checkup but it was difficult with Quinn sitting so close, near enough that she could smell the soap he used in the shower and see the fine blond hairs on the back of his hand.

'How are you feeling?' he asked as she took Beth's temperature. 'Is your cold gone? You sound much better.'

'I'm fine,' she replied. She could hardly tell him she'd been fine all along and that her gravelly, nasal voice hadn't been due to a cold but to the hours she'd spent crying over him. She avoided eye contact, choosing instead to stay focussed on Beth.

'I'm planning on taking the girls on a holiday if you

can give Beth the all-clear,' Quinn said as Ali got Beth to lie down on the examination bed.

'A holiday?' Taken by surprise, she glanced his way.

He was nodding. 'I think we all need a break. I'm taking the girls to Queensland. I have flights booked to leave in two days.'

'Two days?'

Beth's laparoscopic scars were healing well and her digestive system was reportedly working perfectly from top to bottom so Ali couldn't see any reason why Beth couldn't get on a plane to Queensland. 'You're good to go,' she told her, as she helped her sit up and get down from the examination table.

'Great,' Quinn replied on her behalf, before adding, 'I need to speak to Malika quickly but I'd like a chance to speak to you too. I know we booked your last appointment—can you give me a few minutes?' He was watching her closely with his gorgeous blue eyes and Ali had the sense that he was feeling nervous although she couldn't imagine what about.

Despite her resolutions, she would still do anything for him, especially when he looked at her as though he was afraid she was going to disappear. But she had no plans to go anywhere so she could only assume that he did, that somehow his nervousness was tied into this trip. What did he need to tell her? She had to know.

'Why don't I take the girls outside? We can wait for you in the garden,' she replied.

Ali gave the girls each a drink and a piece of cake from the kitchen and made a pot of jasmine tea to take out to the garden. The last of the daffodils were nodding their heads in the flower beds but even the burst of yellow in the spring sunshine wasn't enough to lift her spirits. She could feel Quinn vanishing from her life, bit by bit, and with each little step he took away from her she could feel another piece of her heart breaking. But still she waited.

Quinn came into the garden just as Ali was pouring the tea. She watched him walk towards her, his powerful, muscular thighs flexing under the denim of his jeans as he crossed the lawn. She concentrated hard, trying to commit each movement to memory, wondering when she would see him again. Even though he was walking in her direction, another little piece of her heart broke with each step.

She passed a cup of tea across the table, making him sit opposite her. She wanted to be able to watch him while the girls were otherwise occupied on the swing.

'It's good to see you,' he said as he took the tea. 'I've missed you.'

She'd missed him too but she'd convinced herself that a clean break was the best way, the only way, to get through this. 'I'm sorry I didn't call in to see Beth once she was discharged. I've been swamped at work, one of our doctors has had some family emergencies...' she managed a smile '...which left us a bit short-staffed.'

'You look tired. Has it been very busy?'

Looking tired was a polite way of telling her she looked washed out. Sleepless nights were to blame for that, not busy days, but Ali chose not to tell him the real reason. She shook her head and changed the subject instead. 'How did you go with Mum?' she asked.

He picked up the tea, wrapping his hands around the cup until she could scarcely see the china as it got lost in his grip. His long, slender fingers beckoned to be stroked but she tucked her hands under her thighs and resisted temptation as he bent his head over the tea and inhaled deeply. 'She wanted to know if I've made a decision about coming back to work. She's agreed to let me have another couple of weeks.'

'Will you be back from Queensland then?'

'Mm-hmm.'

Something about his noncommittal response set off alarm bells in Ali's head. She felt a snap as another piece of her heart broke. He was keeping something from her. Had he already made his decision? What wasn't he telling her? There was only one way to find out.

'Do you have any idea what you might decide?' she asked.

His azure eyes had gone a shade darker. When they weren't at their brilliant best she knew something was wrong. She was sure something was bothering him.

He shook his head. 'No, that's partly the reason for this trip. Everyone is struggling with being in the house now that Julieanne is gone. Helen has gone to Hong Kong to stay with her sister and I think we all need a break. I know I need to make some decisions about the future but I don't think I'm in the right environment to do that. I need to take a step away.'

'Away from what?'

'Away from here, before this starts to feel permanent. I need to work out what's best for my family.'

'I see.'

'Do you?'

Ali nodded. 'You need to get away from the memories and the history. It's the right decision. You need to find a place where the three of you can be happy.' Another crack opened in her heart and Ali felt as though someone had slid a knife into it. She waited for the knife to be twisted.

'But I'd like you to come too.'

'Why?'

'I'm happy when I'm with you and I would like to see where our relationship could go. No one knows us up there, there'd be no expectations about how I should be feeling, about how we should be behaving. Do you think you could manage a week away?'

He seemed to be forgetting that his daughters would be there too. They might have some expectations. She wondered if he was worried about having his daughters all to himself. Was he worried about managing? He'd mentioned concerns regarding that a few times. Did he see her as a substitute nanny with sexual privileges or as something more? She didn't know. All she knew was that she couldn't go with him. She couldn't afford to get pulled back into his life.

'I can't go with you. It would leave the clinic short-staffed.'

'You could organise a locum if you wanted to.'

She knew he was right, she could organise a locum if she wanted to join him badly enough, but she needed to be strong. 'Our patients have had the run-around lately, with doctors coming and going,' she told him, 'and, besides, the locum we had is going on holiday... Where am I going to find another one at such short notice?' Did he think she could just run off with him at his fancy?

At least he had the good grace to look sheepish at leaving them in the lurch.

'Would you at least consider it? If you can find a locum, you could join me in a week.'

She had no intention of running away with him, no matter how tempting it sounded. She didn't want a fling and she certainly wasn't prepared to be a nanny with benefits. But if he'd made her a different offer, if he told her he loved her, that he couldn't live without her, that she was all he needed to make his life complete, she knew she'd be on the first plane to Queensland. But there were no such declarations. There were no promises of everlasting love. There was no happily-ever-after in sight.

'I can't go with you,' she repeated, and she felt the knife twist in her heart.

'It's just a holiday.' His body looked relaxed as he almost lounged in the chair but his eyes were intense as he looked at her.

It was her turn to feel nervous now and she felt herself wanting to squirm under the intensity of his gaze. 'I know.' It was just one week and that was the problem. He wasn't making any promises about the future.

'Is this about Scott?' he asked. 'Because I want to apologise for my behaviour. I was an ass. What happened between the two of you is none of my business.'

'No.' She shook her head and forced herself to maintain eye contact. It was important that he hear her this time and believed her. 'This has nothing to do with Scott. I've moved on.'

Ali was grieving for the babies she would never give birth to and the life she would never have with Quinn. Scott's rejection was nothing compared to that.

'So it's just about me?'

She could tell him what it was about. This was her chance. But she didn't want to see his face when she told him. She didn't want to see his face when his perception of her changed. She didn't want to see that realisation in his eyes, that moment when he learnt she was flawed. So she took the coward's way out. She stayed silent. She nodded.

'Okay. I guess that's important to know.'

He stood up and called to the girls.

The alarm bells were pounding in her head. She watched him leave, not knowing when or if she'd see him again. He didn't say goodbye, he didn't look at her, and Ali knew this was the final blow. Her head felt like it was exploding as her heart shattered.

Quinn had been gone for a week. Ali had tried to keep occupied but work wasn't proving to be the distraction it usually was. Her brother and his wife were visiting from Melbourne for the weekend and she hoped they might provide her with the diversion she so desperately craved. But she hadn't bargained on having to deal with the news they brought with them.

Ali stared blankly at her brother, unsure whether she'd heard him correctly. Was this the reason for the visit? Had he just told her they were expecting their first baby?

She had thought her week couldn't get any worse, but it turned out she was wrong.

'Ali, I'm sorry,' Tomas said. 'We didn't know how to tell you. Kim thought it would be best coming from me.'

Tomas had got up early and cornered her in the kitchen. Cornered was probably a harsh description but that was how she felt. But they had always been close, he was only eighteen months older than her and had always been protective, and Ali knew this situation must be hard for him, and she wasn't going to make it any worse.

'Don't be silly. I'm happy for you, really. Congratulations.' Ali stepped forward and gave her brother a hug. She was happy for him, he and Kim would be fabulous parents. She'd known it was inevitable that they would have a family and hearing about other people's pregnancies was something she'd have to learn to deal with.

Kim's pregnancy wasn't unexpected but she did wonder why it had to happen now, on top of everything else that was going on in her life. But this pregnancy wasn't about her and she would do her best to say all the right things. She was surprised, though, to find how much it hurt. She hadn't thought her heart was capable of hurting any more. She'd thought Quinn had done a good job of breaking it irreparably but there was obviously a tiny bit left and this news had pierced what little remained.

Her phone buzzed on the kitchen bench as she released her brother from her hug. Quinn's name appeared on the screen. She couldn't imagine what he could want or that she'd happily answer a call from him but it gave her the perfect excuse not to prolong this conversation.

'I have to take this,' she said, 'but tell Kim I'll come and find her as soon as I'm finished. It's good news, Tomas, you'll be wonderful parents.'

Ali answered her phone as she climbed the stairs. She needed the privacy of her own room as she didn't think she could hold it together for much longer.

'Hi, how are you?' Quinn's voice was the final straw. He sounded as though he actually cared about the answer.

Ali burst into tears.

'Ali? What's wrong?'

'My brother's wife is pregnant. I'm going to be an auntie.'

'Congratulations. They're happy tears, then?'

'No,' she hiccoughed. 'I don't want to be an auntie.'

'Why on earth not?'

'Because I want to be the one having babies.'

She was trying to be happy for Tomas, she really was, but she was also envious. Actually, if she was honest she'd admit she was insanely jealous and suddenly it all become too much. She couldn't keep it inside her any longer. It all came flooding out. All her heartache and broken dreams poured out of her in a torrent directed at Quinn. 'All around me people are having the life I thought I wanted. My ex-boyfriend is getting married, my brother is having a baby, you're off finding yourself or whatever it is you're doing, and here am I, still here, doing the same things I've been doing for years and will be doing for the rest of my life,' she said between sobs.

'I invited you to come with me.'

'I know.' She knew she sounded like a selfish cow but her life sucked.

'You have plenty of time to have a family of your own.'

'No, actually, I don't,' she said. 'It's not that simple. There won't be any pregnancies, accidental or otherwise, for me.'

'What are you talking about?'

'I can't have children. Not naturally.'

'What?'

'I've had a hysterectomy.'

'What? When? Why?'

'It was the beginning of this year.'

There was silence at the other end of the line. A long silence and Ali was just about to ask if he was still there when he spoke.

'What was wrong?'

'Fibroids.'

More silence.

'But a full hysterectomy? What about a myomectomy?'

'I tried that first but the fibroids grew back and I had such severe menorrhagia that it was unlikely I would ever fall pregnant as an embryo would never be able to implant successfully. It was the biggest decision I've ever had to make but I still have my ovaries. I thought even if I couldn't get pregnant that would leave me other options, other ways of becoming a mother, and that was all I ever wanted.'

'Why didn't you tell me before?'

That wasn't the question he should be asking. The question really should be why was she telling him now? But she knew why. She knew why she'd chosen this moment and it had nothing to do with timing, it was all about geography. She could still remember the way Scott had looked at her. The look that had said she was flawed, that she was less of a woman. She didn't want to see that look in Quinn's eyes too, she couldn't handle that. It was much better to tell him when she didn't have to look at him. Or him at her.

But that's not what she told Quinn. 'There never seemed to be the right time and I wasn't sure if we had that sort of relationship,' she said.

'What sort?'

'The sort where I would burden you with my troubles.'

'That's exactly the sort of relationship I thought we had.' Quinn's deep voice thundered through the phone and Ali had to hold the phone away from her ear before his next sentence was delivered in a far quieter manner. 'You know all the intimate details of my life and I feel I know nothing about you.'

She hadn't wanted him to know all about her.

'I wish I could be there for you,' he said.

That's your choice, she thought, but she kept silent. She couldn't get into a long discussion now. She couldn't lay her soul bare any more, she had shared enough secrets for one day. She didn't want to hear any platitudes from Quinn. He would need time to absorb the information and then she would see what he would do with it. Then she would know what sort of man he was. 'I have to go,' she told him. 'I have to go and congratulate my sister-in-law.'

Ali had hoped that telling Quinn would ease her fears but she realised that until she knew what his reaction was, those fears remained. Until she knew what sort of man he was she wasn't going to be able to relax and, as it turned out, he wasn't the man she'd hoped for.

The following day the blows kept coming. Ali was driving past Julieanne's house when a sign caught her eye. Mounted in front of the fence was a 'For Sale' sign.

Quinn must have decided not to return.

That was the final blow.

He wasn't coming back.

The last, tiny piece that remained of her heart popped like a bubble and there was nothing left.

CHAPTER ELEVEN

Ali and Quinn

ALI'S WORST FEARS were realised. Quinn knew the truth and now it was over.

It had been two weeks since he had taken the girls to Queensland, six days since she'd spoken to him and five days since Julieanne's house had been put on the market. In a perfect world he would have been back today. In a perfect world he would have declared his undying love and devotion to her despite her flaws. But it seemed her world was far from perfect.

Still, she couldn't resist driving past Julieanne's house on her way home from work in the hope that Quinn would be there. She drove past every day, hoping to find he'd decided to return.

Thinking she might never see Quinn again was far worse than knowing she'd never be pregnant. That pain paled in comparison with the thought that Quinn was lost to her. He was the love of her life. There were other ways she could become a mother but there was only one

Quinn. He was the one she'd been waiting for. He was the one with the power to break her heart.

But today was just like every other day. There was nothing to see. The house sat and stared at her. It was empty and dark. There was no sign of life, no sign of Quinn.

Ali drove on past the neighbour's house until something registered in her subconscious. Something was different. She reversed her car and took a proper look.

The 'For Sale' sign now had a big yellow sticker across it that read 'Sold'.

It was over.

He wasn't coming back.

'Alisha, there's someone at the door for you.'

Malika's voice carried up the stairs to Ali's room. As she came downstairs she saw her mother walking down the hallway with Quinn's daughters in tow.

'Come, girls, I'm baking a cake, you can help me,' Malika was saying.

Ali frowned. What were Beth and Eliza doing here?

As she stepped into the hall from the staircase it dawned on her. There was only one reason why the twins would be here.

She turned to her left.

Quinn stood in the doorway.

His broad shoulders filled the frame. She absorbed the sight of him, all glorious six feet of him, from the tips of his blond hair to his busted nose to his powerful thighs. He was wearing a pale blue polo shirt that made his brilliant blue eyes seem darker than usual, his gorgeous arms were lightly tanned and his muscular chest strained against the fabric of his shirt.

She'd almost forgotten how gorgeous he was.

Her heart was pounding, leaving her breathless and light-headed. Her hands were shaky and she suspected her knees were too.

He was back.

'What are you doing here?' Her voice shook as she asked the question.

'I came to see you. We need to talk.'

His voice was rich and deep and rumbled through her.

'I don't think there's anything left to say.'

'Believe me, there's plenty,' he said, as he stepped into the house and closed the gap between them. Ali could feel all her cells straining towards him as the air crackled with tension.

'You'd better come in, then,' she said, as she raised one eyebrow and stepped back, trying to break the invisible connection.

She led him into the lounge. The same room where they had sat after Julieanne had died, but this time he didn't need to sit by the fire. He folded himself into a couch.

Her heart was in her throat and her hands were clammy.

'Can I get you something?' she asked. 'Tea?' Nervousness was making her throat dry and her voice was tight and forced.

'No. Thank you.' His words were short and clipped, making her wonder if he was unsettled too.

His uncertainty relaxed her enough to let her perch on the same couch as him, albeit at the opposite end.

'I would have been here sooner,' he said, 'but I couldn't get all three of us on the same flight.'

'Sooner?' Her voice was squeaky.

'Yes. I needed to talk to you but I wasn't going to have the conversation over the phone. Some things are best said face to face.'

She thought she knew what was coming but it wasn't anything she wanted to hear. She didn't want to have this conversation. Not again. She'd told him everything he needed to know and she'd seen his reaction. She'd seen the 'For Sale' sign go up on Julieanne's house almost before she'd hung up the phone.

She went on the offensive. 'You didn't waste any time putting the house on the market. You didn't need to tell me in person that you're not coming back.'

'You think our conversation was the catalyst for that?'

'Wasn't it?'

'No. I was ringing you that day to tell you I was going to sell the house, but you completely sidetracked me with your news and I forgot. I can't believe you waited until you could tell me over the phone about what you've been through, but that wasn't what prompted me to sell the house. I bought that house for Julieanne and the children. I don't want to live there, it was never mine. There was nothing in it that belongs to me, there was nothing of any value to me there except for my daughters. It had to be sold. I signed the contract today.'

'Are you buying something else?' Ali could feel her

hopes rising. Maybe he was planning on staying. 'Are you taking the job at the clinic?' It had been two weeks and she knew he'd promised her mother an answer.

Quinn was shaking his head and with each shake Ali's hopes deflated.

'No. General practice isn't for me. I miss the autonomy and pressure of army medicine. I've been offered a permanent defence force posting.'

'Is the posting here?'

'No. Brisbane.'

So nothing had changed. He definitely wasn't coming back.

'This was Julieanne's life,' he explained. 'I was only here for the girls and they are happy in Brisbane. We need the change of scenery, a fresh start. The only reason I have come back, the only reason I would stay if I had to, is for you.'

'For me?'

His statement took her by surprise, so much so that she didn't object when he moved closer on the couch and took her hands in his. 'I don't want to live Julieanne's life but I don't want my old life back either. I want a new life. With you. Responsibility and duty have been the two words that have defined my life. It started when I was trying to live up to the responsibility of being the perfect son, so desperate for my father's approval, and escalated ten years ago when Julieanne fell pregnant. I will always have the responsibility of Beth and Eliza but I have done my duty by Julieanne and now it is time to start again. I want to take the girls to Queensland but I want you there with us.'

She could hear what he was saying but she couldn't make sense of it. Not yet. 'But my life is here.'

'It doesn't have to be.'

Ali pulled her hands from Quinn's hold. She couldn't think straight while he was touching her. His hands on her skin still had the power to send her blood racing around her body, bringing every cell and nerve ending to life, and it was impossible to think clearly when all she wanted was to let him take her in his arms.

'You want me to leave my life here to move to Queensland with you?' She took a deep breath and tried to focus on what he had said. 'As what? Your girlfriend? A nanny with benefits?'

He was shaking his head. 'A permanent posting with the army means no overseas assignments, no transfers. I'll be home every night. I don't need a girlfriend or a nanny, although I do like the sound of the benefits.' He grinned and her heart flip-flopped. 'When I met you my life split into two. There was "Before Ali" and "After Ali" but I don't want the "after" part to mean after our relationship has ended. I want it to mean after you came into my life and stayed there. I want it to mean "with you". I need you. I want a partner, a lover, a soul mate, a friend, a wife. I want you.' He paused and took her hands again and she didn't resist. 'I love you.'

'You love me?'

'Of course I love you,' he said, as if it was the most natural thing in the world. As if it wasn't the most un-expected thing for her to hear. 'I knew the day I met you that you are the person I am supposed to spend the rest of my life with. I want to share my life with you. I want you to share your life with me. I want you to marry me.'

'Marry you?'

'Yes. I want you to be my wife. But on one condition. We don't keep secrets from each other. You have to tell me all your secrets in person, no more hiding behind long-distance phone calls. You have to trust me.'

'I don't have any more secrets to share but I can't marry you.' She wished it was different. She knew she could have everything she wanted with Quinn but she also knew it wouldn't be enough for him.

'You're not already married, are you?'

Ali shook her head.

'Well, then, of course you can marry me. If you want to. I know I'm asking you for a lot. To give up your life here and move with me, but I promise I will make you happy.'

'It's not that.'

'Are you still worried about it being too soon? I'm a divorcee, not a widower, and I have been for a long time. Long enough to know what I want and I want you. I need you. I want to marry you and I don't care what anyone else thinks. Julieanne even gave us her blessing so that means the girls are the only ones who are allowed to object and I know they won't, they adore you.'

'Julieanne knew about us?'

'No, she suspected I had feelings for you and encouraged me to act on those. She wanted me to be happy. I need you for that. You have to marry me.'

'I can't,' she said, and her heart split apart a little more with each word as she tried to explain. 'I always thought I'd grow up, have a career, get married and juggle motherhood and medicine. I always dreamt of being a mother one day. I never imagined I'd be childless and probably single, that work would be my only constant, but that's how my life was turning out. And then I met you and I knew I'd been waiting for you all my life. I would give up everything I have and everything I've ever dreamt of having just to have you. I love you but I can't marry you.'

'Why on earth not? Love is the perfect reason.'

'It's *because* I love you. I know you want more children and I can't give you that. After my hysterectomy everything changed. My heart aches for the children I will never bear. It hurts but I know your love could ease that ache. I know that you can heal me but I can't give you what you want.

'I can still remember the way Scott looked when he told me he was leaving because his dream of becoming a father was to do it the traditional way, with a pregnant wife. In my own eyes I was less of a woman because I no longer had a womb but to know that *he* saw me the same way... I don't ever want you to look at me the way he did. With a look that said I was flawed. I couldn't stand to see that look in your eyes. You would be choosing me over a baby and I don't want you to regret that choice. I want to be enough for you but I know I won't be.'

Quinn's fingers brushed her cheek. Her skin felt damp under his touch but she wasn't aware until that moment that she was crying. Another tear spilled from her lashes and ran down her cheek. Quinn leant forward and kissed it away. His lips were warm and gentle and made her wish things were different. He moved closer and pressed his lips to hers. This kiss was soft and she could taste the salt from her tears. He wrapped his arms around her and there was nowhere else in the world she wanted to be. Ever.

He was the love of her life, could they have for ever?

'I know what I'm doing,' he whispered. 'Nothing is more important to me than my daughters and you. I know how lucky I am to have my girls and I want you to share my life with me. I will choose you every time and I will never regret it.

'I know I said I'd like to do it all again and, yes, I would like to think I could do a better job the second time round, but I won't do it without you. I don't *want* to do it without you. You are the love of my life. You are the person I am supposed to be with. I'm not giving up anything to be with you. If you marry me, I am gaining everything. I want you to choose to become part of my family but I don't want you to give up your dreams for me. I want to help you make them come true. We should get married because we love each other and everything else we will work out together. If we decide we want to extend our family, we will do that together. If you need to have children of your own, we will explore our options together. We can adopt. Or investigate surrogacy.'

'You would do that for me?'

'Of course. I would do anything for you.'

'You don't think I'm flawed?'

He sat back, releasing her from his embrace, and considered her with his azure eyes. 'I think you are perfect.

A woman is not defined by her anatomy. Your surgery does not take away the fact that you are gorgeous, kind, smart and loyal and I am desperately in love with you. The only thing wrong with you is you seem to be having trouble making a decision, and I don't think I can stand much more of this. I love you and I want to make a life with you. We are perfect for each other. We belong together. Please say you'll marry me.'

Ali could feel Quinn's words putting her heart back together again, connecting all the shattered pieces, and suddenly everything seemed so clear and simple. The answer was obvious.

'Yes,' she said. There was nothing else she *could* say. There was nothing else she wanted other than to spend the rest of her life with this man. 'Yes, I will marry you. I don't know how I ever thought I could live without you. I love you.'

'Thank you. I promise to be the best husband you can possibly imagine. For ever,' he said, before claiming her lips with his.

Ali melted into him. Giving herself up to him utterly and completely. She loved him more than she'd ever thought was possible and it was the most amazing feeling in the world.

* * * * *

A DOCTOR
TO REMEMBER

BY
JOANNA NEIL

Published in Great Britain 2014
by Mills & Boon, an imprint of Harlequin (UK) Limited,
Eton House, 18-24 Paradise Road, Richmond, Surrey, TW9 1SR

© 2014 Joanna Neil

ISBN: 978 0 263 90746 9

Harlequin (UK) Limited's policy is to use papers that are natural,
renewable and recyclable products and made from wood grown in
sustainable forests. The logging and manufacturing processes conform
to the legal environmental regulations of the country of origin.

Printed and bound in Spain
by Blackprint CPI, Barcelona

Dear Reader

I couldn't help wondering what it must be like to lose your memory and not know anyone around you. How would it be to forget the people you once loved—even perhaps someone you'd hoped you might one day marry?

How would that feel—for both people involved? And would that love stand the test of time? Maybe it's possible—but what if something has gone terribly wrong? Something that is now forgotten?

These were the emotions I wanted to explore when I wrote about Saffi and Matt.

Saffi faces a huge challenge after she is hurt in an accident, but fortunately Matt is there to lend a helping hand as she recovers. Will they manage to find their way to true love when there are so many pitfalls along the way?

I hope you enjoy reading their story.

With love

Joanna

Recent titles by Joanna Neil:

SHELTERED BY HER TOP-NOTCH BOSS
RETURN OF THE REBEL DOCTOR
HIS BRIDE IN PARADISE
TAMED BY HER BROODING BOSS
DR RIGHT ALL ALONG
DR LANGLEY: PROTECTOR OR PLAYBOY?
A COTSWOLD CHRISTMAS BRIDE
THE TAMING OF DR ALEX DRAYCOTT
BECOMING DR BELLINI'S BRIDE

**These books are also available in eBook format
from www.millsandboon.co.uk**

CHAPTER ONE

So, HERE SHE was at last. Saffi stretched her limbs and walked across the grass to the clifftop railing, where she stood and looked out over the bay. After several hours on the coach, it was good to be out in the fresh air once more.

From here she could see the quay, where fishermen stacked their lobster pots and tended their nets, and for a while she watched the brightly coloured pleasure boats and fishing craft as they tossed gently on the water. Seagulls flew overhead, calling to one another as they soared and dived in search of tasty tidbits.

In the distance, whitewashed cottages nestled amongst the tree-clad hills, where crooked paths twisted and turned on their way down to the harbour. This little corner of Devon looked idyllic. It was so peaceful, so perfect.

If only she could absorb some of that tranquillity. After all, wasn't that why she was here, the reason she had decided to leave everything behind, everything that had represented safety and security in her life—

even though in the end that security had turned out to be something of a sham?

A small shiver of panic ran through her. Was she doing the right thing? How could she know what lay ahead? Had she made a big mistake in coming here?

She pulled in a shaky breath, filling her lungs with sea air, and then let it out again slowly, trying to calm herself. She'd been living in Hampshire for the last few years, but this place ought to be familiar to her, or so she'd been told, and it was, in a way, in odd fragments of memory that drifted through her brain, lingered for a moment, and then dissolved in mist as quickly as they'd come.

'Perhaps it's what you need,' her solicitor had said, shuffling the freshly signed papers into a neat bundle and sliding them into a tray on his desk. 'It might do you some good to go back to the place where you spent your childhood. You could at least give it a try.'

'Yes, maybe you're right.'

Now the warm breeze stirred, gently lifting her honey-gold hair and she turned her face towards the sun and felt its caress on her bare arms. Maybe its heat would somehow manage to thaw the chill that had settled around her heart these last few months.

A lone seagull wandered close by, pecking desultorily in the grass, searching for anything edible among the red fescue and the delicate white sea campion. He kept an eye on her, half cautious, half hopeful.

She smiled. 'I'm afraid I don't have any food for you,' she said softly. 'Come to think of it, I haven't actually had anything myself since breakfast.' That seemed an awfully long time ago now, but she'd been thinking so hard about what lay ahead that everything else, even food, had gone from her mind. Not that forgetfulness was unusual for her these days.

'Thanks for reminding me,' she told the bird. 'I should go and find some lunch. Perhaps if you stop by here another day I might have something for you.'

She felt brighter in herself all at once. Coming here had been a big decision for her to make, but it was done. She was here now, and maybe she could look on this as a new beginning.

She moved away from the railing, and glanced around. Her solicitor had made arrangements for her to be met at the Seafarer Inn, which was just across the road from here. It was an attractive-looking building, with lots of polished mahogany timbers decorating the ground-floor frontage and white-painted rendering higher up. There were window-boxes filled with crimson geraniums and trailing surfinias in shades of pink and cream, and in front, on the pavement, there were chalkboards advertising some of the meals that were on offer.

There was still more than half an hour left before her transport should arrive, plenty of time for her to get some lunch and try to gather her thoughts.

She chose a table by a window, and went over to the bar to place her order. 'I'm expecting a Mr Flynn to meet me here in a while,' she told the landlord, a cheerful, friendly man, who was busy polishing glasses with a clean towel. 'Would you mind sending him over to me if he asks?'

'I'll see to it, love. Enjoy your meal.'

'Thanks.'

The solicitor had told her Mr Flynn had been acting as caretaker for the property these last few months. 'He'll give you the keys and show you around. I think he's probably a semi-retired gentleman who's glad to help out. He seems very nice, anyway. When I wrote and told him you don't drive at the moment he offered to come and pick you up.'

So now all she had to do was wait. There was a fluttery feeling in her stomach, but she went back to her table and sat down. She felt conspicuous at first, being here in a bar full of strangers, but now that she was tucked away in the corner she felt much more comfortable, knowing that she was partially shielded by a mahogany lattice.

For her meal, she'd chosen a jacket potato with cheese and a side salad, and she had only just started to eat when a shadow fell across her table. She quickly laid down her fork and looked up to see a man standing there.

Her eyes widened. Was this Mr Flynn? He wasn't at all what she'd been expecting, and her insides made a funny kind of flip-over in response.

Her first impression was that he was in his early thirties, tall, around six feet, and good looking, with strong, angular features and a crop of short, jet-black hair. He was definitely no elderly caretaker, and seeing such a virile young man standing there came as a bit of a shock.

He, in turn, was studying her thoughtfully, a half-smile playing around his mouth, but as his dark grey glance met hers it occurred to her that there was a faintly guarded look about him.

'Saffi?'

'Yes.' She gave him a fleeting smile. 'You must be… You're not quite what I expected…um, you must be Mr Flynn…?'

He frowned, giving her a wary, puzzled glance. 'That's right. Matt Flynn.' There was an odd expression around his eyes and in the slight twist to his mouth as he watched her. He waited a few seconds and then, when she stayed silent, he seemed to brace his shoulders and said in a more businesslike fashion, 'Your solicitor wrote to me. He said you wanted to look over the Moorcroft property.'

'I… Yes, that's right…' She hesitated, suddenly unsure of herself. 'I was hoping I…um…' She glanced unseeingly at the food on her plate. 'I…uh…' She looked up at him once more. 'I didn't mean to keep you waiting. Do you want to leave right away?'

He shook his head. 'No, of course not—not at all. I'm early—go on with your meal, please.' He seemed perplexed, as though he was weighing things up in his mind, but she couldn't imagine what was going on in his head. Something was obviously bothering him.

'Actually,' he said, after a moment or two, 'I'm quite hungry myself. Do you mind if I join you?' He smiled properly then, the corners of his eyes crinkling, his mouth making a crooked shape. 'The food here's very good. The smell of it's tantalising as soon as you walk in the door.'

'Yes, it is.' She began to relax a little and waved him towards a chair. 'Please…have a seat.'

'Okay. I'll just go and order, and be back with you in a minute or two.'

Saffi nodded and watched him as he walked to the bar. His long legs were clad in denim and he was wearing a T-shirt that clung to his chest and emphasised his muscular arms and broad shoulders, causing an unbidden quiver of awareness to clutch at her stomach. Her heart was thudding heavily.

It was strange, acknowledging that she could have such feelings. For so long now it had seemed she'd been going through life on autopilot, stumbling about, trying to cope, and feeling her way through a maze of alien situations. She didn't know where men fitted into all that.

He came back to the table and sat down opposite her, placing a half-pint glass of lager on the table. He studied her thoughtfully. 'Your solicitor said you've been mulling over your options concerning Jasmine Cottage. Are you planning on staying there for a while?' He looked around. 'Only I don't see any luggage, except for a holdall.'

'No, that's right, I'm having it sent on. I thought it would be easier that way. There's quite a lot of stuff— I'll be staying for a while until I make up my mind what to do…whether to sell up or stay on.'

'Uh-huh.' There was a note of curiosity in his voice as he said, 'I suppose it would have been easier for you if you had a car, but your solicitor said you sold it a few weeks ago?'

'I… Yes. I was… I…' She faltered momentarily. 'It

was involved in a rear-end collision and I had it repaired and decided I didn't need a car any more. I lived quite near to the hospital where I worked.'

It was a fair enough excuse, and she didn't want to go into the reasons why she had suddenly lost her confidence behind the wheel. All sorts of daily activities had become a challenge for her in the last few months.

'Ah, I see…at least, I think I do.' He gave her a long, considering look. 'Are you worried about driving for some reason?'

He hadn't believed her lame excuse. She winced. 'Perhaps. A bit. Maybe.' She hoped he wasn't going to ask her any more about it.

He sat back for a moment as the waitress brought his meal, a succulent gammon steak and fries. He was quiet, absorbed in his own thoughts, as though he was troubled by something. Whatever it was, he appeared to cast it aside when the girl had left and said, 'Are you planning on working at a hospital here in Devon?' He sliced into the gammon with his knife.

She shook her head. 'No, at least, not right away. I'm going to take a break for a while.'

It still bothered her that she had to say that, and as she lifted her iced drink to her lips she was dismayed to see that her hand shook a little. She put the glass down and took a deep breath, hoping that he hadn't noticed. 'What about you…what do you do? I'm guessing you're not a semi-retired caretaker, as my solicitor suggested.'

A variety of conflicting emotions crossed his face and Saffi gazed at him uncertainly. He seemed taken aback, somehow, by her question.

His dark brows lifted and his mouth made an ironic twist. After a moment, he said, 'No, actually, caretaking is just a minor part of my week. I'm an A and E doctor, and when I'm not on duty at the hospital I'm on call as a BASICS physician, weekends and evenings mostly.'

Her eyes grew large. 'Oh, I see. We have something in common, then, working in emergency medicine.'

Being a BASICS doctor meant he worked in Immediate Care, as someone who would attend injured people at the roadside, or wherever they happened to be. These doctors usually worked on a voluntary basis, so it was up to the individual doctor if they wanted to take a call.

'Yes, we do.' He nodded, and then looked her over once more, a sober expression on his face. He seemed… resigned almost. 'You don't remember me at all, do you?'

Saffi's jaw dropped in consternation. 'Remember you? Should I?' No wonder his manner had seemed so strange. Her stomach was leaden. So much for a new beginning. Even here it seemed she had come face to face with her vulnerabilities. 'Have we met before?'

'Oh, yes. We have.' He said it in a confident, firm voice and she floundered for a second or two, thrown on to the back foot. Of course there would be people here she had known in the past.

'I'm sorry.' She sent him a worried glance. 'Perhaps it was some time ago?' She was desperately hoping that his answer would smooth away any awful gaffe on her part.

'We worked together at a hospital in London.'

'Oh.' Anxiety washed over her. 'Perhaps you were working in a different specialty to me?'

He nodded. 'That's true, I was working in the trauma unit. But I definitely remember you. How could I forget?' His glance moved over her face, taking in the soft blush of her cheeks and the shining hair that fell in a mass of soft curls around her face. His eyes darkened as though he was working through some unresolved torment.

She exhaled slowly, only then realising that she'd been holding her breath. 'What were the chances that we would run into each other again here in Devon?' she said, trying to make light of things, but she looked at him with troubled blue eyes.

'I guess it was bound to happen some time. After all, we both knew your aunt, didn't we? That's another thing we have in common, isn't it?'

She hesitated. 'Is it? I…I don't know,' she said at last on a brief sigh. He'd taken the trouble to come here, and said they knew one another—perhaps she owed him some kind of explanation.

'The thing is, Matt, something happened to me a few months ago…there was an accident, and I ended up with a head injury. I don't remember exactly what went on, only that I woke up in hospital and everything that had gone before was a blank.'

He made a sharp intake of breath. 'I'm sorry.' He shook his head as though he was trying to come to terms with what she had told him. 'Your solicitor mentioned you had some problems with your memory, but I'd no idea it was so profound.' He reached for her, cupping his hand over hers. 'What kind of accident was it? Don't you remember anything at all?'

'Not much.' His hand was warm and comforting, enveloping hers. He was a complete stranger to her, and yet she took heart from that instinctive, compassionate action.

'They told me I must have fallen down the stairs and banged my head. I shared a house with another girl— my flat was on the upper floor—and apparently my friend found me when she came home at the end of her shift at the hospital. She called for an ambulance, and they whisked me away to Accident and Emergency.'

She went over the events in her mind. 'It turned out I had a fractured skull. The emergency team looked after me, and after that it was just a question of waiting for the brain swelling to go down, so that they could assess the amount of neurological damage I had been left with. I was lucky, in a way, because there's been no lasting physical harm—nothing that you can see.' She gave a brief smile. 'Except for my hair, of course. It used to be long and shoulder length, but they had to shave part of my head.'

'Your hair looks lovely. It suits you like that.'

'Thank you.' She moved restlessly, and he released her so that she was free to take another sip of her cold drink. Her throat was dry, aching. 'I remember bits and pieces. Some things come back to me every now and again, and I manage to keep hold of them. Other memories seem to float around for a while and then disappear before I can picture them clearly.'

'I'm so sorry, Saffi. I can't imagine what that must be

like.' His grey eyes were sombre and sympathetic. 'You must be taking a leap in the dark, coming here, away from everything you've known for the last few years. Or perhaps you remember Devon, and Jasmine Cottage?'

She frowned. 'No. I don't think so. Some of it, perhaps.' Her lips flattened briefly. 'I'm hoping it'll all come back to me when I get to the house.'

He nodded. 'I was really sorry when your aunt died. She was a lovely woman.'

'Yes.' She said it cautiously, unwilling to admit that she couldn't remember very much about the woman who had left her this property in a picturesque village situated near the Devon coast. Everyone told her they'd been very close, but the sad truth was she simply had no clear recollection of her benefactor. It seemed wrong to come here to take up an inheritance in those awful circumstances, but all those who knew her back in Hampshire had persuaded her it was the right thing to do. Only time would tell.

'Apparently she died before I had my accident, and I'd been to her funeral. All this business with the property had to be put to one side while I was recovering in hospital.' She glanced at him. 'Had you known my aunt for a long time?' She was suddenly keen to know how he was connected to her relative, and how he came to be caretaking the property.

He appeared to hesitate before answering and she wondered if this was something she ought to have known, some part of the way they'd known one another. 'We met a few years back, but then I went to work with the air ambulance in Wales, so I didn't see much of her until I came to work in Devon last summer. After that, she called on me from time to time to help fix things about the place.'

'I'm glad she had someone. Thanks for that.' She smiled at him, and made light conversation with him while they finished their meals. Her emotions were in a precarious state and she didn't want to enquire right then into how she'd known Matt in the past. Perhaps he understood that, or maybe he had his own reasons for not bringing it up. He seemed concerned, and clearly he had been thrown off balance by her loss of memory.

They left the inn together a short time later and went to his car, a fairly new rapid-response vehicle equipped with a blue light, high-visibility strips and badges.

He held open the passenger door for her and she slipped into the seat. The smell of luxurious soft leather greeted her, and she sat back and tried to relax.

Matt set the car in motion and started along the coast road, cruising at a moderate pace so she had the chance to take in the scenery on the way.

She gazed out of the window, watching the harbour slowly recede, and in a while they left the blue sweep of the bay behind them as he drove inland towards the hills. The landscape changed to rolling green vistas interspersed with narrow lanes lined with clusters of pretty cottages decorated with hanging baskets full of bright flowers.

He sent her a quick, sideways glance. 'Is this meant to be a kind of holiday for you—a chance to recover from everything that has happened? Or are you more concerned with sorting out your aunt's estate?'

'I suppose it's a bit of both, really. I was beginning to feel that I needed a break, a change of scenery at least, and although it was a sad thing that my aunt passed on, it gave me an opportunity to get away. I...' She hesitated momentarily, then went on, 'There's no one else left in my family, so it's down to me to sort out what's to be done with the property.'

Perhaps she'd managed to come to terms with all that before the accident, but since then she'd felt her isolation keenly. Being unable to remember people around her meant that she was cut off from all that was familiar, and it left her with an acute sense of loneliness.

'And do you think you'll manage all right?' he said, cutting in on her thoughts. 'If you're not working, I mean?' He saw her hesitation and pulled a wry face. 'Am I overstepping the mark? You'll have to let me know if I do that—I'm afraid I tend to get carried away and say what's on my mind. '

She shook her head. 'That's all right. I appreciate you being open with me.' She frowned. 'I'm not sure how I'd handle going back to medicine just yet. But I have enough money to keep me going for now, until I find my feet. After my parents died some years ago, it seems that I sold the property and invested what they left me. So at least I don't have any worries on that score.'

'Perhaps that's just as well. It looks as though you have more than enough on your plate right now.'

He concentrated on the road for a while as he negotiated a series of bends, and then, after following a winding country lane for about half a mile, Saffi suddenly became aware of an isolated farmhouse coming into view. It was set back from the road amidst fields, a little gem in the surrounding greenery.

'That's the house, isn't it?' she said, excitement growing inside her as they drew closer. It was a long, rambling property, with a couple of side-on extensions that had been added to the main house over the years, giving it three different roof elevations. It was pleasing on the eye, with the traditional white rendering throughout and slate roofs over all. The window-frames were mahogany, as was the front door. A trailing jasmine shrub sprawled over the entrance wall, its bright, yellow flowers making a beautiful contrast to the dark evergreen leaves.

'Do you remember it?'

'No. But my solicitor showed me a photograph. It's lovely, isn't it?'

He nodded, and parked the car on the drive. 'Here, you'll need the keys.'

'Thank you.' She stood for a moment or two, gazing at the house, and then she slowly walked up to the front door. The scent of jasmine filled the air, sweetly sensuous, instantly calming. Saffi breathed it in and suddenly she was overwhelmed as her mind captured the image of a dear, slender woman, a nurturing, gentle soul.

'Oh…Annie…Annie…'

Her eyes filled with tears, the breath caught in her throat, and she heard Matt saying urgently, 'What is it, Saffi? What's wrong? Have you remembered something?'

She was shaking. 'My aunt…it was just as though

she was here…I could feel her… But she's gone, and I don't think I can bear it…'

He hesitated momentarily, and then wrapped his arms around her. 'It's all right, Saffi. I know it's hard, but it's good that you remember her.'

She didn't move for several minutes, overtaken by grief, but secure in his embrace, glad of the fact that he was holding her, because but for that she might have fallen. Her legs were giving way as emotion wreaked havoc with her body, leaving her fragile, helpless.

'I'm sorry,' she said after a while, ashamed of her weakness and brushing away her tears with her fingers. 'The memory of her just came flooding back. I wasn't expecting it.'

'Do you remember anything else?' he asked cautiously. 'About the house, your work…your friends?' He was looking at her intently, and perhaps he was asking if she had begun to remember anything at all about him and the way they'd known one another.

She shook her head. 'All I know is that I was happy here. I felt safe. This is home.'

He let out a long breath, and then straightened up, as though in that moment he'd come to some sort of decision. 'Well, that's good. That's a start.' He didn't add anything more, didn't try to tell her about the past, or give any hint as to what their relationship might have been. Instead, he seemed to make an effort to pull himself together, reluctantly releasing her when she felt ready to turn back towards the door.

'I should go in,' she said.

'Do you want me to go in with you? You might still

be a bit shaky…and perhaps I ought to show you around and explain what needs to be done with the animals. I mean, I can look after them till you find your feet, but maybe you'll want to take over at some point.'

She stared at him. 'Animals?'

'You don't know about them?'

She shook her head. 'It's news to me.' She frowned. 'You're right. Perhaps you'd better come in and explain things to me.'

They went into the house, and Saffi walked slowly along the hallway, waiting in vain for more memories to come back to her. Matt showed her into the kitchen and she looked around, pleased with the homely yet modern look of the room. The units were cream coloured and there were open shelves and glass-fronted cabinets on the walls. A smart black cooker was fitted into the newly painted fireplace recess, and an oak table stood in the centre of the room.

'I bought some food for you and stocked the refrigerator when I heard you were coming over here,' Matt said. 'Your solicitor said you might need time to settle in before you started to get organised.'

She smiled. 'Thanks. That was thoughtful of you.' She checked the fridge and some of the cupboards and chuckled. 'This is better stocked than my kitchen back in Hampshire. We were always running out of stuff over there these last few months. I had to write notes to remind myself to shop, because my flatmate was worse than me at organisation.'

'I can see I'll need to keep an eye on you,' he murmured. 'We can't have you wasting away.' His glance ran over her and a flush of heat swept along her cheek-bones. She was wearing jeans that moulded themselves to her hips and a camisole top that outlined her feminine curves, and she suddenly felt self-conscious under that scorching gaze.

'I...uh...I'll show you the rest of the house if you like,' he said, walking towards a door at the side of the room. 'Unless it's all coming back to you?'

She shook her head. 'It isn't, I'm afraid.' She followed him into the dining room, where the furniture followed the design of the kitchen. There was a cream wood Welsh dresser displaying patterned plates, cups and saucers, and a matching table and upholstered chairs.

'The sitting room's through here,' Matt said, leading the way into a sunlit room where wide patio doors led on to a paved terrace.

She glanced around. It was a lovely room, with accents of warm colour and a sofa that looked soft and comfortable.

'I think you'll find it's cosy of an evening with the log-burning stove,' he murmured.

'Yes.' She had a fleeting image of a woman adding logs to the stove, and a lump formed in her throat.

'Are you okay?'

She nodded. 'I guess I'll need a plentiful supply of wood, then,' she said, getting a grip on herself. 'Where did my aunt get her logs from, do you know?'

'There's a copse on the land—your land. It should supply plenty of fuel for some time to come, but your aunt did a lot of replanting. Anyway, I've filled up the log store for you, so you won't need to worry about that for quite a while.'

'It sounds as though I owe you an awful lot,' she said with a frown. 'What with the groceries, the wood and…you mentioned there were animals. I don't think I've ever had any experience looking after pets—none that I recall, anyway.' Yet no dog or cat had come running to greet them when they'd first entered the house. It was very puzzling.

'Ah…yes. We'll do a quick tour upstairs and then I'll take you to see them.'

There were two bedrooms upstairs, one with an en suite bathroom, and along the corridor was the main bathroom. Saffi couldn't quite work out the layout up here. There were fewer rooms than she'd expected, as though something was missing, but perhaps her senses were off somehow.

'Okay, shall we go and solve the mystery of these pets?' she murmured. Maybe her aunt had a small aviary outside. She'd heard quite a bit of birdsong when they'd arrived, but there were a good many trees around the house that would have accounted for that.

They went outside to the garden, and Saffi caught her breath as she looked out at the extent of her property. It wasn't just a garden, there was also a paddock and a stable block nearby.

'Oh, no. Tell me it's not horses,' she pleaded. 'I don't know anything about looking after them.'

'Just a couple.' He saw her look of dismay and relented. 'No, actually, Annie mainly used the stable block as a store for the fruit harvest.'

She breathed a small sigh of relief.

Fruit harvest, he'd said. Saffi made a mental note of that. On the south side of the garden she'd noticed an archway in a stone wall, and something flickered in her faulty memory banks. Could it be a walled garden? From somewhere in the depths of her mind she recalled images of fruit trees and glasshouses with grapes, melons and peaches.

They walked by the stable block and came to a fenced-off area that contained a hen hut complete with a large covered wire run. Half a dozen hens wandered about in there , pecking the ground for morsels of food.

'Oh, my…' Saffi's eyes widened. 'Was there anything else my aunt was into? Anything I should know about? I mean, should I ever want to go back to medicine, I don't know how I'll find the time to fit it in, what with fruit picking, egg gathering and keeping track of this huge garden.'

He laughed. 'She was quite keen on beekeeping. There are three hives in the walled garden.'

Saffi rolled her eyes. 'Maybe I should turn around right now and head back for Hampshire.'

'I don't think so. I hope you won't do that.' He gave her a long look. 'I don't see you as a quitter. Anyway, it's not that difficult. I'll show you. Let's go and make a start with the hens.'

He led the way to the coop. 'I let them out in the morning,' he explained. 'They have food pellets in feeders, as well as water, but in the afternoon or early evening, whenever I finish work, I give them a mix of corn and split peas. There's some oyster shell and grit mixed in with it, so it's really good for them.' He went over to a wooden store shed and brought out a bucket filled with corn. 'Do you want to sprinkle some on the ground for them?'

'Uh…okay.' This had all come as a bit of a jolt to her. Instead of the peace and quiet she'd been expecting, the chance to relax and get herself back together again after the trauma of the last few months, it was beginning to look as though her days would be filled with stuff she'd never done before.

She went into the covered run, leaving Matt to shut the door and prevent any attempted escapes. An immediate silence fell as the birds took in her presence.

'Here you go,' she said, scattering the corn around her, and within seconds she found herself surrounded by hens. Some even clambered over her feet to get to the grain. Gingerly, she took a step forward, but they ignored her and simply went on eating. She shot Matt a quick look of consternation and he grinned.

'Problem?' he asked, and she pulled a face.

'What do I do now?'

He walked towards her and grasped her hand. 'You just have to force your way through. Remember, you're the one in charge here, not the hens.'

'Hmm, if you say so.'

He was smiling as he pulled her out of the run and shut the door behind them. 'They need to be back into the coop by nightfall. As long as their routine isn't disturbed, things should go smoothly enough. They're laying very well at the moment, so you'll have a good supply of eggs.'

'Oh, well, that's a plus, I suppose.'

He sent her an amused glance. 'That's good. At least you're beginning to look on the positive side.'

She gritted her teeth but stayed silent. Now he was patronising her. Her head was starting to ache, a throbbing beat pounding at her temples.

'And the beehives?' she asked. 'What's to be done with them?'

'Not much, at this time of year. You just keep an eye on them to make sure everything's all right and let them get on with making honey. Harvesting is done round about the end of August, beginning of September.'

'You make it sound so easy. I guess I'll have to find myself a book on beekeeping.'

'I think Annie had several of those around the place.'

They made their way back to the house, and Saffi said quietly, 'I should thank you for everything you've done here since my aunt died. I'd no idea the caretaking was so involved. You've managed to keep this place going, and I'm very grateful to you for that.'

'Well, I suppose I had a vested interest.'

She frowned. 'You did?'

He nodded. 'Your aunt made me a beneficiary of her will. Didn't your solicitor tell you about it?'

She stared at him. 'No. At least, I don't think so.' She searched her mind for details of her conversations with the solicitor. There had been several over the last few weeks, and maybe he'd mentioned something about another beneficiary. She'd assumed he meant there was a small bequest to a friend or neighbour.

The throbbing in her temple was clouding her thinking. 'He said he didn't want to bother me with all the details because of my problems since the accident.'

He looked at her quizzically and she added briefly, 'Headaches and so on. I had a short attention span for a while, and I can be a bit forgetful at times…but I'm much better now. I feel as though I'm on the mend.'

'I'm sure you are. You seem fairly clear-headed to me.'

'I'm glad you think so.' She studied him. 'So, what exactly did you inherit…a sum of money, a share in the proceeds from the livestock…the tools in the garden store?' She said it in a light-hearted manner, but it puzzled her as to what her aunt could have left him.

'Uh…it was a bit more than that, actually.' He looked a trifle uneasy, and perhaps that was because he'd assumed she'd known all about it in advance. But then he seemed to throw off any doubts he might have had and said briskly, 'Come on, I'll show you.'

He went to the end extension of the property and unlocked a separate front door, standing back and waving her inside.

Saffi stared about her in a daze. 'But this is… I didn't notice this before…' She was completely taken aback by this new discovery. She was standing in a beautifully furnished living room, and through an archway she glimpsed what looked like a kitchen-diner, fitted out with golden oak units.

'Originally, the house was one large, complete family home, but your aunt had some alterations made,' he said. 'There's a connecting door to your part of the house and another upstairs. They're locked, so we'll be completely separate—you'll have a key amongst those I gave you.'

She looked at the connecting door, set unobtrusively into an alcove in the living room.

'I'll show you the rest of the house,' he said, indicating an open staircase in the corner of the room.

She followed him up the stairs, her mind reeling under this new, stunning revelation. No wonder she'd thought there was something missing from the upper floor when he'd taken her to look around. The missing portion was right here, in the form of a good-sized bedroom and bathroom.

'You're very quiet,' he murmured.

'I'm trying to work out how this came about,' she said in a soft voice. 'You're telling me that my aunt left this part of the house to you?'

'She did. I'd no idea that she had written it into her will or that she planned to do it. She didn't mention it to me. Does it bother you?'

'I think it does, yes.'

It wasn't that she wanted it for herself. Heaven forbid, she hadn't even remembered this house existed until her solicitor had brought it to her attention. But her aunt couldn't have known this man very long—by his own account he'd only been in the area for a few months. And yet she'd left him a sizeable property. How had that come about?

All at once she needed to be on her own so that she could think things through. 'I should go,' she said. 'I think I need time to take this in. But...thanks for showing me around.'

'You're welcome.' He went with her down the stairs. 'Any time you need me, Saffi, I'll be here.'

She nodded. That was certainly true. His presence gave a new meaning to the words 'next-door neighbour'.

She'd come here expecting to find herself in a rural hideout, well away from anyone and anything, so that she might finally recuperate from the devastating head injury that had left her without any knowledge of family or friends. And none of it was turning out as she'd hoped.

Matt had seemed such a charming, likeable man, but wasn't that the way of all confidence tricksters? How could she know what to think?

Her instincts had been all over the place since the accident, and perhaps she was letting that trauma sour her judgement. Ever since she'd woken up in hospital she'd had the niggling suspicion that all was not as it seemed as far as her fall was concerned.

She'd done what she could to put that behind her, but now the question was, could she put her trust in Matt, who seemed so obliging? What could have convinced her aunt to leave him such a substantial inheritance?

CHAPTER TWO

SAFFI FINISHED WEEDING the last of the flower borders in the walled garden and leaned back on her heels to survey her handiwork. It was a beautiful garden, filled with colour and sweet scents, just perfect for the bees that flew from flower to flower, gathering nectar and pollen. Against the wall, the pale pink of the hollyhocks was a lovely contrast to the deep rose colour of the flamboyant peonies. Close by, tall delphiniums matched the deep blue of the sky.

'You've been keeping busy, from the looks of things,' Matt commented, startling her as he appeared in the archway that separated this part of the garden from the larger, more general area. 'You've done a good job here.'

She lifted her head to look at him, causing her loosely pinned curls to quiver with the movement. He started to walk towards her, and straight away her pulse went into overdrive and her heart skipped a beat. He was overwhelmingly masculine, with a perfect physique, his long legs encased in blue jeans while his muscular chest and arms were emphasised by the dark T-shirt he was wearing.

'Thanks.' She viewed him cautiously. She hadn't seen much of him this last week, and perhaps that was just as well, given her concerns about him. In fact, she'd wondered if he'd deliberately stayed away from her, giving her room to sort herself out. Though, of course, he must have been out at work for a good deal of the time.

It was hard to know what to think of him. He'd said they'd known one another before this, and she wanted to trust him, but the circumstances of his inheritance had left her thoroughly confused and made her want to tread carefully where he was concerned. What could have led her aunt to leave the house to be shared by two people? It was very odd.

To give Matt his due, though, he'd kept this place going after Aunt Annie's death—he'd had the leaky barn roof fixed, her closest neighbours told her, and he'd made sure the lawns were trimmed regularly. He'd taken good care of the hens, too, and she ought to be grateful to him for all that.

'I see you've made a start on picking the fruit.' He looked at the peach tree, trained in a fan shape across the south wall where it received the most sunshine. Nearby there were raspberry canes, alongside blackberry and redcurrant bushes.

She gave a wry smile. 'Yes…I only had to touch the peaches and they came away from the branches, so I guessed it was time to gather them in. And I had to pick the raspberries before the birds made away with the entire crop. Actually, I've put some of the fruit to one side for you, back in the kitchen. I was going to bring it over to you later today.'

'That was good of you. Thanks.' He smiled, looking at her appreciatively, his glance wandering slowly over her slender yet curvaceous figure, and making the breath catch in her throat. She was wearing light blue denim shorts and a crop top with thin straps that left her arms bare and revealed the pale gold of her midriff. All at once, under that all-seeing gaze, she felt decidedly underdressed. Her face flushed with heat, probably from a combination of the burning rays of the sun and the fact that he was standing beside her, making her conscious of her every move.

She took off her gardening gloves and brushed a stray tendril of honey-blonde hair from her face with the back of her hand. 'There's so much produce, I'm not quite sure what my aunt did with it all. I thought I might take some along to the neighbours along the lane.'

'I'm sure they'll appreciate that. Annie sold some of it, flowers, too, and eggs, to the local shopkeepers, and there were always bunches of cut flowers on sale by the roadside at the front of the house, along with baskets of fruit. She trusted people to put the money in a box, and apparently they never let her down.'

'That sounds like a good idea. I'll have to try it,' she said, getting to her feet. She was a bit stiff from being in the same position for so long, and he put out a hand to help her up.

'Thanks.' His grasp was strong and supportive and that unexpected human contact was strangely comforting. Warm colour brushed her cheeks once more as his gaze travelled fleetingly over her long, shapely legs.

'You could do with a gardener's knee pad—one of those covered foam things…'

'Yes, you're probably right.' She frowned. 'I'm beginning to think that looking after this property and the land and everything that comes with it is going to be a full-time job.'

'It is, especially at this time of year,' he agreed. 'But maybe you could get someone in to help out if it becomes too much for you to handle. Funds permitting, of course.'

She nodded, going over to one of the redwood garden chairs and sitting down. 'I suppose, sooner or later, I'll have to make up my mind what I'm going to do.'

She waved him to the seat close by. A small table connected the two chairs, and on it she had laid out a glass jug filled with iced apple juice. She lifted the cover that was draped over it to protect the contents from the sunshine. 'Would you like a cold drink?'

'That'd be great, thanks.' He came to sit beside her and she brought out a second glass from the cupboard beneath the table.

She filled both glasses, passing one to him before she drank thirstily from hers. 'It's lovely out here, so serene, but it's really hot today. Great if you're relaxing but not so good when you're working.' She lifted the glass, pressing it against her forehead to savour the coolness.

'How are you coping, generally?'

'All right, I think. I came here to rest and recuperate but the way things turned out it's been good for me to keep busy. I've been exploring the village and the seaside in between looking after this place. The only thing I've left completely alone is anything to do with the beehives. I think I'm supposed to have equipment of some sort, aren't I, before I go near them?'

'There are a couple of outfits in the stable block. I can show you how to go on with them, whenever you're ready.'

She nodded. 'Thanks. I'll take you up on that. I'm just not quite ready to tackle beekeeping on my own.' She drank more juice and studied him musingly. Despite her reservations about him, this was one area where she'd better let him guide her. 'Did you help my aunt with the hives?'

'I did, from time to time. She needed some repairs done to the stands and while I was doing that she told me all about looking after them. She said she talked to the bees, told them what was happening in her life—I don't think she was serious about that, but she seemed to find it calming and it helped to clear her thoughts.'

'Hmm. Perhaps I should try it. Maybe it will help me get my mind back together.'

'How's that going?'

She pulled a face. 'I recall bits and pieces every now and again. Especially when I'm in the house or out here, in the garden...not so much in the village and round about. I was told Aunt Annie brought me up after my parents died, and I know...I feel inside...that she loved me as if I was her own daughter.'

Her voice faltered. 'I...I miss her. I keep seeing her as a lively, wonderful old lady, but she was frail towards the end, wasn't she? That's what the solicitor said...that she had a heart attack, but I don't remember any of that.'

'Perhaps your mind is blocking it out.'

'Yes, that might be it. Even so, I feel as though I'm grieving inside, even though I can't remember everything.' She was troubled. Wouldn't Matt have been here when she had come back to see her aunt, and again at the time of the funeral? Everyone told her she'd done that, that she'd visited regularly, yet she had no memory of it, or of him.

She straightened her shoulders, glancing at him. 'Anyway, I'm glad I came back to this house. I was in two minds about it at first, but somehow I feel at peace here, as though this is where I belong.'

'I'm glad about that. Annie would have been pleased.'

'Yes, I think she would.' She studied him thoughtfully. 'It sounds as though you knew her well—even though you had only been back here for a short time.'

She hesitated for a moment and then decided to say what was on her mind. 'How was it that you came to be living here?' She wasn't sure what she expected him to say. He would hardly admit to wheedling his way into an elderly lady's confidence, would he?

He lifted his glass and took a long swallow of the cold liquid. Saffi watched him, mesmerised by the movement of his sun-bronzed throat, and by the way his strong fingers gripped the glass.

He placed it back on the table a moment later. 'I'd started a new job in the area and I was looking for a place to live. Accommodation was in short supply, it being the height of the holiday season, but I managed to find a flat near the hospital. It was a bit basic, though, and after a while I began to hanker for a few home comforts…'

'Oh? Such as…?' She raised a quizzical brow and he grinned.

'Hot and cold running water, for a start, and some means of preparing food. There was a gas ring, but it took forever to heat a pan of beans. And as to the plumbing—I was lucky if it worked at all. It was okay taking cold baths in the summer, but come wintertime it was bracing, to say the least. I spoke to the landlord about it, but he kept making excuses and delaying—he obviously didn't want to spend money on getting things fixed.'

'So my aunt invited you stay here?'

He nodded. 'I'd been helping her out by doing repairs about the place, and one day she suggested that I move into the annexe.'

'That must have been a relief to you.'

He smiled. 'Yes, it was. Best of all was the home-cooked food—I wasn't expecting that, but she used to bring me pot roasts or invite me round to her part of the house for dinner of an evening. I think she liked to have company.'

'Yes, that was probably it.' Her mouth softened at the image of her aunt befriending this young doctor. 'I suppose the hot and cold running water goes without saying?'

'That, too.'

She sighed. 'I wish I could say the same about mine. I would have loved to take a shower after doing all that weeding, but something seems to have gone wrong with it. I tried to get hold of a plumber, but apparently they're all too busy to come out and look at it. Three weeks is the earliest date I could get.'

He frowned. 'Have you any idea why it stopped working? Perhaps it's something simple, like the shower head being blocked with calcium deposits?'

'It isn't that. I checked. I've a horrible feeling it's to do with the electronics—I suppose in the end I'll have to buy a new shower.' Her mouth turned down a fraction.

'Would you like me to have a look at it? You never know, between the two of us, we might be able to sort it out, or at least find out what's gone wrong.'

'Are you sure you wouldn't mind doing that?' She felt a small ripple of relief flow through her. He might not know much at all about plumbing, but just to have a second opinion would be good.

'I'd be glad to. Shall we go over to the house now, if you've finished what you were doing out here?'

'Okay.' They left the walled garden, passing through the stone archway, and then followed the path to the main house. Out in the open air, the hens clucked and foraged in the run amongst the patches of grass and gravel for grain and food pellets, and ignored them completely.

'So, what happened when you tried to use the shower last time?' Matt asked as they went upstairs a few minutes later.

'I switched on the isolator switch as usual outside the bathroom and everything was fine. But after I'd switched off the shower I noticed that the isolator switch was stuck in the on position. The light comes on, but the water isn't coming through.'

'I'll start with the switch, then. Do you have a screw-driver? Otherwise I'll go and get one from my place.'

'The toolbox is downstairs. I'll get it for you.'

'Thanks. I'll turn off the miniature circuit-breaker.'

He went off to disconnect the electricity and a few minutes later he unscrewed the switch and began to inspect it. 'It looks as though this is the problem,' he said, showing her. 'The connections are blackened.'

'Is that bad? Do I need to be worried about the wiring?'

He shook his head. 'It often happens with these things. They burn out. I'll pick up another switch from the supplier in town and get someone to come over and fix it for you. I know an electrician who works at the hospital—I'll ask him to call in.'

'Oh, that's brilliant...' She frowned. 'If he'll do it, that is...'

'He will. He owes me a favour or two, so I'm sure he won't mind turning out for this. In the meantime, if you want to get a few things together—you can come over to my place to use the shower, if you like?'

'Really?' Her eyes widened and she gave him a grateful smile. 'I'd like that very much, thank you.'

She hurried away to collect a change of clothes and a towel, everything that she thought she would need, and then they went over to his part of the house.

She looked around. The first time she had been here she'd been so taken aback by his revelation about the inheritance, and everything had been a bit of a blur, so she hadn't taken much in.

But now she saw that his living room was large and

airy, with a wide window looking out on to a well-kept lawn and curved flower borders. He'd kept the furnishing in here simple, uncluttered, with two cream-coloured sofas and an oak coffee table that had pleasing granite tile inserts. There was a large, flat-screen TV on the wall. The floor was golden oak, partially covered by an oriental patterned rug. It was a beautiful, large annexe—what could have persuaded Aunt Annie to leave him all this?

'I'm afraid I'm on call today with the first-response team,' he said, cutting into her thoughts, 'so if I have to leave while you're in the shower, just help yourself to whatever you need—there's tea and coffee in the kitchen and cookies in the jar. Otherwise I'll be waiting for you in here.'

He paused, sending her a look that was part teasing, part hopeful. Heat glimmered in the depths of his grey eyes. 'Unless, of course, you need a hand with anything in the bathroom? I'd be happy to help out. More than happy…'

She gave a soft, uncertain laugh, not quite sure how to respond to that. 'Well, uh…that's a great offer, but I think I'll manage, thanks.'

He contrived to look disappointed and amused all at the same time. 'Ah, well…another day, perhaps?'

'In your dreams,' she murmured.

She went upstairs to the bathroom, still thinking about his roguish suggestion. It was hard to admit, but she was actually more than tempted. He was strong, incredibly good looking, hugely charismatic and very capable…he'd shown that he was very willing to help out with anything around the place.

So why had she turned him down? She was a free spirit after all, with no ties. The truth was, she'd no idea how she'd been before, but right now she was deeply wary of rushing into anything, and she'd only known him for a very short time.

Or had she? He'd said they'd known one another for quite a while, years, in fact. What kind of relationship had that been? For his part, he was definitely interested in her and he certainly seemed keen to take things further.

But she still wasn't sure she could trust him. He was charming, helpful, competent...weren't those the very qualities that might have made her aunt want to bequeath him part of her home?

She sighed. It was frustrating to have so many unanswered questions.

Going into the bathroom, she tried to push those thoughts to one side as she looked around. This room was all pearly white, with gleaming, large rectangular tiles on the wall, relieved by deeply embossed border tiles in attractive pastel colours. There was a bath, along with the usual facilities, and in the corner there was a beautiful, curved, glass-fronted shower cubicle.

Under the shower spray, she tried to relax and let the warm water soothe away her troubled thoughts. Perhaps she should learn to trust, and take comfort in the knowledge that Matt had only ever been kind to her.

So far, he had been there for her, doing his best to help her settle in. She had been the only stumbling block to his initial efforts by being suspicious of his motives around her aunt. Perhaps she should do her best to be a little more open to him.

Afterwards, she towelled her hair dry and put on fresh clothes, jeans that clung to her in all the right places, and a short-sleeved T-shirt the same blue as her eyes. She didn't want to go downstairs with wet hair, but there was no hairdryer around so she didn't really have a choice. Still, even when damp her hair curled riotously, so perhaps she didn't look too bad.

Anyway, if Matt had been called away to work, it wouldn't matter how she looked, would it?

'Hi.' He smiled as she walked into the living room. 'You look fresh and wholesome—like a beautiful water nymph.'

She returned his smile. 'Thanks. And thanks for letting me use the shower. Perhaps I ought to go back to my place and find my hairdryer.'

'Do you have to do that? I'm making some lunch for us. I heard the shower switch off, so I thought you might soon be ready to eat. We could take the food outside, if you want. The sun will dry your hair.'

'Oh...okay. I wasn't expecting that. It sounds good.'

They went outside on to a small, paved terrace, and he set out food on a wrought-iron table, inviting her to sit down while he went to fetch cold drinks. He'd made pizza slices, topped with mozzarella cheese, tomato and peppers, along with a crisp side salad.

He came back holding a tray laden with glass tumblers and a jug of mixed red fruit juice topped with slices of apple, lemon and orange.

'I can bring you some wine, if you prefer,' he said, sitting down opposite her. 'I can't have any myself in case I have to go out on a job.'

'No, this will be fine,' she told him. 'It looks wonderful.'

'It is. Wait till you taste it.'

The food was good, and the juice, which had a hint of sparkling soda water in it, was even better than it looked. 'This has been a real treat for me,' she said a little later, when they'd finished a simple dessert of ice cream and fresh raspberries. 'Everything was delicious.' She mused on that for a moment. 'I don't remember when someone last prepared a meal for me.'

'I'm glad you enjoyed it.' He sent her a sideways glance. 'Actually, Annie made meals for both of us sometimes—whenever you came over here to visit she would cook, or put out buffet-style food, or occasionally she would ask me to organise the barbecue so that we could eat outside and enjoy the summer evenings. Sometimes she would ask the neighbours to join us.' He watched her carefully. 'Don't you have any memory of that?'

'No...' She tried to think about it, grasping at fleeting images with her mind, but in the end she had to admit defeat. Then a stray vision came out of nowhere, and she said quickly, 'Except—there was one time... I think I'd been out somewhere—to work, or to see friends—then somehow I was back here and everything was wrong.'

He straightened up, suddenly taut and a bit on edge. Distracted, she sent him a bewildered glance. 'I don't know what happened, but the feelings are all mixed up inside me. I know I was desperately unhappy and I think Aunt Annie put her arms around me to comfort me.' She frowned. 'How can I not remember? It's as though I'm distracted all the while, all over the place in my head. Why am I like this?'

It was a plea for help and he said softly, 'You probably feel that way because it's as though part of you is missing. Your mind is still the one bit of you that needs to heal. And perhaps deep down, for some reason, you're rejecting what's already there, hidden inside you. Give it time. Don't try so hard, and I expect it'll come back to you in a few weeks or months.'

'Weeks or months…when am I ever going to get back to normal?' There was a faint thread of despair in her voice. 'I should be working, earning a living, but how do I do that when I don't even know what it's like to be a doctor?'

He didn't answer. His phone rang at that moment, cutting through their conversation, and she noticed that the call came on a different mobile from his everyday phone. He immediately became alert.

'It's a job,' he said, when he had finished speaking to Ambulance Control, 'so I have to go. I'm sorry to leave you, Saffi, but I'm the nearest responder.'

'Do you know what it is, what's happened?'

He nodded. 'A six-year-old boy has been knocked down by a car. The paramedics are asking for a doctor to attend.' He stood up, grim-faced, and made to walk across the terrace, but then he stopped and looked back at her. He made as if to say something and then stopped.

'What is it?' she asked.

He shook his head. 'It's nothing.'

He made to turn away again and she said quickly, 'Tell me what's on your mind, please.'

'I wondered if you might want to come with me? It might be good for you to be out there again, to get a glimpse of the working world. Then again, this might not be the best call out for you, at this time.' He frowned. 'It could be bad.'

She hesitated, overwhelmed by a moment of panic, a feeling of dread that ripped through her, but he must have read her thoughts because he said in a calm voice, 'You wouldn't have to do anything. Just observe.'

She sucked in a deep breath. 'All right. I'll do it.' It couldn't be so bad if she wasn't called on to make any decisions, could it? But this was a young child…that alone was enough to make her balk at the prospect. Should she change her mind?

Matt was already heading out to the garage, and she hurried after him. This was no time to be dithering.

They slid into the seats of the rapid-response vehicle, a car that came fully equipped for emergency medical situations, and within seconds Matt had set the sat nav and was driving at speed towards the scene of the accident. He switched on the flashing blue light and the siren and Saffi tried to keep a grip on herself. All she had to do was observe, he'd said. Nothing more. She repeated it to herself over and over, as if by doing that she would manage to stay calm.

'This is the place.'

Saffi took in everything with a glance. A couple of policemen were here, questioning bystanders and organising traffic diversions. An ambulance stood by, its rear doors open, and a couple of paramedics hid her view of the injured child. A woman was there, looking distraught. Saffi guessed she was the boy's mother.

Matt was out of the car within seconds, grabbing his kit, along with a monitor and paediatric bag.

With a jolt, Saffi realised that she recognised the equipment. That was a start, at least. But he was already striding purposefully towards his patient, and Saffi quickly followed him.

Her heart turned over when she saw the small boy lying in the road. He was only six…six years old. This should never be happening.

After a brief conversation with the paramedics, Matt crouched down beside the child. 'How are you doing?' he asked the boy.

The child didn't answer. He was probably in shock. His eyes were open, though, and Matt started to make a quick examination.

'My leg…don't touch my leg!' The boy suddenly found his voice, and Matt acknowledged that with a small intake of breath. It was a good sign that he was conscious and lucid.

'All right, Charlie. I'll be really careful, okay? I just need to find out where you've been hurt, and then I'll give you something for the pain.'

Matt shot Saffi a quick look and she came to crouch beside him. 'He has a fractured thigh bone,' he said in a low voice so that only she could hear. 'He's shivering—that's probably a sign he's losing blood, and he could go downhill very fast. I need to cannulate him, get some fluid into him fast, before the veins shut down.'

He explained to Charlie and his mother what he was going to do. The mother nodded briefly, her face taut, ashen.

Saffi could see that the boy's veins were already thin and faint, but Matt managed to access one on the back of the child's hand. He inserted a thin tube and taped it securely in place, then attached a bag of saline.

The paramedics helped him to splint Charlie's leg, but just as they were about to transfer him to the trolley the boy went deathly pale and began to lose consciousness.

Matt said something under his breath and stopped to examine him once more.

'It could be a pelvic injury,' Saffi said worriedly, and Matt nodded. He wouldn't have been able to detect that through straightforward examination.

'I need to bind his pelvis with a sheet or something. He must have internal injuries—we need to get more fluids into him.'

One of the paramedics hurried away to the ambulance and came back with one of the bed sheets. Matt and the two men carefully tied it around the child's hips to act as a splint, securing the suspected broken bones and limiting blood loss. Saffi noted all that and moved forward to squeeze the saline bag, trying to force the fluid in faster.

Matt glanced at her, his eyes widening a fraction, but

he nodded encouragement. She'd acted out of instinct and he must have understood that.

A minute or two later, the paramedics transferred Charlie to the ambulance, and Matt thrust his car keys into Saffi's hands. 'I'm going with him to the hospital,' he said. 'Do you think you could follow us? I'll need transport back afterwards. Are you still insured to drive?'

She stared at the keys. She'd not driven since the accident, not because she didn't know how but because, for some reason, she was afraid to get behind the wheel. It didn't make sense—her accident had been nothing to do with being in a car.

'Saffi?'

'Y-yes. I'll follow you.' She had to know if the boy was safe.

He left her, and she went to the car, opening the door and sliding into the driver's seat. She gripped the wheel, holding onto it until her knuckles whitened. She couldn't move, paralysed by fear. Then she saw the ambulance setting off along the road, its siren wailing. Charlie was unconscious in there, bleeding inside. His life was balanced on a knife-edge.

Saffi wiped the sweat from her brow and turned the key in the ignition. She had to do this. Her hand shook as she moved the gear lever, but she slowly set the car in motion and started on the journey to the nearest hospital.

Matt was already in the trauma room when she finally made it to her destination. 'How is he? What's happening?' she asked.

'It's still touch and go. They're doing a CT scan right now.'

'Do you want to wait around to see how he goes on?'

'I do, yes.'

'Okay.' She thought of the boy, looking so tiny as he was wheeled into the ambulance. Tears stung her eyelids and she brushed them away. She was ashamed of showing her emotions this way. Doctors were supposed to be in control of themselves, weren't they?

It had been a mistake for her to come here. She wasn't ready for this.

Matt put his arm around her. 'It'll be a while before we know anything,' he said. 'We could go and wait outside in the seating area near the ambulance bay. They'll page me when they have any news.'

She let him lead the way, and they sat on a bench seat next to a grassed area in the shade of a spreading beech tree.

He kept his arm around her and she was glad of that. It comforted her and made her feel secure, which was odd because in her world she'd only known him for just a few days.

She was confused by everything that was happening and by her feelings for Matt. Her emotions were in chaos.

CHAPTER THREE

'ARE YOU OKAY?' Matt held Saffi close as they sat on the bench by the ambulance bay. 'It was a mistake to bring you here. I shouldn't have put you through all that—it's always difficult, dealing with children.'

He pressed his lips together briefly. 'I suppose I thought coming with me on the callout might spark something in you, perhaps bring back memories of working in A and E.'

'It did, and I'm all right,' she said quietly. 'It was a wake-up call. Seeing that little boy looking so white-faced and vulnerable made me realise I've no business to be hanging around the house feeling sorry for myself.'

'I don't think you've been doing that. You've had a lot to deal with in these last few months, first with your aunt's death and then the head injury coming soon afterwards. Your aunt was like a mother to you, and losing her was traumatic. No one would blame you for taking time out to heal yourself.'

'You'd think I'd remember something like that, wouldn't you?' She frowned. 'But I do keep getting these images of how she was with me, of moments we shared. The feelings are intense, but then they disappear. It's really bewildering.'

'It's a good sign, though, that you're getting these flashbacks, don't you think? Like I said, you should try not to get yourself too wound up about it. Things will come back to you, given time.'

'Yes.' She thought of the little boy who was so desperately ill, being assessed by the trauma team right now. 'I can't imagine what Charlie's parents must be going through. This must be a desperate time for them. What are his chances, do you think?'

'About fifty-fifty at the moment. He lost a lot of blood and went into shock, but on the plus side we managed to compensate him with fluids and we brought him into hospital in quick time. Another thing in his favour is that Tim Collins is leading the team looking after him. He's a brilliant surgeon. If anyone can save him, he's the man.'

He sent her a thoughtful glance. 'You came up with the diagnosis right away, and knew we had to push fluids into him fast. That makes me feel a bit less guilty about bringing you out here, if it was worth it in the end.'

She gave him a faint smile. 'It was instinctive...but there was no pressure on me at the time. I don't know how I would cope by myself in an emergency situation. There's been a huge hole in my life and it's made me wary about everything. I doubt myself at every step.'

He nodded sympathetically. 'At least it was a beginning.' He stretched his legs, flexing his muscles, and glanced around. 'Shall we go and walk in the grounds for a while? It could be some time before they page us with the results.'

'Okay. That's a good idea. Anything would be better than sitting here, waiting.'

They walked around the side of the hospital over a grassed area where a track led to a small copse of silver-birch trees. There were wild flowers growing here, pinky-white clover and blue cornflowers, and here and there patches of pretty white campion.

Beyond the copse they came across more grass and then a pathway that they followed for several minutes. It led them back to the hospital building and they discovered an area where wooden tables and bench seats were set out at intervals. Saffi looked around and realised they were outside the hospital's restaurant.

It was late afternoon, and there were few people inside the building, and none but themselves outside. They chose a table on a quiet terrace and Saffi sat down once more.

'I'll get us some drinks,' Matt said, and came back a few minutes later with a couple of cups of coffee. 'This'll perk you up a bit,' he murmured. 'All you need is a bit of colour in your cheeks and you'll soon be back to being the girl I once knew.'

'Will I?' She looked at him, her eyes questioning him. 'You don't think she's gone for ever, then?'

He shook his head. 'No, Saffi. The real you is there, under the surface, just waiting to come out.'

He sat beside her and she sipped her coffee, conscious that he was watching her, his gaze lingering on her honey-coloured hair and the pale oval of her face.

After a while, she put down her cup and said thoughtfully, 'How well did you and I know one another?'

He seemed uncomfortable with the question, but he said warily, 'Well enough.'

His smoke-grey glance wandered over the pale gold of her shoulders and shifted to the pink, ripe fullness of her lips. Sudden heat flickered in his eyes, his gaze stroking her with flame as it brushed along her mouth, and despite her misgivings an answering heat rose inside her, a quiver of excitement running through her in response.

He was very still, watching her, and perhaps she had made some slight movement towards him—whatever the reason, he paused only for a second or two longer, never lifting his gaze from her lips, and as he leaned towards her she knew instinctively what he meant to do. He was overwhelmingly masculine, achingly desirable, and she was drawn to him, compelled to move closer, much closer to know the thrill of that kiss. Yet at the same time a faint ripple down her spine urged caution as though there was some kind of hidden danger here, a subtle threat to her peace of mind.

A clattering noise came from inside the restaurant, breaking the spell, and she quickly averted her gaze. She'd wanted him to kiss her, yearned for it, and that knowledge raced through every part of her being. Through all her doubts and hesitation she knew she was deeply, recklessly attracted to him.

She took a moment to get herself together again, and

when she turned to him once more she saw that there was a brooding, intent look about him, as though he, too, had been shaken by the sudden intrusion.

'You didn't really answer my question,' she said softly. '"Well enough" hardly tells me anything. Why are you keeping me in the dark?'

He looked uncomfortable. 'I...uh...I think it's probably better if you remember for yourself—that way, you won't have any preconceived ideas. In the meantime, we can get to know each other all over again, can't we?'

She stared at him in frustration, wanting to argue the point. Why wouldn't he open up to her about this? But his pager went off just then and he immediately braced himself.

'They're prepping Charlie for surgery,' he told her after a moment or two. 'I'll go and find out what came up on the CT scan.'

'I'll go with you.'

'Are you sure you're ready to do this?' He looked at her doubtfully.

'Yes. I'm fine.' She'd now recovered from her earlier bout of tearfulness and she should be more able to cope with whatever lay ahead. Perhaps she just hadn't been ready to face that situation... It was one thing coming back to medicine, but quite another to find herself caught up in the middle of one of the worst possible incidents. No one, not even doctors, wanted to come across an injured child.

'Hi, boss,' the registrar greeted Matt as they arrived back in the trauma unit.

Saffi looked at Matt in astonishment. He was in

charge here? That was another shock to her system. No wonder he exuded confidence and seemed to take everything in his stride.

'Hi, Jake. What did they come up with in Radiology?'

Jake showed them the films on the computer screen. 'It's pretty bad, I'm afraid.'

Saffi winced when she saw the images, and Matt threw her a quick glance and said quietly, 'You know what these show?'

She nodded. 'He has a lacerated spleen as well as the leg injury, and there's definitely a fracture of the pelvis.'

'He's lost a lot of blood but he's stable for the moment, at any rate,' Jake said. 'We don't know yet if he'll have to lose the spleen. Mr Collins will take a look and then decide what needs to be done. The boy's going to be in Theatre for some time.' He hesitated. 'You know, there's nothing more you can do here. You'd be better off at home.'

'I know, you're right,' Matt agreed with a sigh. 'Thanks, Jake.'

He walked with Saffi back to the car park a few minutes later. 'You weren't too sure about driving here, were you?' he said. 'How did it go?'

'It was difficult at first, but then it became easier.' She pulled a face. 'I suppose I should have persevered a bit more before getting rid of my car.'

He opened the passenger door for her. 'I suspected there was more to it when you sold your car...some kind of problem with driving. It might not be a bad idea to get yourself some transport now that you've made a start…keep up the good work, so to speak. It would be a shame if you were to lose your nerve again.'

She studied him thoughtfully as he slid behind the wheel and started the engine. Then she said in a faintly accusing tone, 'You did it on purpose, didn't you—giving me the keys? What would have happened if I'd refused? How would you have managed to get home?'

'Same way as always. I'd have cadged a lift back with the paramedics or hailed a taxi. Sometimes the police will drive the car to the hospital for me.' His mouth twitched. 'I was pretty sure you could do it, though. You're not one to give up easily.'

She frowned. 'That makes two trials you've put me through in one day—I suppose I can expect more of this from you? Do you have some sort of interest in me getting back on form?'

He thought about that. 'I might,' he said with a smile. 'Then again…' He frowned, deep in thought for a second or two. 'Perhaps it would be better if…' He broke off.

'If…?' she prompted, but he stayed annoyingly silent, a brooding expression around his mouth and eyes. What was it that he didn't want her to remember? What had happened between them that he couldn't bring himself to share? It was exasperating not being able to bring things to mind in an instant. Would she ever get to know the truth?

An even darker thought popped into her head… he had grown on her this last week or so, but would she still feel the same way about him if she learned what was hidden in their past? Perhaps that was what haunted him.

He parked up at the house, and she left him to go back to the annexe alone. It had been a long, tiring day for her so far, and she needed to wind down and think things through.

'Will you let me know if you hear anything from the hospital?'

'Of course. Though I doubt they'll ring me unless there's any change for the worse. No news is good news, so to speak.'

'Okay.'

She hadn't expected to remember so much of her work as a doctor, but it had started to come back to her when Charlie's life had hung in the balance. What should she do about that? Was she ready to return to work? Would she be able to cope on a day-to-day basis?

Anyway, she wasn't going to decide anything in a hurry. For the moment she would concentrate on getting back to normality as best she could. She would do as her doctor had suggested, and take advantage of her time here in Devon to recuperate, by doing some gardening, or wandering round the shops in town, and exploring the seashore whenever the weather was good.

The very next day she made up her mind to go down to the beach. They were enjoying a few days of brilliant sunshine, and it would have been sheer folly not to make the most of it.

The easiest way to get there from the house was via

a crooked footpath that ended in a long, winding flight of steps and eventually led to a small, beautiful cove sheltered by tall cliffs. She'd been there a couple of times since her arrival here, and she set off again now, taking with her a beach bag and a few essentials...including sun cream and a bottle of pop.

The cove was fairly isolated, but even so several families must have had the same idea and were intent on enjoying themselves by the sea.

She sat down in the shade of a craggy rock and watched the children playing on the smooth sand. Some splashed at the water's edge, while others threw beach balls or dug in the sand with plastic buckets and spades. Her eyes darkened momentarily. This was what Charlie should be doing, enjoying the weekend sunshine with his family.

There'd been no news from the hospital about the little boy, and she'd thought about giving them a call. But she wasn't a relative, and none of the staff at the hospital knew her, so she doubted they would reveal confidential information. She had to rely on Matt to tell her if there was anything she needed to know. He would, she was sure. She trusted him to do that.

She frowned. He was so open with everything else. Why was he so reluctant to talk about their past?

A small boy, dressed in blue bathing trunks, came to stand a few yards away from her. He was about four years old, with black hair and solemn grey-blue eyes, and he stood there silently, watching her. There was an empty bucket in his hand.

She smiled at him and put up a hand to shield her eyes from the sun. 'Hello. What's your name?'

'Ben.'

'I'm Saffi,' she told him. 'Are you having a good time here on the beach? The sand's lovely and warm, isn't it?'

He nodded, but said nothing, still staring at her oddly, and she said carefully, 'Are you all right? Is something bothering you?'

He shrugged his shoulders awkwardly and she raised a questioning brow. 'You can tell me,' she said encouragingly. 'I don't mind.'

'You look sad,' he said.

Ah. 'Do I?' She smiled. 'I'm not really. It's too lovely a day for that, isn't it?'

He nodded, but his expression was sombre, far too wise for a four-year-old.

'Are you sad sometimes?' she asked, prompted by a vague intuition.

He nodded again. 'It hurts here,' he said, putting a hand over his tummy.

Saffi watched him curiously, wondering what could be making him feel unhappy. Being here on the beach and being out of sorts didn't seem to go together somehow.

'Do you feel sad now?' she asked.

He shook his head. 'I did, a bit, 'cos I don't see Daddy every day, like I used to. But it's all right now.'

'Oh. Well, that's good. I'm glad for you. Are you on holiday here with your daddy?'

He shook his head. 'We live here.'

She looked around to see if his father was anywhere

nearby, and saw a man just a few yards away, in rolled-up jeans and tee shirt, kneeling down in the sand, putting the finishing touches to a large sandcastle. When he stood up and looked around, Saffi's throat closed in startled recognition.

Matt came towards them. 'What are you up to, Ben? I thought you were coming down to the sea to fill up your bucket. Or have you changed your mind about getting water for the moat?'

Then he looked at Saffi and his eyes widened in appreciation, taking in her curves, outlined by the sun top and shorts that clung faithfully to her body. 'Hi...I wondered if I might see you down here some time.'

She nodded vaguely, but inside she was reeling from this new discovery. Matt had a son? That meant he was married—or at least involved with someone. It was like a blow to her stomach and she crumpled inside. Was this what he'd been trying to keep under wraps? No wonder she'd been guarded about her feelings towards him... her subconscious mind had been warning her off...but weren't those warnings all too late?

Ben was looking at Matt with wide-eyed innocence. 'I do want to finish the moat. I was just talking to the lady.'

'Hmm.' Matt studied him thoughtfully. 'You know what we've said about talking to strangers?'

The boy nodded. 'But she's not a stranger, is she? I know her name. She's Saffi.'

Matt made a wry face, trying unsuccessfully not to smile at that marvellous piece of childish logic.

He shook his head, looking at Saffi. 'I guess I don't

need to introduce you to one another. Ben seems to have taken care of all that for me.' He lightly ruffled the boy's hair. 'He's going to be staying with me for a week or so.'

'Oh, I see,' she said slowly, and then with a dry mouth she added quietly, 'I didn't realise you had a child. You didn't say anything about him.'

He raised his brows in surprise. 'You think I have a child? Heavens, no—that's not going to happen any time soon. I'm not planning on getting involved in any deep, long-term relationships.' He frowned. 'Once bitten, as they say…'

Saffi stared at him, feeling a mixture of relief and dismay at his words. He wasn't married. That was something at least. But as to the rest, she didn't know what to think. He'd spoken quickly, without giving the matter much thought, but it was clear his feelings were heartfelt. Once bitten, he'd said. Who had hurt him and made him feel that way?

Matt seemed to give himself a shake to get back on track and said, 'Ben's my nephew, my sister's child. I should have told you right away, but I think I was a little bit distracted with this talking-to-strangers business. I barely took my eyes off him while I finished off the drawbridge, yet he managed to wander off. I could see him, out of the corner of my eye, talking to someone, but you have to be so careful… It can be a bit of a nightmare, taking care of children.'

'Well, yes. I can see that it must be worrying.' She was still caught up in his comment about long-term relationships. So, when he flirted with her it was nothing more than a bit of fun, a light-hearted romance. Of course it was. Why would she have expected anything more? She barely knew him.

At least it was out in the open, though, and she would be on her guard even more from now on. She didn't think she was the sort of woman who would be content with a relationship that wasn't meaningful. Or was she? Her mind was a blank where past boyfriends were concerned.

Matt turned to Ben once more, crouching down so that he was at the boy's level. 'I think you and I need to have another serious chat some time, Ben. Do you remember we talked about strangers?'

Ben nodded.

'That's good. So, what would you say if a stranger came up to you and asked if you'd like a sweet?'

Ben thought about it. 'Um… Yes…please?' he answered in an overly polite voice, and Matt groaned.

'I've a feeling it's going to be a long conversation,' he murmured, getting to his feet. 'Do you want to sort through those pebbles in the other bucket, Ben? See if you can pick out the smallest.'

'Okay.' Ben went to do as Matt suggested.

Saffi smiled. 'How is it that you're looking after him?'

'Gemma's ill—my sister, that is. She hasn't been well for some time, but late last night she rang me and said she was feeling much worse. I went over there and decided she needed to be in hospital. She didn't want to go, and kept saying it was just stress, but I insisted. At the very least, I thought she needed to have tests.'

Saffi sucked in a quick breath. 'I'm sorry. That must

have been upsetting—for you and for Ben—for all of you.'

'Yeah, it was a bit of a blow.'

'How has he taken it? He must miss his mother.'

'He's not doing too badly. I explained that she was poorly and needed to rest, and he thinks he's spending time with me so we can have fun together.' He looked at Ben once more. 'Why don't you put some of those pebbles on the wall of the sandcastle, while I talk to Saffi?'

The boy nodded, his eyes lighting up with anticipation. 'Okay.'

'What's wrong with her?' Saffi said, once the boy was absorbed in his new pursuit. 'Do you mind me asking?'

He shook his head. 'No, that's all right. We're not sure what the problem is, exactly. She's been feeling tired and nauseous for a few weeks now, with a lot of digestive problems, and yesterday she was vomiting blood.'

He glanced at Ben, to make sure he couldn't hear. 'That's why I took her to the hospital, so that the doctors can find the source of bleeding and cauterise it. They'll start doing a series of tests from tomorrow onwards to find out what's causing the problem.'

'It's good that your sister can rely on you to take care of things,' Saffi said. 'But how is it going to work out, with you looking after Ben? You have to be on duty at the hospital throughout the week, don't you?'

'Yes, but he'll be at day nursery some of the time, and for the rest he'll be with a childminder until I'm free to look after him. We'll muddle through, somehow.'

He smiled at her. 'Anyway, it's good to see you here. Do you want to help us finish off this sandcastle? Ben's been nagging me to bring him down here and get on with it since breakfast this morning. Of course, he's not satisfied with plain and simple. The bigger, the better.'

She went over to the castle. 'Wow. It looks pretty good to me.' There were towers and carved windows and walls that surrounded different levels. 'It's fantastic,' she said, and Ben beamed with pleasure at her praise.

She looked at Matt. 'You must have been working on this all afternoon.'

'Pretty much,' Matt agreed. 'There's no slacking with this young man. He knows exactly what he wants.'

She watched the little boy arrange small pebbles on top of the castle's main wall. He did it with absorbed concentration, placing each one carefully.

'Shall I make some steps just here, around the side?' Saffi asked, kneeling down, and Ben nodded approvingly.

Matt knelt down beside her and added some finishing touches to the drawbridge. After a while he sat back on his heels and surveyed his handiwork.

'That's not looking too bad at all,' he mused, wiping the beads of sweat from his forehead with the back of his hand.

Saffi smiled at his boyish satisfaction. 'You look hot. Do you want a drink?'

He nodded and she rummaged in her canvas beach bag until she found the bottle of pop. 'Here, try some of this.'

He drank thirstily, and when he had finished she offered the bottle to Ben. He took a long swallow and then went back to work with the pebbles.

She glanced at Matt, who was studying the castle once more. 'Has there been any news from the hospital?' she asked, having a quick drink and then putting the bottle back in her bag.

He nodded. 'I rang the hospital just before we left the house. Tim managed to repair Charlie's spleen, and stabilised the pelvis. He'll be non-weight-bearing for a while, and he'll have to wear a spica cast for a few weeks, while the fractures in his leg and pelvis heal, but he should gradually return to his normal activities. He came through the operation all right and Tim thinks he should recover well.'

'I'm so glad about that.' Saffi gave a slow sigh of relief. 'I don't suppose you found out how he is in himself?'

'He's obviously frail and shocked right now, but children are very resilient. They seem to get over things far quicker than we expect.'

He glanced at Ben. 'It all makes me thankful that it didn't happen to my own family. Though I guess I have Gemma to worry about now.'

Kneeling beside him, Saffi laid a comforting hand on his arm. 'You did the right thing, taking her to hospital. I'm sure they'll get to the root of the problem before too long.'

'Yes, I expect so.' He looked at her hand on his arm and overlaid it with his own. His fingers gently clasped hers and his gaze was warm as it touched her face softly. 'You're very sweet, Saffi. It's good to have you here.'

She smiled in response, but they broke away from one another as Ben urged them to look at his creation.

'That's great,' Matt told him. 'I think we can say it's actually finished now, can't we?'

'It's wonderful,' Saffi said.

She sat back and watched Matt and Ben, their heads together, admiring their handiwork.

A tide of warmth ran through her. What was not to love about Matt? She was drawn to him despite her misgivings. He was everything any woman could want... and yet instinct told her she had to steel herself against falling for him.

Didn't she have enough problems to contend with already? He wasn't the staying kind, he'd more or less said so, and the last thing she needed was to end up nursing a broken heart.

CHAPTER FOUR

SAFFI HEARD A rustling sound behind her and turned around to see that Ben had come into the garden. He stood, solemn faced, just a few yards away from her.

'Hello,' she said with a smile. 'You're up and about bright and early. Are you ready for school?'

He nodded, not speaking, but watched as she tended the flowers at the back of one of the borders. It was breakfast-time, but she'd wanted to get on with the work before the sun became too hot.

'I'm putting stakes in the ground so that I can tie up the gladioli,' she told him, guessing that he was interested in what she was doing but unwilling to talk to her. 'See? I've wrapped some twine around the stem.'

He stayed silent but seemed content to stay and watch her as she worked, and she wished there was some way she could bond with him, or at least reach out to him. What could be going on inside his head? Of course, he must be missing his parents. The disruption going on in his family was a lot for a four-year-old to handle.

'Sometimes the flower stems get too heavy and fall over,' she told him, trying to include him in what she was doing, 'or they might bend and break. Tying them like this keeps them standing upright.'

He nodded almost imperceptibly, and they both stood for a while, looking at the glorious display of flowers on show. There were half a dozen different colours, and Saffi was pleased with the end result of her work.

'It's time we were setting off for nursery school, Ben.' Matt came to find his nephew and smiled at Saffi. 'Hi.' His gaze was warm and in spite of her inner warnings her heart skipped a beat as her glance trailed over him.

'Hi.'

He was dressed for work in his role as the man in charge of A and E and the trauma unit, wearing a beautifully tailored suit, the jacket open to show a fine cotton shirt and subtly patterned silk tie.

'It's looking good out here,' he said, glancing around. 'You definitely have green fingers.'

Saffi glanced down at her grimy hands and made a face. 'In more ways than one,' she said with a laugh. 'I suppose I'd better go and clean up. I need to make a trip to the shops to get some food in. The cupboard's bare.'

'Uh-huh. That won't do, will it?' His glance drifted over her, taking in her dark blue jeans and short-sleeved top. There was a glint in his dark eyes. 'We can't have you fading away and losing those delicious curves.'

Her cheeks flushed with heat, but he added on an even note, 'I can give you a lift into the village if you like. But we need to leave in ten minutes.'

'Oh…' She quickly recovered her composure. 'Okay, thanks. I'll be ready in two ticks.'

She hurried away to wash her hands, and met up with

Ben and Matt at the front of the house a short time later. They were waiting by the rapid-response vehicle, and as she slid into the passenger seat she asked softly, 'Are you on call again today?'

He nodded. 'Just this morning.'

She was puzzled. 'How does it all fit in with you working at the hospital?'

'Well enough, most of the time. There are some mornings or afternoons when I'm in the office, or attending meetings, rather than being hands on, so to speak, like today, so I fit in outside jobs when I can. Otherwise the call centre has to find other people who are available.'

He smiled. 'At least it means that this morning I can take Ben to nursery, rather than handing him over to Laura, his childminder. His routine's already disturbed, so I want to make things easier for him as best I can. He's been a bit unsettled, with one thing and another.'

'I noticed that,' she said softly. She glanced behind her to see Ben in his child seat, playing with an action figure. 'He's very quiet this morning. I suppose that's understandable, in the circumstances.'

Matt nodded. He parked up outside the day nursery and Saffi went with him to see where Ben would be spending the next few hours. The school was a bright, happy place with colourful pictures on the walls and stimulating puzzles and craft activities set out on the tables for the children.

The staff were friendly and welcoming, and one of the women took Matt to one side to speak to him while Saffi helped the boy with his coat.

Matt came back to Ben a moment or two later. 'All

being well, your daddy will be coming to fetch you at lunchtime,' he said, bending down to give him a hug. Ben's face lit up at the news. 'If he can't make it for some reason, Laura will come as usual. Anyway, have a good time…we'll see you later.'

Saffi and Matt waved as they left the school and went from there to the village store, where Saffi stocked up on essentials like bread, eggs and cheese. Later, as they walked back to the car, she talked to him about Ben's father.

'Does he work away from home a lot of the time?' she asked as they stowed her groceries in the boot alongside all the medical equipment. 'Only, the other day when we were at the beach, Ben told me he feels upset sometimes about not seeing his father so much.'

'Mmm…that's a difficult one. He *is* away a lot of the time…he works for a computer company and goes out to set up systems or resolve problems for business clients in the banking industry or health services. Sometimes it means he has to travel to Scotland, or Wales, or wherever the customer happens to be based. If their systems go down for any reason, he has to sort it out and recover any lost data.'

'Is that why Ben gets anxious—because his father's working life is unpredictable?'

'Possibly. Though he and Gemma have been going through a bad patch lately. That might be something to do with it. They decided to separate, and I think Ben has picked up on the tension. They haven't told him about the split, but most likely he's sensed some of the vibes.'

'I'm sorry. It must be really difficult for everyone.'

'It is, but at least James is home right now. I haven't actually spoken to him, but apparently he called the day nursery to let them know, and he also left a message for Gemma to say he would pick up Ben today—up to now I've tried calling him to let him know that Gemma is ill, but I haven't been able to reach him. I think he must have changed his number.'

'Oh, I see.' She sent him a quick glance. 'It's a bad time for you just now, having to look after Ben and with your sister in hospital. How is she? Is there any news?'

He grimaced. 'Not too much as yet. They're still trying to find what's causing her problems—they've done blood tests, and an endoscopy to check out her stomach and duodenum, and they've taken a biopsy. They're keeping her in hospital because she's very anaemic from loss of blood, and she's lost a lot of weight recently. Obviously, they want to build up her strength.'

'From what you've told me, I'd imagine she must have stomach or duodenal ulcers.'

'Yes, that's right, but the tests have shown they aren't due to any bacterial infection.'

His grey eyes were troubled and she said softly, 'It's worrying for you…if there's anything I can do to help, you only have to ask. I could watch over Ben for you any time you want to go and visit her.'

'Thanks, Saffi.' He squeezed her arm gently. 'I appreciate the offer…but Ben wants to see his mother whenever possible, so I'll probably take him with me.'

She nodded. 'Well, the offer still stands…if there's anything I can do…if you want to talk… A trouble shared is a trouble halved, as they say.' She waited while he closed the boot of the car. 'Do you have any other family?'

'Only my parents, but they don't live locally, and, like me, they're both out at work during the week, so they're not really able to help. And Gemma was desperate to have Ben stay close by.'

'It's good that you were able to look out for him.'

He nodded. 'The other alternative was foster-care, and I didn't want that for him.' His mobile phone trilled, and he quickly took the call, becoming quiet and alert, so she guessed it was the ambulance control centre at the other end of the line.

He cut the call and glanced at Saffi. 'Looks like you get to come along for the ride once again,' he said, a brow lifting questioningly.

She pulled in a quick breath, doubts running through her. Was she up to this? What if it was another child, like Charlie, whose life stood on the brink? Part of her wanted to pull out, to shut herself off from anything medical, but another, more forceful, instinct urged her to face up to her demons.

She nodded. 'Where are we going?' she asked, easing herself into the passenger seat a moment later.

'A riding stables—or, at least, an area close by them. A girl has been thrown from her horse.'

Saffi winced. 'That could be nasty.'

'Yeah.' He hit the blue light and switched on the siren and Saffi clung on to her seat as they raced along the highway, heading away from town towards the depths of the countryside.

A few minutes later, he slowed down as they turned

off a leafy lane on to a dirt track that ended at a wide wooden gate, bordered on either side by a rustic fence and an overgrown hedgerow.

Saffi saw a small group of people gathered around a young woman who was lying on the ground. Someone was holding the reins of a horse, and a little further away two more riders stood silently by their mounts. Everyone looked shocked.

Matt stopped the car and removed his jacket, tossing it onto the back seat. He grabbed his medical kit and hurried over to the girl, leaving Saffi to follow in his wake. There was no sign of the ambulance as yet.

'What happened here?' he asked. 'Did anyone see how she fell?'

'The horse reared,' one of the bystanders said, her voice shaking. 'Katie lost her hold on him and fell. Then Major caught her in the back with his hoof as he came down again.'

'Okay, thanks.'

Matt kneeled down beside the injured girl. 'How are you doing, Katie?' he asked. 'Do you have any pain anywhere?'

'In my neck,' she said in a strained voice. 'It hurts if I try to move.'

Saffi could see that she was completely shaken, traumatised by finding herself in this situation. For Saffi, it was heart-rending, knowing how serious this kind of injury could be. If there was a fracture in any of the neck bones, causing spinal-cord damage, this young woman might never walk again.

'All right,' Matt said in a soothing voice. 'It's best if

you try to keep as still as possible, so I'm going to put a neck brace on you to prevent any further injury. Once that's in place I'll do a quick examination to make sure everything's all right. Okay?'

'Yes.' The girl was tight-lipped, ashen-faced with pain. She was about seventeen or eighteen, a slender girl with long, chestnut hair that splayed out over the grass.

Saffi helped him to put the collar in place, carefully holding Katie's head while Matt slid it under her neck. Then he fastened the straps and began his examination, checking for any other injuries.

'Shall I start giving her oxygen through a mask?' Saffi asked. Any damage or swelling in the area could eventually deprive the tissues of oxygen and add to the problem.

'Yes, please.' He went on checking the girl's vital signs. 'Heart rate and blood pressure are both low,' he murmured a short time later, glancing at Saffi. 'We need to keep an eye on that. I'll get some intravenous fluids into her to try and raise her blood pressure.'

She nodded. 'She's losing heat, too. Her skin's flushed and dry. We should get her covered up as soon as possible.'

'Yes, it's most likely neurogenic shock. But first we need to get her on to a spinal board. I'll go and fetch it from the car.' He gave a brief smile. 'Last time I saw it, it was underneath a large sack of chicken feed.'

She pulled a face. 'Oops.'

He was soon back with the board, and quickly en-listed a couple of onlookers to help him and Saffi logroll their patient onto the board. 'We need to do this very carefully, no jolting. Is everyone ready?'

On a count of three they gently laid Katie on the board and then Matt covered her with a blanket before securing the straps.

As if on cue, the ambulance finally arrived, and Saffi sighed with relief.

Matt made sure the transfer into the vehicle went smoothly, and once Katie was safely inside, a paramedic stayed beside her to watch over her. The driver closed the doors and then walked round to the cab. Matt spoke to him briefly and a few seconds later Katie was on her way to the hospital.

'I'll follow her and see how she gets on,' Matt said. 'Do you want to come with me or should I call for a taxi to take you home?'

'I'll go with you,' Saffi said quickly. 'I want to know what the damage is.'

'Come on, then. I'll ask the paramedics if they can drop you off at home when they've finished at the hospital.'

He was as worried as she was, she could tell, from the way his mouth was set in a grim line. When they were almost at their destination, though, he relaxed enough to ask, 'How are you coping with all this...coming with me on callouts?'

'All right, I think. It's like stepping into the un-known...I'm a bit scared of what I'll find.'

'But you decided to come along anyway. That must have been hard for you...I could see you were in two minds about joining me.' He sent her a sideways glance. 'So what made you do it in the end?'

'I felt I had to see things through.' Her lips made a flat line. 'After all, this was my career before I fell down the stairs and lost my memory. I need to know if I can go back to it at some point.'

'Do you think that will happen?'

She sighed. 'I don't know. It's one thing to stand to one side and watch, but it's a whole different situation making decisions and holding someone's life in your hands.'

He nodded agreement. 'Yes, I can see how that would be difficult.'

He turned his attention back to the road, pulling up at the hospital a few minutes later. They hurried into the trauma unit.

'Hi, there,' Jake greeted him at the central desk, and smiled at Saffi. 'Are you here to find out about the girl from the riding accident?'

'We are,' Matt said. 'What's been happening so far? Have you been in touch with her parents?'

'They're on their way...should be here in about half an hour. She's been down to X-Ray and right now the neurologist is examining her reflexes. Her blood pressure's still low, so we're giving her dopamine to improve cardiac output.'

'And the heart rate? Has that improved?'

'It's getting better. She's had atropine, two milligrams so far.'

'Good. That's something, at least. Now, these X-ray films—'

'Coming up.' Jake brought up the pictures on the screen and Matt sucked his breath through his teeth.

'That's a C7 fracture. She'll need to go for surgery to get that stabilised. See if Andrew Simmons is available to come and look at her.'

'I will. I think I saw him earlier in his office.'

'Okay. She'll need her pain medication topped up and steroids to bring down the inflammation.'

'I'll write it up. Gina Raines is her specialist nurse. I'll let her know.'

Matt's head went back. 'Gina?'

Saffi frowned. It was clear he was startled by this information for some reason.

'Yes, she generally works at the community hospital, but she transferred over here a couple of days ago on a temporary contract. She's pretty good at the job, from what I've seen.'

'Oh, yes,' Matt said. 'She's certainly well qualified. She was always keen to get on.' His expression was guarded and Saffi wondered what had brought about this sudden change in him. Had he worked with Gina before this? From the sound of things, he knew her fairly well.

'It's all right, Jake,' he said briskly, getting himself back on track. 'I'll go and speak to her myself. Perhaps you could concentrate on chasing up Andrew Simmons.'

'I'll do that.'

Matt turned to Saffi, laying a hand lightly on her elbow. 'Are you okay to go home with the paramedics? They have to go through the village on the way to the ambulance station.'

'Yes, that's fine, as long as they don't mind helping me transfer my groceries from your car.'

'I'm sure they'll be okay with that.'

He seemed concerned about her and Saffi smiled at him. 'Don't worry about me. I know you want to see to your patient and I understand that you're busy.'

He relaxed a little. 'They'll be in the restaurant, getting coffee, I imagine, but I asked them to page me when they're ready to go.'

She walked with him to the treatment bay where Katie was being looked after by a team of doctors and nurses. The girl was still wearing the rigid collar that protected her cervical spine, and she looked frightened, overwhelmed by everything that was happening. A nurse was doing her best to reassure her. Was this Gina?

The nurse's glance lifted as Matt entered the room and there was an immediate tension in the air as they looked at one another.

'Well, this is a surprise,' she said. There was a soft lilt to her voice. She was an attractive woman with green eyes and a beautifully shaped mouth, and dark brown hair that was pinned up at the back in a silky braid. 'It's been quite a while, Matt.'

'It has. I—uh—wasn't expecting to see you here.'

'No. I'm standing in for the girl who went off on maternity leave.'

'Ah.' He cleared his throat, and Saffi guessed he was more than a little disturbed by this meeting. 'So, how's our patient doing?'

'She's very scared.'

'That's only natural.' He walked over to the bedside and squeezed Katie's hand gently. 'Your parents are on their way, Katie. They should be here soon.'

He spoke in a calm, soothing voice, comforting her as best he could and answering her questions in a positive manner. After a while, the girl seemed a little less tense.

Gina looked at him in quiet satisfaction as they

walked away from the bedside. 'You were always good with the patients,' she murmured. 'You seem to have the magic touch.'

'Let's hope her faith in me isn't misplaced,' he said, his mouth making a taut line.

Gina glanced at Saffi, and her eyes widened a fraction. 'Saffi. I thought you were based in Hampshire? Are you working here now?'

'Um. No. I'm just visiting.' She was flummoxed for a while after Gina spoke to her. It seemed that the nurse knew her, as well as Matt, and that made her feel more confused than ever. How many more people would she come across that she didn't recognise?

'Saffi's been in an accident,' Matt said, giving the nurse a strangely intent look. His pager bleeped and he quickly checked it, before adding, 'She has amnesia and she's here to recover.'

'Oh, I'm sorry.'

'It's all right.' Saffi was suddenly anxious to get away, her mind reeling with unanswered questions. Just how well did Matt and Gina know one another? Quite closely, she suspected, from the way Gina looked at him. Would they be getting back together again?

Her mind shied away from the thought. She realised she didn't want to think of Matt being with another woman, and that thought disturbed her and threw her off balance.

'I'd better leave you both to your work,' she murmured. 'I should be going now, anyway.' She turned to Matt. 'Was that the paramedics paging you a moment ago?'

He nodded. 'They're waiting by the desk. I'll take you over to them.'

'No, don't bother. You stay here and look after your patient.'

He frowned. 'If you're sure?'

'I am.'

'Okay, then. Bye, Saffi.'

'Bye.' She nodded to Gina and hurried away. More than ever she felt as though she needed to escape. How was it that Matt had crept into her heart and managed to steal it away?

The paramedics were a friendly pair, making up for the stress of the job they were doing with light-hearted humour. Word of the exchange between Matt and Gina must have travelled fast, because they were chatting about it on the journey home.

'Is she another conquest in the making, do you think?' the driver said with a smile.

His partner nodded. 'I wouldn't be surprised. I don't know how he does it. I could do with a bit of his charisma rubbing off on me.'

They both chuckled, and Saffi kept quiet. Heaven forbid they should see her as yet another woman who had managed to fall for the good-looking emergency doctor. Just how many girls had fallen by the wayside where Matt was concerned?

The paramedics dropped her off at the house and then left, giving her a cheerful wave.

She started on some chores, desperate to take her mind off the image of Matt and Gina being together. It bothered her much more than she liked to admit. She'd wanted to stay free from entanglements, but somehow Matt had managed to slide beneath her defences and now she was suffering the consequences.

Some time later, she glanced through the local newspaper, studying the advertisements for cars. One way or another, she had to steer clear of Matt before she became too deeply involved with him. She could finish up being badly hurt, and she'd been through enough already, without adding that to her troubles. Having her own transport would be a start. But was she ready to get back behind the wheel? That one time she'd driven Matt's car was still seared on her brain.

Around teatime, she went out into the garden to feed the hens. She filled up a bucket with grain from the wooden shed but as she was locking the door a huge clamour started up, coming from the chicken run. Filled with alarm, she hurried over there. Had a fox managed to get in? But hadn't Matt told her there was wire mesh under and around the base of the pen to keep scavengers out? Besides, there were solid walls and fences all around the property.

The hens were squawking, making a huge din, scurrying about, flapping their wings in distress, and she was startled to see that, instead of a fox, it was Ben who was behind the disturbance.

He was running around, shouting, waving his arms and shooing the hens from one end of the compound to the other. How had he managed to get in there? She looked around and saw an upturned plastic flower tub by the side of the gate. He must have climbed on it to reach the door catch.

'Ben! Stop that right now.' Matt strode towards the enclosure as though he meant business.

Ben stood stock-still, his face registering dismay at being caught doing something wrong, swiftly followed by a hint of rebellion in the backward tilt of his head and in the peevish set of his mouth.

Matt opened the door to the run and he and Saffi both went inside.

'I know you think it's fun to get the hens running about like this,' Matt said, 'but they're not like you and me…they could die from fright. You have to be careful around them.'

Ben's brow knotted as he tried to work things out in his head, and Saffi wondered if he actually knew what it meant to die from fright. He certainly knew from Matt's tone of voice that it wasn't a good thing. In the meantime, the hens went on squawking, still panicked.

'I'm sorry about this, Saffi,' Matt said. 'He's been fractious ever since I fetched him from the childminder.'

'It's not your fault.' She frowned. 'I thought he was supposed to be with his father this afternoon?'

'He was, for a while, but apparently James was called away again.'

'Oh, I see.' She made a face. 'That can't have helped.'

'No. Anyway, I'll take him away and leave you to get on.' He turned to Ben and said firmly, 'Come on, young man, we're going back to the house.'

The boy went to him as he was told, but there were tears of frustration in his eyes and Saffi's heart melted. He was obviously upset about his father and overwhelmed at being in trouble, and maybe all he needed was some kind of distraction therapy.

She cut in quietly, 'Perhaps it would help him to learn how to look after the hens instead of scaring them. I could show him how to feed them, if you like.'

Ben looked at him with an anxious expression and Matt smiled, relenting. 'That's a good idea. Thanks, Saffi.' He looked at Ben. 'You know, it's kind of Saffi to do this, so make sure you behave yourself.'

Ben nodded, the tears miraculously gone, and Saffi showed him how to grab a handful of corn and scatter it about. He watched as the hens started to peck amongst the sand and gravel and giggled when they nudged his feet to get at the grain.

'You're doing really well,' Saffi told him. 'Your dad would be proud if he could see you now.'

'Would he?' He looked at her doubtfully, and then at Matt.

'Oh, yes,' Matt agreed. 'He would. Shall I take your picture? Then you can show him next time you see him.'

'Yeah.' Ben threw down some more grain, showing off and smiling widely at the camera, and Matt snapped him on his mobile phone. He showed him the photo and the little boy grinned in delight.

'I want to show Mummy.' Ben's expression sobered instantly and tears glistened in his eyes once more. 'I want Mummy.' His bottom lip began to tremble.

Matt put an arm around him and gave him a hug. 'I know you do. We'll go and see her at the hospital after tea.'

'We could pick some flowers for her,' Saffi said. 'I think she'd like that, don't you?'

'Yeah.' Ben rubbed the tears from his eyes and looked at her expectantly. 'Can we do it now?'

'Okay. Let me finish up here and we'll find some for you.'

They made sure the hens were contented once more and then Matt locked up and removed the flower tub from the gate while Saffi went with Ben into the walled garden, carrying a trug and scissors.

'I wonder what your mummy would like?' Saffi said, looking around. 'What do you think, Ben?'

'Those ones.' He pointed to a trellis that was covered with delicate sweet-pea blooms, and Saffi nodded.

'That's a good choice, Ben. I think she'll love those.' She started to cut the flowers, frilly pink-edged blooms along with pale violet and soft blues, placing them carefully in the trug on the ground. The four-year-old went down on his knees and put his nose against them, breathing in the scent.

She smiled. 'These were Aunt Annie's favourites. She planted them every year.' She put down the scissors and handed him the basket. 'I think that's enough now. Why don't you take them into the kitchen and I'll find a ribbon to tie round the stems?'

'Okay.' Ben hurried away, taking extra care with his treasure trove.

'You remembered…' Matt was looking at her in wonder, and Saffi stared at him, not knowing what he was talking about. 'Your Aunt Annie,' he prompted, 'planting sweet peas.' She gasped, stunned by the revelation.

She laughed then, a joyful, happy laugh, full of the excitement of new discovery. 'I remember her showing me how to grow them when I was a small child,' she said, suddenly breathless with delight. 'And then we picked them together and made up little wedding baskets for some children who were going to be bridesmaids.' She laughed again, thrilled by the memory and the unlocking of part of her mind that she had thought was gone for ever.

Matt put his arms around her. 'I'm really glad for you, Saffi.' He hesitated, then asked on a cautious note, 'Has it all come back to you?'

She shook her head. 'No, but I do remember living here when I was a child. She was a wonderful woman. She always had time for me and I loved her to bits.' There was sadness with the memory, and as he heard the slight shake in her voice, Matt held her close, knowing what she was going through.

'I think you've absorbed a lot of her qualities,' he said softly. 'You were so good with Ben just now. I'm not sure I would have handled the situation as well as you did. But now you've given him something to look forward to.'

She smiled up at him. 'He's not a bad boy, just overwhelmed with what's going on in his life right now. He's bewildered by what's happening to him. I feel the same way sometimes, so I think I understand something of what he's going through. His world has turned upside down.'

He sighed, gently stroking her, his hand gliding over her back. 'I know. I wish I could make things right for him...and for you. It was great just now to see you laugh.

It lights up your face when you do that,' he said huskily, 'and when you smile, I'm helpless… I tell myself I must keep away, and not go down that road but, no matter how much I try to hold back, I just want to kiss you…I'm lost…'

Inevitably, the thought led to the action, and slowly he bent his head and brushed her lips with his. It was a gentle, heart-stopping kiss that coaxed a warm, achingly sweet response from her. As her lips parted beneath his, he gave a ragged groan as though he couldn't stop himself, and he held her tight, drawing her up against him so that her soft curves meshed with his long, hard body and her legs tangled with his muscular thighs.

She ran her hands over him, loving the feel of him. Elation was sweeping through her, the ecstasy of his kisses sending a fever through her blood and leaving her heady with desire—a desire that seemed altogether familiar all at once. She needed him, wanted him.

Had she been wrapped in his arms this way at another time? Her feelings for him were so strong… She loved being with him this way, feeling the thunder of his heartbeat beneath her fingers—could it be that she simply couldn't help falling for him? He'd been so caring, so supportive and understanding of her. Or was there more to it…had she felt this way for him long before this, before her memory had been wiped out?

'You're so beautiful, Saffi,' he whispered, his voice choked with passion. 'It's been so tough, being with you again after all this time, longing to hold you…and yet…I just can't help myself…'

He broke off, kissing her again, his hands moving

over her, tracing a path along her spine, over the rounded swell of her hip, down the length of her thigh. It felt so good to have him touch her this way. It felt right…as though this was how it should be.

Her hand splayed out over his shoulder, feeling the strength beneath her palm. 'I want you, too,' she said. She ached for him, but her mind was suddenly spinning with unanswered questions. 'What happened to us, Matt? After all this time, you said…were we together back then?'

A look of anguish came over his face. 'In a way,' he said.

'In a way…?' She broke away from him, looking at him in bewilderment. 'What do you mean? What kind of answer is that?'

'I can't…' He seemed to be waging some kind of inner battle, struggling to get the words out, and finally he said in a jerky, roughened voice, 'I can't tell you how it was. I'm sorry, but…' he sucked in a deep breath '…I think this is something you need to remember for yourself.'

His eyes were dark with torment. 'I shouldn't have kissed you. I don't want to take advantage of you, Saffi… and perhaps for my own self-preservation I should have held back. I should have known better.'

She stared at him in bewilderment. What did he mean when he talked about self-preservation? What was so wrong in them being together—was he so determined against commitment? What was it he'd said before— *once bitten*? Had he been so badly hurt in the past that he didn't want to risk his heart again? But as she opened her mouth to put all these questions to him, his phone began to ring.

At the same time Ben came out of the house, looking indignant. 'I thought we were going to the hospital to see Mummy?' he said crossly. 'You've been ages.'

Matt braced his shoulders. 'We'll go soon,' he told the little boy.

'Do you promise?'

'I promise.' He looked at Saffi and held up the phone, still insistently ringing. 'I'm sorry about this,' he said on a resigned note. 'It might be about the girl in the riding accident.'

'It's all right. Go ahead.' She was deeply disappointed and frustrated by the intrusion, but she took Ben's hand and started towards the house.

The moment of closeness had passed. He might not be forthcoming about what had gone on between them before, but whatever his reasons one thing was for sure... it was much too late now for her to guard against falling for him. She had so many doubts and worries about him, but he'd grown on her and she didn't want to imagine life without him. She was already in love with him.

He pressed the button to connect his call. 'Hello, Gina,' she heard him say, and her heart began to ache.

CHAPTER FIVE

'CAN I DO that?' Ben watched Saffi as she picked runner beans, carefully dropping them one by one into a trug. It was the weekend and the sun was shining, and the only sounds that filled the air were birdsong and the quiet drone of bees as they went about their business. A warm breeze rippled through the plants, making the leaves quiver.

'Of course you can. Here, let me show you how to do it. We snap them off where the bean turns into stalk—like this, see?' He nodded and she added, 'Why don't you try picking some of the lower ones and I'll do these up here?'

'Okay.'

They worked together amicably for a while, with Ben telling her about his visits to the hospital. 'Mummy's still poorly,' he said. 'She's got lots of…um…acid… inside her, and it's hurting her. They don't know why she's got it.'

'I'm sorry to hear that, Ben. But the doctors are looking after her, and I'm sure they'll soon find out what's causing her to be poorly.'

'Yeah.' His eyes grew large. 'Uncle Matt says they're going to take some pictures of inside her tummy.'

'That's good. That should help them to find out what's wrong.' Saffi guessed he meant they were going to do a CT scan. She winced inwardly. That sounded as though they suspected something quite serious was going on.

'Hi, Saffi.' Matt came to join them in the garden, and immediately she felt her pulse quicken and her stomach tighten. He was dressed in casual clothes, dark chinos and a tee shirt in a matching colour, and it was easy to see why women would fall for him. His biceps strained against the short sleeves of his shirt and his shoulders were broad and powerful. He looked like a man who would take care of his woman, protect her and keep her safe.

'Hi.' She tried to shut those images from her mind, but even so her heart turned over as she recalled the meeting between him and the nurse. They'd known each other for a long time, and from the tension that had sparked between them she guessed there was still a good deal of charged emotion on the loose.

'It's a beautiful day,' she said, trying to get her thoughts back onto safer ground. 'Do you have plans for today, or are you on call?'

He shook his head. 'I don't have any plans. It's not really possible to make any while I'm looking after Ben.' He sent her a thoughtful, hopeful glance. 'I suppose we could all go down to the beach after breakfast, if you'd like to come with us?'

'Yay!' Ben whooped with excitement. 'Come with us, Saffi.'

Saffi smiled at the four-year-old. He hadn't said a lot to her over these last few days, being quiet and introspective, but if he wanted her to go with them, that was a heartening sign. It made her feel good inside to know that he had warmed to her.

'I'd like that,' she said. She sent Matt a questioning glance. 'What would you be doing if you didn't have to look after Ben? How do you usually spend your weekends?' She didn't know much about his hobbies or interests, but from the looks of him he must work out quite a bit at the gym.

He shrugged. 'Sometimes I swim—in the sea, or at the pool—or I might play squash with a friend. I go to the gym quite often. On a day like this, when there's a breeze blowing, a group of us like to go kite-surfing at a beach a bit further along the coast. There's a good southerly wind there and a decent swell.'

'Kite-surfing? I'm not sure if I know what that is.'

'You go out on the sea on a small surfboard, and with a kite a bit like a parachute. The wind pulls you along. It's great once you've mastered the skill.'

Her mouth curved. 'It sounds like fun. Why don't you join your friends? I'll look after Ben on the beach. We can watch the surfing from there. What do you think, Ben?'

'Yeah.' He was smiling, looking forward to the trip.

Matt frowned. 'I can't do that. It's too much to ask of you.'

'No, it's fine, really.' She started to move away from

the vegetable garden, but at the same time Ben went to Matt to tug on his trousers and claim his attention.

'I want to see the kites…please, Uncle Matt,' Ben pleaded.

Saffi sidestepped him, trying to avoid a collision, and caught her heel against one of the bean canes.

'Ouch!' She felt a stab of pain as she untangled her foot from the greenery.

'What is it? Have you twisted your ankle?' Matt looked at her in concern, reaching out to clasp her arm as she tried to look behind her at her calf.

She shook her head. 'No. It's a bee sting.'

'Come into the house. I'll have a look at it.' He turned to Ben, who was watching anxiously. 'She'll be fine, Ben. Bring the trug, will you? Can you manage it?'

'Yes, I'm strong, see?' The little boy picked up the basket and followed them into the house.

'Sit down.' Matt showed her into the kitchen and pulled out a chair for her at the table. He reached for a first-aid kit from a cupboard and brought out a pair of tweezers. 'Let's get that sting out. Put your leg up on this stool.'

She did as he suggested. She was wearing cropped cargo pants, and he crouched down and rolled them back a little to expose the small reddened, inflamed area where the bee had stung her. Then he carefully pulled out the sting with the tweezers. Ben watched every move, his mouth slightly open in absorbed concentration.

'Okay, now that's out, we'll get something cold on the leg to help take down the swelling.' He fetched a bag of frozen peas from the freezer and laid it over the tender area. 'Are you all right?'

'I'm fine.' She made a wry face. 'It's not a good start to my beekeeping, is it?'

He smiled. 'I expect you disturbed it. They don't usually sting if you're calm with them and keep your movements slow. When you're working with the hives it might help if you go to them between ten o'clock and two in the afternoon, when most of the bees are busy with the flowers…and make sure you always wear protective clothing. That's what Annie told me.'

He looked at her leg, lifting the frozen plastic bag from her. 'That's not quite so inflamed now. I'll rub some antihistamine cream on it, and it should start to feel easier within a few minutes.'

'Thanks.' She watched him as he smoothed the cream into her leg, his head bent. He was gentle and his hands were soothing, one hand lightly supporting her leg while he applied cream with the other. She could almost forget the sting while he did that. She studied him surreptitiously. His black hair was silky, inviting her to run her fingers through it.

'How are you doing?' He lifted his head and studied her, and she hastily pulled herself together. She felt hot all over.

'I'll be okay now. Thanks.'

'Good.' He held her gaze for a moment or two as though he was trying to work out what had brought colour to her cheeks, and then, to her relief, he stood up. 'Do you want to stay and have breakfast with us, and then we'll head off to the beach? I'm not sure what we're having yet. Toast and something, maybe.'

'That sounds good.' She straightened up and made herself think about mundane things. It wouldn't do her any good to think about getting close up and personal with Matt. Look what had happened last time. He was fighting his own demons, and she was worried about all the other women who might try to take her place.

'I could take Ben with me to collect some eggs. How would that be?' She stood up.

'Dippy eggs and toast soldiers!' Ben whooped again and licked his lips in an exaggerated gesture. 'I love them.'

'Sounds good to me,' Matt agreed. 'But are you sure you don't want to rest your leg for a bit longer?'

'I'll be fine. Why don't you ring your friend and make arrangements to do some kite-surfing? We'll be back in a few minutes.'

She collected a basket from her kitchen and took Ben with her to the hen coop. There she lifted the lid that covered the nesting boxes and they both peered inside.

'I can see two eggs,' he said happily, foraging amongst the wood shavings. 'And there's some more.' He looked in all the nest boxes, carefully picking out the eggs and laying them in the basket. He counted them, pointing his finger at each one in turn. 'There's six.'

'Wow. We did well, didn't we?' Saffi closed the lid on the coop and made everything secure once more. 'Let's go and wash these and then we'll cook them for breakfast.'

'Yum.' Ben skipped back to the house, more animated than she'd seen him in a while.

Over breakfast they talked about kite-surfing for a while, and about how Saffi was coping with the day-to-day running of the property.

'It's fine,' she said. 'It's quite easy once you get into a routine—but, then, I'm not going out to work at the moment, so that makes a big difference.'

Thinking about that, she looked over to Ben. Keeping her voice low she said, 'At least you must be able to see your sister every day, with working at the hospital. How is she? Have they managed to find out what's causing her problems? Could it be anything to do with stress, with the marriage problems, and so on?'

'It's always possible, I suppose. But they're still doing tests—she'll be going for a CT scan on Monday.'

'It must be a worry for you. Do you manage to get together with your parents to talk things through?'

He nodded. 'They've been coming over here to visit her as often as they can. I think my mother will have Ben to stay with her next weekend.'

'That should give you a bit of a break, at least, and I expect Ben will look forward to staying with his grandmother for a while.'

She glanced at the boy, who was placing the empty top piece of shell back onto his egg. He was getting ready to bang it with his spoon.

'Humpty Dumpty,' he said, and they both smiled.

Still dwelling on news from the hospital, Saffi asked, 'Have you heard anything more about the girl who fell from her horse? How's she doing?'

'She's had surgery to stabilise the neck bones, and she's on steroids to bring down the inflammation, as well as painkillers. They'll try to get her up and about as soon as possible to make sure she makes a good recovery. I think she'll be okay. She's young and resilient and she has a lot of motivation to get well again.'

'That's a big relief.'

'Yes, it is.' He seemed pensive for a second or two, and Saffi wondered what was going through his mind.

She glanced at him and said tentatively, 'At the hospital, you seemed quite surprised to see the nurse… Gina. I had the feeling…were you and she a couple at one time?'

Perhaps they still were, or maybe he was planning to resume their relationship… Her mind shied away from the thought.

His mouth flattened. 'We dated for a while.'

'Oh.' She absorbed that for a moment or two. Wasn't it what she had expected? 'Did something happen to break things up? I suppose you moved to different parts of the country?' And now they were reunited once more in Devon…what was there to stop them taking up where they had left off? A shiver of apprehension ran down her spine.

'Gina wanted to take things to a more serious level.' He grimaced. 'I wasn't looking for anything more than a fun time.'

She winced inwardly. Was this the way he treated all women? Hadn't he admitted as much? As far as she and Matt were concerned, at least he'd had the grace to say he didn't want to take advantage of her.

'That must have been upsetting for her.'

'Yes, I guess it was.'

She frowned. She couldn't see him simply as a man who played the field without any consideration for the feelings of the girls he dated. But if he did, there must surely be a reason for his behaviour. She didn't want to see him as a man who was only interested in seducing women with no thought for the consequences.

They finished breakfast and cleared away the dishes, and Matt started to get his kite-surfing gear together.

'I hope you're all right with this,' he said. 'We're usually on the water for about an hour.'

'I can keep Ben amused for that long, I'm sure.' She smiled. 'Are we about ready to go? I think the waiting's too much for him. He's running around like a demented bee.'

Matt laughed, and a few minutes later he crammed his kite and small surfboard into the back of the rapid-response car and they set off.

'How can you answer an emergency call if you're out on the water?' she asked with a quizzical smile as he drove along the coast road.

'I can't. I'd have to turn them down, and ask them to find someone else to go in my place, but if anything should happen when I'm back on dry land I'll be prepared. Usually I get to enjoy my weekends, but you never know.'

They went a few miles down the road until they arrived at the surfers' beach, a sandy cove, bound by rugged cliffs that were covered with lichens and here and there with moor grass and red fescue.

Matt parked the car and Saffi looked out over the sea as he changed into his wetsuit. He was wearing swimming shorts under his clothes, but it was way too distracting, seeing his strong, muscular legs and bare chest with its taut six-pack. 'From the looks of those people surfing, it must be an exhilarating experience,' she said.

'It is,' Matt agreed. 'If you're interested, I could teach you how to do it—just as soon as we get a day on our own. Do you do any water sports?'

'Um…I've a feeling I do. I know I can swim, anyway, and I think I might like to learn kite-surfing. It's mostly men who do the sport, though, isn't it?'

'Not necessarily. A lot more women are getting into it nowadays. You'd start with a trainer kite and learn simple techniques first of all.' He looked at her expectantly and she nodded.

She was getting her confidence back now, feeling stronger day by day, and maybe it was time to accept some new challenges.

'Maybe I'd like to try,' she said, and he gave her a satisfied smile. She breathed in the salt sea air. It was good to be with him out here, and to look forward to more days like this, but didn't she know, deep down, that she was playing with fire? She was getting closer to him all the time, when the sensible thing would be to keep her distance. It was quite clear he wasn't looking for any serious involvement.

He introduced her to his friends and she and Ben watched from the beach as they went out onto the water. Saffi walked along the sand with the contented little boy, helping him to collect shells in a plastic bucket, looking up every now and again to see the surfers wheeling and diving, letting the wind take them this way and that.

Ben kicked off his shoes and splashed in the waves that lapped at the shore, while Saffi kept a close eye on him, and then they walked back to the base of the cliff where he could dig in the sand.

She saw the surfers moving over the sea at a fast pace, some of them lifted up by the kites from the surface of the waves, skilfully controlling their movements and coming back down again to ride the water. The wind was getting up now, gusting fiercely, and she rummaged in her beach bag for a shirt for Ben.

'Here, put this on. It's getting a bit chilly out here.'

He stopped digging for a while to put on the shirt and then he gazed out at the sea. 'I can't see Uncle Matt,' he said. 'He's too far away.'

'There are two of them in black wetsuits…I'm not sure, but I think that might be him coming in to the—' She broke off, clasping a hand to her mouth in horror as she saw one of the surfers lifted up by a sudden squall. Was it Matt? His kite billowed, the fierce wind dragging him swiftly towards the cliffside so that he was powerless to do anything to stop it. He was hurtling towards the craggy rock face at speed, and Saffi's stomach turned over in sheer dread. As she watched, he hit the jagged rocks near the foot of the cliff and crumpled on to the sand below.

She saw it happen with a feeling of terror. Was it Matt? It couldn't be Matt…she couldn't bear it.

She sprang to her feet. 'Ben, come with me,' she said

urgently. 'That man's hurt and I have to help him. We need to get the medical kit from the car.'

He didn't argue but left his bucket and spade behind as they hurried up the cliff path to the car. 'Is it Uncle Matt?' he asked.

'I don't know, sweetheart.' She rummaged in her bag for her phone and called for an ambulance.

'Will you make him better?'

She gently squeezed his hand. 'I'll do everything I can. But you must stay with me, Ben. You can't wander off. I need to know you're safe. Promise me you'll stay close by me.'

'I promise.'

'Good boy. It might not be very nice to see the man that's hurt, so you'll probably need to look away.' Heaven forbid it should turn out to be Matt. She studied him. 'Okay?'

He was solemn-faced, taking in the enormity of the situation. 'Okay.'

She whipped open the boot of the car, thankful that Matt had left the keys with her. She pulled out the heavy medical backpack and the patient monitor and then locked up the car once more and hurried back down the path as fast as she could go, with Ben by her side.

They had to make their way carefully over rocks to get to the injured man and all the time she was praying that it wasn't Matt who was lying there. Whoever it was, he was screaming with pain. A small crowd had gathered around him and she said, 'Let me through, please. I'm a doctor.'

People moved aside and she saw that two lifeguards

were already by the man's side. One of them, white-faced, said quietly, 'His foot's twisted round at an odd angle. It's like it's been partly sheared off.'

Saffi pulled in a quick breath. Not Matt, please don't let it be Matt.

'I'll look at him,' she said, shielding Ben from what was going on. 'Would one of you keep an eye on the little boy for me?' She glanced around. 'Perhaps he'd be better over there, out of the way, but where I can still see him.' She pointed to a sheltered place in the lee of the cliff where there was enough sand for him to dig with his hands.

'Sure. I'll do it.'

'Thanks.' She looked down at the kite-surfer and a surge of relief washed through her as she realised it wasn't Matt lying there. It was his friend, Josh. She laid down her pack and knelt beside him.

'Josh, I'm a doctor…I'm going to have a look at you and see if I can make you more comfortable before we get you to hospital. Okay?'

'Okay.' He clamped his jaw, trying to fight the pain, and Saffi went through her initial observations. The foot was purple, with no great blood loss, and he was able to wiggle the toes on his other foot, as well as move his leg.

She didn't think there was any spinal injury but she needed to take precautions all the same, so she asked the lifeguard to help her put a cervical collar around Josh's neck.

Josh's pulse was very fast and his blood pressure was high, most likely because of the excruciating pain. That was going to make it difficult to move him. He might also have other, internal injuries, so the best thing to do would be to administer pain relief.

She asked both lifeguards to help her. 'I'm going to give him drugs to reduce the pain. As soon as I've given him the medication, we'll have to carefully roll him on to his back and set him up with an oxygen mask. Are you all right with that?'

'Yeah, that's okay.'

She glanced at Ben to make sure he was staying put, and then prepared to go on with the procedure. Thankfully, it wasn't likely that he could see much of what was going on, while three people were gathered around Josh. She made sure Josh was as comfortable as possible, looping the oxygen mask over his head.

There was a movement on the periphery of the crowd and she saw that Matt had gone to stand with Ben. She looked at him and he gave her a nod of support.

At the same time, the ambulance siren sounded in the distance, getting nearer.

'Thanks for your help,' she said to the lifeguards as she connected the oxygen cylinder to the tube. 'One last thing…I need one of you to help me get his foot back into the proper position.' If they didn't do that, the circulation could fail and the foot would be useless.

One of the lifeguards hesitantly volunteered. 'I don't know what to do,' he said.

'It'll be all right,' she said, reassuring him. 'I'll talk you through it. We need to give it a tug.'

He swallowed hard, but a few minutes later the foot pinked up, and she could feel that the pulses were present.

She sat back on her heels. The paramedics would help with splinting the foot and getting Josh onto a spinal board. Her work was almost done.

Matt came over to her, holding Ben by the hand, as they transferred his friend to the ambulance a short time later. He'd rolled down the top half of his wet-suit and Saffi couldn't take her eyes off him. He was hunky, perfectly muscled, his chest lightly bronzed. Her heart began to thump against her rib cage and her mouth went dry.

Together, they watched the ambulance move away, and as the crowd dwindled and people returned down the path to the beach Matt drew her to him, putting his free arm around her.

'You were brilliant,' he said. 'I thought about coming over to you to help, but I could see you had everything under control, the whole time. You were amazing. How did it feel?'

'Feel?' She stared at him blankly for a moment, not understanding what he was saying, and then realisation came to her in a rush. Without any conscious thought she'd acted like a true A and E doctor.

'I didn't think about what I was doing,' she said, her eyes widening. 'All I know is I was terrified it might be you who was injured, and I was desperate to make sure you were all right. I couldn't think beyond that. The adrenaline must have taken over.'

'That's my girl.' He hugged her close and kissed her swiftly on the mouth.

His girl? Her heart leapt and she returned his kiss with equal passion, a fever beginning to burn inside her. How did he manage to do this to her every time, to make her want him more than anything, more than any other man?

Where had that thought come from? She didn't remember any other man in her life before this. There must have been, surely? But somehow she was certain that Matt was the one man above all who could stir her senses and turn her blood to flame.

Ben started tugging at Matt's wetsuit. 'Can we go down to the beach? I want to make another sandcastle.'

Matt gave a soft groan and reluctantly broke off the kiss. 'Perhaps I should never have started that,' he said raggedly. 'Wrong place, wrong time.' He frowned. 'It's always going to be like that, isn't it?' he added with a sigh. 'I have to keep telling myself I must stay away, but when I'm with you it's so hard to resist.'

And she should never have responded with such eagerness, Saffi reflected wryly. She knew what she was getting into, and going on his record so far it could only end in sorrow, so why couldn't she keep her emotions firmly under lock and key?

CHAPTER SIX

'HAVE YOU THOUGHT any more about going back to work in A and E?' Matt asked. He'd popped home from the hospital to pick up his laptop, and Saffi was glad to see him, and even more pleased that he'd stopped to chat for a while. She missed him when he wasn't around.

It was lunchtime and she was hosing down the chicken run, a chore she did once a week to make sure the birds' living quarters were scrupulously clean. The hens were out on the grass, exploring the pellets of food she'd scattered about.

Matt seemed keen to know what she planned to do workwise, and she guessed it was because he cared enough to want her to be completely well again. Being able to do the job she'd trained for was a big part of that recovery process.

'I think it would do you good to go back to working in a hospital,' Matt said. 'It could help to bring back some memories.'

She nodded. 'I've been thinking the same thing. I'm just not sure I'd cope with the responsibility—what if I've forgotten some of the techniques I knew before?'

'I know it would be a huge step for you after you've spent the last few months getting yourself back on track, but you did so well looking after Josh—I think you proved yourself then.'

'Maybe.' She was hesitant. Was she really ready for it? He seemed to have a lot of faith in her.

'How is Josh?' she asked, switching off the hose and laying it on the ground. 'His foot was in a pretty bad state, wasn't it?'

'Yes, but he went up to Theatre and Andrew Simmons pinned it with plates and screws, and did a bone graft. It'll take a while to heal, and he'll need physiotherapy, but I think he'll be all right eventually.' He gave her a look of new respect. 'You saved his foot, Saffi. If you hadn't restored the circulation he could have been looking at an amputation.'

'I'm just relieved that he's all right.' She was thoughtful for a second or two. 'One thing I'll say—it's definitely put me off kite-surfing. Are you sure you want to go on doing it? I was worried sick when I thought you might have been hurt.'

'Were you? I'm glad you care about me.' He ran his hands down her arms in a light caress. 'I understand how you feel about trying it out. That's okay. And as for the other—I'm always careful to avoid going close to cliffs or rocks. You don't need to worry about me.'

'That's a relief.'

He studied her briefly. 'So what do you think about going back to work?'

'I don't know. Perhaps I could do it…but I always thought I would know when the time was right because

I'd have recovered all of my memories. It doesn't seem to be happening that way, though, does it?'

'Amnesia can be strange,' he murmured, 'but, actually, you've been doing really well. You've remembered your aunt and your career, and all the time, day by day, you're getting small flashes of recall. Perhaps by going back to your job things will begin to come back to you more and more.' He shooed a hen out of the flower border, where she'd been trying to eat one of the plants. 'Go on, Mitzi, back with the others.'

'You could be right. I don't know why it matters so much to me...but I feel...it's like I'm only half a person.' She looked at him in despair, and he took her into his arms.

'I can't bear to see you looking so forlorn,' he said. 'You mustn't think like that—anyway, you look pretty much like a whole person to me,' he added in a teasing voice. 'So much so that I think about you all the time...I can't get you out of my mind. You're beautiful, Saffi...and incredibly sweet. Look how you coaxed Ben to come out of himself.'

He gave her a gentle squeeze, drawing her nearer, and his words came out on a ragged sigh. 'It's getting more and more difficult for me to keep my resolve. Every time I look at you I want to show you just how much I want you.'

Having his arms around her was a delicious temptation but she couldn't give in to it, could she? Much as she wanted to believe every word he said, she had to make a strong effort to resist. At least, she had to do better than she'd managed up to now.

'Hmm...' She looked into his smoke-grey eyes. 'From what I've heard, that's what you say to all the girls.'

He pressed a hand to his heart as though she'd wounded him. 'It's not true. Would I do that? Would I?'

'I think that's open to debate,' she murmured.

He gave her a crooked smile. 'You're gorgeous, Saffi, and that's the truth, and I feel great whenever I'm with you. I have to keep pinching myself to believe that I'm actually living right next door to you.'

He was saying all the things she wanted to hear, but did she really want to end up as just another conquest? She couldn't get it out of her head what the paramedics had said. He had a way with women.

'You certainly do live next door—and that's another thing about you that confuses me,' she commented on a musing note, trying to ease herself away from him. 'I still haven't figured out why my aunt would leave part of the house to you. It doesn't make any sense to leave a house to be shared by two people who aren't related.'

She rubbed her fingers lightly over her temples in a circling motion to get rid of a throbbing ache that had started up there. Having him so close just added to her problems. She couldn't think straight.

'It's just another of those mysteries that I can't solve...' she murmured, 'but perhaps one day I'll get to the bottom of it. At the moment my mind's like a jig-saw puzzle with lots of little bits filled in.'

He became serious. 'I'm sure things will come back to you if you start to live the life you once had. I mean it. Going back to work at the hospital could be the best thing for you. I need another doctor on my team, and you would be perfect. You could work part time if it suits you—in fact, that would probably be the best option to begin with.'

'You need someone? You're not just trying to find a job for me?'

'We're desperately short of emergency doctors. I'd really like you to say yes, Saffi, not just for me but also for your own well-being. We'll get clearance for you to work again from the powers that be, and maybe arrange for someone to work with you for a while. I'd keep an eye on you to begin with until you get your confidence back.'

He looked so sincere she knew he would watch over her, and part-time work did seem like the ideal solution for her at the moment. It would give her the best of both worlds and allow her time to adjust.

She swallowed hard. 'Okay,' she said. 'I'll do it.'

'Yay!' He swooped her up into his arms once again and kissed her firmly, a thorough, passionate kiss that left her breathless and yearning for more.

'That's wonderful, Saffi.' He looked at her, his grey eyes gleaming, his mouth curved in a heart-warming smile. 'We should celebrate. Let me take you out to dinner this evening.'

She smiled back at him. 'I'd like that,' she said, 'except...' she frowned '...I'm expecting a visitor at around nine o'clock. He's bringing some stuff I left behind in Hampshire—a few books, my coffee-maker, glassware, things like that. My flatmate has been looking after them for me, but Jason offered to bring them here.

Apparently he's coming to Devon to take a few days' holiday.'

Matt frowned. 'Jason? You know this man? I thought you didn't remember anyone from where you lived?'

'No, I don't know him. I mean, I did, apparently, according to my flatmate. She's the only one I recalled after the accident, but even that was just bits and pieces that came back to me before I left Hampshire. Jason's a complete blank in my mind.'

'It seems odd that he's coming over so late in the evening?'

'I suppose it is, but he told Chloe he has to work today. He'll head over here as soon as he's finished.'

'That makes some kind of sense, I suppose.' He was still doubtful, a brooding look coming into his eyes as though he was already weighing up Jason as some kind of competition. His dark brows drew together. 'He must be really keen to see you if it can't wait till morning. Did your flatmate tell you anything about him?'

She could see he was suspicious of the man and his motives. 'No, she didn't, not really…not much, anyway. She mentioned something about us dating a few times. I remember he came to see me when I was in hospital, but I was getting distressed whenever I had visitors—they were all strangers to me and I was a bit overwhelmed by everything that was happening to me. I think the doctors advised her to let me remember things in my own time.' A feeling of unease washed through her. 'I feel bad about it…all those people I was supposed to know…'

'It wasn't your fault, Saffi.' He held her tight. 'Look,

how about this—we could go for an early dinner. What do you think? I really want to spend some time with you. I'll make sure you're back here in time to meet up with this Jason...' he pulled a face '...even though I'd rather you weren't going to see him.' His eyes darkened. 'I don't like the idea of him taking up where you left off.' Once again, he was at war with himself. 'I hate the thought of you dating someone else.'

'I'm not dating him. I don't even know him.' She nodded thoughtfully. 'An early dinner sounds like a good compromise. But what will you do about Ben... or will he be coming with us? I don't mind, if that's what you want.'

He shook his head. 'His father's going to look after him. He's back from sorting out the latest crisis, and he says he's going to stay home for a few days.'

'Oh, that's good news.' She smiled. 'Ben will be really happy to see him.'

'Yeah. Let's hope he doesn't get unsettled again when James has to leave.'

She winced. 'You're right, he's really come out of himself this last couple of weeks. Do you think James will take him to see Gemma in hospital?'

'He said he would. He wants to know the results of the CT scan they're doing.'

Of course...they would be doing the scan today. Matt had told her about it. He must be worried sick about what it might reveal.

He checked his watch. 'I have to go. It's almost time I was back on duty. I'll see you later. Dinner for about seven o'clock? Would that be all right?'

She nodded. 'I'll look forward to it.'

'Good. I'll book a table.'

It was only after he'd left for work that she realised she'd done it again—that she'd agreed to spend time with him when she should be putting up some barriers between them. Did she really want to end up like Gina, still hankering after him years later, when their relationship had run its course? And how would she get on with Gina if they had to work together? Had she made a mistake in agreeing to it?

She shook her head. It was done now, and she may as well throw caution to the wind and look forward to the evening.

What should she wear? After she'd showered and started her make-up later on in the day, she hunted through her wardrobe and picked out a favourite wine-coloured dress, one that she'd brought with her from Hampshire. It was sleeveless, with a V-shaped neckline and pleated bodice, a smooth sash waist and a pencil-line skirt. She put the finishing touches to her make-up, smoothing on a warm lip colour and adding a hint of blusher to her cheeks.

When Matt rang the doorbell at half past six, she was finally ready.

'Hi,' she said. 'I wasn't sure you'd make it here on time. I know how things can be in A and E. It isn't always easy to get away.'

'I handed over to my registrar.' He gazed at her, his eyes gleaming in appreciation as he took in her feminine curves, outlined by the dress, and her hair, which was a mass of silky, burnished curls. 'You look lovely,

Saffi. You take my breath away—you're the girl of my dreams.'

Her cheeks flushed with warm colour at the compliment. He looked fantastic. He must have showered and changed as soon as he had got home from work because his black hair was still slightly damp. He wore an expensively styled suit that fitted perfectly across his broad shoulders and made him look incredibly masculine.

They went out to the car and he drove them along the coast road to the restaurant. He was unusually quiet on the journey, a bit subdued, and she wondered if something had happened at work to disturb him. Was it something to do with his sister? Or perhaps he was simply tired after a stressful day. She remembered feeling like that sometimes after a bad day at work.

It might not be a good idea to bombard him with questions right away, though. If he wanted to talk to her about whatever it was that was bothering him, he would be more likely to do it after he had relaxed into the evening a little.

He took her to a pretty quayside restaurant, and they sat at a table by the window, from where they could look out at the boats in the harbour.

'It's lovely in here,' she said, looking around. 'It's very peaceful and intimate.' There were screened alcoves with candlelit tables, a glass-fronted display cabinet showing mouth-watering desserts, and waiters who hovered discreetly in the background. 'It makes me want to skip the meal and go straight for the dessert,' she said, eying up the assortment of gateaux and fruit tarts.

He laughed. 'You always did go for the dessert.'

'Did I?' Her brow puckered. 'Have we done this before?'

He nodded cautiously. 'Don't worry about it,' he said. 'Just relax and enjoy the food.'

She tried to do as he suggested, but at the back of her mind she was trying to work out why, if they had been a couple at one time, they had drifted apart, with her working in Hampshire and Matt here in Devon. What wasn't he telling her?

Through the starter of freshly dressed crab served with asparagus spears and mayonnaise they talked about her starting work in a week's time, and then moved on to generalities, but Matt said nothing about what might be troubling him. They chatted and she could tell he was making an effort, being as considerate and thoughtful as ever.

He ordered a bottle of wine, and Saffi took a sip, studying him as the waiter brought the main course, sirloin of beef with red wine sauce. 'You're not yourself this evening,' she said softly, when they were alone once more. 'What's wrong?'

He blinked, and then frowned slightly. He wasn't eating, but instead he ran his finger around the base of his wine glass. 'I'm sorry. It's nothing. I'm just a bit preoccupied, that's all, but I didn't mean to spoil the evening.' He smiled at her. 'You were saying you were thinking of buying a new car?'

'Well, I'll need one if I'm going to start work. But that's not important right now. I want to know what's wrong, Matt. Something's troubling you. Is it your sister?'

He sighed heavily and then nodded. 'I've seen the results of the tests and the CT scan. They've diagnosed Zollinger-Ellison syndrome.'

She pulled in a quick breath. 'Oh, no...no wonder you're feeling down... I'm so sorry, Matt.' It was bad news. She laid her hand over his, trying to offer him comfort, and he gave her fingers an answering squeeze.

She really felt for him. Zollinger-Ellison syndrome was an illness caused by a tumour or tumours in the duodenum and sometimes in the pancreas, too. They secreted large amounts of the hormone gastrin, which caused large amounts of stomach acid to be produced, and in turn that led to the formation of ulcers. It was a very rare disease and there was around a fifty per cent chance that the tumours might be malignant. 'How is she? Does she know about it?'

'Yes, she knows. Obviously, it was a huge shock for her, but she was trying to put on a brave face for Ben.'

'Will they try surgery?'

He nodded. 'As a first stage of treatment, yes. The Whipple procedure would be the best option, but it's difficult and very specialised surgery, as you probably know. If the tumours have spread to other parts of her body they won't even consider it. We'll just have to take things one step at a time.'

'It's hard to take in. I've heard it might go better if the patient has chemotherapy before surgery as well as afterwards.' She reflected on that for a while, knowing just how terrible it must be for Gemma and Matt to have to go through all this heartache.

She said, 'If there's anything I can do...does Gemma want any more books, or magazines, anything that will help to take her mind off things? I could perhaps find her some DVDs if she'd prefer?'

'Thanks, Saffi. I think she still has some of the magazines you sent last week. Maybe some comedy DVDs might help to take her mind off things for a while. Perhaps we can sort something out between us? I tried taking her fruit and chocolates but, of course, she has to be careful what she eats. Some things disagree with her.'

'We'll find something.'

They went on with their meal for a while, but somehow the pleasure in tasting the perfectly cooked meat and fresh vegetables had waned. She said quietly, 'Do your parents know?'

'Yes, I phoned my mother this afternoon. She was at work—she's a vet up in Cheltenham. She was so upset she said she was leaving everything and coming over right away.'

'I expect that will be good for Gemma.'

He nodded. 'My father's a GP in Somerset. He's going to try and get a locum to cover his practice for a while.'

'Your parents are divorced, then? I hadn't realised. Did that happen a long time ago?'

'When I was a child, yes.' His eyes were troubled. 'I was about eight years old when they broke up. Gemma was younger. It was fairly traumatic for both of us...

though I suppose it often is for the children if it's a fairly hostile split.'

He leaned back in his seat as the waiter came to clear the dishes and take their order for dessert. He swallowed some of his wine, and then refilled Saffi's glass.

'We chose to stay with my mother—Gemma and I. My father could be distracted by work and we didn't always get to see much of him.' He pulled a face. 'Then about three years later my mother had a sudden illness that affected her kidneys and we were taken into foster-care for a while.'

Saffi sucked in a breath. 'Is she all right now? It must have been a double blow to go through the break-up of your family and then to have that happen.' She frowned, trying to imagine what it would have been like to endure such an emotional upset.

'I think she's all right. While she was in hospital, they managed to prevent the worst of the kidney damage, but she has to take medication now to control her blood pressure and cholesterol, to make sure there aren't any further problems. She sees a specialist once a year, and things seem to be going well for her, as long as she follows the dietary advice he's given her.' He was quiet for a moment. 'I think she's the reason I wanted to study medicine.'

The waiter brought dessert, a pear tatin with vanilla ice cream, and Saffi ate, almost without knowing what she was eating. 'I'd no idea you had such a troubled childhood,' she said. 'But I suppose it was better for you once your mother was out of hospital?'

'Yes, it was.' He toyed with his food. 'Gemma and I

had been in separate foster-homes for quite a long time, and that was tough. We were taken away from everything that made us feel safe.' He lifted his glance to her. 'But I don't suppose it was much worse than what you went through. After all, your parents died, didn't they?'

'They did, but I was quite young when that happened. And I had Aunt Annie. She stepped in right away and was like a mother to me. My uncle was there as well until two or three years ago, so he became a father figure for me.'

She dipped her spoon into the tart and savoured the taste of caramelised fruit on her tongue. 'Did you see much of your father back then?'

'Quite a bit. We'd spend time with him whenever he had a free weekend, but then he married again and his wife already had children of her own. We didn't get on all that well with them. We tried, of course, but they were older than me and Gemma and I think they resented us.'

'Oh, dear. That doesn't sound good. It must have been awkward for you.'

He smiled. 'Probably, as children, you take these things more or less in your stride. It's only when you get to adulthood and you look back that you realise it could have been a lot better, or maybe that you could have handled things differently. I was more or less okay with my father getting married again, but when my mother did the same thing I wasn't too happy.' He pulled a face. 'I was quite rebellious for a time.'

Saffi studied him thoughtfully as he signalled to the waiter and ordered two cappuccinos. 'Do you think it's had an effect on you?' she asked when the waiter left. 'Now, I mean, as an adult.'

He mused on that for a while. 'Possibly. I suppose it makes you cautious. But it's probably worse when you're an adolescent. Your emotions are all over the place anyway then. At one time I began to think I didn't really belong anywhere. I looked out for Gemma—that was the one thing that was constant.'

'Maybe that's why you can't settle into relationships now—the reason you bale out when things start to get serious—because deep down you think it could all go wrong and then it would be heart-wrenching for you all over again.'

He looked startled for a second or two, but he mused on that for a while, and then he frowned. 'I hadn't thought of it that way,' he said. He gave a crooked smile. 'I think you could be right. Men are supposed to be tough, but even they can have their hearts broken.'

She stirred brown sugar crystals into her coffee and stayed silent, deep in thought. *Once bitten?* Had some woman broken his heart in years past? Perhaps that had reinforced his conviction that he must steer clear of getting too deeply involved. Was it the reason he seemed to have so much trouble dealing with his feelings for her?

Maybe it might have been better if she'd never worked out the cause of his reluctance to commit long term. If he started going over past decisions in his mind, would he soon start to have second thoughts about seeing Gina again?

When they left the restaurant, it was still fairly early, and they walked along the quayside for a while, looking at the yachts in the harbour. He put his arm around her bare shoulders and said softly, 'I'm sorry for weighing you down with my problems. I wanted this to be a pleasant evening.'

'It was. It is. Perhaps we should do it again some time.' Her face flushed a little as she realised how pushy that sounded, and she added hurriedly, 'I mean, when you're not so troubled and you can relax a bit more.'

He smiled. 'I'd really like that.' They stopped by a railing and looked out over the bay in the distance, formed by tall cliffs and a long promontory. Waves lapped at the shore and splashed over the rocks. Further out, a lighthouse blinked a warning to any passing ships.

After a while, he checked his watch and said soberly, 'I suppose we should start heading for home. I wish we didn't have to break up the evening like this. I want to be with you...' He smiled wryly. 'I'm beginning to resent this Jason before I've even met him.'

He linked his fingers in hers as they started to walk back to the car. It felt good, just the two of them, hand in hand, and she, too, wished the evening didn't have to end.

It was still well before nine o'clock when they arrived home, but Saffi was dismayed to find that there was a black car parked on the drive. As she and Matt approached the house, the driver's door opened and a man stood up and came to greet them. He was tall, with crisply styled brown hair and hazel eyes. He wore a beautifully tailored dark suit.

'Saffi, it's so good to see you again.' Before she could guess his intention, Jason had put his arms around her and drawn her to him in a warm embrace. Beside her, she felt Matt stiffen.

Saffi froze. Jason was a virtual stranger to her and she had no idea how to react. She had the strong feeling he would have kissed her, too, but he seemed to gain control of himself just in time and released her. Maybe he realised she wasn't responding to him as he might have expected.

She felt bad about her reaction. 'I...uh...Jason... hello. I don't think you know Matt, do you? He lives in the annexe over there.' She waved a hand towards the end of the building. 'He's been really helpful to me, one way and another, these last few weeks.'

Jason frowned, and it seemed like an awkward moment, but Matt nodded a guarded acknowledgement of him and said, 'She's been through a bad time, so I've been looking out for her. I mean to go on doing that.'

Something in the way he said it made Saffi glance at Matt. Perhaps he'd meant it as a subtle warning, but Jason didn't seem put out.

She said, 'Thanks for coming over here, Jason. It was good of you to do that.'

'I was glad to. I wanted to see you again.'

'You came to see me in hospital, didn't you?'

He nodded. 'I'd have visited more often, but the nurses wouldn't let me. Then your flatmate kept sending me away, saying you weren't up to seeing people. Can you believe it—after all we meant to one another? I'm just so glad that we can finally be together.'

She heard Matt's sudden intake of breath and she made a shuddery gasp. It was no wonder he was alarmed by what Jason was saying. It had come as news to her, too.

Her cheeks flooded with sudden heat. How could she tell Jason that she didn't know him? He seemed to think things were exactly as they had been before—that they could go back to whatever relationship they'd had before she'd suffered her head injury.

'I…I'm still having trouble remembering things, Jason,' she said in a soft voice. 'I'm sorry, but I still don't know who you are and I don't think we can go back to how we were. It's not possible.'

Jason shook his head. 'I know it was a bad thing that happened to you, Saffi, but I'm not going to give up on what we had. Even if you've lost your memory, we can start again.'

Saffi looked at him, a feeling of apprehension starting up in her stomach. 'I don't think that's possible, Jason. Things are different now. I'm not the same person I was back then, back in Hampshire.'

'I don't believe that's true, Saffi. People don't change, deep down. And I won't give up on you. How can I? I won't rest until things are back to how they should be. You mean everything to me, Saffi. We love one another. We were practically engaged. It'll be the same again, you'll see.'

Saffi stared at him in disbelief. Engaged? Was it true? Matt was looking stunned by the revelation and she felt as though the blood was draining out of her. A feeling of dread enveloped her. How could she even consider being with another man when in her heart she knew she wanted Matt?

But wasn't that the worst betrayal of all, wanting to have nothing at all to do with a man she was supposed to have loved?

Distraught, she looked at Matt. She was shattered by everything Jason had said.

'Let's not get ahead of ourselves,' Matt said, his gaze narrowing on Jason. 'Whatever was between you two before this has to go on the back burner. She's in shock. She doesn't know you. You have no choice but to let it go for now.'

CHAPTER SEVEN

MATT HELPED JASON to unload the boot of his car, and between the three of them they carried Saffi's belongings into the house. The men seemed to have come to a mutual agreement that there would be no more talk of what had gone on in the past, and gradually Saffi felt the shock of Jason's announcement begin to fade away. Had they really been on the point of getting engaged?

After a while she managed to find her voice once more and she tried to make general conversation, wanting to ease the tension that had sprung up between the two men.

Neither of them said very much, but when they had finished the work, they both followed her into the kitchen. Matt was making no attempt to return to the annexe, and she suspected he had no intention of leaving her alone with Jason.

'My coffee-maker,' she said with a smile, unpacking one of the boxes. 'I've really missed it. Who's for espresso?'

She spooned freshly ground coffee into the filter and added water to the machine. It gave her something to do, and helped to take her mind off the awfulness of her situation. She'd been thoroughly shaken by events, so much so that her hands were trembling. Turning away, she tried to hide the tremors by going to the fridge and pouring milk into a jug.

Matt was frowning, his dark eyes watching Jason, assessing him. 'How long will you be staying in Devon?' he asked, and Saffi was grateful to him for taking over the conversation for a while. She felt awkward, out of her depth and she had no idea what to do about it.

'A couple of weeks,' Jason answered. 'I've booked into a hotel in town.'

Saffi handed him a cup of coffee. 'Chloe said you were taking some time off work...' She pulled a face. 'I don't even know what it is that you do.'

'I'm a medical rep. I generally work in the Hampshire area, and sometimes further afield if an opportunity crops up.'

'And you were working near to here today?'

'That's right, but I'd already made up my mind to come and see you. I just wanted to be near you, Saffi.' His gaze was intent, his hazel eyes troubled. 'We were so close before the accident. I want to be with you and make it like it was before. We can do that, can't we?'

She looked away momentarily, unable to face the yearning in his expression. He seemed to be in such an agony of emotion—how was it that she could have forgotten him, feel nothing for him, and yet apparently they had been so close? She was overwhelmed by guilt.

'I don't know what to say to you, Jason. I don't know what to do.' She frowned, trying to work things out in her mind. Why did this have to happen…especially now, when she cared so much for Matt? But how could she simply turn Jason away? That would be heartless, like a betrayal of whatever relationship they'd once had. Was she the kind of person who could do that?

She said quietly, 'I know this must be very difficult for you. Perhaps we could get to know one another again…take it slowly…but I can't make any promises. I don't know how things will turn out. Things have changed. I'm not the same person any more.'

'What are you trying to say to me?' Jason's mouth made a flat line. 'Are you telling me you feel differently because you're with him?' He looked pointedly at Matt, a muscle in his jaw flicking.

She closed her eyes for a second or two, a tide of anxiety washing through her. 'Yes, I think I am.' She let out a long, slow breath. She'd said it. Admitted it. She'd known what the consequences might be when she couldn't stay away from Matt. She'd flirted with danger. Matt didn't want a long-term relationship, he had been clear on that, but she'd gone ahead anyway, getting herself in deeper and deeper.

Standing beside her, she saw Matt brace his shoulders. His lips were parted slightly as though on a soft sigh…of relief, or was he concerned now because she might want their relationship to be more serious? He didn't say anything, though, but looked fixedly at Jason.

Jason's mouth was rigid. 'You don't love her,' he said. 'You can't possibly care for her as I do. You've only known her for five minutes…how can that compare with what Saffi and I have shared?'

Matt pulled a wry face. 'Actually, you're wrong about that. I've known Saffi for years. The irony of it is that she doesn't remember me either.'

Jason looked stunned. After a second or two he recovered himself and said briskly, 'So, we're on an even footing. We'll see who comes out of this the winner, won't we?'

'True.'

Saffi stared at both of them, a wave of exasperation pulsing through her. 'Have you both finished discussing me as though I'm some kind of commodity to be shifted from one place to another as you please?' she enquired briskly. 'I think it's time for you both to leave.'

Stunned by her sharp rebuke, they did as she asked, albeit with great reluctance. Jason said goodbye, stroking her arm in a light caress, hesitant, as though he wanted to do more, perhaps to take her in his arms. Finally, he went to his car and drove off towards town.

Matt stood on the drive, watching him turn his car onto the country lane.

Saffi raised her brows questioningly. 'You're still here,' she said.

He gave her a wry smile. 'I'm just making sure you're safe,' he murmured, and then with a gleam in his eyes he added, 'If you begin to feel anxious in the night, or you want some company, you only have to bang on the wall and I'll be there in an instant.'

'Hmm…thanks for that, I appreciate it. But don't hold your breath, will you?' she murmured.

His mouth made an amused twist. 'You think I'm joking. Believe me, I'm not. Are you sure you don't want me to stay? After all, a few minutes ago you admitted you had feelings for me.' He moved closer as if to take her in his arms but she dragged up a last ounce of courage and put up a hand to ward him off.

'I can't do this, Matt,' she said huskily. 'I want to, but I can't. Not now. My whole life has been turned upside down and I don't know what to do or what to think. I need some space.'

He laid his hands lightly on her shoulders. 'I'm sorry. It's just that I hate to think of you being with that man—with any man. Seeing him with you has come as such a shock it's making me reassess everything.' He frowned. 'I don't mean to put pressure on you, Saffi, but you must know I want you...I need you to know that. I want you for myself. I want to protect you, to keep you from harm, in any way I can.'

'I'm not sure you would feel the same way if I hadn't lost my memory.' She shook her head. 'It makes a difference, doesn't it?'

'I don't know. All I know is I've always wanted you, Saffi. I've tried to fight against it, but I can't help myself. It seems like I've longed for you for ever and a day.'

Wanting wasn't the same as loving, though, was it? She daren't risk her happiness on a man who couldn't settle for one woman in his life. More and more she was growing to understand that it was what she wanted above all else—to have Matt's love and to know that it was forever.

'Things are all messed up,' she said softly. 'I don't know who I am or how to respond any more.'

Briefly, he held her close and pressed a gentle kiss to

her forehead. 'Just follow your instincts,' he said, 'and know that I'm here for you, whenever you need me.'

He was still watching her as she went back into the house and closed the door. Alone once more, Saffi leaned back against the wall and felt the spirit drain out of her. Everything that she was, or had been, was locked up inside her head. Why didn't she know what had happened between her and Jason? Why had she and Matt parted company all those years ago? If only she could find the key to unlock the secrets hidden in her mind.

Jason came to call for her the next day, after Matt had left for work, and they spent time walking in the village and exploring the clifftop walks nearby. Perhaps he'd had time to think things through overnight, because he seemed to be doing everything in his power to help ease her mind. He made no demands of her, so that after a while she was able to relax a little with him. He told her about his job as a representative for a pharmaceutical company, and how it involved meetings with hospital clinicians, GPs and pharmacists.

In turn, she told him about her love for the house she'd inherited, the time she spent in the garden or looking after the hens and the beehives.

'I'll have to collect the honey soon,' she told him. 'You could help if you want. I could find you some protective clothing.'

'I could never have imagined you doing such things,' he said with a grin. 'You were always so busy, working in A and E. You loved it. It was your passion.'

'Was it?' She couldn't be certain, but it felt as though he was right. 'I'll be doing it again in a few days' time.'

He frowned. 'You will? Are you sure you're up to it? How are you going to manage things at the house if you do that? The garden's huge. That's a full-time job in itself, without the hassle of looking after the hens.'

'It's not so bad. Matt helps with everything, especially the bigger jobs around the place, like repairing fences or painting the hen coop. He's been keeping the lawns trim and so on. Besides, I'll only be working part time to begin with.'

'Even so, you don't need all this bother. You've been ill, Saffi. Why don't you sell up and come back to Hampshire? Life would be a lot easier for you there, and you would have friends around you.'

She shook her head. 'I don't remember anyone back there and I wasn't getting better. I was frightened all the while, and I didn't know why. It's different here. I love this house. It's my home, the place where I spent my childhood and where I felt safe.'

Jason wasn't happy about her decision, and she knew he wanted her to return to Hampshire with him, but he said no more about it. She saw him most days after that, while Matt was out at work, and he was always careful not to push things too far. Perhaps he was hoping her memory would return and they could take up where they had left off, but that didn't happen.

Although she knew Matt hated her being with Jason, he didn't try to persuade her against seeing him. Instead, he was there every evening, helping her with whatever needed to be done about the place. She discovered one of the hens, Mitzi, had a puncture wound in her leg and he cleaned it up while she gently held the bird to stop her from struggling.

'I think she might have broken the leg,' he said with a frown. 'I'll use some card as a splint and bind it up. Then we'll take her along to the vet.' He looked around. 'It's hard to see how she's managed to hurt herself— unless she was panicked in some way and fell against the timbers.'

'Perhaps we should keep her separate from the others for a while?'

He nodded. 'I'll sort out something for her. I think there's an old rabbit cage in the shed. I'll scrub it out and make it as good as new and it should make a good place for her to rest up.'

'Okay. Thanks.' She smoothed Mitzi's feathers. 'You'll be all right,' she said soothingly. 'We'll look after you.'

The vet prescribed antibiotics, a painkiller and splinted the leg properly. 'Keep her quiet for a few days, away from the other hens. She should heal up in a few weeks. Bring her back to me next week so that I can see if the leg's mending okay.'

'We will, thank you.' They went back to the house and settled her down in her new home.

'Maybe we could let her out on the grass on her own when she's feeling a bit more up to it?' Saffi suggested. She went over to the garden table and poured juice into a tumbler.

'Yes, we can do that. If it looks as though she's going to flap about too much, we'll pop her back in the cage.'

He sat down on one of the redwood chairs and she slid a glass towards him. He stared into space for a while, unseeing, and she guessed his thoughts were far away.

'Are you all right? Are you thinking about your sister? Have they operated on her? You said they were deciding on the best course of treatment.'

'That's right. They had to find out how far the disease had gone…whether it had spread beyond the pancreas and duodenum, but it seems she's in luck as far as that goes. They're bringing in a specialist surgeon to perform the Whipple procedure.'

She stood at the side of him and reached for his hand, wanting to comfort him as best she could. It was major surgery, a complicated procedure where part of the pancreas and the small intestine were removed, along with the gall bladder and part of the bile duct. After that had been done, the remaining organs would be reattached.

'When will they do it?'

'Next week. She's having a course of chemotherapy first to try and make sure it goes no further than it already has. They're going to do minimally invasive surgery, through laparoscopy, so there should be less chance of complications.'

Saffi bent down and put her arms around him. 'If you hadn't insisted on taking her to hospital, things could have been much worse. You've done everything you can for her, Matt.'

'Yeah.' He sighed. 'It just doesn't seem like nearly enough.'

'You're looking after Ben again, aren't you? Has his father gone back to work?'

He nodded. 'James is worried sick about Gemma and about the effect it's having on Ben. He was at the hospital all the time, but now he has to go away on an urgent callout. He's going to make sure he's back here when she has the surgery. I think this illness has really shaken him up.'

'I don't suppose Ben's reacting too well to all the changes going on in his life. Perhaps he can help me with the honey—not the collecting of it but afterwards, when I put it into jars?'

'I think he would enjoy that. When are you planning on doing it?'

'At the weekend.' She made a wry face. 'I thought I would open up the hives on Saturday, around lunchtime, when, like you said, most of the bees would be out and about.'

'Good idea. I'll give you a hand.'

She smiled at him. 'Thanks. I wasn't looking forward to doing it on my own for the first time.' Jason had said he had to be somewhere else on that particular morning, and she wondered if he had a problem with bees, or was worried about being stung. He still maintained she ought to sell up and leave everything behind.

Matt shot her a quick glance. 'How do you feel about going into work next week?'

Her mouth made a brief downward turn. 'I'm a bit apprehensive, to be honest. I'm worried that being able to help Josh might have been a once-only thing, and that I was working purely on instinct. I feel pretty sure

I know what I'm doing, but I'd hate to come across something that I couldn't handle.'

'I don't think that's going to happen, because the way you were with Josh everything you did seemed skilful and automatic, as though it was part of you. And after talking to you the hospital chiefs are confident that you'll be fine. But if you're worried, you could come to the hospital with me tomorrow, just to observe and help out…if you want to. There's no pressure.'

'That's probably a good idea. I might get to know one way or the other if it's going to work out.'

'Okay. That's a date.' He grinned. 'Not the sort I'd prefer, but I guess it'll have to do for the time being.'

He picked her up in the morning after breakfast and drove her to the hospital. 'I'll introduce you to everyone, and after that you can just watch what's going on, or you can work alongside me,' he said as they walked into A and E. 'If you feel uncomfortable at any time, just let me know.'

She looked around. Everything seemed familiar to her, and perhaps that was because she'd been here before with the little boy, Charlie, who had broken his leg and pelvis in the road accident. He was doing well now, by all accounts. She hadn't taken it all in then, but now she saw the familiar layout of an emergency unit.

'I think I'd like to work with you,' she said. 'If you'll show me where everything is kept.'

He put an arm around her shoulder and gave her a quick hug. 'Brilliant. I know you can do it, Saffi. It'll be as though you've never been away, you'll see.'

She wasn't so sure about that to begin with, but gradually, as the morning wore on, she gained in confidence, standing by his side as he examined his patients and talking to him about the problems that showed up on X-ray films and CT scans. It was a busy morning, and they finally managed to take a break several hours after they had started work.

'It's finally calmed down out there,' she said, sipping her coffee. 'It's been hectic.'

He nodded. 'You seem to be getting on well with Jake, our registrar, and the nurses on duty.'

'They've been really good to me, very helpful and kind.' Except that Gina Raines had come on duty a short time ago, and straight away Saffi had become tense. She wasn't sure why, but she had a bad feeling about her. Maybe it was because she knew she and Matt had been involved at one time, but that was over now, wasn't it? So why should that bother her now? As soon as she had seen her, though, a band of pain had clamped her head and her chest muscles had tightened.

She frowned. 'They all know about my head injury. I know we talked about telling them, but it feels odd.'

'I thought it best to be straight with everyone from the start, to explain what we're doing and why you're here. They're a good bunch of people. You'll be fine with them.'

'Yes. I think it will work out.' She took another sip of coffee and all of a sudden her pager went off. Matt checked his at the same time, and stood up, already heading towards the door. Saffi hurried after him.

'A five-year-old is coming in with her mother,' the

triage nurse said. 'The little girl had just finished eating a biscuit at a friend's house when she felt dizzy and fainted. Now she can't get her breath.'

Matt and Saffi went to meet the mother in the ambulance bay, and quickly transferred the child to a trolley. It was clear to see that she was struggling to get air into her lungs, and a nurse started to give her oxygen through a mask.

'She's been saying her tummy hurts,' the distressed mother said, 'and she's been sick a couple of times in the car. She's getting a rash as well.'

They rushed her to the resuscitation room and the child's mother hurried alongside the trolley, talking to her daughter the whole time, trying to soothe her.

'Has Sarah had any problems with fainting before, or with similar symptoms?' Matt asked.

'She's never fainted, but she does have asthma, and she had a bit of a reaction to peanuts once.'

'Did she see her GP about the reaction?'

The woman shook her head. 'It was quite mild, so we didn't bother.'

'All right, thanks,' Matt said. 'You can stay with us in Resus. The nurse will look after you—if you have any questions, anything at all, just ask her.' He indicated Gina, who went to stand with the mother as they arrived in the resuscitation room.

It looked very much as though Sarah was having a reaction to something she'd eaten. Her face was swollen, along with her hands and feet. Saffi handed Matt an EpiPen, an automatic injector of adrenaline, and he smiled briefly, knowing she had intercepted his thoughts.

'Thanks.' He injected the little girl in the thigh, and Saffi handed him a syringe containing antihistamine, which he injected into the other leg. Then he began his examination, while a nurse worked quickly to connect the child to the monitors that gave readings of heart rate, blood pressure and blood oxygen. Everyone was worried about this little girl who was fighting for her life.

'Blood pressure's falling, heart rate rising. Blood oxygen is ninety per cent.'

'Okay, let's get a couple of lines in to bring her blood pressure up. I'll intubate her before the swelling in her throat gets any worse. And we need to get her legs up to improve her circulation—but be careful, we don't want to cause more breathing problems.'

After five minutes the child was still struggling with the anaphylactic shock. 'I'll give her another shot of adrenaline,' Matt said, 'along with a dose of steroid.'

The medication was already in Saffi's hand and she quickly passed it to him. They had to work fast. This was a life-threatening condition and they had to do everything they could to bring down the swelling and restore her life signs to a safe level.

Matt looked concerned, anxious for this small child, but he followed the treatment protocol to the letter.

'Her breathing's still compromised,' Saffi murmured. 'Should we give her nebulised salbutamol via the ventilator circuit?'

'Yes, go ahead. It should open up the air passages.'

A short while later they could finally relax and say

that the child was out of immediate danger. They were all relieved, and Matt took time out to talk to the girl's mother and explain the awful reaction that the girl had experienced.

'We'll send her to a specialist who will do tests,' he said. 'We need to know what caused this to happen. In the meantime, we'll keep her here overnight and possibly a bit longer, to make sure that she's all right. We'll give you an EpiPen and show you how to use it so that you can inject Sarah yourself if anything like this happens again. You'll need to bring her straight to Emergency.'

He took the woman to his office so that he could talk to her a bit more and answer any of her questions.

Saffi went home later that day, satisfied that she had managed a successful day at work. She felt elated, thrilled that she was back on form, workwise at least.

Matt came to find her in the garden the next day when she was getting ready to open up the beehives. She'd brought out the protective clothing and laid it down on the table in preparation.

'Two new skills in one week,' he said with a smile. 'You're really up for a challenge, aren't you? You did really well yesterday. How did it feel to you, being back in a hospital?'

'It was so good,' she said, returning the smile. 'Like you said, it felt as though I'd never been away. I remembered everything about medicine, and how much I love being a doctor, the way Jason said I did.'

His brows drew together at the mention of Jason. 'How are you getting on with him?' he asked cautiously.

'Have you remembered how it was with you two before the accident?'

She shook her head. 'From time to time I get flashbacks, of places we've been, or brief moments we've shared, the same as I do with you and me, when we were once together, but they're so fleeting that I can't hold onto them.' Her glance met his. 'You still don't like him being here, do you?'

He winced. 'It shows? I thought I was doing a pretty good job of hiding it.' He moved his shoulders as though he was uncomfortable with the situation. 'Of course, he's been quite open about the fact that he wants you back, and I can scarcely blame him for that. You're a special kind of woman, and who wouldn't want to be with you? But I wish he'd stayed back in Hampshire.'

She studied him for a moment or two, frowning. 'It's more than that, isn't it? You really don't like him.'

'I think it's odd that he hasn't come to find you before this. I would have moved heaven and earth to find you if I was in his shoes.'

His brow furrowed. 'He's putting pressure on you— subtle pressure, but it's there all the same. He says you were practically engaged, but "practically" isn't the same as having a ring actually on your finger, is it? I can't help wondering if he's exaggerating.'

'Does that matter? Wouldn't you do the same if you really cared about someone?'

'I do care about someone—I care very deeply for *you*, Saffi. I've never felt this way before—you can't imagine how badly it hurts to see you with someone else.'

She pressed her lips together. She didn't want to hurt him. It grieved her to see the pain in his eyes, but she was torn. She loved Matt, deeply, intensely, but didn't she owe Jason something, too?

To turn her back on him would be a betrayal. He would feel she hadn't even given him a chance. She didn't want to hurt anyone, but she desperately wanted Matt.

She lifted her arms to him, running her palms lightly over his chest. 'Isn't that a kind of pressure you're using, too? I don't want to see you hurting, Matt. That's the last thing I want.'

He gave a ragged sigh, the last of his willpower disintegrating as her hands trailed a path over his chest and moved up to caress the line from his neck to his shoulders.

He pulled her to him and kissed her fiercely, all his pent-up desire burning in that passionate embrace. His hands smoothed over her, tracing every feminine curve, filling her with aching need.

She clung to him, her fingers tangling in the silk of his hair, loving the way his body merged with hers, the way his strong thighs moved against her, and longing for him to say to her the one thing she wanted to hear.

She wanted his love, needed it more than anything in the world, but would it ever be hers?

'Saffi, I'm lost without you… What am I to do?' His voice was rough around the edges and she could feel his heart thundering in his chest.

The sun beat down on them and she felt heady with longing, fever running through her as his hand cupped

her breast and his thumb gently stroked the burgeon-
ing nub. A quivery sigh escaped her, and she looked
up at him, her gaze meshing with his. More than anything, she wanted to give in to her deepest desires, to
have him make love to her without any thought for the
consequences.

But she couldn't do that. Not until she knew the truth
about her past, about what had happened to spoil their
relationship and send her headlong into Jason's arms.

Slowly, she came down to earth, and began to gently
ease herself away from him.

Even as she did so, a small voice called in the distance, 'Uncle Matt, I finished my picture. Come and
see.'

Matt gave a soft groan, releasing her and gazing at
her with smoke-dark eyes full of regret.

'We have to sort out this thing with Jason,' he said
huskily. 'I'm not going to share you with any man, in
body or in spirit.'

CHAPTER EIGHT

'HEY, YOU'VE BEEN out and bought yourself a new car!' Matt looked admiringly at Saffi's gleaming silver MPV. 'It looks great, doesn't it?'

'I'm pleased with it,' Saffi said, glad that he liked her choice. 'I need one so that I can get to and from work, so I went ahead and took the plunge yesterday.'

'I wonder how I managed to miss that? You must have put it straight in the garage while I was busy with something else.'

'Yes, I did. I was a bit overwhelmed by the time I arrived home—getting back behind the wheel and so on.'

Frowning, he put an arm around her. 'I would have gone with you if you'd said. Did you have any problems finding what you wanted?'

She shook her head. 'Actually, Jason went with me to the showroom.'

She felt Matt stiffen, and added hastily, 'I didn't have much choice in the matter. He came to see me and insisted on going along with me.'

'How can he insist on anything? He's not your keeper.'

She winced. 'True. But I feel so guilty about forgetting him… I'm finding it hard to make him understand that I need some space.'

'He's playing on your emotions.'

'Maybe. Anyway, he wasn't too happy with my choice of car. He thought I should have gone for something smaller, but I like the flexibility of this one. You can fold down the seats to create more storage space. That might come in useful if I ever have to carry medical equipment around with me.'

He smiled. 'Do you think you might want to try your hand at being an immediate care doctor?'

She chuckled. 'Perhaps I'd better not try to run before I can walk. But you never know.'

'Hmm.' He sobered. 'How does it feel to drive? I mean, you said you were a bit worried about it.'

'It's okay, I think. I didn't actually have a problem bringing it home, anyway.'

'That's good. One more hurdle out of the way.'

'Let's hope so. I thought I could drive us to the vet's with Mitzi after work today, if that's all right with you? Unless you'd like me to go on my own?'

'No, I'll go with you. I want to hear what the vet has to say. It's good to see other professionals at work, and it's useful to get their advice. You never know when it might come in handy. Besides, I like spending time with you. You know I do.' He frowned. 'I'd do it a lot more if it wasn't for Jason hanging around.'

He turned to go back into the house to get ready for work. 'I'll see you at the hospital in two ticks.'

'Okay.' She set off for the hospital, still smiling at

what he'd said. He liked spending time with her. It made her feel warm inside.

They met up in A and E a short time later, and even though this was her first official day at work, everything went smoothly. She treated a child who had come in with a broken collarbone after playing football at school and a girl who had dislocated her shoulder in a fall. There was also a tricky diagnosis where a boy had fallen and felt disorientated…it turned out to be a case of epilepsy.

Matt left her to get on with things pretty much on her own, but she was aware he was keeping an eye on her all the while. He needn't have worried, though, because she was absolutely sure of what she was doing, and after a while the whole team relaxed and treated her as one of themselves, as if she'd been there for years.

At lunchtime Matt disappeared, and she guessed he'd gone to check up on Gemma. She was having her surgery today, and although Matt had been as calm and as efficient as ever as he went about his work, she knew that he was worried about her.

When he returned to A and E after about half an hour, he said quietly, 'Shall we go and get a coffee?'

'That would be good. I'm ready for one.' She walked with him to the staffroom. 'How is Gemma?'

'She's still in Theatre, but everything's going well so far. Her vital signs are okay, which is good.' He fetched two coffees and they went to sit down. 'James is in the waiting room. He's in bad shape. He's terrified something might go wrong.'

'Whatever happened to break them up, it seems as though he really cares about her.'

He nodded. 'I think he does. I'm fairly sure it's his job that's the trouble, because he's away from home so often.'

'Can't he get some other kind of work?'

'That would be the best answer, and I think he realises it now. He says he's applying for posts close to home. His qualifications are good, so he shouldn't have too much trouble finding something suitable.'

She sipped her coffee. 'It's been a scary time for both of you.'

'Yeah.'

'Even so, I envy you, having a family, having someone close. I sometimes wish I'd had a brother or a sister. My aunt wasn't able to have children, so there weren't even any cousins.'

He looked at her, his eyes widening a fraction. 'Is that a new memory?'

'Oh!' She gave a laugh. 'Yes, it was. Perhaps you were right about me coming back to work. It must be opening up new memory pathways.'

They went back to A and E a few minutes later, and Saffi became engrossed once more in treating her patients.

She left for home a few hours before Matt, and spent the afternoon getting on with chores. Jason had wanted to meet up with her, but she'd put him off as she needed to make a trip to the grocery store.

'I could go with you,' he'd said. 'I just want to be with you.'

'I know, Jason, but I'd sooner do this on my own. Anyway, I'm going to the hairdresser and then to the vet's surgery later.' She didn't want to be with him for too long. She'd much rather be with Matt, and she suspected Jason knew that.

After Matt arrived home, she gave him time to grab a bite to eat and then she put Mitzi into a carrier ready for the journey to see the vet.

'Is there any news of Gemma?' she asked as they went over to her car. She slid into the driver's seat and Matt climbed in beside her.

'Well, she's out of surgery and in Intensive Care. Her blood pressure's very low and she's had several bouts of arrhythmia—they're obviously concerned. She's in a lot of pain, too, so they're giving her strong drugs.'

'At least she came through it, Matt.' She laid her hand on his arm. 'She's young, and that's in her favour.'

'Yeah, there is that.' He breathed deeply. 'And James is at her bedside. If she wakes up, she'll see him right away.'

She started the engine. 'Where's Ben today?'

'He's with my mother. She's staying at Gemma's house so that he's in familiar surroundings.'

'That's good. This is bound to be upsetting for him.'

A few minutes later she turned onto the tree-lined road where the vet's surgery was situated. They didn't have to wait long before they were called into his room and he examined Mitzi's leg once more.

'That seems to be healing up nicely,' he said. 'Sometimes the leg becomes crooked, but it looks as though she's doing really well. I'll give you some more antibiotics for the wound, and a few painkillers, although I think she probably won't need them for too long.'

Mitzi's ordeal was over in a few minutes and they put her in the carrier once more then went back to the car.

Saffi drove back to the village. There was a fair amount of traffic on the main road at this time of the evening, and she checked her rear-view mirror regularly along the way.

After a while, she noticed that a black car was edging into view, coming close up behind her. She frowned. Whoever was driving it had been following her for some time, getting nearer and nearer, and now she was beginning to feel uneasy. Because of the shadows she couldn't see the driver's face clearly, but seeing that car had sparked something in the darker regions of her mind. She was sure something like this had happened to her before, that she'd been followed along a busy road.

She indicated to turn off the main road, and breathed a soft sigh of relief as the black car made no signal to do the same. It had all been in her imagination. The car wasn't following her. It was going straight on.

She drove onto the country lane, and after a while she glanced into her rear-view mirror once more. The car was there again, right behind her. She gripped the steering-wheel tightly. Her heart was thudding heavily.

'Saffi, what's wrong?' Matt's voice sounded urgent. 'You're as white as a sheet.'

'I'm not sure,' she managed, 'but I think I'm being followed.' She pulled in a shaky breath. 'It's probably nothing. It's just that…'

She broke off, switching on her indicator and carefully bringing the car to a halt in a lay-by. Beads of sweat had broken out on her brow.

She looked in the mirror once more. The black car had slowed down, too, as though the driver was unsure of himself, but then at the last moment he pulled away and went on down the country lane.

Saffi leaned back in her seat and let the fear drain out of her. The image of that black car was imprinted on her mind.

'Can you tell me what happened?'

'I don't know. Perhaps I made a mistake.'

'You were frightened, Saffi. What was it that scared you? Is it because you were in a collision once before? Did it happen because someone was following you?'

She swallowed hard. 'I think so. I can't remember clearly. It was a dark-coloured car. Something happened...I think I was rammed from behind...then a man stepped out of the car and came over to me.' She searched her mind for anything more, but the image faded and she couldn't bring it back. 'All I know is I was terrified.'

He undid his seat belt and leaned towards her, wrapping his arms around her. 'No wonder you were scared. It would be a bad experience for anyone.' He stroked her hair. 'Did you report it to the police?'

She frowned. 'I don't think so. I don't know what happened after he came over to me.'

They sat for a while with Matt holding her until her heart stopped thumping and she felt as though she could go on.

'Would you like me to drive the rest of the way?'

She shook her head. 'No, thanks. I'll do it. I'll be all right now.' She wanted to stay in his arms, but at the same time she needed to overcome her fears. Slowly, she eased away from him.

He frowned. 'Okay...if you're sure.' He fastened his seat belt once more and she started the car, driving cautiously until they arrived home.

'If you want me to be a passenger in the car over the next few weeks until you're over this, that's fine by me,' Matt said after she'd settled Mitzi back in her cage.

'Thanks.' She smiled at him. 'I think I'll be okay.'

Somehow knowing what it was that had caused her worries about driving was enough to ease her mind. Whatever had happened was in the past and not something that she need be concerned about now. It was like a weight off her mind, and it meant that when she drove to work the next day she was calm and the journey was uneventful.

'You seem to have settled in here well,' Gina said, as she assisted her with a young patient who needed sutures in a leg wound. 'Are you getting to know your way around?'

'I think so,' Saffi answered. 'Everyone's been very helpful.'

'Yes, I found that, too.'

'Ah, of course—you came here just a few days before I started, didn't you?' She glanced at Gina, who was wearing her brown hair loose this morning, so that it fell in soft waves to the nape of her neck. 'You're covering for a maternity leave? What will you do when that contract finishes?'

'I'll go back to the community hospital. They let me do this as a way of gaining experience in other departments. The nursing chief is good like that. She thinks variety will make for better nursing, so she was willing to allow the transfer.'

'She's probably right.'

Saffi tied off the last suture and gave her small patient a smiley-face badge. 'You were very brave,' she said.

Gina stayed behind to clear the trolley while Saffi went off to examine a six-year-old who had breathing difficulties and a barking cough. The nurse seemed friendly, and she hadn't anticipated that. She'd wondered if there might be some tension between them since Gina had dated Matt, but working with her had been much easier than she'd expected.

Matt had gone to see his sister before coming into A and E this morning, and Saffi busied herself going about her work. Whenever she had a brief free moment she thought about the dilemma she was in, and what she should do about Jason. He'd been easygoing, good company, and she could perhaps see some small reason why they might have been a couple before the accident that had blighted her life.

She didn't have any feelings for him, though, and she was fairly certain that even if she were to spend several more weeks in his company she still wouldn't feel anything for him. Was that because something inside her had changed after her head injury, or was it because she had fallen in love with Matt?

What could she say to him? He would be going back

to Hampshire in less than a week and he was begging her to go with him.

And what should she do about Matt? Emotionally, she was totally bound up in him. He wanted her and they were good together, but there was no future in the relationship that she could see. Wasn't she inviting heartache?

Matt walked briskly into A and E, breaking into her thoughts, and quickly glanced through the list of patients who were being treated. 'Any problems so far?' he asked, and the registrar shook his head.

'It's all under control.'

Saffi glanced at Matt, trying to gauge his mood. His expression was serious, and she wondered if everything was all right with his sister.

'How is she?' she asked.

His mouth flattened. 'She's feeling pretty awful at the moment. There are all sorts of tubes that have to be left in place for a while, as you know, and one of the insertion points is infected. They've taken swabs to find out what bacteria are involved, and put her on strong antibiotic cover in the meantime.'

'I'm sorry.'

The triage nurse cut across everyone's conversation just then, saying, 'Red alert, people. We've a child coming in by ambulance. Suspected head injury after a fall on a path at home. Estimated arrival ten minutes.'

Everyone was immediately vigilant, ready to do their designated jobs.

When the boy, Danny, was brought into the resuscitation room, Saffi's heart lurched. He was about the same age as Ben, and he looked so small and vulnerable, white-faced, his black hair stark against the pillows.

'He's been vomiting on the way here,' the paramedic said, but by now the child had slipped into unconsciousness.

Immediately, Matt began his assessment, while Saffi quickly set up a couple of intravenous fluid lines. A nurse connected Danny to monitors and Matt began a thorough examination of his small patient.

Once his vital signs had stabilised and Matt was satisfied there were no other major injuries, he said, 'Okay, let's get him over to Radiology for a CT head scan.'

Matt and Saffi went with the child. She was apprehensive, dreading what the scan might reveal. Head injuries like this were always serious and could be life-threatening. Danny's parents must be frantic with worry.

Seeing the results of the scan on the computer screen, Matt's jaw tightened. Saffi was filled with anxiety.

'Call Theatre,' Matt told Gina, who was assisting. 'Tell them I'm on my way with a four-year-old who has a subdural haematoma.'

'Are you doing the surgery?' Gina asked.

He nodded. 'There's no one else available right now. Prep the child and I'll go and scrub in as soon as I've spoken to the parents.' He looked at Saffi. 'Do you want to come and scrub in as well?'

'Yes. I'd like to.'

Everything happened very quickly after that. He explained to the parents that blood was leaking into the tissues around their child's brain and because it had no way of escaping it was building up dangerous pressure inside Danny's head. Left untreated, it could cause brain damage.

To prevent that, Matt had to make a hole in the boy's skull in order to release that pressure and remove any blood clots that had formed.

The boy's parents were stunned, and obviously terrified about what was happening to their child, but they signed the consent form and soon Danny was on his way to Theatre.

As soon as Danny had been anaesthetised, Matt worked quickly and carefully, aided by computer monitoring, to make a burr-hole in the child's skull. Saffi suctioned the wound to remove a huge clot that had formed, and then Matt controlled the bleeding with cauterisation and finished the procedure, inserting a drainage tube into the operation site.

Danny was still in danger, as Saffi knew only too well from her own experience of head injury, but at least he could be treated with drugs now to keep him sedated and bring down the swelling on the brain. The worry was whether he would have suffered any brain damage, but that might not become clear for some time.

Afterwards, Danny was taken to the recovery room where he was to be cared for by a specialist nursing team. Matt supervised the transfer. 'We'll send him over to Intensive Care just as soon as they're ready to receive him.'

He and Saffi started back down to A and E, and Matt said quietly, 'Are you due to go off home now? It must be about time for your shift to end.'

'Yes, it is. Why? Do you want me to stay for a bit longer?'

'I wondered if you have time for a coffee in my office. I need to record my case notes, but we could talk for a while.'

'Okay.' She followed him into the office and watched as he set up the coffee-machine in a small alcove.

He passed her a cup a few minutes later, and she stood with him, sipping the hot drink and admiring his strong, wonderfully capable hands and his long, powerful body as he leaned back against the worktop. They talked for a while, about his sister, their work, and the way her memory was coming back in fits and starts.

He put his arm around her, and she looked up at him.

'I'm glad I came to work with you,' she murmured. 'You're very good at what you do. Everyone here respects you and would do anything for you. And you were so efficient, so quick at getting Danny up to Theatre and then operating on him.'

'Sometimes you have to work fast.'

She nodded. 'I thought you were brilliant.'

He pretended to swagger. 'Well, I do my best.'

She smiled up at him, settling into his embrace, gazing at him in love and wonder. 'I mean it. You're a good teacher, too…I've watched you show junior doctors how to carry out difficult procedures. You're very patient.'

'You do realise this is all going to my head, don't you? I shall be too big for my boots at this rate.' He gave that some consideration. 'Hmm. Perhaps I'd better stop you from saying any more.' He drew her towards him and bent his head, capturing her lips with his own.

His kiss was gentle at first, exploring the sweetness of her mouth with such tenderness that it seemed he was brushing her lips with fire. Her body tingled with exhilaration. And all the time he was coaxing her to move in closer, his hand smoothing over the base of her spine and urging her against him. 'You're everything I want in a woman, Saffi,' he said in a roughened voice. 'I don't think you know what you do to me.'

'What do I do to you?' she asked mischievously, revelling in the way her soft curves were crushed against his hard body.

'Ahh…' he groaned, as though he was in pain. 'You know exactly what it is.' His dark gaze moved over her, and the breath snagged in his throat. 'I need you, Saffi. It makes my heart ache to think of you with another man.'

'I'm not with another man.'

'You are. You know who I mean…Jason.' He sucked in a shuddery breath. 'Will you be seeing him this afternoon?'

'Oh.' She gave a small sigh. 'Yes. He said he wanted to take me to a place along the coast.'

His eyes closed briefly as though he was trying to shut out the picture that formed in his mind. 'Promise me you won't fall for him, Saffi.'

'I'm not dating him, Matt. I'm just trying to help him…it must have been such a shock for him, knowing he was like a stranger to me. I thought, if we got to know one another, he might realise we have nothing.'

'Things don't quite work out like that, though, do

they…the way we expect? You might suddenly remember what it was you had before.'

'Matt…'

He kissed her again, quelling the words before she could get them out, and her mind spun in a heady vortex of desire and longing, and all the while mixed up with it was a spiralling fear that uneasy suspicions might tear them apart.

She loved him. How could she ever leave him for another man? But, on the other hand, would he eventually tire of her and leave her for someone else? Someone like—

The image of a dark-haired temptress with sultry green eyes swam into her vision. In her mind, the girl was standing in a bedroom doorway, one hand resting on the doorjamb. She was dishevelled, her shirt falling open to show her bra and a skirt that was unbuttoned at the waist. Saffi recoiled as though she'd received a blow to the stomach. 'No…oh, no…'

'Saffi?' Matt looked at her in consternation. 'What is it? Has something happened?' He stared at her, trying to work out what was going through her mind. 'Is it another memory?'

'I…she…yes…she was there…she was with you…' She broke away from him, aghast at the images that had swirled through her mind.

The colour drained from Matt's face. 'Saffi, it's not what you think. You have to believe me.'

She shook her head, as though that would shake off the picture that was splashed across her vision like the pages of a magazine.

She stared at him, shocked to the core. 'You know what I'm seeing, don't you?' His words were like an admission of guilt, even though he was denying it. 'No wonder you wouldn't tell me what had happened between us.'

He moved towards her, reaching out to hold her, but she backed away.

'You…you ch-cheated on me… Oh, no…'

She felt sick, her stomach was churning, her chest heaving. The image, once forgotten, was now burned on her mind.

'How could you? We were in love and you cheated on me with Gina.'

Matt looked agonised. 'I tried to explain, but you wouldn't listen. I didn't cheat on you, Saffi. I know it must have looked that way, but I didn't.'

'She told me…she said you wanted her…that it was all over between you and me. How can I believe you when she told me herself what was going on?' She turned away from him and rushed to the door. 'I have to get out of here.'

She heard him calling after her, but she ignored him and kept on going, out of the door, desperate to get away. The department's emergency phone began to ring, and as she stepped into the main area of the emergency unit she heard Matt's pager bleep. She knew he couldn't come after her now, and she fled to the car park, thankful that she had been able to make her escape.

CHAPTER NINE

'YOU'RE VERY QUIET today. Has something happened between you and Matt?'

Jason watched Saffi keenly, but she tried to avoid his gaze. They were sitting on the grass in a picnic area high up on the moor, overlooking a magnificent bay. 'I noticed that you keep trying to avoid him by going into the house whenever he's around in the garden. You did that yesterday and again this morning.'

'I'd rather not talk about it,' she said. 'Could we finish up here and go back to the house, do you think?' She hadn't wanted to come out at all this afternoon, but he'd persuaded her to come with him on a picnic and now she was regretting it. Her heart simply wasn't in it. She needed to be on her own, to think things through.

'But it's beautiful out here, don't you agree? It might help you to relax if we stay for a little longer. I picked this spot especially…it's peaceful and shaded from the sun, and we can see over the moor for miles.'

'I know. I'm sorry.' It was true that this was a lovely place to spend an afternoon, and for the most part she'd appreciated the peaceful riverside walk. They'd followed the path through the woods and come to this idyllic place, where they could sit and look at the coastline in the distance.

But she didn't want to be here with Jason. She wanted to be with Matt, but every time she thought about him her stomach turned over and she felt panicky and sick inside. How could he have let her fall in love with him all over again only to have the beautiful bubble of illusion burst in her face?

'Have some food,' Jason suggested, rummaging in the hamper and bringing out a pack of sandwiches. 'You've hardly eaten anything.'

'No, I'm not hungry. Thanks all the same.'

He held up a plastic container. 'How about a jellied fruit pot?'

'No, really. Thanks. You thought of everything, the food was excellent and this place is perfect, but I want to start back now.' Her head was hurting as the blood pounded through her veins and her forehead was hot.

He frowned. 'But I thought we could—'

She started to pack away the paper plates and packaging. 'Stay here, if you like,' she said, unable to cope any longer with his prevarication, 'but I'm going home.'

'Ah, come on, Saffi, don't be like that. I thought we might stay here for a bit and then wander down to the inn later on. We could head down that way now, if you want.'

She stood up. 'You're not listening to me, Jason. We've already been out for a few hours, when I didn't want to come here at all. It's my fault, I should never have agreed. But now I'm going home.'

She started to walk across the moorland, taking a short cut to where they'd left the car. Jason caught up with her and fell into step beside her.

'You've fallen out with him, haven't you?' he guessed, and when she didn't answer he said with quiet satisfaction, 'Well, I can't say I'm sorry. I'm glad he's out of the picture.' He gazed at her, his eyes filled with longing. 'You and I belong together, Saffi. I knew we were right for each other the moment we met.'

'I don't know about that,' she said. 'I still don't remember how it was before I hurt my head.'

He smiled. 'Perhaps if I kissed you, it would all come flooding back.'

A faint tremor ran through her. 'No,' she said, perhaps a little too firmly. 'That's not a good idea.'

He was quiet after that, walking along with her to the car, making desultory conversation.

It was a huge relief finally to be back at the house and when he asked if he could come in, she said softly, 'I want to be alone for a while, Jason. I think I'll go and lie down for a bit.'

She had a sick headache, and perhaps it was a result of the strain of these last few days, or maybe it was because everything was coming unglued inside her head and her memories were returning thick and fast. She'd longed for that to happen these last few months, but now she wished she could go back to her state of blissful ignorance.

At work in A and E it took a real effort not to let her unhappiness show. She spoke to Matt about their patients or anything medical, but whenever he tried to talk about what had happened between them she cut him off.

'I don't want to hear it, Matt,' she said in a fractured voice. 'We've been through this before. It's over.' Even though she'd managed to say it, inside she was falling apart. His expression was tortured, and she guessed he was full of regret for the way things had ended all over again. Her stomach churned to see the pain in his features, but it was all of his own doing, wasn't it? She couldn't be with a man who had cheated on her. Wasn't there always the chance he might do it again? Hadn't his love for her been strong enough to overcome temptation?

She finished her shift at the hospital and hoped Jason would stay away from her. She hadn't exactly been good to him the day before. But he turned up again a couple of hours after she returned home, full of plans for where they might go.

'We could drive over to Rosemoor and look around the garden,' he suggested. 'You'd love it there. There's an arboretum and a cottage garden—all the things you like.'

She shook her head. 'Not today, Jason. I think I'll just stay here and potter in the garden. There's quite a lot of tidying up to do.' She could see he was disappointed and she added gently, 'I know this is your holiday and you want to be with me, but I'm not in the best of moods. Perhaps you'd do better to look up old friends or go out and about by yourself.'

'No. I'll stay with you,' he said, and her heart sank. Sooner or later, she would have to tell him it would never work out for them. Perhaps she'd seen something in him at one time and they'd been good together, but, whatever it was, it had gone. It had taken her less than a fortnight to discover that they weren't suited.

She doubted she'd ever find love again. Matt had ruined her for that. For her, he was the one and only, but it looked as though he hadn't felt the same way about her. What had gone on between him and Gina was in the past, of course, but it could well happen again when he tired of her and she couldn't handle that.

Jason sat on the rustic bench and watched her as she carried out everyday gardening tasks, dead-heading flowers and pulling up the occasional weed. They talked as she worked, and he told her more about his job as a rep, and how they'd met up when he'd come to the hospital pharmacy back in Hampshire as she had been fetching medication for a patient.

She'd started to gather seed pods from the aquilegia when Ben wandered into the garden. 'Hi,' he said, giving her a big smile. 'What are you doing?'

'I'm collecting these pods from the flowers,' she said, showing him. 'They're full of seeds, see?' She shook some out into a small bowl. 'I'll put them into envelopes so that they can dry out, and then next year I can plant them in the ground. They'll grow into flowers.'

'Can I have some? When Mummy comes home, we can put them in the garden.'

'That's a good idea. I'll give some to your Uncle Matt to keep for you.' She didn't want him deciding to see what they tasted like. 'How is your mother? Have you been to see her?'

He nodded vigorously. 'We're going in a little while—me and Uncle Matt. She's feeling a bit better. She was sitting in a chair when we went to see her yesterday.' His eyes shone with excitement. 'My daddy's coming back home to live with us.'

'That's great, Ben.' She gave him a hug. 'I'm so pleased for you.'

Jason cleared his throat noisily, drawing her attention away from Ben, and when she turned towards him he said, 'All this talk about planting seeds—surely you're not thinking of staying here?'

She frowned. 'Yes, of course. I thought you realised that's what I wanted to do. I wasn't sure what I was going to do when I first came back here, but now I know it's what I want more than anything.'

'But I thought you would go back with me to Hampshire. You know that's what I want. We talked about it.'

She stared at him, aghast. How could he have assumed so much? She searched her mind for anything she might have said that could have given him the idea she had agreed to his suggestion, and came up with nothing.

'I'm not leaving here,' she said.

Ben tugged on her jeans. 'Can we go and look for some eggs?'

'Yes, okay.' She glanced at Jason and saw that he was scowling at the boy. He obviously didn't like the interruption.

'Jason,' she murmured, 'it looks as though I'm going to be spending some time with Ben now, and then I plan to have a quiet evening. Like I said, I'm not the best company today. Perhaps it would be best if you went back to your hotel.'

'We haven't had much time together,' he complained, 'with you working, and people dropping by.'

'People?' she echoed.

'All these distant neighbours that come by for flowers or vegetables—it wouldn't be so bad if they took the stuff and went away, but they stay and chat. And now the boy's come along to take up your time.'

Ben looked confused, sensing that something was wrong. Saffi put a comforting arm around the child and said, 'I like chatting with my neighbours, and I want Ben to feel that he can come round here whenever he wants.'

She hesitated, bracing herself for what had to be said. 'I think you should go, Jason. This isn't going to work out the way you hoped. I don't know how it was before, but I can't care for you the way you want. We're just not suited.'

'You feel that way because you've been ill, you suffered a bad head injury and it's taking time for you to get things back together again. We'll be fine. Give it time, Saffi.'

She shook her head. 'I'm sorry, Jason. I don't mean to hurt you, but you're so keen to see things the way they were that you're not giving any thought to the way I am now and what I feel and think.'

'We could work it out. You just have to give it time.'

He couldn't accept what she was telling him, and he countered everything she put to him with an argument of his own.

In the end, she said sadly, 'I can't do this any more, Jason. Please, go.'

Ben tugged once more at her jeans and she nodded, looking down at him. 'Yes, we'll go and see the hens.'

Jason left in a huff, and Saffi winced. Could she have been a bit more tactful or given him more time? Maybe, from his point of view, he had good reason to feel put out.

She went with Ben to the hen house and helped him to collect the eggs from the nesting boxes. 'Shall we see if Mitzi's left any for us?'

He nodded and they went over to the rabbit hutch. Matt had attached a wire run to the cage so that she could stretch her legs, and Ben was gleeful when he found two large brown eggs nestling in the wood shavings.

Matt came over to them as they started back towards the house. 'You've been busy,' he said, looking at the basket.

'We found six!' Ben said gleefully. 'They're for tea.' He thought about it. 'I could eat them all.'

Matt chuckled. 'You must be hungry. Do you think you could take them into the kitchen? Be careful.'

'I will.' Ben went off, holding the basket very still so as not to disturb the eggs.

Matt looked at Saffi, searching her face for some clue as to how she was feeling. 'How are you?' he asked.

She shrugged. 'I'm okay.'

He grimaced. 'I'd have done anything not to upset you.'

'Then perhaps you should have told me what happened before I started to care for you all over again,' she said sharply. 'You should have thought about it in the first place before you decided to two-time me with Gina. Or perhaps you imagined I wouldn't find out?'

His face was contorted with grief and regret. 'It didn't happen, Saffi—it wasn't what you thought.'

'Wasn't it?' Her eyes widened in disbelief. 'It seemed pretty straightforward to me. I dropped by your place one night when you weren't expecting to see me, and Gina came out of the bedroom. What am I supposed to make of it?'

'She was trying to get back with me. When you came by after your shift finished she took advantage of the situation and made it seem as if we'd been together.'

She was scornful. 'You've had a long time to think that one up, haven't you? There's no future for us, Matt. I told you at the time, I believe what I saw, and what she said. She told me you were getting back together. Why would I think differently?'

'Because you know me, and I'm telling you that's how it was.' His eyes darkened with sorrow. 'Or perhaps I'm wrong about that, and you never really knew me at all.'

'Obviously you're right about that.' There was pain in her eyes as she flung his words back at him. 'I thought I knew you, but you deceived me and I was devastated—twice over. I don't know how you could do that to me.' Her mouth tightened. 'And why *didn't* you tell me what had happened between us when we met up again instead of letting me find out weeks later?'

His brows shot up. 'Are you kidding? If I'd done that

I would never have had the chance to show you who I really am all over again. You wouldn't have had anything to do with me.' His mouth flattened. 'You can't imagine how difficult it's been for me to stay silent, or how hard it was for me to watch and wait for your memory to return, knowing all the while that you might cut me out of your life all over again.'

'You were right,' she said stiffly. 'That's exactly what I'd do. I couldn't be with anyone who played around.'

'I told you I didn't do that. I tried to explain, but you wouldn't listen and instead you left within the week and started a new life in Hampshire.' His grey eyes were bleak. 'You wouldn't take my calls, you wouldn't see me when I went over there—you wouldn't even speak to me at your aunt's funeral. Where does trust come into all this, Saffi?' There was an edge of bitterness to his words as though he was finally coming to accept what had happened to them.

He said nothing for a while, deep in thought as though he was trying to work things out in his head. Then at last he said, 'You're right. There's no future for us, because it seems to me that without trust there's nothing at all. I knew I should never have allowed myself to get close to you all over again. I was just setting myself up for heartbreak, wasn't I?'

She turned away from him as Ben came out into the garden once more. Her throat was aching and her eyes burned with unshed tears. She couldn't answer him, and she escaped into the house, her heart pounding, her throat constricted.

She wished she'd never remembered how he'd

cheated on her. Then she could have gone on loving him in blissful ignorance instead of having to suffer this awful heartache. More than anything, she wanted to be with him, but how could their relationship ever work out with that awful betrayal hanging over them? How was she even going to cope with working alongside him?

Back in A and E the next day she was busy with her patients and managed for the most part to stay out of Matt's way. At lunchtime she went over to the intensive care unit to look in on Danny and find out how he was doing.

'His intracranial pressure is down,' the nurse told her, 'and we've done another CT scan, which shows everything's going along nicely. There's no sign of the blood clot building up again.'

'So you'll be removing the drainage tube soon?'

'In a day or so, I should think. He's doing really well. We're very pleased with him.'

Saffi was relieved. Danny was sitting up in bed, talking to his parents, and it looked as though his mother was showing him pictures in a story-book. She said cautiously, 'Is there any sign of brain damage?'

The nurse shook her head. 'Thankfully, no. He's a very lucky boy.'

'He is.' Smiling, Saffi went back down to A and E to finish her shift. She was glad Danny was doing so well. Things could have turned out so differently if it hadn't been for Matt's prompt action.

'Shall I help you with the patient in Room Three?' Gina asked, cutting in on her thoughts. 'It's an infant with a bead lodged in her ear. You might need me to distract her while you try to get it out.'

'Yes, okay. Thanks, Gina.' Saffi frowned. It was an uncomfortable feeling, working with this woman, now that she'd remembered everything that had happened between her and Matt. She had to dredge up every ounce of professionalism she possessed in order to do her job properly, without letting her emotions get in the way.

'Are you all right?' Gina was studying her closely. 'Matt said you were recovering new memories all the time. Has it upset you?'

Saffi closed her eyes briefly. 'It has. It was bound to, don't you think?' She looked at Gina, beautiful, green-eyed, her hair shining with health. Was it any wonder that Matt's head had been turned, especially if Gina had made a play for him?

'There's nothing going on between us, you know,' Gina said quietly. 'I'm engaged to be married—look.' She held out her left hand, showing her sparkling diamond ring.

'Oh, I see.' Saffi's brows drew together. 'Congratulations.' She hesitated. 'That wasn't actually what was bothering me.'

'No.' Gina's voice was flat. 'Matt said you'd remembered me being in his bedroom.' She winced. 'I wanted to get back with him after he'd finished with me, so I went to see him when I knew you were busy at work. He was friendly enough, but he didn't want anything to do with me as a girlfriend and wanted me to leave, so I said was feeling ill…a bit sick, faint, and so on. I lied to you, Saffi.'

Saffi stared at her, shock holding her still, rooted to the spot. Had she made a terrible mistake?

'I was desperate to make him want me. He said perhaps I should lie down for a while, undo my skirt to ease the pressure on my waist, and I did as he said. Only I undid a few more buttons on my blouse than was necessary. He just drew the curtains and left me alone. After a while, he came to see if I was all right.'

She swallowed hard. 'I wanted him to love me, but he just saw me as a friend. I felt so unhappy, and when you turned up after your shift had ended, I wanted to finish things between you, the way he'd finished things with me. I thought, maybe, if he didn't have you, he might turn to me after all.' She pressed her lips together. 'He never did.'

Saffi let out a long, shuddery breath. 'It was all a lie? All of it?'

Gina nodded. 'I'm sorry. I know what I did was stupid, hurtful. It's just that I was hurting too, inside.'

Saffi's head was reeling. All this time she'd refused to listen to Matt. She'd believed what Gina had said at the time, and she'd sent Matt away. Without trust, he'd said, there was nothing at all. He would never forgive her.

'Saffi, I really am sorry.'

Saffi nodded. It took everything she had to keep going and she said now, 'I'm glad you told me.' She took in several long breaths to steady herself. What was she to do?

She gazed around her without seeing for a moment or two. Then gradually, the sights and sounds of the hospital came back into view and she said dully, 'We'd better go and see what we can do about this bead.'

She made herself go into the room and talk soothingly to the little girl and her mother. 'I'm going to look inside your ear with this,' she said to the two-year-old, showing her the otoscope. 'It won't hurt, I promise.'

When she could see the shiny object, way down in the ear canal, she tried to gently remove it using special forceps, but when that didn't do the trick, she asked Gina for suction equipment. After a few seconds, much to the mother's relief, she'd retrieved the bead.

She left the room a few minutes later, leaving Gina to talk to the patient and her mother and clear away the equipment. The only thing on her mind was to find Matt and talk to him, though how she was going to persuade him to forgive her lack of trust was beyond her right now. He'd seemed to have made up his mind, finally, that there was no point any longer in trying to win her back. He'd decided she wasn't worth the effort.

'He went out on a call,' Jake told her, 'and I think he's going to be tied up in meetings all afternoon. Do you want me to pass on a message?'

'No, that's all right, Jake. Thanks. I'll catch up with him later.'

She arrived home feeling washed out and dreadful. How could she have been so blind, so certain that she'd had things right all this time?

She was pacing the floor of her living room when Jason turned up at the house, and she groaned inwardly.

This was the last thing she needed, but some part of her insisted that even though he would never win her round she should let him say his piece. Wasn't that where she'd gone wrong with Matt, by not listening to him?

They went back into the living room.

'I'm going back to Hampshire tomorrow,' Jason told her.

'So soon? I thought you had another couple of days here?'

'No.' He shook his head. 'I have to go and see the head of a regional pharmacy service. It's a new contact for me, and my bosses didn't want me to miss it.'

She smiled. 'It sounds as though your job is going really well. You must be pleased.'

He shrugged. 'I work hard and make a lot of contacts, but I could have done without that one right now. I need more time here to persuade you that we belong together.'

'It's never going to happen, Jason,' she said, unhappy because she had to hurt him yet again. 'I don't know how it was before, but I can't see how we were ever a couple, to be honest. I don't think I've changed so much from how I was before the accident.' She still felt the same way about Matt as she'd always done, so how could it be any different with Jason? Something had to be wrong somewhere.

'You're being very cruel to me, Saffi. How can you say these things to me?'

She sent him a troubled look. 'I don't mean to be cruel. I'm trying to be straightforward with you, so that you don't have any illusions as to how it will be.'

'But I love you, and you loved me. How can that all have changed?'

Her expression was sad as she tried to explain, 'I don't think it was ever that way. It feels to me as though you've conjured something up in your mind and made it into something that never was. It's what you want to believe.'

He moved closer to her. 'You're my blonde, beautiful, blue-eyed angel,' he said. 'How could I not love you?'

'It isn't love, Jason. You're infatuated with someone you can't have. Don't you see that?'

'All I see is you and me, together.'

He slid an arm around her and pulled her to him. 'I'm not letting you go, Saffi. You're mine, and sooner or later you'll see that I'm right.'

He tried to kiss her and she pushed him away. 'No, Jason, stop it.'

'It'll all come right, you'll see.' He ignored her protests and backed her up against the wall, clasping her wrists and pinning her there with his body.

'I said no, Jason. Get off me. Let go of me.' She struggled, trying to wriggle free, and as they tussled he somehow knocked over a stool. It fell against the wall with a crash, and it made her realise how determined he was. 'Jason, this is crazy,' she said. 'Let me go.'

He tightened his grasp on her wrist and she stared up at him, frightened, afraid of what he might do. A startling image flashed across her mind, of another place, another time, when he'd grabbed her wrist in that very same way.

'Oh, no...no...' she cried. 'This can't be happening,

not again.' The last time he'd held on to her this way they'd been at the top of a flight of stairs. She'd tried to get away from him, and the next thing she'd known she'd been tumbling down and down and then there had just been blackness until she'd woken up in hospital.

'You're the reason I fell down the stairs. You were trying to stop me from breaking up with you.' Her voice was rising with panic. 'Please, Jason. Think about what you're doing. Do you want it to happen all over again? Are you deliberately trying to hurt me?'

He didn't get the chance to answer because all at once there was the sound of a key scraping in a lock, and Matt came rushing into the room through the connecting door.

'Let go of her,' he said in an ominously threatening voice. His jaw was clenched in anger and there was the fierce promise of retribution in his grey eyes.

Jason paled with fright. 'What are you doing here?'

'Never mind that. Do as I said. Let her go.'

Jason hesitated for a few seconds too long, and Matt was on him right away, putting an arm around his neck and yanking him backwards, while at the same time hooking his leg from under him.

Matt gave him a push and Jason fell to the floor. Standing over him, his foot firmly placed over Jason's arm, Matt glanced at Saffi.

'Are you all right?'

Saffi resisted the urge to rub her sore wrists, and nodded. She was winded, breathing hard after the skirmish, and her heart was pounding as she wondered what she would have done if Matt hadn't intervened. Perhaps a knee to the groin would have done the trick?

'Let me up,' Jason said, struggling to get to his feet.

Matt pushed him back down with his other foot. His balance and his strength were incredible, and Saffi realised his sessions at the gym had definitely paid off.

'What do you want me to do with him? Do you want to call the police?' Every time Jason made a move, Matt pushed him down again.

'I don't know,' she said, filled with anxiety. 'Do you think he'll come back and try again?'

'I won't. I won't do that.' Jason's voice shook as he became more desperate.

Matt ignored him. 'I don't think it's very likely,' he said, looking at Saffi. 'If he does, he'll certainly regret it, because I'll do more than drag him off you next time. He'll wish he'd never been born.'

'I just want him out of here,' she said, and Matt nodded.

He grasped Jason by the collar of his sweatshirt and dragged him to his feet. 'You heard what she said. Get out of here, and don't come back.'

He pushed him towards the front door and pulled it open wide. 'Get in your car and don't come within twenty miles of her, don't phone her, don't email, don't write to her. If you try to contact her in any way, we'll get an injunction against you. Are you clear on all that?'

Jason nodded, his face ashen. He must have realised he didn't stand a chance against Matt, who was so much fitter and stronger than he was. He didn't say another word but hurried over to his car and drove away as though he was terrified Matt would come after him.

'Thank you for coming in and rescuing me,' Saffi said when Matt returned to the living room. 'I thought you would be out all day. I thought I was completely alone with him.' The after-effects of her ordeal suddenly kicked in and she began to tremble. Feeling behind her for a seat, she sank down into the sofa and clasped her hands in her lap.

Matt came to sit beside her. After a moment of hesitation, as he appeared to be at war within himself, he wrapped his arms around her and held her until the trembling stopped. Then he said softly, 'I'll make you a hot, sweet drink. That should help you to feel better.'

She nodded silently. She would have gone after him, but her legs were weak and all the energy had drained out of her. The shock of Jason's assault and the memory of how her fall down the stairs had come about were too much for her to take in. She started to shake all over again.

'Here, drink this.' Matt handed her a cup of tea and helped her to clasp her hands around it. He sat with her as she tried to gain control of herself.

'Thank you for this.' She swallowed some of the reviving tea and then slid the cup down onto the coffee table. 'I can't tell you how glad I am that you came through that door when you did.' She sent him a puzzled look. 'But I don't understand how you were there, how you knew to come to me.'

'I was afraid something like this might happen. Ben told me that you were talking in the garden yesterday.

He said Jason was cross when you said you weren't leaving here and he was angry when you asked him to go, and that started warning bells in my head.' He grimaced. 'I cancelled all my meetings so that I could be here, just in case I was needed.'

'You did that, even though I'd been so awful to you?' She clasped his hand, needing that small contact.

'I was already watching out for trouble after you were followed the other night.'

'By the black car?'

He nodded. 'I'm fairly sure it was Jason in the car. He must have thought you were on your own—perhaps the headrests obscured his vision. Did you tell him you were going to the vet's surgery?'

She frowned, thinking about it. 'I don't remember. I was busy and then... Oh, yes...he wanted to take me out and I said I couldn't go with him because I had to take Mitzi to the vet.'

'He must have been waiting there, ready to follow you home.'

'But why would he do that?'

'He's obsessed with you. He must have followed you before. How was your other car damaged in a rear-end collision? Do you have any recollection of it?'

She nodded slowly, covering her face with her hands as the incident came back to her in bits and pieces. Getting herself together after a minute or so, she said, 'It was when I wanted to finish things with him...he took to following me. When I wouldn't stop the car, he drove me off the road.' She looked at Matt. 'He's out of his mind, isn't he? Perhaps we should have called the police after all, or tried to persuade him to get treatment?'

'I doubt the police would do anything without proof. Were there any witnesses?'

She shook her head.

'And when you fell down the stairs?'

'No.' It came out as a whisper, and she began to shake all over again. 'He must have left me there at the foot of the stairs, knowing I needed help. But he did nothing. Apparently, it was Chloe who called for the ambulance when she arrived home from work. I don't know how long I was lying there.'

He put his arms around her and drew her to him, gently stroking her silky hair. 'It's over now, Saffi. He won't trouble you again.' They stayed together that way for some time, and eventually he said softly, 'It looks as though your memory's come back in full force.'

She gave him a tremulous smile. 'It does, doesn't it?' She gazed up at him, her brow puckering. 'But why did I lose it so completely? I can understand partial amnesia because it was a bad head injury, but such a total loss is unusual—people don't often recover their memories after such a loss.'

'There's probably a combination of reasons. The head injury is one, as you say, but your mind could have been shutting out the bad things, all the emotional trauma that you didn't want to face…like your relationship with Jason.'

'And the end of my relationship with you. That has been the worst of all.' She looked at him anxiously, passing her tongue lightly over her dry lips. 'Matt—I spoke to Gina before I left work today. She told me that she'd lied to me.' Her gaze meshed with his. 'I'm so sorry I doubted you. You were right all along—I should have trusted you.'

'We'll have to start again, won't we…and make a pact to always trust one another?'

'Does that mean you forgive me?' She looked at him in wonderment. 'Do we have some kind of a future together?'

He looked into her blue eyes. 'We'd better have a future. I'm not going to lose you again, Saffi. It's been hell on earth for me these last few days…these last few years, even.'

'But you don't believe in long-term relationships, do you? Wasn't that why you finished things with Gina, because you didn't want any kind of commitment?'

'I thought that was the reason at the time. It was what I told myself. But the truth is, Gina and I were never right for one another. She wanted to get serious, but I knew it would never work.'

He hesitated. 'I never looked for commitment. But then I met you, and I could feel myself getting in deeper and deeper, knowing that you were the one woman I could love. But all the time I was afraid that it would go wrong, that it would end the way it always did with people I cared about…my parents, even my sister was lost to me when we ended up in separate foster-homes. I was afraid to love you in case I lost you. And then the very worst happened. You thought I'd cheated on you.'

He drew in a shuddery breath. 'It made me even more wary of getting involved. When I met up with you again, here in Devon, I was so afraid of being hurt all over again. I told myself I needed to keep my distance, but it was too difficult and I ended up not being able to stay away. And after you remembered what had happened with Gina, I was devastated all over again. It was like my worst nightmare. I thought I'd lost you for ever.'

She lifted a hand to his face and stroked his cheek. 'You haven't lost me. I love you, Matt. I think I knew it almost from the first.' She gently drew him towards her until their lips touched, and he gave a ragged groan, kissing her fiercely, with all the longing and desperation that had built up inside him.

'Will you marry me, Saffi?' His voice was husky with need. 'I couldn't bear to lose you again.'

'Yes…yes, I will…' She wrapped her arms around him, loving the way he ran his hands over her body, over every dip and curve. She kissed him because she loved him, because she wanted him, because she needed him to know that she would be his for evermore.

When they at last stopped to gather breath, she said softly, 'Aunt Annie thought we were meant for each other, you know. She knew how much I loved you and she always had faith in you, even when I was floundering. That must be the reason she left you part of the house. She wanted us to be together, and she knew we'd have to find some way of making it work if we both lived here.'

He chuckled. 'Yes, I'd worked that one out. She was right, wasn't she? I know she couldn't have expected it to happen so soon, but her plans were all intact. She didn't leave anything to chance.'

She snuggled into him, nuzzling his neck and planting soft kisses along his throat. 'I love you so much.'

'And I love you, beyond anything. That's why I came to work in Devon. I knew, sooner or later, you would come to visit Annie and I would do everything I could to win you round. I just had to see you again.' He gave a wry smile. 'And then when you turned up and hadn't a clue who I was, I thought maybe here was my chance to get you to love me all over again.'

'Well, you managed that all right.'

'I did, didn't I? That must say something about true love lasting for ever.' He kissed her again. 'Are we too late for a summer wedding, do you think?'

She smiled up at him. 'I shouldn't think so. I'm sure we'll manage to sort something out.'

'That's good…that'll be perfect.' He gently pressured her back into the cushions and eased himself against her, and after that neither of them had any inclination to move apart for a long, long time.

* * * * *

Special Offers

Every month we put together collections and longer reads written by your favourite authors.

Here are some of next month's highlights— and don't miss our fabulous discount online!

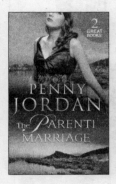

On sale 21st February

On sale 28th February

On sale 21st February

Work hard, play harder...

Welcome to the Gold Coast, where hearts are broken
as quickly as they are healed. Featuring some of the
rising stars of the medical world, this new four-book
series dives headfirst into Surfer's Paradise.

Available as a bundle at
www.millsandboon.co.uk/medical

Join the Mills & Boon Book Club

Want to read more **Medical** books?
We're offering you **2 more** absolutely **FREE!**

We'll also treat you to these fabulous extras:

- Exclusive offers and much more!

- FREE home delivery

- FREE books and gifts with our special rewards scheme

Get your free books now!

visit www.millsandboon.co.uk/bookclub
or call Customer Relations on 020 8288 2888